JUGLUCK
THE HARE

*For Ash,
with 'prupest'
and 'saztaculous' wishes

Phum*

SilverWood

THE PUZZLE OF THE TILLIAN WAND

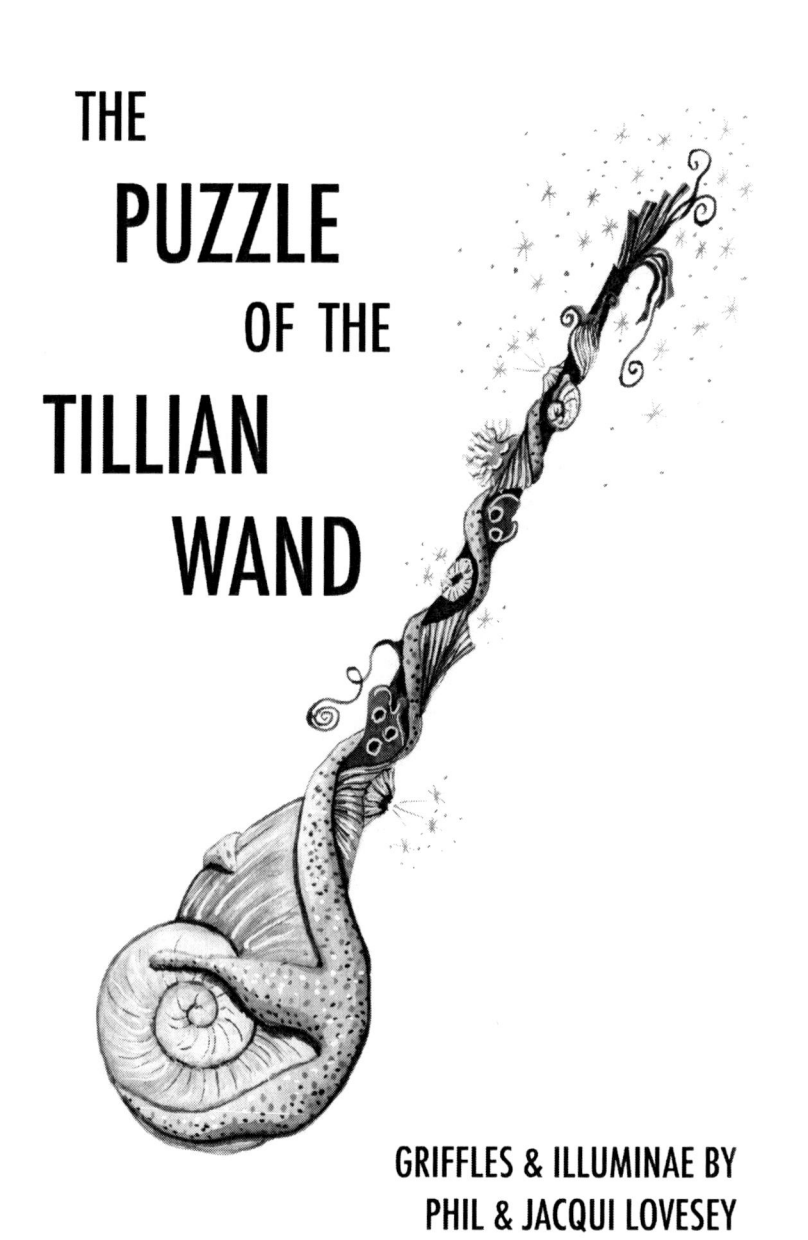

GRIFFLES & ILLUMINAE BY
PHIL & JACQUI LOVESEY

Published in 2015 by the authors

SilverWood Books
30 Queen Charlotte Street, Bristol, BS1 4HJ
www.silverwoodbooks.co.uk

Copyright © Phil and Jacqui Lovesey 2015

To discover more about Matlock the Hare and Winchett Dale,
visit www.matlockthehare.com this very sun-turn…

The right of Phil and Jacqui Lovesey to be identified as the authors
of this work has been asserted by them in accordance with the
Copyright, Designs and Patents Act 1988.

All rights reserved. No part of this publication may be reproduced,
stored in a retrieval system, or transmitted in any form or by any means,
electronic, mechanical, photocopying, recording or otherwise,
without prior permission of the copyright holder.

ISBN 978-1-78132-287-1 (paperback)
ISBN 978-1-78132-288-8 (hardback)
ISBN 978-1-78132-289-5 (ebook)

British Library Cataloguing in Publication Data
A CIP catalogue record for this book is available from the British Library

Set in Baskerville and Almendra by SilverWood Books
Printed on responsibly sourced paper

Acknowledgements

The authors would very much like to acknowledge and offer their most sincere thanks to the many saztaculous folk whose majickal-support has made this book a reality.

May all your pid-pads continue to be peffa-crumlush ones…
Barry Moth, Hazel Lambert, Betie and Agatha; Kym Mcrory; Kerry Lacey; Precious Lacey; Grace Humberstone; Robert Shaw; Susan L Hughes; Douglas and Tess Barnett; Rachel Anne Kay; Julie Moore; Andy and Cat Fereday; Simon and Sal; Peter and Jax Lovesey; Kay Isobel Goodliffe; Susan Tudor-Coulson; John West; Emma 'Ickleweb' Gregory; Team Denson; Lara Pressburger; Suzanne; Cathy Brown; John Grisswell; Paul A Withers (Pawprint Wildlife); Louise Whiddett.

And finally, Saffron Russell, for services above and beyond, in providing cover designs, ideas and graphic wizardry to bring our website and the world of Winchett Dale majickally to life in so many ways.

This book is dedicated to you all…

Phil & Jacqui Lovesey, December 2014

Also by Phil and Jacqui Lovesey:

The Riddle of the Treffelpugga Path

Contents

Map of Winchett Dale	8
What is a 'Majickal-Hare'?	9
The Task	15
1. Questions, Snoffibs and the Dale Vrooshfest	17
2. The Krettles, the Second Task and the Lid-Machine	44
3. Ledel, Vrooshed-Robes and the Todel Bear	81
4. Laffrohn, Alvestra and the Vroffa-Tree Inn	108
5. Grik, Baselott and the Nullitts	135
The Dale Vrooshfest…	175
6. Goole, Garrick and the Ripped-Robes	177
7. Luck, Flutebeaks and Soriah	196
8. Kringle, Fellic and Drutted-Secrets	241
9. Ayaani, Eyesplashers and Garrick's Castle	270
10. Vrooshers, Colley-Rocks and Vroffa'd Witches	299
The Tillian Wand	333
11. The Icy Seas, Legends and Statues	335
12. Heights, Krellits and Sea-Wizards	380
13. Betrayals, Treachery and Sisters	409
14. Tillian, the Tower and the Puzzle	425
15. Gifts, Even'ups, and Trials	466
Griffle Glossary	475
The Dale Bugle	481

Map of Winchett Dale

What is a 'Majickal-Hare'?

All hares, it is widely acknowledged, are 'majickal' to one degree or another, although this is perhaps less accepted by those of us living out here in The Great Beyond. And if this makes little or no sense, then it is as well to remember that *our* lives don't make a lot of sense to the creatures of Winchett Dale, either – excepting perhaps, a shared appreciation for the majickal qualities of all hares.

Griffled quite simply, dear reader, dale-creatures would find our lives just as different and confusing as anything we might ever encounter in Winchett Dale, and were you to ever stumble upon the entrance to Trefflepugga Path, hidden high in the crumlush Derbyshire Peaks, then take its winding, constantly changing route down into the dale itself, this would become all too immediately apparent, from the very first pid-pads you took into Wand Wood, then down into the village itself.

But more of Winchett Dale, and all the creatures who live there, later…

For now, these griffles concern themselves with the most majickal business of the ascension of hares, a sacred practice that has existed since Oramus first created Trefflepugga Path, together with the moon, the stars, and each and every saztaculous thing in the twinkling-lid above. Indeed, there are some that think the ascension of hares may well have been the most peffa-important of *His* plans in the very first place.

There are, as far as we know, four kinds of majickal-hare.

The first live alongside us, out here in The Great Beyond, in family groups and droves, rarely glimpsed during the day, lying flat in forms, ears to their backs, hoping not to be disturbed, usually in open fields and lush grasslands. Brown in colour, they are born with their eyes open, alert and seemingly ready for whatever life may have in store for them from the very first blinksnap. To see one is a peffa-rare pleasure, but if you do, and dare to look into its bright majickal eyes, you might well get a small inkling as to just why it is that so many myths, spuddles and legends have been written and griffled about these saztaculous creatures in cultures the world over.

The second kind of hare are true 'majickal-hares'; hares that have been chosen to make the long and perilous journey along Trefflepugga Path and down into any one of the waiting dales, there to serve their apprenticeship under a Most Majelicus hare-master; to learn and be taught the ways of ancient-dalelore – to walk on their hind legs, dress in their saztaculous green robes, long purple shoes and caps, and eventually to read the many majickal-driftolubb books that will provide them with the essential potionary and wand-wielding skills they'll need during their time as a true 'majickal-hare'.

Once trained and their apprenticeship is complete, majickal-hares are then left in their various dale homelands to tend the immediate needs of the resident creatures, plants and trees who live there; from sorting out the most gobflopped squabbles, to conjuring saztaculous vrooshers, as and when the need arises.

The third kind of hare are Most Majelicus hares, the briftest of all majickjal-hares; those few that have successfully completed three tasks to prove themselves worthy of this most shindinculous majickal accolade, and the wearing of the saztaculous red robes that accompanies it. After becoming Most Majelicus, they spend their sun-turns searching for hares back out in The Great Beyond, taking apprentices back to the dales, passing their knowledge, experience and wisdom to a new generation.

Thus, the circle on this good Earth is complete; from hare, to majickal-hare, to Most Majelicus hare, leaving just the final ascension to that of a Majickal Elder – the fourth kind of hare – achieved when the hare is finally taken into Oramus' most eternal-care to join the ranks of other blue-robed Majickal Elders, whose combined ethereal governance over all Oramus' many lands, seas and dales becomes their sole duty from that sun-turn forth…

…except, perhaps, when they're eating niff-soup, or busy squabbling amongst themselves, or failing to reach any kind of a decision in the many separate Elder committees and councils that were once ironically designed by Oramus to make the whole business of ethereal governance a good deal simpler in the first place. Indeed, some peffa-wise Majickal Elder hares have sometimes wondered if Oramus didn't have a *fifth* and final ascension in *His* saztaculous and eternally shindinculous mind when *He* planned the four-stage ascension, but seeing as *He* has never really been glimpsed (saving shadowy appearances on the surface of the occasional full-moon) no one has ever really been able to griffle to *Him* as to what *His* true intentions and purposes really were.

In the meantime, the Majickal Elders content themselves as best they can with the knowledge that their blue-robes of office signify to others that they have risen to the peffa-highest of all places for any hare that once hid and sheltered in open fields back out in The Great Beyond, leaving the vexing possibility of a fifth ascension for Oramus' *Himself* to finally reveal, if and when *He* sees fit to do so.

And until that distant sun-turn arrives, all hares, of whatever office, rank and stature, must simply wait…

…which, if you were Matlock, the majickal-hare of Winchett Dale, would suit you from the tops of your brown ears to the tips of your long purple shoes – and most other places in between. For Matlock, it has to be said, is one of the few majickal-hares that really rather likes waiting. Not that he'd ever see it as 'waiting', as such – more, he'd see plenty of other things he'd much rather be doing instead, mostly in and around his cottage garden, his potionary, Wand Wood and the village of Winchett Dale itself. Indeed, this ability of simply being able to get on with what he thinks is necessary at the time, rather than worrying about any sort of 'greater scheme of things' was one of the main reasons Chatsworth, his Most Majelicus master, had chosen Matlock to be his apprentice when he'd first set eyes on him as a leaping leveret way out in The Great Beyond. For no matter what was going on, Matlock always busied himself with his own chores; searching for food in hedgerows, building his form, seemingly oblivious to any lurking predators or dangers, completely absorbed by whatever he'd set his mind on. After just a single sun-turn observing Matlock in this way, Chatsworth knew the young leveret to be the peffa-perfect choice for his next apprentice, and had taken him back along Trefflepugga Path, the path itself then choosing Winchett Dale to be Matlock's brand new home and training ground.

And some might wonder just why it was that Trefflepugga Path chose Winchett Dale of all the majickal-dales. Even Chatsworth, as a Most Majelicus hare had no idea of the path's true intentions, save for the fact that it always seemed to take creatures where it best thought they needed to go, and that this was in some strange and majickal way connected to Oramus' will, and therefore wasn't really ever open to dispute or negotiation. Trefflepugga Path had decided on Winchett Dale, so it was there that Matlock began his apprenticeship in what was generally acknowledged to be the most peffa-glopped-up and clottabussed of all the majickal-dales.

Peffa-glopped-up? Clottabussed? Confusing griffles indeed, but not perhaps if you were to actually spend a snutch of sun-turns in Winchett Dale amongst the creatures, watching them pid-padding about their daily lives. You might even find yourself using some of their griffles too, as Dalespeak can be peffa, peffa-catching…

And what would be your first impressions of this most crumlush place? Certainly, its unspoilt beauty would shine through; from the limestone cliffs of Twinkling Lid Heights, to the dense forest of Wand Woods, the crisp, clear waters of Thinking Lake, the sweeping grasslands of Chiming Meadows, and finally the wooden houses of the village itself, cosily clustered around a saztaculous tree at its very centre. You might even notice an inn on the far side of the village-square, with creatures drinking guzzworts and griffling loudly, as landlord Slivert Jutt tried his jovial best to keep order and stop any unnecessary singing – although, as no one really knows what 'unnecessary' means in Winchett Dale, you'd also probably realise that his efforts in this regard were – perhaps somewhat inevitably – rather unnecessary in themselves.

And of the creatures? Well, some would look like animals you might vaguely recognise from your own time out in The Great

Beyond. But here any similarity would soon end, as you discovered that nearly every creature 'griffled', albeit what they actually had to say might sound rather glopped-up at times. Which is why it's worth remembering that life as seen through the eyes of Winchett Dale – or any of the other majickal-dales, for that matter – is peffa, peffa-different to ours…which is perhaps the main reason why Oramus made it that way in the first place.

Some Useful 'Griffles' for your Journey...

Briftest – (adj) What you know as 'the best'.
Chickle – (v) To laugh.
Clottabus – (n, colloquial) A bit of a fool. *Clottabussed* – foolish, but mostly harmless.
Creaker – (n) Door.
Crumlush – (adj) The feeling you get inside when all's *saztaculoulsy* well. Cosy, warm, lovely.
Driftolubb – (n) A book. Part of a set of *driftolubbs* used by majickal-hares to find spells, potions and *vrooshers*.
Excrimbly – (adj) Excited.
Fuzzcheck – (sl) When everything's *saztaculoulsy* fine.
Gobflop – (n) to fail at something.
Glopped-up – (n phrase) When something has gone wrong.
Glubbstool – (n) When something has gone *peffa*-wrong!
Griffle(s) – (n) Word(s)
Juzzpapped – (n) Tired, exhausted.
Lid – (n) Sky. *Twinkling-lid* (n) being a night sky full of stars.
Majelicus – (adj) *Peffa*-majickal, the most majickal majick, that can't be *vrooshed* from books, tinctures or potions. The very heartbeat of our majickal world.
Nifferduggle(s) – (n) Sleeping. To go to *nifferduggles* is sometimes the most *crumlush* part of our *sun-turn*…
Oidy – (adj) Tiny, *peffa*-small.
Peffa – (adj) Very.
Pid-pad – (v) To walk. Humans tend to '*bud-thud*'; whereas we, more delicate creatures of the dale simply *pid-pad*. Except Proftulous, who *lump-thumps*, and oidy creatures who sometimes *scrittle*.

Russisculoffed – (n) Irritated. From the gutteral noises made by *Russicers* if you go too near to them while they are hoarding *shlomps*. Be warned, they much prefer their *schlomps* to you!
Saztaculous – (adj) Incredible, fantastic.
Shindinculous – (adj) Something that is so *peffa-saztaculous* that it shines out.
Sisteraculous – (n) The absolute being of you. The complimentary part of your *softulous* (body) that if you really take the time to listen to, has some truly *shindinculous* answers to questions you never thought to even ask. Something so many have forgotten how to trust, but we at Winchett Dale rely on most *glopped-up sun-turns*!
Snutch – (n) A few.
Stroff – (v) To be taken to pass into Oramus' most eternal care.
Sun-turn – (n) A day. The period of *time* it takes for the sun to rise and fall, before leaving just the *saztaculous twinkling-lid*. Twenty-eight of them make a *moon-turn (*or 'month', as you would *griffle*.)
Twizzly – (n) To feel scared; something rather scary.
Vilish – (adv) Quickly. From the noise made by a woodland creature rushing through the undergrowth, searching for berries, or trying to escape a hungry predator!
Vroosher – (n) A wand-assisted majick spell. From the *saztaculous vrooshing* noise they make!
Yechus – (n) horrible, awful, hideous; something that might be *peffa-glopped-up*.

Armed with these few griffles, the wary traveller should have little difficulty in easily pid-padding around Winchett Dale. However, in the unlikely event of you ever getting lost, a more comprehensive glossary can be found waiting for you at the end of your journey…

The Task

1.

Questions, Snoffibs and the Dale Vrooshfest

Matlock had often suspected that some even'ups were simply made for friends, brottle-leaf brew and griffling in his cottage garden at the edge of Wand Wood. As such, the even'up in question was almost peffa-perfect; the lid above twinkling with stars, a slight autumnal breeze settling over Matlock and his two briftest friends – Proftulous the dworp, and Ursula Brifthaven Stoltz, a visiting white hare-witch from across the Icy Seas. An even'up fluff-thropp flew in slow circles high above their heads, greeping exquisitely to the moon that shone down and bathed them all in its crumlush glory.

"So," Proftulous griffled, finishing the last of his brew and wiping his yechus lips with a ganticus paw, "there still be a snutch of things that I just don't be understanding at all."

Ursula screwed her white hare's face into a frown. "Just a snutch of things? I would be thinking there would be grillions of them, dworp."

Proftulous thought about this for a moment then began silently counting on his paws, frowning heavily as he tried to recall all the things he found confusing.

"I have a feeling in my Sisteraculous," Matlock whispered into Ursula's long white ear, "that this could take a peffa-long time."

"And I have a feeling," she warned him, "that you are far too close to my ears. Just because you have completed the first task to becoming Most Majelicus doesn't mean you can sit so close."

"Sorry," Matlock apologised, swiftly leaning away as Proftulous moved onto counting his yechus toes, mumbling to himself all the while.

Ursula's stern face didn't change. "And you would also do as well to remember, Matlock, that you only solved the riddle of Trefflepugga Path because you had a lot of tzorkly help from many of us – including that clottabussed dworp of yours." She looked at Proftulous. "What will you do, when you run out of fingers and toes to count?"

Proftulous looked up. "Count?"

"Because that's what you're doing, isn't it?" Ursula griffled. "Trying to count all the things you don't understand, like the great clottabussed splurk you are?"

Proftulous blinked, confusion written ganticus on his yechus face. "Well, methinks the biggest problem is that I don't remember how to be counting in the first place. So I's having peffa-difficulty trying to remember anything else, I really am."

She sighed. "And I wonder why I'm not even the least surprised by that." She turned to Matlock. "Are you *really* sure your dworp is Most Majelicus?"

Matlock nodded, looking over at his oldest friend. "Fairly. Although, at times, even I'm not completley sure, to be honest. I mean, he did eat nearly a full set of majickal-driftolubbs, so somewhere inside that glopped-up head there's supposed to be all sorts of Most Majelicus majick and wisdom just waiting to be used."

Ursula took another long, hard look at Proftulous. "Of course, it also helps to remember that he's spent most of his life living here in Winchett Dale, with you as his briftest friend. I'm supposing that explains a ganticus amount about his cottabussedness."

Matlock tried his briftest not to feel offended. He already had a lot to thank Ursula for, and the last thing he wanted on such a crumlush even'up was to have a russisculoffed white hare-witch on his paws. For even though she had helped him complete the first task to becoming Most Majelicus, she had also proved herself a more than formidable friend. He knew all too well that just one swish from her wand could vilishly send out a bright blue vroosher

18

that would easily turn him into any number of glopped-up and yechus creatures in the oidiest blinksnap. "I think it'll take time before Proftulous' Most Majelicus nature really surfaces," he tried diplomatically; keen not to upset either of his two friends. "After all, it's peffa-early sun-turns, yet."

"Well, that is time that I don't have," Ursula griffled, finishing the last of her brottle-leaf brew. "It's already late, and I have a long journey back home across the Icy Seas." She stood and made ready to leave, pid-padding to where her waiting broom lay against the side of the cottage, its vroffa-branches already beginning to frizz and glow bright red as she approached. "So I will be leaving you two to your counting, griffling and generally being splurked."

"But I know what it is, now!" Proftulous suddenly cried, a ganticus smile spreading over his yechus face. "I know one of the things that I don't be understanding!"

"Just one?" Ursula called back, shrugging. "Progress, I suppose. Even for you, dworp."

"Well, what is it?" Matlock asked, a little glopped that Ursula was about to leave and to end what had been such a peffa-pleasant even'up so far. For no matter how stern she was, he enjoyed her company, and also knew full well that the moment she was gone, Proftulous would find a a way to turn the griffversation round to his all time peffa-favourite subject – tweazle-pies, the one thing he could griffle about almost as endlessly as he could eat the yechus pies themselves. Indeed, in all the years they had been friends, Matlock, even as a majickal-hare, couldn't even begin to estimate the amount of tweazle-pie griffversations he'd had to endure with Proftulous. On the one paw, it was an oidy price to pay for having a dworp as a peffa-loyal friend (and over time he had learned how to mostly close his long hare's ears to the endless pie-related griffles), but on the other, Matlock did sometimes wonder if there wasn't something more excrimbly to griffle about than the needs of Proftulous' continually rumbling crimple.

"What be what?" Proftulous griffled, trying to remember Matlock's question.

"What's the thing that you've finally remembered?" Matlock sighed, trying not to grind his hare's teeth.

Proftulous stared blankly back. "I's trying to be remembering something?"

Matlock took a deep hare's breath, waving a paw at Ursula as she mounted her broom across the way. "I don't suppose it really matters, now."

Ursula waved back, expertly gripping her broom, as suddenly a deafening roar filled the small cottage garden and she took to the lid, streaking towards the stars, leaving Matlock wondering just when and where he would see her again.

"Well, old friend," he griffled to Proftulous, "I guess that leaves just the two of us."

Proftulous nodded enthusiastically, lump-thumping after Matlock as he collected the brew-mugs and headed inside the cottage. "I's be thinking that p'raps we could be making ourselves a slurpilicious tweazle-pie, Matlock. T'would be the most peffa-saztaculous end to the even'up, wouldn't it be, Matlock? Wouldn't it?"

"It would," Matlock slowly agreed, his mind still on a distant white hare-witch flying back to her home across the Icy Seas, "but for two things."

"And what they be?" Proftulous griffled, trying to help Matlock wash the mugs in the small kitchen sink, but just making his usual peffa-glopped mess.

"Well, firstly," Matlock explained, "I don't have any tweazles in the cottage…"

"That be one problem Proftulous can solve right now!" the excrimbly dworp eagerly griffled. "I's be lump-thumping out into Wand Wood and stroffing a snutch of 'em so we can pie and pastry 'em all up! Honestly, Matlock, we'll be sat down and all crunching on slurpilicious tweazle-pies before you can griffle…"

"Before I can griffle that I *never* eat tweazle-pies," Matlock quietly reminded him. "Ever. Do I?"

Proftulous slapped the side of his yechus head, his ganticus ears drooping a little. "You be right, Matlock. I be clean forgetting you's only like eating niff soup, or niffs and a cloff-beetle salad. I's be such a clottabus. Must be all this Most Majelicus business. I've not been feeling very fuzzcheck since I ate all those griffles from your majickal-driftolubbs. I think they be playing all sorts of

Ursula waved back, expertly gripping her broom, as suddenly a deafening roar filled the small cottage garden and she took to the lid...

glubbstooled tricks with me memory, I really do."

Matlock frowned, drying his paws on a long-haired frittle sitting on the sink-top, before it shook itself dry and scrittled happily back into the garden. "I wonder where Ayaani is?"

Proftulous brightened at this. "Now that much I *can* be remembering," he griffled. "She be gone somewhere, and she hasn't got back yet."

"Indeed, but the question is where?"

"What question?"

Matlock sighed, making his way into his potionary, its tables and shelves heaving with all kinds of jars, majickal-equipment and exotic tinctures. "The question of where she is, of course. Honestly, how can you forget the question?"

"That's it!" Proftulous shouted, nodding his yechus head so vilishly that a stottle-beetle, for reasons it alone only knew had decided to spend the best part of the even'up nifferduggling deep inside Proftulous' left ear, suddenly shot across the potionary, knocking into several jars before finally landing on the window sill and chickling loudly. "That's the thing I've tried to be remembering all this time, Matlock! 'Tis all about questions! The question even'up! 'Tis tonight, at the inn! The ganticus question even'up! Can we be going, Matlock? Can we be going for all sorts of guzzworts and questions?"

"I'm really not sure that it's such a good idea, really," Matlock tried.

"But 'tis a *competition*, Matlock," Proftulous stressed, his yechus eyes alive with excrimblyness. "Those that gets the most questions all correctly answered wins the most saztaculous things."

"What things?" Matlock half-heartedly asked, already sensing that he didn't have it in him to disappoint the eager dworp, and realising that to finish the even'up at the Winchett Dale Inn would at least put an end to all tweazle-pie griffversations, which surely had to be a good thing – or at least peffa-preferable to his current situation. "What are the prizes?"

"Well, it don't be mattering to us, does it?" Proftulous smiled back. "We's too clottabussed to be winning anything, anyway."

"'Tis a fair point," Matlock agreed. "Even if it is made by a dworp."

"A *Most Majelicus* Dworp," Proftulous corrected him.

"Yes, well, we have to keep peffa, peffa-quiet about all that," Matlock warned him. "Dworps aren't supposed to be Most Majelicus. If too many folk discover you are, then there could be ganticus trouble."

"But no one from Winchett Dale's going to griffle anything about it," Proftulous griffled. "Besides, they all still think I'm the most clottabussed dworp in all the dales. There's not one creature, tree, plant or leaning-shrivver that'd ever believe that I be Most Majelicus, Matlock, you know that. After all, I don't really be looking the part, do I?" He puffed out his large chest proudly. "I still be looking just as glopped-up, yechus and clottabussed as always, don't I?"

"Indeed, you do," Matlock smiled. "Peffa, peffa-yechus and clottabussed."

"And glopped-up?"

"Oh, completely," Matlock agreed. "Possibly the most glopped-up dworp in the eternal history of all the dales, my good friend."

Content with Matlock's verdict, Proftulous headed for the front creaker of the cottage. "We's got to be hurrying," he griffled. "We don't wants to get there before all the tweazle-sandwiches and guzzworts have gone."

"I'm not so sure there'll be too many folk queuing up for tweazle-sandwiches," Matlock griffled.

Proftulous turned, frowning as he raised a paw and pointed a long and yechus claw. "Well that's where you could be peffa-wrong, Matlock. And not for the first time, either."

"What do you mean?"

Proftulous lowered his voice to a confidential whispgriffle. "Tonight's question even'up is going to be a special one. There be teams coming from all over the many dales. Visiting teams of peffa-clever creatures, not just us Winchett Dale folk. There'll be creatures we've never seen before, and chances are some of 'em will be all too willing to get their glopped-up paws and claws on my tweazle-sandwiches."

Matlock took a moment to try and take the news in. "There's going to be *visiting* teams? To a Winchett Dale question even'up? Are you sure about this?"

Proftulous nodded. "Completely. It's going to be right fuzzcheck,

Matlock. Teams of three can be taking part, which means you and me can be a team, just like we are in real life." He smothered Matlock in an excrimbly hug, which, as he stood two hares tall, meant Matlock rather wished he hadn't.

Matlock managed to extricate himself, shaking his head and standing back a pid-pad or two, trying not to sneeze or heave. Being hugged by Proftulous was possibly even worse than being cuddled by a swamp-glopped disidula, something to be avoided at all costs, if possible. "Teams of three?"

"S'right. So, me and you's going to be the briftest team, ever."

Matlock took a breath. "But Proftulous, there's only two of us."

Proftulous frowned. "And that be different to 'three', is it?"

Matlock nodded. "It's one short, really."

"One short what?" Proftulous griffled. "One short tweazle? Because I can find one of those if you need one! Plenty of short tweazles around this time of year." He rubbed his ganticus crimple. "Make for the briftest, most slurpilicious crunch, they do, the short ones."

Before Matlock could even think of a response, he was interrupted by a most welcome tugging at the hem of his green robe, looking down to see Ayaani, his dripple by his feet, waiting to be lifted into his hood. "Ayaani," he gratefully griffled, holding her up to his face, "Am I glad to see you."

She smiled. "The dworp has been griffling about tweazles again?"

"Pretty much," Matlock nodded. "Where have you been?"

"To get this," she griffled, producing an oidy twig, no bigger than one of Matlock's toes, and thinner than a murpworm. "It's for the dworp."

"For Proftulous?" Matlock griffled, frowning slightly before whispgriffling in her ear. "What is it?"

"A twig," Ayaani replied, her small dark eyes staring straight back intently.

"A twig?"

Ayaani nodded in the way that dripples do when they're peffa-serious – peffa-slowly. She held out an oidy paw to Proftulous, offering him the twig. "For you, dworp."

Proftulous, who it has be griffled, had never exactly been

the briftest of friends with Matlock's dripple, narrowed his eyes suspiciously.

"Take it," she instructed.

Proftulous carefully reached out a ganticus paw. "It not be going to be biting me, is it?"

"Just take it!" she snapped. "It's your very own wand. Every Most Majelicus dworp should be having one."

Proftulous gasped in pleasant surprise. "My own wand? My actual and very own all Proftulously Most Majelicussy wand?"

Ayaani yawned, an oidy squeeking noise coming from her open mouth. "Something like that, dworp, yes."

He turned the twig in his paw, marvelling at it. "A wand that I can be doing most saztaculous vrooshers with?"

Ayaani vilishly shook her furry dripple's head, her face suddenly serious again. "*No*," she firmly griffled to him. "*Never* for vrooshing, dworp, ever. You can't be seen to be doing vrooshers, or being the oidiest bit Most Majelicus. It be too dangerous. You know that."

Proftulous sighed, his voice almost pleading. "Not even the oidiest, oidiest vroosh, when I can be vrooshing meself a peffaganticus tweazle-pie?"

"One vroosh, and I take the wand back," Ayaani warned. "I went a long way into Wand Wood to find it for you, so you must use it wisely, and only if you really, *really* have to."

Matlock gently popped her into his long velvet hood. "Any good at answering questions, Ayaani?" he griffled, trying to change the subject. "Because apparently there's a question even'up at the inn tonight, and it's open for teams of three."

Ayaani blinked. "What? You, me, and who else?"

"Me, of course" Proftulous griffled, putting the oidy twig into the leather tweazle-pouch he kept tied around his ganticus waist. "I can be answering all kinds of questions."

Ayaani narrowed her eyes. "About what?"

Proftulous thought for a snutch of moments, his large brow furrowed in ganticus concentration as a heavy silence filled the cottage.

"It's all going to go peffa-glopped, I just know it," Ayaani eventually sighed. " Let's just go and get the gopflopping humiliation over with as vilishly as possible."

So it was that moments later, all three friends left Matlock's crumlush cottage; Ayaani safe in Matlock's hood, Proftulous lump-thumping alongside, excitedly griffling about all the tweazle-sandwiches he would soon be eating, as they made their way along the well pid-padded pathways through Wand Wood towards the village of Winchett Dale.

All was quiet, apart from Proftulous' griffling, allowing Matlock to simply enjoy the place he probably loved the most, feeling quite crumlush under a twinkling-lid, savouring being at one with the trees, creatures, and all the hidden majick of the woods. Ayaani, as dripples often do, had already started gently snoring in his hood, her short arms wrapped around his neck, nifferduggling soundly to the rhythm of his soft pid-padding. All, it seemed to Matlock, was peffa-perfect. He felt saztaculously content with the world, knowing that it had almost been a year to the sun-turn since he'd trod this very same pathway to begin his journey to complete the first Most Majelicus task – the solving of the ancient riddle of Trefflepugga Path. Which, of course, hadn't been nearly as easy as he'd thought it would be. Indeed, there were some twizzly times along the way that he would prefer to forget – and yet, in solving the task, he'd met Ursula Brifthaven Stoltz, Proftulous had become Most Majelicus, his dripple had learned to griffle, and he'd even come by the way of a Most Majelicus hawthorn wand for his very own use. And if all that seems peffa-lucky, then perhaps it's because Matlock had always appreciated the simpler things in his life, making him *feel* peffa-lucky, perhaps the most peffa-lucky majickal-hare in the histories of all the majickal dales.

He was just in the middle of deciding what herbs from his garden he would add to his niff-soup the following morn'up, when his thoughts were rudely interrupted by a familiar officious voice, urgently calling out his name in a twizzly panic through the quiet of the moonlit woodland.

"Serraptomus?" Matlock griffled as a short, rotund, wheezing krate dressed in a tattered tweed jacket pulled up breathlessly in front of them. "What in Balfastulous' name is the matter?"

Serraptomus held up a paw, doubled over and fighting for breath. As a krate, whose duties are normally officious, Serraptomus was hardly used to running at all, and the vilish pid-pads he'd taken seemed to have knocked the very breath out of him.

"Is he stroffing?" Proftulous asked, pointing at the coughing krate. "I hope he not be, because even though he can be peffa-officious and bossy, he can still sometimes be making crumlush things from wood."

Which was true, Serraptomus, Winchett Dale's most officious krate, had also proved himself to be a competent whittler and carver, though for just how much longer, Matlock wondered as he rubbed his back to stop him coughing, was anyone's guess. Certainly, it didn't seem that exercise was doing him any good at all. "I don't think all this rushing around suits you," Matlock griffled, straightening Serraptomus' tweed jacket. "Perhaps better to stick to your woodwork from now on?"

Serraptomus nodded, taking a huge breath. "Normally, I would," he finally griffled, trying his briftest to adopt the officious tone favoured by all krates of the dales. "But this, Matlock, is something of a peffa-emergency."

"Emergency?"

Serraptomus nodded again, finally being able to take regular breaths. "The snoffibs have arrived!"

Matlock simply stared back, unable to spot even the oidiest beginnings of any 'emergency' at all. "Snoffibs?"

Serraptomus pointed a short, stubby paw urgently back up the path. "They're at the inn already, Matlock! Three of them, the peffa-cleverest snoffibs I've ever seen, all eager and ready for the question even'up to begin. Their heads be all full of *grillions* of facts and answers, Matlock, grillions and grillions of them!"

"But I've never even heard of snoffibs," Matlock griffled, a little confused.

"Me, neither," Proftulous added. "Never be hearing anything about no snoffibs, ever, and I've lump-thumped around a fair-few dales in my time, believe me I has."

Serraptomus' officious jaw dropped. "You've *never* heard of snoffibs?" He vilishly scratched at an itch on the back of his krate's head. "But surely *everybody's* heard of snoffibs?"

"Clearly not," Matlock griffled. "If we don't know what they are."

Disturbed from her hooded slumbers, Ayaani stretched and

yawned. "Snoffibs," she griffled, "are griffled to be the peffa-cleverest creatures in all the dales. They spend all their time in Snoffib Dale, learning answers to grillions and grillions of questions. And if they're going to be at the inn tonight, then I suggest we all pid-pad straight back to the cottage for a brew, because there really won't be the oidiest point trying to beat them. Once again, it'll all go peffa, peffa-glubstool and everyone will be chickling at us."

Matlock narrowed his eyes at her. "How do you know all that?"

She shrugged. "I know lots of things. You just never think to ask, that's all."

"Because you've only just learned how to griffle," Matlock pointed out.

Which was also true. For traditionally – and according to majickal-dalelore – dripples are totally silent creatures, born mute, whose sole duty is to be a noiseless familiar for majickal-hares, tending to their needs for niff-soup and endless supplies of trupplejuice and brottle-leaf brews, whilst also tidying their cottages and allowing their majickal-hare masters to go about their business of being saztaculous and majickal, without worrying about chores, food or any other such glopped-up matters. And while some may think that this represents something of a thankless life for the hard-working dripple, it's also worth remembering that for whatever bizarre and peffa-strange reasons, dripples choose this life for themselves, born to it, it seems, from the very first blinksnap they open their eyes as drip-kittens, already knowing that one sun-turn they will be able to choose their majickal-hare master and begin their peffa-important dripple-duties.

Another crucial connection between majickal-hares and dripples concerns their life together. Each are born on the very same sun-turn, and will finally pass together into Oramus' most eternal care on the very same sun-turn, also – bonded in life and subsequently in the majickal hereafter, for all eternities. Ayaani had chosen to spend the rest of her years with Matlock, faithfully serving him as his dripple-familiar, doing so willingly as dalelore dictates; without ever griffling a single griffle. But no longer. In solving the riddle of Trefflepugga Path, and for reasons Matlock himself couldn't even begin to fathom, Ayaani had begun to griffle – only the second dripple from all the dales that had ever been known to make even the oidiest noise, whatsosever.

"Well?" she griffled, yawning and hugging his neck. "How much longer are we going to stand around here for? Let's pid-pad back to the cottage. There's no point in going to any sort of question even'up if snoffibs are going to be there."

Serraptomus officiously waved a short, stubby paw. "Absolutely not! I forbid it! Winchett Dale needs your services more than ever before, Matlock. You must go to the inn and beat these snoffibs, or else our beloved village will be the chickling-stock of all the dales."

"But it already is," Proftulous griffled. "Every dale-creature knows Winchett Dale be the most peffa-glopped and clottabussed of all the dales."

"But don't you see?" Serraptomus insisted. "If we can win the competition, then our good and crumlush dale will no longer be something to chickle at. And with you three as a team, we simply *have* to win. After all, who else has a majickal-hare, a griffling dripple and a clottabussed dworp to represent them?"

Proftulous enthusiastically nodded. "Indeed, and I not just simply be clottabussed, Serraptomus, I also be Most Maj—"

Matlock vilishly silenced him with a bliff in the ribs and a long, hard stare.

"You're also *what*, Proftulous?" Serraptomus suspiciously asked.

"He's also most pleased at the thought of eating all the tweazle-sandwiches," Matlock vilishly griffled, shooting Proftulous another look.

Serraptomus considered this in his most officious mind for a snutch of moments, seemingly satisfied. "Of tweazle-sandwiches, there will be a ganticus supply, good dworp. Enough, I suspect, even for you."

Proftulous broke into a ganticus smile at the news. "Then I be griffling that as far as my name be Proftulous, and I be named after the oldest star high in the twinkling-lid, that I be willing to be taking on that challenge, Serraptomus." He turned to Matlock. "What say we go to the inn, and you and Ayaani do all the clever answering of the questions, while I be filling my crimple with tweazles?"

Matlock took a deep hare's breath, before – much to Ayaani's disappointment and Proftulous' excrimbly joy – finally agreeing; all four creatures then making their way out from Wand Wood, over the wooden walkway of Grifflop Marshes, across the River Winchett and finally down into the village of Winchett Dale itself.

Normally, at this time of the even'up, most creatures would be getting ready for nifferduggles, but on the even'up in question (ironically, perhaps, the 'question even'up') the whole village was still awake and peffa-excrimbly, eagerly crowded around the entrance to the inn, leaning through the open windows, peffa-keen to see and hear what was going on inside.

When a lone tilted-graggle spotted Matlock and the others making their way into the square, a ganticus round of pawplause broke out, as everyone began chanting Matlock's name, reaching out to eagerly shake his paw and playfully bliffing him on the back as he was ceremoniously shown to a specially reserved table inside the packed inn.

Landlord Slivert Jutt vilishly delivered a fregle of guzzworts and a ganticus plate of tweazle-sandwiches for Proftulous, as Serraptomus officiously appealed for calm, before loudly clearing his throat in what was probably a totally unnecessary manner. "Good creatures of Winchett Dale," he griffled, "and all our many esteemed visitors who have travelled far and peffa-wide from other dales, I bid you all a most shindinculous and fuzzcheck welcome to our humble inn for this saztaculous question even'up."

"I got's meself a question," a short-legged trullip asked from the back. "You be getting fatter, Serraptomus, or is it that your clothes be getting smaller?"

Serraptomus ignored the chickling, still trying his briftest to be officious, then going on to welcome and announce the visiting teams, which, as far as Matlock could tell, occupied most of the other tables in the inn; some clearly simply there for the guzzworts, others taking the competition far more seriously, and the rest simply looking rather confused, even at this early stage. Many dales were represented, including a saztaculously dressed team from Alfisc Dale, an oidy team of cloff-beetles from Scrittle Dale and a team of bearded-hicklegoats from Svaeg Dale who were already beginning to chew the table.

"Which ones are the snoffibs?" Matlock griffled to Ayaani as she sat in his lap sipping the frothing top of his guzzwort.

She looked around the inn, taking her time, before finally

She looked around the inn, taking her time, before finally pointing to the three strange, four-eyed creatures silently sitting at the very next table. "Them," she griffled, pointing. "They be snoffibs."

pointing to the three strange, four-eyed creatures silently sitting at the very next table. "Them," she griffled, pointing. "They be snoffibs."

Proftulous, his mouth full of tweazle-sandwiches, immediately turned to the creatures, offering a greasy, glopped-up paw. "Even'up, good snoffib folk," he cheerfully griffled, a glopp of drool running down his chin. "We be the Winchett Dale team, and we's going to be right beating you."

The snoffib pulled a disgusted face, flinching and refusing to shake Proftulous' paw, its lizard's skin flushing an alarming deep red.

"Well, not me, personally," Proftulous explained, cramming another sandwich in. "I just be here for the food, really. My briftest friend Matlock will be the one beating you, 'cause he be a majickal-hare who is simply the briftest majickal-hare there is."

Feeling rather awkward, Matlock thought he should at least wave politely at the peculiar looking trio. "Even'up," he griffled. "Please ignore my friend. He can get things an oidy bit clottabussed at times."

The snoffib, clearly having no wish to griffle with such lowly creatures, rearranged his chair and turned his back to them.

"And now," Serraptomus proudly griffled, having announced all the other teams, "'Tis my most honourable pleasure to finally introduce to you all…"

"Get on with it!" someone called out from the back.

"…the team from Winchett Dale – Matlock, his dripple thing, and Proftulous!"

Landlord Sliver Jutt pid-padded over, whispgriffling in Serraptomus' ear for a snutch of moments as everyone waited.

"But as it's just been pointed out to me by good Mr Jutt, keeper of this most fine hostelry…"

"*Please* get on with it," the voice from the back griffled.

Serraptomus ignored it. "Because most of us here already know who Matlock, his dripple thing and Proftulous are, then they don't really need an introduction."

Proftulous quickly raised an eager paw. "S'true, Serraptomus. All we be needing is more of Slivert's slurpilicious tweazle-sandwiches."

The three snoffibs all turned to Matlock, becoming rapidly

russisculoffed with delays to proceedings, their grey skin now flushing pulsing greens and reds. "Can you possibly shut that dworp thing of yours up, hare?"

"I find the briftest way is simply to let him eat," Matlock griffled. "The more he eats, the less he griffles."

The snoffibs pulled a face, as Slivert Jutt replenished Proftulous' plate with another ganticus pile of tweazle sandwiches, before making his way back to the middle of the crowded inn and calling for silence, savouring the moment as all eyes fell upon him. "Right," he griffled. "Are we all being ready for the questions?"

"Yes!" Proftulous loudly griffled, filling his paws with more food.

"Is the right answer!" Jutt griffled as a ganticus cheer filled the inn, ringing right out to the village square. "The first pointy-thing will be awarded to Winchett Dale! Well done, Proftulous. You got's enough sandwiches, over there?"

Proftulous looked at the plate. "No."

"Is another right answer! Because you's *never* be having enough tweazles to eat! Winchett Dale now has another pointy-thing!"

"Which makes two points," Proftulous corrected him. "Even *I* be knowing that much, Slivert."

"*Another* pointy-thing to Winchet Dale!" Jutt roared, as once again the whole inn shook with ganticus cheers and pawplause, the excrimbly creatures crammed at the window eagerly passing the saztaculous news back to the waiting crowd outside. "Though, to be honest, I don't quite know how many pointy-things that be making."

The nearest snoffib stood, outrage in all four eyes, the whole of his head shaking, flushing the deepest reds and purples. "This… this is peffa-outrageous! I've never known anything as glopped up!" Silence gradually fell over the inn as everyone looked at the peffa-russisculoffed creature. "Landlord, how can you possibly even *begin* to griffle that this is any sort of proper and decent question even'up?"

"It be peffa-simple," Proftulous replied from behind a mouth rammed with half-eaten sandwiches. "You begins by opening your mouth, then you just goes and griffles it."

"Correct!" Jutt cried, turning to the crowd. "Another right answer for Winchett Dale! We be winning this right easily! Don't know how, though."

"Me neither, Slivert," Proftulous griffled. "Not the oidest idea. Far too clottabussed, me."

"Another point to Winchett Dale!" Jutt roared, as the inn erupted, creatures whooping and chickling, clinking their guzzwort-jugs high in the air.

"That be more right answers than I can ever be counting!" Jutt griffled, turning to the excrimbly crowd. "What you think that we just declares Winchett Dale the winner right now, to save everyone else looking all clottabussed – especially those snoffibs over there?"

"Fuzzcheck idea, Slivert!" Proftulous called over the loud cheers.

"He's done it again!" Jutt cried. "It *is* a fuzzcheck idea, because it be one of *my* ideas! So that be yet another pointy-thing to Winchett Dale!"

The snoffib stood once more, now puce with rage, unable to conceal the utter russisculoftulation in its shaking voice. "Just…just how much longer is this farce going to go on?"

"Until it be ending, probably," Proftulous calmly replied, motioning to Slivert for another plate of sandwiches. "Which also gives us another pointy-thing for a another correct answer, methinks."

"But," the snoffib loudly objected, "these aren't *questions*! They're not questions at all!"

Matlock, who had spent the time watching with a contented smile, met the snoffib in the largest of its four eyes. "Well, just what are they then?"

"They're not *proper* questions!" He pointed a long, thin claw at Matlock accusingly. "You! You're supposed to be some sort of majickal-hare, supposedly clever. You know full well these aren't proper questions!"

Matlock considered this as silence fell over the inn and everyone waited on his griffles. "You're right," he eventually griffled. "I am a majickal-hare. And as such, I can read, make potions and tinctures, and sometimes even do saztaculous vrooshers with my wand. But

I really don't know that that makes me 'clever'. But I will griffle this, as far as I know, there are no 'proper' questions that I can really think of – only perhaps, 'proper' answers to just some questions."

"What in Oramus' name are you griffling about, hare?" the snoffib demanded, his two teammates nodding in support. "You know very well that I'm griffling about proper questions for a question even'up. Hard questions. Peffa-difficult questions! Questions we can peffa-easily answer to show just how much more we snoffibs know than any other dale creatures! Not easy, clottabussed, glopped-up questions that even a sandwich-eating dworp can answer!"

"Aah, but he *did* answer them, didn't he?" Matlock reminded the puffing snoffib. "And you *didn't*. None of you. Imagine that, three of the peffa-cleverest snoffibs from Snoffib Dale – beaten by a clottabussed dworp? And as for your griffles about *difficult* questions, I griffle you this – if you can answer them so easily, then by definition, that has to make them easy-questions for *you* in the first place. So, what you've been struggling with is accepting the fact that the questions Proftulous answered were far too peffa-difficult for you – even though you griffled that they were really much too easy." He gave the shocked, open-mouthed snoffibs his familiar curling hare's smile. "I suggest you devote more time into looking into the real meaning and truth behind questions, instead of trying to remember answers. And, as such, my question to you all is this – which is more important; remembering answers, or asking the right questions?"

No-one griffled a single griffle for a long snutch of moments until a competing dilva-beetle from a nearby table raised an oidy wing to attract Matlock's attention. "I've no idea what you're on about, hare," it griffled in a peffa-high voice. "But it sort of sounded alright, didn't it, fellas?" He nodded at his other two oidy teammates who both shrugged and nodded uncertainly back.

The snoffib rounded on them. "It sounded," he angrily griffled to the startled beetle, "exactly the sort of glubbstooled, gobflopped nonsense I'd expect from a majickal-hare who's spent too many moon-turns in this most glopped-up dale!" He marched straight to the centre of the inn, the other two snoffibs following close behind, turning to everyone, his face flushing and swirling in a changing sea of raging colour.

"Methinks it's going to go peffa-glopped any blinksnap now," Ayaani whispgriffled into Matlock's long ear as he gently stroked the top of her soft head.

"My name is Dr Irapus Klaxon," the irate snoffib loudly announced, turning to his two teammates. "This is Dr Ritellal Crumble. And this…this is Spig."

"How come he's not a doctor?" someone immediately called out.

"Spig's only here because Dr Forticus Grik couldn't make it," Klaxon explained as the unfortunate Spig looked at his feet somewhat shamefully, flushing an embarrassed pink. "Spig *will* be a peffa-clever doctor one sun-turn, but at the moment, he still has far too many answers to learn. Many moon-turns of hard study will be required."

"Bet you can't wait for that, eh, Spiggy?" a slow-jarrock griffled from the front, chickles breaking out around it.

"Enough of your mocking!" Klaxon barked. "Spig's progress is our concern, not yours!" He turned to Slivert Jutt. "You, landlord! You are somehow going to somehow find it within yourself to ask one peffa-difficult question that only *we* can answer, in order that *we* can win the prizes, and can finally go home from this wretched, clottabussed place!"

"Seems fair," Jutt griffled.

"Of course it's fair!" Klaxon griffled. "We win. We *always* win. We *have to* win. Because we are snoffibs!" He took a breath, staring at everyone, daring them with all four unblinking eyes to griffle even the oidiest griffle. Creatures crammed at the windows waited expectantly for Jutt to painfully think of a question.

"Is it going to take long?" Klaxon asked.

Jutt closed his eyes, scratching his head, making a series of strange guttural noises, concentration filling his landlord's face. At length, he opened his eyes. "A question only you can answer?" he griffled.

"Yes," Klaxon nodded, beginning to get excrimbly. "A peffa, peffa, *peffa*-difficult question. A question about anything."

Slivert thought for another snutch of moments, before finally nodding to himself. "All right. Are you ready?"

"Indeed. Ready to win and get the prize."

"You sure?"

"Completely. Get on with it."

"Right," Jutt griffled, frowing slightly as he formulated his question. "What is…anything?"

"What is *anything*?"

"S'what I griffled," Jutt nodded. "What is anything?"

Klaxon frowned. "But it's not even a question!"

"Indeed, it does be one," Jutt proudly insisted. "You just griffled me to ask you a question about anything, so I be asking you what *is* anything?"

Klaxon flushed bright greens and purple. "But…but…" he stammered, balling his thin fists, "…it doesn't even have an *answer*! Anything is just *anything*. Anything can *be* anything! 'Tis the most glopped-up question I've ever heard!"

Jutt courteously bowed. "A grillion thanks, Dr Klaxon. I do be having my standards to be keeping up, after all."

Spig humbly raised a small, lizardlike hand with a quietly griffled suggestion for Jutt. "Perhaps, if you could griffle us a question about… say…the moon, or the stars in the twinkling-lid, then Dr Klaxon and Dr Crumble would be able to answer it. For they both consider themselves to be the briftest lidgazers in all the dales, you see."

Jutt frowned, confused. "Lidgazers? What be they, then?"

"Creatures who study maps of the twinkling-lid," Spig replied. "They know the name of every star, every constellation. Sometimes they be called astronomers."

Jutt tried his briftest to understand. "And what in Balfastulous' name be a 'constellation' when it be at home, young Spig?"

"'Tis a group of stars," Spig replied. "They can sometimes form shapes and pictures high in the twinkling-lid, with spuddles and legends surrounding them. Many creatures griffle of the majickal power of the constellations."

Jutt looked into all four eyes of the earnest-faced young snoffib for a long time, before finally turning to Matlock. "Pictures and spuddles from stars? This be true, Matlock?"

"It's true," Matlock confirmed from his table.

Jutt smiled, patting the cautious snoffib on the shoulder. "Then I can be confirming that you have just been answering a peffa-difficult question correctly, young Spig. And as such, I take great pleasure in making you the winner of the Winchett Dale Inn question even'up!"

An appreciative round of pawplause broke out, everyone congratulating the confused young snoffib as he desperately tried to divert the attention onto his two scowling teammates. "I really couldn't have done it without good Dr Klaxon and Dr Crumble," he weakly griffled, trying to ignore their frowns.

"So that simply leaves the presentation of the crumlush prizes to the winning team," Jutt announced, nodding to Serraptomus to take over as he vilishly disappeared behind the bar.

Serraptomus duly stepped forward, officiously puffing out his krate's chest, keen to do the honours. "Indeed, Slivert. And I think we'd all agree that we've all had the most saztaculous even'up so far." He went through the business of slowly thanking all the other visiting teams while Jutt continued to loudly search behind the bar. "Slivert, you got those prizes, yet?"

"Slight problem," Jutt griffled, shrugging his shoulders. "I've just remembered that the prizes were three ganticus plates of tweazle-sandwiches. And Proftulous has already eaten 'em."

"Oh, my flipperjubbles!" Serraptomus moaned as gradually the gobflopped news filtered to the waiting crowd of excrimbly creatures outside, inevitably causing the loudest round of pawplause and chickling of the entire even'up. A loud chant of '*Proftulous be eating all the prizes!*' soon begin to ring around the square.

Klaxon turned to Serraptomus, fury in all of his four eyes. "This even'up," he griffled above the raucous noise, russisculoffed colours chasing themselves over his whole body, "has been a complete glopp-up from the peffa-first moment to the ridiculous, clottabussed last one! You should be ashamed! Your dale can't even organise a question even'up without eating the prizes! Winchett Dale is still the biggest joke of all the dales! It always has been, and always will be!" He turned on the chanting room. "Just look at them – fools – each and every clottabussed one! What are you going to do, Serraptomus, when come the morn'up you have to host the Dale Vrooshfest, eh? Or do you simply want me to pid-pad up to Trefflepugga Path right now and tell the grillions of creatures that are currently on their way not to bother?"

Serraptomus, turning pale, called for silence around the inn. "What did you just griffle?"

"That tomorrow's Dale Vrooshfest here in Winchett Dale will be just as badly organised and glopped-up as tonight's question even'up," Klaxon gleefully replied, a thin smile spreading over his oidy mouth. "And then, it won't just be me that sees just how glubbstooled everything is here – it'll be every creature in all the dales."

Serraptomus slowly swallowed, his nervous gulp clearly audible around the shocked inn. "The Dale Vrooshfest…is…here… tomorrow?"

Klaxon nodded, softly chickling. "And your very own majickal-hare didn't even think to tell you? How peffa, peffa-careless of him." He turned to Matlock. "Peffa-careless of you, indeed, hare."

"I knew of no such thing," Matlock protested, murmurs filling the inn, creatures shaking their heads and whispgriffling to each other. "I've been away for many moon-turns, completing my first Most Majelicus task. I've no idea what you're grifling about."

"Then perhaps," Klaxon griffled, milking the moment, "you'd have been far wiser to have stayed at home, instead."

His teammate, Dr Crumble earnestly stepped forward. "Once every seven years, the dales hold their Dale Vrooshfest, when majickal-hares compete for the honour of becoming *Briftest Majickal-Hare of All the Dales* by demonstrating their most saztaculous and shindinculous vrooshers. Thousands of creatures attend, and as such are making their way along Trefflepugga Path right now, in anticipation of seeing this most ganticus and peffa-splendid majickal-festival – right here, tomorrow morn'up."

Matlock tried to take it all in. "And Winchett Dale has been chosen to host it?"

Crumble nodded. "After a peffa-long and important selection process. Many dale's compete for the honour of holding the Dale Vrooshfest – the winners spend many, many moon-turns preparing for it, getting every oidy detail ready and making it all peffa-perfect for their thousands of arriving guests and dignitaries."

"And the last one was seven years ago?" Matlock asked Crumble, who seemed slightly more reasonable to griffle with than the formidable Dr Irapus Klaxon. "That's why I haven't heard of it before. I wasn't even *in* these dales seven years ago. I was still just a hare, out in The Great Beyond."

"Perhaps," Crumble agreed, "Although I'm surprised no-one here thought to griffle you a single griffle about it."

Matlock turned towards the sea of shocked, clottabussed and blank faces belonging to his fellow creatures, sighing heavily. "The thing is," he confidentially griffled to Crumble, "knowing them as I do, it doesn't really surprise me that much at all." He turned to the door, spotting Serraptomus trying to sneak away though the silent crowd. "Serraptomus! Why didn't *you* know about this? You're supposed to be our officious krate! You've lived in this dale for many more years and moon-turns than I have. You're supposed to know everything that's going on. Why didn't you tell us something as peffa-important as this was about to happen?"

Serraptomus turned, looking vacantly at the beamed ceiling in the heavy silence. "I…I…er…I…think I forgot."

"You *forgot*? You honestly forgot something as ganticus as a Dale Vrooshfest? How?" Matlock griffled, aghast. "How, Serraptomus?"

Down at Matlock's side, Proftulous pulled at his green robe with a paw covered with yechus remains of tweazle-sandwiches. "It be easy," he griffled. "I be forgetting things lots of times. We all do."

"But," Matlock insisted through gritted hare's teeth, "not necessarily something as important as this." He turned to the rest of the inn. "How many others of you knew about this Dale Vrooshfest?"

The visiting teams from all the other dales raised their paws, wings, hands, oidy beetly legs and talons, whilst Winchett Dale's own creatures somewhat inevitably simply looked at each other blankly, scratching their heads while trying their briftest to remember.

An immaculately dressed team-member from Alfisc Dale broke the awkward silence. "Frankly, we're only here for the vrooshfest, good hare. We arrived a sun-turn early to get the briftest seats for tomorrow morn'up. The last thing we ever wanted to do was come to your question even'up. It just helped pass some time, really."

All the other teams slowly nodded in agreement, apart from the three snoffibs, all too keen to griffle that for them, the question even'up was the main event, and that to waste a sun-turn at the Dale Vrooshfest would be to miss the peffa-important chance to be safely back in Snoffib Dale, learning new answers for lots more peffa-difficult questions.

"I have a question for you," Matlock griffled to them, his mind reeling from the unexpected news. "How in Balfastulous' name was Winchett Dale ever chosen as hosts? It makes no sense at all."

"Well," Klaxon griffled, his voice calmer now, pleased he finally had an audience eagerly awaiting one of the many grillions of answers he had in his large, lizardy head, "now this is a peffa-easy question for me."

"Good," Matlock griffled. "I'd be much obliged if you answered it."

Klaxon made a show of clearing his throat. "There are three factors deciding which dale will be chosen; the first being that the size of dale is sufficiently ganticus enough to hold the many thousands of excrimbly spectators and visitors. The second – that the Dale Vrooshfest has never been held in the chosen dale before…"

"And the third?" Matlock griffled, not really wanting to hear the answer, his hare's eyes firmly fixed on Serraptomus, still blankly staring at the beamed ceiling.

"That the most officious krate from the chosen dale agrees wholeheartedly to put in place saztaculously efficient plans to ensure the many elaborate preparations are carried out in accordance with the *Dale Vrooshfest Committee*'s highest expectations."

"Serraptomus?" Matlock called over to the wincing krate. "Did you hear all that?"

Serraptomus nodded miserably. "I just forgot, Matlock, honestly." He turned, eyes imploring and beginning to well-up rather unofficiously. "It was all such a long time ago. I sort of made some plans in my head…I think…and then just…forgot about them."

Proftulous suddenly looked up. "What we all be griffling about?"

"The Dale Vrooshfest," Slivert Jutt griffled from behind the bar. "The one Serraptomus be all forgetting about, so now grillions of creatures from all the other dales will be coming here tomorrow morn'up and be seeing just how glopped-up we are – again."

Proftulous considered this for a snutch of moments, before eventually standing and lump-thumping over to Serraptomus and wrapping a ganticus paw over the trembling krate's upset shoulders. "Well," he griffled, "I don't be knowing about any Dale Vrooshfests, and I doubt there's many in this dale who do. But one thing I will griffle is this; I don't like to see folk getting eyesplashy and twizzly over something that they can't be stopping, or changing. Because, good folk, whatever happens tomorrow sun-turn, however much we all gobflop, however much this dale becomes the chickling-stock of all the dales…"

"Nothing new there, then," a voice called from the window.

"…when the sun-turn finally be over and everyone's gone, then come the even'up the only thing that'll matter to us is that we're able to get back into our beds and be all crumlushly nifferduggling like we normally do." He effortlessly lifted Serraptomus up onto his ganticus shoulders, misjudging the ceiling and painfully bliffing the krate's head on a low roof-beam. "And I don't be seeing a single oidy reason why our Serraptomus should be eyesplashy about it all glopping-up – because, after all, it's what we do best. We are the briftest gloppers in all the dales, and methinks that to be anything else – just wouldn't be us."

The listening creatures nodded their heads in agreement.

"So let us all hold our clottabussed heads up high tomorrow morn'up. Let the grillions come to our dale," Proftulous took a large breath, puffing his chest out proudly, "and let them see just how saztaculously Winchett Dale can *really* glopp-up a Dale Vrooshfest! We not be ready, we not be prepared, and we all be forgetting all about it– but one thing we shall never be forgetting is that we are, shall be, and always *will* be – the briftest gloppers in all the dales!"

Pawplause and cheers erupted like a ganticus case of cracksploding Trikulum powder as Proftulous carried Serraptomus outside to the waiting crowd, all now eagerly beginning to chant, '*We are the briftest gloppers in the dales!*' as Matlock watched with a heavy heart from inside the inn.

"Well, I wish we could stay to see just how glopped-up it'll get tomorrow," Klaxon griffled, signalling to Crumble and Spig that it was time to leave. "I'm peffa-sure it'll be remembered by everyone for a long, long time. However, we have to go because…"

"I know, I know," Matlock sighed, feeling quite juzzpapped at just the thought of the morn'up's inevitable chaos, "you have too many difficult answers to be learning and remembering."

Klaxon bowed slightly. "Indeed, we do. But I wish you the peffa-briftest of luck, hare." He held out a long, thin hand to shake. "And if your question even'up was anything to go by, then I suspect you're going to need every oidy bit of it."

Matlock smiled. "It'd be fuzzcheck that, wouldn't it?"

"What would?"

"If luck did actually come in bits and pieces, and you could somehow carry it around and use it."

Klaxon smiled back. "Indeed, it would. But unfortunately, you can't. But I still wish you well, hare, I really do."

Matlock scooped a sleeping Ayaani up into his hood then bade farewell to the other visiting teams, slowly pid-padding out of the inn into the autumnal night, watching the crowd of Winchett Dale's excrimbly, chanting creatures parading Serraptomus around the village square, knowing in his Sisteraculous that no matter how many saztaculous vrooshers he could conjure, there was simply far too little time for the dale to ever be prepared for what was going to happen the following morn'up.

Yet, as he looked up at the stars high in the twinkling lid, all crumlush in the deep-blue night, he wondered if for once, Proftulous' clottabussed griffles hadn't been right. Surely, no matter what happened, no matter how much things went gobflopped, Winchett Dale would do as it always did, and somehow get by to glopp-up another sun-turn – and, perhaps most peffa-importantly, everyone really would be safely nifferduggling in their beds at the end of it. And nothing about Winchett Dale would have changed at all; it would simply be yet another clottabussed sun-turn in this most clottabused of all the majickal-dales.

Taking a deep hare's breath, he began to pid-pad out of the village, the cries and chants receding as he made his way back into the welcoming darkness of Wand Wood towards the shindinculous promise of his own cottage and the crumlush bed which awaited him there.

The Krettles, the Second Task and the Lid-Machine

Of all its many majickal-mysteries, Trefflepugga Path holds one to be its most consistent – its very *inconsistency*. The path itself runs like a central vein between all the majickal-dales, providing a possible route for creatures to cross from one dale to the other, but (and here is the most consistent inconsistency) only *if it allows you to*. With entrances to each dale to be found in various places across its ever changing length, the unwary traveller might well assume that it would be a relatively simple matter to leave one dale, travel along the path, then duly arrive at the chosen dale of your intended destination. However, this would expose the folly of your decision, as from the very first pid-pad you took along Trefflepugga Path, it alone would decide the destiny of your journey. You may wish to travel from Currick Dale to Snoffib Dale, Svaeg Dale to Grupple Dale, Alfisc Dale to Krilt Dale – however, where you actually ended up would depend solely on the will of the path, and where it decided you should really be.

And this alone isn't the only inherent danger, for the path may well decide (for reasons most unsuspecting creatures never realise) that your journey is simply to be an unending one, or that you will be victim to one of its many twizzly perils and be stroffed, leaving your softulous and bones to be chewed upon and crunched by the savage long, long-nosed krellits who wait in the path's many shadows for just such a slurplicious opportunity.

However, it's also worth bearing in mind that if you set out along Trefflepugga Path and it finds your journey to be a reasonable one, then it's also perfectly possible that it might allow you a relatively safe passage to your final destination without so much of a hint of a single twizzly danger presenting itself along the way. Mostly, these instances are rare, but as such, the ganticus migration of creatures from all the dales to the Dale Vrooshfest is one of them, with the majority of creatures who set out along Trefflepugga Path arriving safely in the hosting dale. Only once in dale history has this not been the case – the infamous Dale Vrooshfest of Frods Dale – when every creature making the journey had to pid-pad for three long and desperately dangerous moon-turns along its ever changing landscape, before finally finding themselves bizarrely and reluctantly back in their own dales, most of them considering the whole gobflopping experience a most peffa-twizzly waste of time. And as Trefflepugga Path (although it's undoubtedly alive) has never been known to griffle, to this very sun-turn no explanation of what came to be known as the 'Frods Dale Glopp-up' was ever given, or has ever been found.

Since then, however, most journeys to and from Dale Vrooshfests have passed without too much incident, almost as if somehow Trefflepugga Path fully agrees with both the festival and the choice of hosting dale, which was something Matlock was all too aware of as he made his way slowly back through Wand Wood that even'up. No matter what would happen the next morn'up, Trefflepugga Path would most likely grant safe passage to the hoards of visiting creatures, and even he, as a majicjkal-hare, knew there was absolutely nothing he could do to change its will.

He wondered too, about just what he would be required to do at the vrooshfest; who would be his opponents, how the contest would be scored, who would decide the winner? And while an oidy bit of him quite liked the peffa-unlikely thought of being crowned *Briftest Majickal-Hare of All the Dales*, for the most part he simply wanted the whole sun-turn to pass without too much gobflopping. Yes, inevitably, it would all go peffa-glubbstooled (this was Winchett Dale, after all), but hopefully all would be well come the even'up.

He was so deep in these thoughts that he hadn't even noticed what was perhaps one of the strangest and most unexpected sights to see in Wand Wood looming in the darkness just a few pid-pads away. There, off the small path and partially hidden by the stout trunks and dense canopies of a snutch of bossatt-trees, stood the beginnings of what looked like a ganticus curved stone structure, which as Matlock approached and he craned his hare's neck to see up into the twinkling-lid, he could only assume to be some sort of ivy-clad tower…

The more he looked and cautiously pid-padded towards it, the more he began to notice a most peffa-peculiar thing about the arched windows running up its length – they were all upside down. Further, the ivy appeared to be growing *down* the ganticus circular tower, its roots high at the very top, reaching out like an umbrella of angry, twisting claws, the entire tower looking as if it had been somehow unearthed, up-ended, then thrown with ganticus force into the trembling earth below.

And yet all around him nothing moved, not an oidy creature scrittled through the undergrowth, or a single leaf rustled in the breezeless night. The whole sight was one of the most peffa-curious Matlock had ever seen.

Ayaani stirred in his hood, climbing up onto his shoulder to peek out. "Methinks we should leave," she urgently whispgriffled in his long hare's ear. "There be much twizzly danger here, Matlock. I feel it in my Sisteraculous. Too much danger. We must pid-pad away, vilish!"

Matlock narrowed his hare's eyes, scrutinising the tower, a powerful extrapluff shaking his whole body and telling him exactly what he must do. "I can't," he whispgriffled to his twizzly dripple. "I have to go inside." He lifted her out and gently set her on the ground. "Go to the cottage, fetch my Most Majelicus wand and bring it straight back here."

Ayaani reluctantly nodded, knowing that as a dripple, it was always her first duty to follow her master's orders and instructions. She set off, scrittling away up the path and towards the cottage as vilishly as her oidy legs would take her, knowing that all her warning griffles would be in vain, for when Matlock had an extrapluff, he would always follow it, regardless of whatever anyone else griffled. And this, she also realised, was just one of those times.

Matlock watched her leave then turned back to the tower, standing at the base where it met the rough forest floor, the gaps between up-turned crenulations looking like black doorways set into the rough stone. He was just peering inside, gingerly poking his head into the darkness, when suddenly a smiling candlelit furry head with pink ears and the most peffa-crumlush and welcoming smile burst into his view, startling him to cry out in shock, the only noise in the eerily silent wood.

"So sorry," the friendly creature replied. "Didn't mean to be giving you a peffa-twizzly fright. Do forgive me."

"Who…who are you?" Matlock griffled, taking a breath and trying to control his vilishly beating heart.

The creature held out a pink paw and gently pulled at the side of Matlock's cheek. "Lily," she griffled, beaming widely in a way that made Matlock's whole softulous feel quite crumlush. "Lily Krettle. And this," she griffled, as another equally friendly furry face suddenly appeared at her side, "be my husband, Jericho. Together, we be the keepers of the second Most Majelicus Task."

A shudder shook Matlock at the mere mention of it.

Jericho Krettle smiled at him. "You not be expecting to be starting it so soon, then?"

Matlock blinked in shock. "What? Starting it? The second task? Now?"

The Krettles both smiled and nodded warmly.

"But I can't," Matlock griffled, "I'm not sure that I'm ready, and there's going to be a vrooshfest and a peffa-important sun-turn for the dale tomorrow morn-up, and…"

Lily Krettle chickled and gently led Matlock through the gap in the stone. "Now, you'll not be surprised to know that there's many of you majickal-hares what be griffling the peffa-same things about not being ready when me and Mr Krettle shows up and be all surprising them."

Jericho Krettle nodded. "But as soon as they've been told what to do, there's not one of them that doesn't set off immediately on the second task. So you's just the same as all the others, you see?

Pid-pad this way, good hare, there's nothing to be twizzly about. Nothing at all."

Before Matlock could even begin to reply, the crumlushly furry Krettles had led him underneath the tower, Lily holding a candle in her paw to light the cloying darkness, Jericho reaching up to open a thick wooden hatch and letting down a small ladder just above their heads.

"Up we go then," he cheerfully griffled, "and we can be getting on with everything as vilishly as possible."

"You live here?" Matlock griffled, climbing up the small ladder into a large room that he realised would have once been at the very top of the tower. A large, lit twinkleabra rose from the floor, and above his head, tables, chairs and other unrecognisable bits of furniture appeared stuck to the ceiling. "You really live in this tower?"

Lily drew up the ladder and quickly closed the hatch behind her. "Indeed we do. It gets a bit glopped at times, but you'd be surprised how quickly you can get used to everything being downside-upsy."

"You mean, upside-down?"

She smiled, shook her head, her small pink ears wobbling. "No, I mean downside-upsy. Upside-down be the right griffles, but clearly they be all wrong in here. So we's be calling it downside-upsy, don't we Jericho, my lovely?"

Her husband agreed, wrapping a paw round her shoulder and lightly kissing her cheek. "We do, good Lily, we do," he griffled. "But right now we must be taking this hare to his second task, methinks." He turned to Matlock. "Now, you just be following me and Mrs Krettle right down to the bottom of the tower…"

"Which you'd be calling the top," Lily helpfully explained.

"…so you can be listening to our griffles as we be explaining the task to you."

Feeling he really had no other choice, and mindful of the powerful extrapluff he'd had outside, Matlock slowly followed Jericho Krettle up a long, ornate iron spiral staircase in the centre of the tower, passing through different levels full of quite the strangest looking furniture and what looked like heavy chains hanging from vastly elaborate pulley systems, huge black iron wheels slowly turning high above his head, constantly moving with ominous, echoing clanks. Each room they climbed through was dimly lit by just one or two flickering candles throwing eerie shadows dancing on the thick stone walls.

Indeed, if it hadn't been for the crumlush, cheery and welcoming countenance of the Krettles themselves, their jokes and gentle chickles as they climbed, Matlock might have found the tower to have been one of the most peffa-twizzly places he'd ever had the misfortune to pid-pad in. But with Jericho leading the way, and Lily following behind, he felt strangely safe, knowing that although he was pid-padding to what was possibly the last thing he wanted to do – the second Most Majelicus task – he also sensed deep in his Sisteraculous that somehow the time was right, even though it seemed as if he'd barely taken a single hare's breath after solving the riddle of Trefflepugga Path.

And as he also knew, Most Majelicus tasks rarely wait for the most convenient time for majickal-hares to attempt them. If you were called upon to undertake one, you really had no choice – it had somehow already been decided, far away, by creatures and forces that Matlock knew he couldn't even begin to imagine.

At last, they reached the top of the spiral staircase, the three of them stepping off into a ganticus round room with upturned arched windows cut into its thick walls. Jericho Krettle pid-padded to the far side and began pulling on a large, heavy chain as a huge iron wheel turned above his head, causing the spiral staircase to slowly and noisily descend, leaving just a gaping black hole in the floor. Next, Matlock's jaw dropped as Jericho began heaving on another dangling chain, this time slowly raising a ganticus hourglass four times his own size into the room, the floor closing underneath it, the massive structure being gently lowered down onto the wooden floor with a heavy, garrumblooming thump.

"Look around you," Jericho instructed Matlock, panting from his efforts. "What do you notice up here?"

Matlock looked, realising that this was the only room in the tower that seemed to be the *right* way up. Twinkleabras and lamps hung correctly from the ceiling, and tables, chairs and cupboards littered the floor. Indeed, the only things that seemed to hint at the rest of the tower were the upturned windows, with long green curtains hanging at their sides. And, of course, the ganticus hourglass itself – for here, most strangely, the sand inside appeared to be 'falling' from the huge lower glass bowl *up* into the one above it. Matlock also noticed the top seemed very full, with only an oidy amount of sand remaining in the lower bowl, which was so large, he felt sure Proftulous could have easily stood in it.

He really didn't know what to make of any of it.

Lily Krettle pid-padded over to a large cauldron that was bubbling and sprottling over a roaring piff-tosh on the far side of the room. "Methinks the hare be lost for griffles, good Jericho," she griffled, putting on an apron and beginning to chop vegetables with a soot-blackened knife on an old wooden table, each chunking thud echoing round the curved stone walls. "Methinks you'd best be griffling to him what he has to be doing, so he's not being all displeased with us."

"Indeed, good Lily," Jericho griffled back. "We don't wants the hare to be being all displeased with us, do we?" He turned to Matlock. "How about you be being peffa-nice and be helping my good wife prepare those vegetables, so's we can be all having a slurpilicious bowl of soupy-soupy." He gave Matlock an oidy wink. "Only we don't want to be displeasing her, do we? Not be wanting to displease her at all, methinks."

"Er…no, we don't, I suppose," Matlock griffled not quite sure what was going on, or why it was that Jericho Krettle seemed to be suddenly eyeing him intently, as if studying every inch of his hare's face for even the oidiest twitch or movement. "It's probably good if none of us are displeased or russisculoffed in any way."

Jericho smiled, Matlock noticing for the first time just how yellow and sharp his teeth were, yechussly pointed, each one down to a needlepoint at its end. The smile vilishly changed into a comforting smirk, his lips now firmly closed, as if he'd inadvertently given something away. "They be good griffles, hare," he chickled, patting Matlock jovially on the shoulder. "So you go and be doing some chopping and dropping in of vegetables, and we'll all be having the most slurpilicious soupy-soupy, you'll see."

Feeling an oidy bit unsettled, Matlock joined Lily Krettle,

Lily Krettle pid-padded over to a large cauldron that was bubbling and sprottling over a roaring piff-tosh on the far side of the room.

chopping vegetables as she tossed them into the ganticus splutting cauldron. Jericho, meanwhile, busied himself on the other side of the room, checking chains and pulleys, as Lily closely watched Matlock, chopping in absolute silence until the very last vegetable had disappeared into the furiously boiling water.

"Right," she happily griffled, wiping her delicate pink paws on her apron. "That be done, and it all be preparing most nicely. Not long to be waiting now, hare." She turned to him, Matlock wondering if her eyes hadn't become just an oidy bit pinker. "What be your name, then?"

"Matlock," he griffled.

She nodded, leading him gently back by the paw to stand in front of the ganticus hourglass, the last remaining grains of sand still trickling into the upper glass bowl. "Well, Matlock, the time has come when we be griffling to you the nature of your second Most Majelicus task."

He waited as Jericho Krettle adjusted some chains, shifting the hourglass on the hard wooden floor.

"Your task," Lily griffled, "is a finding one. We tell you what you need to be finding, you go and find it – then bring it back here to us." She smiled, Matlock suddenly noticing that her teeth were just as yellow, yechus and sharply pointed as her husband's. "That not be sounding too peffa-difficult, now, does it?"

"I suppose not," Matlock griffled, watching as the last of the sand fell into the top of the hourglass, noticing that it appeared to be speeding up; rushing, almost, to get into the upper-bowl. "But surely it depends on what I have to find?"

"Indeed, it does," Lily Krettle agreed, a thin sliver of yechus drool falling from her lips. "And it also depends on the time you're given to do it." She suddenly dragged her claws over the hourglass, a dreadful scratching sound filling the room as the cauldron boiled ever more ferociously on the far side.

"Time?" Matlock griffled, sensing that he didn't really want to know the answer, watching Jericho Krettle keenly studying the empty bowl of the hourglass, as if something peffa-important was just about to happen.

"Each majickal-hare that undertakes the second Most Majelicus task is given a certain amount of time to be completing it," Lily carefully explained. "If they haven't found what they seek before the sands of their time run out, then…"

"It all goes soupy-soupy for them!" Jericho suddenly cried out. "Hare soupy-soupy! Hare soupy-soupy for Jericho and Lily Krettle!"

Matlock watched in horror as suddenly a majickal-hare appeared in a blinding flash of light in the bottom of the hourglass, its green robes ripped and glopped with mud, frantically hammering its paws on the sides of the glass, muffled screams pleading to Matlock for help, its eyes meeting his, peffa-twizzly with pure fear and terror.

"Let him out!" Matlock cried. "For goodness sake – let him out!"

Jericho Krettle chickled loudly, pulling on the chains with all his might, slowly raising the hourglass and the trapped majickal-hare into the air and towards the horribly bubbling cauldron. "Let him out?" he griffled, puffing and panting. "He be failing the task! His sands be running out. He be all hare soupy-soupy in a snutch of moments!"

"Keep pulling him this way, Jericho, my lovely!" Lily griffled, chickling loudly as she pid-padded over to the cauldron and grabbed a ganticus black wooden spoon to begin stirring the splutting gloop inside. "Let's be having him all boiley-boiley!"

Matlock struggled to breathe, utterly and dreadfully transfixed as Jericho Krettle gleefully hauled on the chains, inching the ganticus hourglass right over the cauldron, the trapped majickal-hare still desperately pounding on the glass, its terrified eyes begging Matlock for help.

"Please," Matlock managed to griffle in the chaos. "Please… don't…"

"It be too peffa-late for any pleases and beggings!" Lily Krettle snarled back, her whole mouth now a ganticus collection of yellow pointed teeth, growing longer with every blinksnap. "He be failing the task and making us all displeased with him. He be for the soupy-soupy now!"

"No!' Matlock screamed, watching in open-mouthed horror as suddenly the entire bottom of the hourglass swung open, sending the terrified majickal-hare plunging straight into the boiling, splutting cauldron. Lily Krettle whooped with joy as she pushed it under, vilishly swirling and stirring, her teeth clacking together like thick yellow claws.

"He be all stroffed!" she cried out, as Jericho bounded over and reached straight down into the boiling soup and vilishly pulled out the soaked green robes, hurling them with a wet, steaming slap onto the cold stone floor.

"More curtains for you, my lovely," he griffled, his own teeth multiplying and become longer as he watched his wife stirring the soup. "Methinks he all be ready for bowling up and eating soon."

Lily Krettle shook her head. "He needs a snutch of moments yet, my lovely," she cheerfully griffled. "Don't wants him all underdone. Plays havoc with me crimple, does underdone hare soupy-soupy." She pointed over at Matlock. "You be explaining the task to that twizzled hare over there, whilst I be finishing this one off. Then, when he's gone we can both be tucking in."

"Alright, my lovely," Jericho griffled, kissing her, their growing, horribly pointed teeth clashing and clacking. "I's be going and doing that."

Matlock watched in stunned shock, his hare's feet rooted to the stone floor, as Jericho Krettle began working on the pulleys once more, closing the trapdoor and returning the ganticus hourglass to the centre of the room. For all his life he wanted to cry out, to pid-pad away as vilishly as possible, but nothing in his softulous seemed to work. Everything he'd just seen had frozen him. None of it seemed real, yet, of course, it *was* real – which made it all a grillion, grillion times worse. He *had* to leave, somehow find the will and energy to escape this dreadful and most glopped-up place, yet still he simply stood, transfixed in peffa-twizzly fear.

A sudden chattering of teeth by his side made his startled head turn. "So let me be explaining this to you," Jericho Krettle griffled. "This be a finding task, and in a snutch of moments, I'll be chaining and heaving this hourglass back over. The sands will begin their journey back into the upper bowl. This time, they will be *your* sands, and your time will have begun. To complete the task, you must find what the task decrees before your sand runs out." He offered Matlock a sight shrug. "And if you fail, then you'll end up all hare soupy-soupy, just like the rest of 'em."

Matlock's gaze followed his pointed claw towards Lily Krettle, still stirring the cauldron and chickling gently to herself. "What…" he finally managed to griffle, "…is it that I have to find?"

"It be a good question," Jericho griffled.

"A peffa-good question!" his wife called across. "A question that not be displeasing to us at all. Not an oidy bit displeasing, is it, my lovely?"

"Not the peffa-oidiest bit," Jericho agreed, blowing her a kiss from behind his terrible teeth. "There be no displeasing in that question whatsoever. It be a good question – but that alone doesn't always make for a pleasing answer, now, does it?"

Feeling he might faint at any minute, desperate to leave as vilishly as possible, Matlock took his deepest hare's breath and tried again. "Please, just griffle me what it is I need to find."

Jericho smiled, his teeth now beginning to suddenly bend and swivel in his drooling mouth, as if each had an independent life, starting to spin like hundreds of tiny sharp tentacles. "A wand," he griffled through them. "You must be finding a wand."

"What sort of wand?" Matlock griffled, trying not to look into the yechus mouth.

"The Tillian Wand," Jericho replied. "The second Most Majelicus task be the finding and bringing back of the Tillian Wand."

Lily laughed from the other side of the room. "That not be sounding too peffa-difficult, now, does it? Just the mere finding of a wand? It be sounding peffa-easy, if you asks me. Right peffa-easy indeed." She pointed a claw at Matlock, her teeth now also spinning as the soup boiled furiously below. "But you'd be surprised how many of your majickal kind never even get the oidiest bit close to it."

"Which means more soupy-soupy for us!" Jericho joyfully exclaimed, bounding over to a large looped iron chain and pulling with all his might, causing the ganticus hourglass to slowly begin to turn. "I'd not be still stood there like a clottabus if I was you, Matlock!" he laughed, hauling on the chain. "I'd be off on my pid-pads as vilishly as possible! Your sands are about to start running out any blinksnap!"

"But where do I begin?" Matlock panicked, looking everywhere, the hourglass almost horizontal, the sand beginning to lurch inside, the whole structure knocking against the backened chains swinging precariously above his head. "Is it here? Here in this tower?"

Krettle shouted at him. "What, you think we're about to be giving you clues, hare? You think this be some sort of gobflopped *game*? I think that be displeasing us muchly, I really do." He set back to the chain, pulling with all his might, the hourglass rising upright, the heavy sand now at the bottom, an oidy trickle already beginning to make its way up into the ganticus top bowl. "Each of these grains of sand be one of your heartbeats, hare," he griffled through swirling teeth. "And the more you get's all twizzly, the more of them you'll be losing – so the more vilishly your time will be running out."

Lily appeared by Matlock's side, a steaming bowl of yechus soup and a wooden spoon in her paw. "Please stay and join us for some soupy-soupy, won't you? You'll be peffa-surprised how slurpilicious your own kind are. Especially when their fur be all nicely boiled off. Some proper crumlush meaty-bits you can pull from the bones." She dug him in the ribs. "And Jericho, well, he just loves all the eyebally-jelly."

Matlock yelped, shrinking from the dreadful offering, the ganticus hourglass finally coming to a loud, clattering standstill behind him.

Lily tutted and shook her head. "See how fast those sands be running now that's you've got all clottabussed and twizzly over just some harmless soupy-soupy?" She pointed at the rising trail of sand getting faster with each blinksnap. "Why, methinks your heart must be beating more vilishly than a hare's back legs in a boiling cauldron."

Matlock tried to breathe and calm himself, but it was peffa-impossible. The more he tried, the faster his heart began to beat, the quicker the sand-trail rose into the upper bowl. "But I've never even heard of the Tillian Wand!" he griffled, eyes frantically searching for any sign of anything that might be a wand.

"And that be pleasing us most greatly," Lily smiled, handing her husband a steaming bowl of soup. "Most pleasing us, indeed. But you should be on your way. Wands don't be finding themselves, you know." She pid-padded back to the cauldron, ladling a large bowl of soup for herself. "And if you really be stuck, hare, then perhaps you should be griffling with the creeping-green. It might even be knowing something peffa-useful."

"Not that it be helping too many of the other hares!" Jericho cried out, soup spilling from his yechus mouth. "The creeping-green always griffles the most peffa-difficult puzzles!" He pointed to a small wooden door set in the darkened recesses of the circular stone wall. "Your journey begins through that door, Matlock. It be time for you to begin."

"And be careful," Lily warned him, a frightful smile spreading over her face. "There be many dangers. We don't want you coming back with cuts and all-bruisy. Makes the meat on you taste peffa-glopped. Likes you all tender and melty, we do."

Feeling as yechus and twizzly as he'd ever felt, yet utterly relieved to be able to leave the terrible room, Matlock vilishly seized his opportunity, swiftly crossing to the creaker to finding another spiral staircase, frantically panting as he raced down, desperate to be back outside, away from the horror of the Krettles; their echoing chickles and shrieks chasing him, step by step, as he blundered further down into the darkness. Finally, he reached the bottom, stumbling and falling, and hurled himself against a thick wooden creaker, peffa-grateful when it shuddered and opened, finally allowing him back into the darkness of Wand Wood.

He stood, holding his aching sides, gasping for breath, trying to make some sort of hare's sense of it all, looking at the upturned tower, hearing the Krettles' muffled cries at the very top, the light of the twinkleabras sending golden shadows ghosting over nearby swaying tree-tops, leaves rustling in the night, their branches obscuring the twinkling lid above.

"It is the most peffa-glopped-up experience, isn't it?" a voice suddenly griffled by his side. "The first time you meet the Krettles."

Matlock turned, gasping as he saw the familiar face of his old Most Majelicus hare-master. "Chatsworth! Thank Oramus you're here!" he blurted out, unable to conceal the twizzly panic in his griffles. "It was truly yechus, in there! It was so glubbstooled and…"

Chatsworth patiently nodded, holding out a paw and putting it to Matlock's frantically beating chest. "The second Most Majelicus task is indeed a finding task, Matlock. But really, the thing you're searching for – the thing you really need to find – is something within yourself."

"The Tillian Wand?"

Chatsworth nodded, standing in his red robes and smiling slightly. "That, too, Matlock. But in order to find it –in order not to be stroffed and eaten by the Krettles – you must find a way to control your twizzliness. You must keep the calmest heart at all times, Matlock. It must beat slowly – or your sands will run out too quickly." He removed his paw, looking Matlock deep into his bright orange hare's eyes. "Those hares that complete the challenge successfully – and unfortunately, there are peffa-few – will have found that strength in themselves, Matlock, and conquered their twizzliness in doing so. 'Tis a vital process to becoming a Most Majelicus hare, and the real purpose of the second task – to teach you to think calmly and clearly in the most glopped-up, glubbstooled and peffa-twizzly situations. For without clarity, Matlock, you will be of no use whatsoever. 'Tis why those who fail are stroffed, just as you saw."

Matlock tried to swallow, his mouth too dry, his paws shaking. "But it was yechus, Chatsworth – truly, peffa yechus!"

"As it was meant to be. The hare who boiled knew the risks, just as you do now. He failed at the task, his sands ran out before he could get to the wand. So he had to be stroffed. *The Most Majelicus Council for all Hares* decrees it thus. Don't think too harshly of the Krettles – they're just doing their job as keepers of the second task."

"But it's…so…" Matlock was almost lost for griffles, "…cruel."

Chatsworth nodded. "And peffa-serious, Matlock, peffa-serious indeed." He reached out both paws, placing them gently on Matlock's shoulders. "Here we both stand in Wand Wood, under the twinkling-lid, just like old times. I have a great fondness for them, Matlock. I know full well you sometimes see me as cold, but believe me, I have never felt that way about you, for you alone out of all the majickal-hare's I have trained as apprentices during my all too short time in these dales, stood paws and ears taller than the rest." He lowered his voice to a whispgriffle and smiled. "We Most Majelicus hare's aren't supposed to have favourites – but you were always mine, Matlock, from the peffa-first moment I saw you out in The Great Beyond. When I bought you back, so excrimbly, and we made our first trip along Trefflepugga Path together, I extrapluffed deep in my Sisteraculous that you would be *different* – so different from all the rest." He winked and smiled. "And you never proved me wrong – not even for the oidiest blinksnap.

"So when the time came for me to nominate my chosen hare, I already knew whose name I would put forward for consideration to undertake the three tasks – yours, Matlock – and only yours. You've completed the first task, and now you must begin pidpadding on your second. My heart might beat slowly in the way of Most Majelicus hares – but it has never beaten with so much ganticus pride, Matlock – ever."

Matlock tried to smile, finding the best he could muster was a gobflopped half-grimace, his long hare's ears still hearing the Krettle's echoing shrieks from up on high. "You're not going to tell me where the wand is, are you?"

Chatsworth shook his head. "It is completely forbidden."

"But you've broken rules before," Matlock insisted. "Laffrohn griffled to me that in order for me to solve the riddle of Trefflepugga Path that you…"

Chatsworth vilishly shot an old paw to Matlock's lips. "Hush!" he urgently griffled. "Let there be no griffling of that, ever! Laffrohn shouldn't have griffled to you about *any* of those things. She was wrong to do that, peffa-wrong. There is much here, Matlock, that you just don't understand. There is too much at stake."

"But I *want* to understand," Matlock desperately griffled. "I *need* to. Everyone keeps griffling that somehow I'm special, and my becoming Most Majelicus is peffa, peffa-important – but no one ever griffles me why. Look at me, I'm just a majickal-hare somehow trying to become Most Majelicus, like so many other hares."

Chatsworth rubbed thoughtfully at his hare's chin. "These matters are for another time."

"But I want the answers *now*," Matlock insisted. "I need to know why it is that I'm somehow so different from the rest."

"They are answers that will only be given by time," Chatsworth griffled, "and not by an elderly Most Majelicus hare that was once your master. Already I have received griffles that I am shortly to be summoned before the *Grand Council of the Majickal-Elders* to answer charges for my conduct relating to your first task. It is best that for now, you concern yourself with this, your second task, the finding of the Tillian Wand."

Matlock's eyes widened at the peffa-glopped up news, knowing exactly what Chatsworth meant in those few griffles. "You're… you're being taken to the Elders?" He could hardly bear to hear himself griffle it. "But, master, that's most glopped-up and peffa-glubbstooled! That's…"

Chatsworth's hares ears dipped slightly. "T'was inevitable, Matlock – and perhaps not before time. I have lived a long and mostly happy life in these dales. My own master, Baselott, will be ready and waiting for me when the time comes. You must not be eyesplashy, Matlock, for I shall leave knowing you are well on your way to wearing these Most Majelicus red robes one sun, and my work here will be carried on through you. T'is the way of all things Matlock. Oramus has decreed that my pid-pads through these many dales are nearly over, so I must leave to face the judgment of the Majickal Elders. But I'm hoping that one fine and saztaculously distant sun-turn it will be my turn to greet you." He gave Matlock a truly peffa-crumlush smile. "And until that time comes, I will simply wait for that shindinculous chance to finally shake your paw as Elder to Elder."

Matlock shook his head, not wanting to hear any more of his master's griffles.

"But now," Chatsworth continued, "you must be getting on with your task, Matlock. Find the Tillian Wand – I know you can do it. I always knew you would." He took a deep hare's breath. "But there are two peffa-important things I must tell you. And you mustn't griffle even the oidiest griffle of them to anyone."

Matlock waited as the trees swished in the breeze.

"When the time comes for you to wear these robes – *my* robes," Chatsworth griffled in his peffa-gravest tones, "then you must."

"Your robes? But I don't understand," Matlock griffled, looking at the red Most Majelicus robes.

"You will when the time comes," Chatsworth replied. "You will feel it as an extrapluff, and although you will want to fight it with all your hare's will and majickal wisdom– you must listen to it. You *must* wear these robes. Will you promise me that?"

Matlock slowly and reluctantly nodded. "And the second thing?" he asked.

"That you find it within yourself to forgive Baselott, my master, for what he has to do."

"Baselott?" Matlock griffled, frowning, feeling completely peffa-beffudled. "But he's a Majickal Elder. What's he going to do?"

Chatsworth closed his eyes as if struggling to find the right griffles. A long pause followed. "Something," he eventually griffled, "that only he can do – but that he *must* do. For you, for me – for all who live in these dales."

Matlock shook his head. "None of this makes even the oidiest amount of sense."

"That's because yours isn't to understand, Matlock. Yours is to do. Yours is to *be* – to find within yourself the peffa-same hare you once were in The Great Beyond, to use those same natural senses that exist in all hares, to sense their majick and find the true way. You will be asked to do many things, Matlock, many peffa-glopped and twizzly things – I simply hope you'll know which heart to follow when those times come."

"What will I have to do?"

Chatsworth tried to smile, reaching out to cup Matlock's cheek in his paw. "I think it's time for you be listening to the creeping-green, good Matlock," he griffled, staring deeply into his eyes. "Put aside your worries for future sun-turns, and turn to the finding of the Tillian Wand. I know you can do it, Matlock, I've never doubted it." He smiled. "And never, *ever*, be doubting yourself. Not even for the oidiest blinksnap, you understand?" He dropped his paw to Matlock's chest, Matlock feeling its calming warmth through his green-robes. "See? You are already less twizzly. The sands will have slowed in the hourglass. Everything is possible, Matlock, everything."

"But where do I find the creeping-green? I don't even know what it is."

Chatsworth softly chickled. "Why waste peffa-valuable hearbeats chasing and looking for something that might very well come looking for you? Sometimes, Matlock, the briftest way to find something is *not* to look for it. For if the creeping-green has something peffa-important to griffle to you, then surely won't it also be trying to find *you*?"

"Put aside your worries for future sun-turns, and turn to the finding of the Tillian Wand. I know you can do it, Matlock, I've never doubted it."

Matlock watched as Chatsworth's paw pointed at the ivy on the side of the upturned tower, seeing it slowly beginning to move, twisting over itself, snaking up and down the curved stone wall, beginning to form griffles made from hundreds of moving leaves and vines.

"Read the griffles, Matlock," Chatsworth instructed. "Remember them, for they are a puzzle – the puzzle of the Tillian Wand. They are the only clues you will get. Most majickal-hares miss them, too peffa-keen to race away and begin searching without a single thought or extrapluff in their heads, blinded by twizzly-panic and nothing else. As such, they are more or less stroffed and souped the blinksnap they leave this tower – but you have this chance, Matlock, to read and remember the puzzle the others so often miss."

Matlock watched the griffles beginning to form, squinting to try and make them out against the stone walls of the upturned tower.

"I stand with you now," Chatsworth griffled to him, "to show you the puzzle of the creeping-green. I'm not meant to be here – far from it. As such, my actions will once again be frowned upon by the Majickal Elders, and I will doubtless face more charges when I'm finally called before them. But the plain fact of the matter is this – and I know peffa-well your hare's ears don't want to hear my griffles – but you are simply too important – for so many reasons, Matlock – that I *had* to be here to give you the briftest possible chance of completing the task."

"You've broken another rule for me?" Matlock griffled, watching as the ivy-griffles became suddenly more distinct in the moonlight, silvered and glistening on the side of the tower.

Chatsworth chickled. "You could griffle it became a bit of a habit for me in the end." He lightly bliffed Matlock's long hare's ears. "Now read them, remember them, for they'll be gone all too soon. Then it will be time for you to begin your journey, just as I must begin preparing for mine."

Matlock turned to the side of the tower, clearly seeing griffles amongst the twisting ivy, screwing up his eyes to distinguish them from the stonework, reading them, his lips moving, trying his briftest to remember them:

Look to the lid, the sand and the sea,
And there reflected in your sands of time,
Four dworps linked in all eternity,
A wand from a broom to make a Tillian shine,
There to be grasped, and taken by one paw,
According to Most Majelicus dalelore.

"But it makes no sense," Matlock griffled, turning to discover that he was now once again quite alone in the woods. "Chatsworth!" he cried out, beginning to get twizzly, feeling his heart beating faster with each griffle. "Where are you? I don't understand what the griffles mean!"

He vilishly pid-padded into the trees, calling Chatsworth's name, searching for the oidiest glimpse of a red robe disappearing into the darkness, but saw nothing.

A sudden scrittling to one side immediately made him turn. He looked down to see Ayaani, his faithful dripple, bursting through the undergrowth, a wand held high in her outstretched paw.

"Ayaani!" he griffled, taking his prized Most Majelicus hawthorn wand. "Have you seen Chatsworth? He was here just a blinksnap ago!"

She shook her soft dripple's head. "I see no Chatsworth. Just trees, and darkness, and now the tower eating the ground."

Matlock turned towards the tower, glimpsing it through the trees, spinning slowly and indeed beginning to somehow dig itself into the shaking ground. "The puzzle-griffles!" he cried to Ayaani, scooping her up and popping her inside his hood. "They'll be buried!"

Panting heavily, he vilishly raced back to the tower, the trees of Wand Wood shaking as the ganticus structure twisted and dug itself further into the ground, the Krettles leaning from an upturned window, pointing and chickling at Matlock below.

"Until we be meeting again!" Lily cried out.

"Until we be making you all soupy-soupy!" Jericho laughed, his yechus teeth still spinning and twirling in his mouth. "You be sure to keep your softulous all slurpilicious for when we be boiling you up, now!"

Matlock tried to block the Krettles' chickling from his long hare's ears, concentrating on trying to compose himself and re-read the ivy-griffles one final time before they disappeared into the shuddering ground. He tried to commit the puzzle to memory, as the ivy-griffles slid slowly passed his eyes and down into the churned up forest floor, the ground majickally closing behind to leave no trace of the tower whatsoever. Indeed, it was as if it had never really been there at all.

"We must pid-pad away, peffa-vilishly!" Ayaani urged from Matlock's hood. "There is still much peffa-twizzly danger here!"

Matlock held up a paw to silence her. "I'm thinking, Ayaani." He closed his eyes, trying to level his breathing in the stilled silence of the woods. "Just give me a snutch of moments to work out what to do." He let out a long slow breath, began to feel his pounding heart beating a little more slowly, trying to focus and recall the ivy-griffles, seeing them clearly in his mind, cementing them into his memory.

"We must go," Ayaani urged.

He opened his eyes, a smile breaking over his majickal-hare's face. "You're absolutely right. We must go. But not back to the cottage, Ayaani."

"Then where?" she griffled, her oidy paws closing around his neck for comfort.

"To find the Tillian Wand," he griffled.

"The Tillian what?"

"Wand," he griffled, as he began pid-padding along the woodland path back towards the village. "And if you're wondering just what it is, then I have to confess, so am I. All I know is that my second Most Majelicus task is to somehow find it and bring it back here. I haven't the oidiest idea what it is, where it is, or even if it's a wand at all." He stopped, craning his neck to look at his alarmed dripple. "But then again, we happen to know some creatures who apparently know all the answers to everything, don't we?"

Ayaani blinked. "The snoffibs?"

"And surely who better to tell us what we need to know, eh? If anyone's going to have an idea of just what the Tillian Wand is – it has to be them. Hopefully they won't have left the dale yet, so we can find them and ask them. 'Tis a peffa-simple plan, Ayaani – and as such one of my more fuzzcheck and saztaculous ones, I think."

Ayaani simply let out a long sigh, sensing in her own oidy Sisteraculous that Matlock's 'peffa-simple plan' would most probably go glopped-up – as they so often did.

When they reached the village, the celebrations were flowing as fast as the guzzworts and trupplejuice, with excited creatures still packed in and around the Winchett Dale Inn, all loudly griffling about the imminent Dale Vrooshfest.

"Where are the snoffibs?" Matlock cried out, pushing towards the crowded doorway and spotting the landlord. "Slivert! I need to find the snoffibs! It's peffa-peffa important!"

"Matlock!" Slivert Jutt griffled, a ganticus smile over his proud face. "Be coming in! See what we've been doing to get all prepared for the vrooshfest tomorrow morn'up! We all be working and thinking peffa-hard about it, and…"

"Not now, Slivert," Matlock tried, looking round the crowded inn. "I really don't have time – literally. I just need to find the snoffibs. Are they here? Are they gone? Where are they?"

A gradual silence fell over the inn, making its way slowly outside to the square.

Slivert frowned slightly. "But we's be thinking you'd be all pleased with us for all the organising and preparing, Matlock," he griffled. "We be doing it so that you can be proud of us when you wins the Dale Vrooshfest for Winchett Dale tomorrow."

Matlock scratched a sudden itch above his eye, trying not to see the obvious disappointment in so many faces. "Look," he griffled to them all, "I'm sorry for not appearing interested, it's just that…"

"We've only gone and found a chair!" Slivert cried out, full of pride.

"A what?"

Slivert nodded eagerly, pointing to a lone chair standing ceremoniously on one of the inn's tables. "A chair, Matlock!" he repeated, peffa-excrimbly, other creatures joining in, pointing and nodding at the lone piece of furniture. "All the other dales will surely be chickling on the other side of their faces when they be seeing just how saztaculous Winchett Dale is at the organising of a vrooshfest."

"But…" Matlock griffled, feeling the oidiest beginnings of

russisculoftulation rising. "...it's just a chair, Slivert. Just *one* chair."

Slivert nodded, clearly missing the point. "And don't she be a beauty?" he griffled, admiring it. "Four legs, a back and seat. They'll all be griffling about our chair tomorrow morn'up, you'll see. It'll be the talk of the dales, this chair will."

Matlock screwed up his face, turning to them all. "Are you really that clottabussed?" he griffled, scratching at his forehead. "One chair? Just *one chair*? For a whole Dale Vrooshfest? It's just... so gobflopped!" He took a breath, looking at the shocked sea of dismayed faces. "All of you, take a long hard look! There are chairs *everywhere* in here! And tables, too! It's an inn, for goodness sake!"

A sharp, collective intake of breath raced round.

"Matlock's right!" an elderly grupp called out. "There *do* be chairs everywhere! Three ganticus cheers for Matlock! He be majickally-finding us more chairs!"

"And tables, too!" an excrimbly fluff-thropp greeped. "Matlock be truly majickal. Surely he be winning the vrooshfest for us tomorrow morn'up with all his cleverness!"

"Just stop!" Matlock cried above the celebrations, unable to control his temper any longer. "All of you! Stop!" He turned to them, his eyes begging for even the oidiest bit of understanding. "Don't you *see*? Does none of you understand just how clottabussed and glubbstooled this is?" He took a breath, hearing just the vilish beating of his own heart in the stunned silence, trying to force the unwelcome image of a ganticus hourglass out of his mind, its sands running faster and faster with each blinksnap. "Please, someone, just answer me."

There was a long silence, filled with much scratching of heads, frittles and various other parts of the creatures' softulousses.

Matlock tried to level his voice. "Look, I don't want to be griffling any griffles that would be hurting anyone..."

"Then don't be griffling them," Slivert Jutt replied, with indisputable dale-logic.

"...but I don't think I've ever known you all to be as clottabussed as this. I mean, what in Oramus' name were you thinking?" He scanned the entire inn, meeting them in the eye. "Your *one* chair – it's just peffa-pathetic, it really is. Unbelievably the most glubbstooled thing I've ever seen and heard. *Ever*!"

An oidy frettle awkwardly raised its peffa-hairy paw. "Sorry, Matlock. We was only trying to…"

"Shut your griffle-hole!" Matlock exploded. "I don't need to know how much you thought you were trying, *any* of you! For Oramus' sake, finding just one clottabussed chair! Don't you even begin to understand?" He angrily pointed to the chair. "This… chair! This glopped-up chair – in its own way griffles *everything* there is to know about each and every one of you…"

"Begging your pardon, Matlock," Slivert unwisely interrupted. "But 'tis only a chair, and as such it's not being able to griffle a single griffle, methinks. And I don't think it be doing you much good to be being so peffa-russisculoffed with us, I really don't. Your eyes be all bulgy, and it's not be making you look peffa-majickal, not one bit. You be needing to get some nifferduggles before the ganticus Dale Vrooshfest, so you can be winning it with a saztaculous vroosher, and…"

"I'm not going to the vrooshfest!" Matlock shouted, causing another sharp intake of breath.

"Why not, Matlock?" an oidy disidula cautiously asked.

"Because," Matlock began, realising as soon as he had griffled it, that any explanation of his task, the upside-down tower, the Krettles, the hare soupy-soupy and the puzzle of the Tillian Wand – would be as lost on them as a blind murpworm in the darkest, most yechus cavern imaginable. Instead, he took a deep hare's breath. "Because I have to pid-pad elsewhere."

"Where's elsewhere?" someone asked.

"Not here," Matlock quietly griffled, feeling suddenly bad at just how angry he'd been with them all, looking at their disappointed faces, sensing their quiet, muddled confusion and hating himself for it. "Just not here," he griffled. "I have to go and find something. It's really peffa-important, that's all I can griffle."

"More important than winning the Dale Vrooshfest?" Silvert griffled. "More important than not making us look like proper gobfloppers in front of all the other dales? We did be finding a chair for you, after all."

Ayaani whispgriffled in Matlock's ear. "We're wasting time,

master. We must leave and find the snoffibs."

Matlock nodded. "I've got to go," he griffled. "Hopefully, one sun-turn, if I find what I'm looking for, you'll all understand."

Not a single creature griffled the oidiest griffle, simply looking, then slowly parting to let their trusted majickal-hare through the shocked silence.

At the wooden creaker, he turned to them. "I'm sorry," he griffled. "It just has to be this way." He tried his briftest to smile and nod at Slivert. "And it really is a crumlush chair, Slivert. Possibly the most crumlush I've ever seen. You're right; four legs, seat, back, the lot."

"Thanking you, Matlock," Slivert quietly replied, idly wiping the bar-top with a paw, not meeting Matlock's gaze. "You just be having a right nice finding-time, and don't be all thinking about how it's going to be go peffa-glopped for us in the morn'up. Just you be coming back when you be ready." He shook his head slightly. "I take it this be something to do with one of those Most Majelicus tasks of yours?"

"It is," Matlock nodded.

"And it's *really* more peffa-important than being here?"

Matlock couldn't answer, which in itself was all Slivert and the others need to hear.

"You'll be finding the snoffibs behind the cottages around the back of the square," Slivert griffled. "I wish you well, Matlock." He turned his back and pretended to wipe tankards. "We all do. You best be pid-padding off, now."

Matlock took what he hoped wasn't his last ever look around the inn before pid-padding outside into the village square, the quietened, disappointed creatures once again parting to let him through, some wishing him well on his journey, others simply looking confused, unable to believe he was actually going to leave them all on the eve of such a peffa-important sun-turn. At the end stood Serraptomus, genuine concern on his officious krate's face.

"You will be back, won't you?" he griffled.

Matlock tried to smile. "I really peffa-hope so, Serraptomus. Can you do your briftest to look after them all until I return?"

Serraptomus shifted awkwardly from foot to foot. "I'll try,

Matlock, I really will, but you know just how glubbstool I am at being officious."

Matlock nodded. "*I* believe in you, Serraptomus."

Serraptomus blushed slightly under his krate's fur then gave Matlock a ganticus hug. "Just you be pid-padding back safely to us, Matlock. That's all we really want, you know."

Matlock extricated himself from Serraptomus' short stubby arms. "Where's Proftulous? I need to griffle with him. It's important."

Serraptomus looked round. "I haven't seen him for some time. Methinks he most probably went to be finding tweazle-nests in Wand Wood. You know what he's like for his tweazle-pies, Matlock."

"Can you get a message to him?" Matlock griffled. "Only I don't have time to find him."

"Of course," Serraptomus griffled, offering an ear so Matlock could whispgriffle into it, "I'll do my briftest to get your griffles to him." He paused, listening to Matlock's instructions, then suddenly stood back, frowning. "Are you *sure*, Matlock? I mean, are you really sure that's going to work? Or even that it's allowed? Only it all sounds most peffa-*un*officious to me."

"I think," Matlock replied, his attention drawn by a large looming shape suddenly billowing up behind the nearest row of cottages, "that it's the briftest I can manage for now, Serraptomus. That is, unless you have any better, more officious ideas?"

Serraptomus looked at his feet. "Er…not, really, Matlock. I'll get your message to Proftulous."

"And keep it a secret, will you?" Matlock griffled, drawn by a ganticus extrapluff that now was the absolute right and proper time to leave, and furthermore, that the large inflating shape was exactly what was going to help him. "Just Proftulous, you and I are to know."

"Nod's as good as a wink to a blind cavern-owl," Seraptomus replied, tapping the side of his officious nose twice, hoping he could still remember Matlock's whispgriffles. "When it comes to the end of the sun-turn, most creatures can always rely on Serraptomus."

"Just try and make that *all* creatures," Matlock griffled, wiping away an oidy mirrit from his shoulder and pid-padding to a small alleyway that led between the cottages and crumlushly tended back-gardens beyond.

Ayaani cowered slightly in his hood at the sight of the ganticus balloon standing between the edge of the village and the River Winchett. "'Tis the snoffibs," she griffled, a paw on each of Matlock's shoulders. "And they be about to leave in a ganticus lid-machine!"

Matlock bounded to the balloon, spotting the three snoffibs throwing branches and timber into a roaring piff-tosh held in a vast iron basket underneath.

"Wait!" he cried at the top of his voice. "Please wait! I need to ask you something peffa, peffa-important!"

The snoffibs, too occupied with ropes and timber, began climbing into a large basket slung underneath the blazing fire, the last of them pulling an anchor rope from the ground, sending the ganticus balloon suddenly lurching dangerously sideways, a spray of splutting cinders showering and sizzling onto the ground below.

Matlock instantly saw the danger – the dangling anchor had caught in the branches of a nearby tree. "Stop!" he screamed, reaching into his green robes for his Most Majclicus wand "Stop, or you'll all be stroffed!"

An unexpected peffablast raced across the dale, blowing the stuck balloon back on itself, the three terrified snoffibs now cowering inside the basket, completely unable to see the danger below.

Matlock brandished the wand, its tip already beginning to glow bright red, aiming for the rope and sending out a bright-red vroosh that circled like a russisculoffed sazpent, vilishly biting through the rope and freeing the petrified snoffibs. Next, he sent another vroosher up to to the rising basket itself, first coiling round, then lifting him clean off his pid-pads and up into the twinkling-lid.

"Hang on!" he cried out to Ayaani, ducking as another shower of red-hot glowing sparks fell all around. "The wand will take us there!"

Sure enough, bit by oidy bit, the clinging vroosher gradually wound Matlock up towards the basket, until finally three peffa-grateful snoffibs were able to heave and haul him over the side to safety.

Matlock put away his wand. "Thank you," he griffled, trying to get his breath back. The balloon was rising more steadily now,

Matlock seeing the vast illuminated canopy above his head looking like a crumlush summer sun drifting though the cold darkness of the twinkling-lid. The fire had calmed too, its gentle heat enough to both inflate the balloon and keep them warm in the basket. Though perhaps, Matlock realised, the griffle 'basket' was rather inadequate. As he was helped to his feet, he saw cupboards neatly set into the sides, and a table and chairs in the centre. In one corner was a battered old armchair, and above it, a candle-lamp swinging in the breeze. He was standing on a fine carpet, albeit slightly blackened and charred in places from falling cinders – but, all in all, it looked to him rather like a living room in a crumlush cottage, save its walls were wicker, and it had no ceiling.

The snoffibs showed Matlock to the armchair, gratefully griffling their thanks for the vroosher that had saved their lives, Dr Irapus Klaxon then ordering Spig to make them all a hearty brottle-leaf brew.

"Quite a view from up here, isn't it?" he griffled.

"You don't travel by Trefflepugga Path, then?" Matlock griffled, reaching out as Dr Ritallel Crumble handed him his warm brew. Ayaani, feeling the need for some calming herself, vilishly climbed from Matlock's hood and took a hearty swig of the slurpilicious brew.

"Trefflepugga Path?" Klaxon replied. "Oh, good gracious, no. We have too much knowledge – too many answers in our minds to risk being stroffed along the path and eaten by long, long-nosed krellits. T'would be a most peffa-glopped-up thing indeed, a loss of so many grillions of thoughts, ideas and facts. We always travel by lid-machine, it's far safer." He flushed a little, the colour running over his head in the dancing firelight. "That is, it always *has* been safer, until just now, until we…"

Dr Crumble came to his rescue, pointing over the side of the basket, his voice excrimbly at what he saw far below. "Look! We're over the path! Come see! There must be grillions of creatures down there!"

Matlock looked down, the wind flapping his long hare's ears as he made out a solid ribbon of flaming torches far below. "They're all on their way to the vrooshfest," he griffled.

Beside him, Klaxon nodded. "And whatever it is they're expect-

Dr Crumble came to his rescue, pointing over the side of the basket, his voice excrimbly at what he saw far below. "Look! We're over the path! Come see! There must be grillions of creatures down there!"

ing in Winchett Dale, I'm quite sure that nothing they've ever experienced will have prepared them for it."

"No," Matlock quietly agreed. "I'm sure it won't."

Klaxon turned to him, all four eyes bright and alert. "A Dale Vrooshfest that for the only time in its peffa-long history won't have a majickal-hare representing the hosting dale." He wagged a small lizardlike finger at Matlock. "I know full well what you're up to, Matlock. Only something peffa, peffa-important would stop a majickal-hare from competing in the vrooshfest." He narrowed all four eyes slightly. "Something as important as a Most Majelicus task, perhaps?"

"Indeed," Matlock quietly agreed. "Another correct answer."

Klaxon nodded, smiling slightly. "Which, I would go as far to presume would be the second task, the finding task – the finding and bringing back of the Tillian Wand?" He watched Matlock's face intently for a snutch of moments. "We snoffibs know many things, Matlock. Our knowledge is second to none in all the dales. That wand you used to save us just now – it's a Most Majelicus one, isn't it? And as such, I am wondering just how it came to be in the paws of a mere majickal-hare like yourself?"

"It's a long story," Matlock cautiously griffled, unwilling to give too much away. "And frankly, none of your business."

Klaxon's thin lips smiled. "Peffa-true. Yet I suspect your ownership of such a wand would be of the most important concern to others. Perhaps, the Majickal Elders? For such a wand has powers that are quite forbidden for the likes of yourself."

"True," Matlock griffled. "But it also has powers that just saved all of your lives."

Klaxon chickled softly. "You think I'm about to tell someone about your wand? I'm not. But I see the panic in your face, the twizzliness. How vilish is your heart beating now, Matlock? How quickly are those sands slipping away in the ganticus hour-glass, I wonder?"

Matlock took a slow breath. "Your knowledge of the second task is quite formidable, Dr Klaxon."

He waved the compliment aside. "Your flattery is quite ridiculous and glopped-up, Matlock. You come to us to seek all that we know about the Tillian Wand. That much is obvious. How things can change so vilishly, eh? For just a short while ago, it was you, as I recall, griffling to me about the nature of questions and answers. Yet here we are, high in the lid, and suddenly you need my answers more than anything else." He licked his lips with a jet-black, leathery tongue. "Which I think places me at somewhat of an advantage."

"I did come to seek your knowledge," Matlock conceded, vilishly ducking a fresh shower of sparks as a strong gust suddenly shook the balloon, rocking the entire basket. "I need to know everything you know about the Tillian Wand. But as I just saved your lives, I think it's a fair exchange."

Klaxon scratched at the side of his neck, calling over to young Spig. "Unravel the hanging sail! It's getting peffablasty! The last thing we want is to be downed somewhere along Trefflepugga Path." He turned to Matlock. "It's why we came up with this, our lid-machine. By flying above it, the path has no power over you. The fire gives us height, the sail gives us direction. The only other way to beat the path's will is, of course, to solve its riddle – something you've already done in your first task?"

Matlock nodded, watching Spig unfurl a large sail over the side of the basket, lashing it to a steering column that allowed the balloon to veer away from the ever-changing path below.

Klaxon leaned closer. "Now that *is* an answer I would give all my lands for – the answer to the riddle of Trefflepugga Path."

"I'd tell you…" Matlock slowly griffled

"But?" Klaxon's four eyes narrowed.

"The answer is different for any creature that tries to solve it. Like the path, it changes all the time. The answer I found only works for me, it would be useless if you tried it."

Klaxon thought for a moment. "I have heard rumours of this, and despite everything, I don't think you're lying."

"Why would I lie?" Matlock asked.

"Because you are desperate for my knowledge about the Tillian Wand. Your life is on the line. Creatures will resort to any sort of glopped-up behaviour if they feel threatened."

Klaxon closed his eyes for a snutch of moments, nodding to himself, recalling facts. "It is the second of the two Most Majelicus tasks and kept by the Krettles. It is a race against time…"

"I already know all this," Matlock griffled through gritted teeth.

Klaxon angrily held up a hand, his face racing puce. "I will *not* be interrupted in the imparting of knowledge, answers and facts!"

"Sorry," Matlock mumbled.

"You will listen, without griffling another griffle!"

Matlock frowned, slightly balling his paws.

"The successful hare," Klaxon continued, "will find and retrieve the wand, bringing it back to the tower before the sands of his time run out – a time that is determined by the beatings of his own heart. The wand will appear only once, and only then only for the merest blinksnap. If the hare isn't in *exactly* the right place, it will vanish, and all will be lost for the hare, as the wand will never appear for it again."

Matlock simply sat, waiting for more.

"Tillian himself was rumoured to be a most peffa-ganticus wizard of the seas. With his wand, he could summon storms, great waves, whirlpools and all the most peffa-yechus creatures that swim, slither and scrittle in the twizzly, dark depths of the oceans. Legend has it that one sun-turn, a grillion moon-turns ago Tillian met his match in Alvestra – a cunning witch. She challenged him to a duel, the winner to gain ultimate power over the seas. Alvestra wagered her broom, Tillian wagered his wand. And so the battle began, far out to sea, Alvestra raining down lightning, Tillian rising from the depths to vroosh ganticus waves high into the air, determined to down and drown her. The contest raged for many sun-turns and deep into the nights, neither able to gain an advantage, both seemingly, equally matched. But Alvestra had guile, and knew full well that the longer it continued, the more vilishly the ganticus Tillian would tire, as she effortlessly flew above, diving down and vrooshing him time and time again.

"And then, when he was at his most exhausted, and the moon at its fullest, Alvestra lured Tillian right across the Icy Seas straight to where a most peffa-powerful lunar tidal surge sent him crashing onto the shore. There he lay, juzzpapped by his efforts, outwitted by a mere witch who simply happened to know all there was about the power of moon and tides."

Matlock imagined the scene, the cunning witch besting the ganticus sea-wizard, and couldn't help but smile. If he'd learned one thing from Ursula, it was that witches, be they white hares or otherwise, were nothing less than peffa-tzorkly and saztaculously clever all of the time. He clasped his paw around an oidy leather potion bottle she'd once given him for safekeeping. Since that sun-turn, he'd tried his briftest to always wear it around his neck as one of his most cherished possessions.

Klaxon cleared his throat. "But as Tillian stroffed, and Alvestra raced to where he lay, Tillian had one final trick to play. Enraged by being beaten, he snapped his wand in two, managing to hurl one half far out into the deepest waters, the other high up into the twinkling-lid, leaving no trace of the ganticus wand for Alvestra to take." He looked at Matlock with all four eyes. "So neither won. Tillian was stroffed, and Alvestra spent the rest of her life searching for any sign of the wand she thought to be rightfully hers. She never found it. It had gone forever."

"But some hares *have* found it," Matlock griffled. "My master found it. Many hares have failed, but others have succeeded, so it can't have been lost forever."

Klaxon nodded. "Indeed, but remember what I griffled earlier. It only appears once to anyone who tries to seek it. *Just once.* Alvestra had her chance as Tillian lay washed-up on the shore. She didn't take it in time, so it was lost to her from that moment. Some griffle that it was Tillian's curse as he lay dying, so russisculoffed was he to lose to a mere witch. Others griffle that it was Oramus who decreed the wand should remain hidden, to prevent such a glopped-up battle ever happening again. But whichever of these peffa-ancient spuddles and legends are true, one thing is certain, Matlock – you will only have one chance to find it. Miss it, and you will be returned to the Krettles to be stroffed."

Matlock tried not to think about it.

"How are they, by the way?" Klaxon suddenly asked.

"Who?"

"The Krettles; Jericho and Lily," he griffled. "I've heard it griffled that they're quite the most crumlush and happy couple you'll ever find – except if you're a hare on the finding task, that is."

"There was a puzzle on the tower," Matlock griffled, ignoring the question. "It grew from the creeping-green."

The snoffib rubbed his chin thoughtfully. "A puzzle? Well, this is interesting, peffa-interesting indeed. And you saw it?"

Matlock nodded as Crumble and Spig, their curiosity roused, pid-padded over to listen.

"And remembered it?" Klaxon griffled, becoming quite excrimbly. "Tell us, Matlock, tell us the puzzle of the Tillian Wand."

Matlock cleared his throat, trying his briftest to ensure that he recited the ivy-griffles without the oidiest mistake:

Look to the lid, the sand and the sea,
And there, reflected in your sands of time,
Four dworps linked in all eternity,
A wand from a broom to make a Tillian shine,
There to be grasped, and taken by one paw,
According to Most Majelicus dalelore.

He watched as the three snoffibs formed a huddle, earnestly nodding or shaking their heads at what each other had to griffle.

"Er…" Crumble asked, raising a paw, "can we hear it one more time, please? But more slowly? Only, we missed the bit about the dworps."

Matlock recited the puzzle again, watching the snoffib-huddle resume. "Does it make any sense?" he asked, wondering if he should take over the steering of the balloon as another peffa-blast rocked the glowing canopy above their heads.

"Sort of," Klaxon eventually announced, breaking the huddle and sending Spig back to steer the sail.

"Sort of?"

"Well…bits of it, I suppose."

"Bits?" Matlock griffled, frowning. "Which bits? I mean, you snoffibs are supposed to know everything."

Klaxon thought for a moment. "The bits that sort of make sense, I suppose. Those bits."

Matlock felt a stirring in his hood as Ayaani whispgriffled in his ear. "Methinks they're as much use to us as Proftulous would be right now."

"But," Matlock tried again, clearing his throat, "Of the bits that 'make sense' to you…"

"Yes?" Klaxon keenly answered.

"What sort of sense do they *actually* make?"

Klaxon stared blankly back for a snutch of moments then vilishly summoned another huddle.

"They don't know, do they?" Ayaani sighed.

The huddle griffled and muttered for another long snutch of moments, before Klaxon eventually turned to Matlock. "We have arrived at, and reached, a conclusion."

"Saztaculous," Matlock griffled, trying his briftest to sound enthusiastic, but an extrapluff telling him not to get too excrimbly. "And what conclusion is it?"

Klaxon raised a warty hand triumphantly into the air, nearly knocking the bottom of the splutting fire-basket as he did so. "The conclusion is – that we shall ask the thinking-machine when we get back to Snoffib Dale!"

Matlock narrowed his eyes. "The…thinking-machine?"

"Please don't tell me they have one," Ayaani griffled. "This is more peffa-glopped than your trip along Trefflepugga Path!"

Crumble nodded enthusiastically. "Indeed, Matlock. Our thinking-machine will tell us all the answers we need to know about your puzzle. It always knows everything."

"But I thought *you* always knew everything!" Matlock griffled, trying not to get russisculoffed.

"Oh, by Oramus no!" Crumble chickled. "'Tis the machine that knows things, Matlock. We just remember the answers. And do the huddles, too. We do a peffa-lot of those."

Matlock took a deep hare's breath. "So that's *it*, is it? That's all you know about the Tillian Wand? That it was part of some ancient spuddle, and only appears once to each creature that seeks it?"

"Pretty much," Klaxon mumbled. "I mean, we never griffled we were experts, did we?"

Matlock rubbed his eyebrows. He was peffa-juzzpapped, and really, all he wanted was his crumlush bed and some fuzzcheck nifferduggles – all of which were frustratingly impossible in the glubbstooled circumstances. "But your machine will be able to solve the puzzle?"

"Oh, abso-peffa-lutely!" Klaxon griffled, brightening. "You just griffle a question to it, and a blinksnap later you have the answer. It's peffa-*peffa* clever!"

"Well, I do hope so."

"It'll know for sure, you'll see!" Klaxon beamed.

Matlock stood and pid-padded to the far side of the basket-room, staring over the side at the dark, drifting landscape far below, feeling the wind on his face, and being reminded of Chatsworth making preparations for his own, final journey. He had no idea if he'd ever find the Tillian Wand, or whether he'd end up being hauled in the ganticus hourglass towards the boiling cauldron – all he did know was that without Chatsworth, Ursula and Proftulous and even the glopped-up, clottabussed creatures of Winchett Dale, the world suddenly seemed like a peffa-lonely place.

Spig awkwardly stepped forward, trying his briftest to help. "I'm sure our thinking-machine will help, Matlock."

"I hope so," Matlock griffled, trying not to think of the alternative, or just how his heart was slowly beginning to quicken once more. "I really peffa-hope so."

3.

Ledel, Vrooshed-Robes and the Todel Bear

For Ursula Brifthaven Stoltz, at that very same moment flying high above the Icy Seas on her thundering vroffa-broom, loneliness was the last thing on her mind. Indeed, as a solitary, Arctic white hare-witch, it was something she'd very much learnt to accept, if not value. For although most dale-witches grouped together in various covens, Ursula's chosen lifestyle demanded that she worked her tzorkly majick alone, mostly from her small stone cottage deep in the Land of the White Hares. And whilst she might decide to occasionally join other witches and covens at meetings of *The League of Lid Curving Witchery* (and here, for the sake of accuracy, it has to be griffled that these 'meetings' mostly consist of ganticus midnight flights, where up to a thousand witches might take to the lid simply for the sheer tzorkly joy of it, flying over dales and generally causing mahem for any unfortunate creatures trying to nifferduggle below) by and large, Ursula stuck to the life she had been born into and prepared for by her mahpa as a leveret – that of the truly solitary white-hare witch.

Solitary, that is, until the time came to settle down with an equally solitary white wizard-hare – something Ursula had never been too particularly keen on, even as a wide-eyed youngster.

"Ursula," her mahpa would griffle to her. "I have spent some time with the Gulbrandsens this sun-turn. Their eldest leveret,

Ledel, is coming on well with his wizarding. I think he will make a good and tzorkly match for you one sun-turn."

And Ursula would shoot her mother a look and mutter something about Ledel Gulbrandsen being the most 'peffa-clottabussed splurk that ever tried to wield a wizard's wand!' before pid-padding angrily from the house to ride away on her broom.

Yet Ursula's mahpa knew that it would simply take time, recognising in her daughter her own youthful obstinance, her unwillingness to even consider taking Ursula's pahpa on her vroffa-broom, despite his almost continual insistence. Because this peffa-important moment is what's known as the 'vroffa-blinksnap' amongst solitary white hares – the instance when a wizard – unable to take to the lid himself – finally receives the honour of flying on the back of a broom of a white hare-witch, signalling the shakey beginnings of their life-partnership and the start of a new life together – provided, of course, the white-hare wizard doesn't fall from the broom whilst in flight – an occurrence that happens far more often than one would think.

Sometimes, Ursula's mahpa would remember just how determinedly Ursula's pahpa would regularly pid-pad the three long hours across the icy landscape, an oidy bunch of arctic flowers in his paw, snow on his robes, ice on his whiskers, simply to have the door immediately slammed in his face as she contentedly watched him pid-pad dejectedly away, yet also knowing that somehow he wouldn't give up, as would return to break her chosen solitude the very next sun-turn.

But this continual insistence, this *tzorkly*-insistence (a hallmark of all white hare-wizards) eventually, little by little, began to pay off. Throughout the long summer nights, Ursula's mahpa began to reluctantly leave a bowl of kerrvaghen soup (cold, of course – he hadn't *nearly* proven himself enough to merit a warm bowl) on the front stone step; silently watching him eat before vilishly shooing him away, calling him a 'Peffa-clottabussed splurk!' and vrooshing him with her wand as he began his lonely journey back home.

"And then," she told Ursula late one night, as they sat together in front of a roaring piff-tosh, "came the sun-turn that your Pahpa *didn't* turn up – the one your grandmahpa had always told me would happen, the sun-turn that I'd need to get my oidy leather potion bottle for."

"Potion bottle?" Ursula had asked.

"Indeed," her mahpa griffled, "just like the one I'm going to give you now."

"But I don't want an oidy potion bottle."

Ursula's mahpa didn't listen, instead fetching a small leather potion bottle and tying it round Ursula's neck with a soft, leather loop. "The potion-bottle of a solitary white hare-witch is the most precious thing a mahpa can give her daughter," she griffled. "Soon, you are to go out into the world and live the solitary lifestyle you have always yearned for."

Ursula nodded eagerly, her mind already full of the imminent joys of leaving home and living by herself.

"But," her mahpa warned her, "the time will come when you are no longer in need of the solitary life, Ursula. A stranger will come who you will think is a clottabussed splurk, just as your pahpa came for me. And gradually, without you even knowing, he'll win your heart."

"That will *never* happen," Ursula confidentially assured her. "Not in a grillion of the most splurked moon-turns!"

Her mahpa softly chickled. "It will. A white-hare wizard will come. And when he does, it will be time to be with him and begin your new life together."

Again, Ursula vehemently shook her young head. "No!" she insisted. "I shall be solitary all my life! It is my tzorkly destiny as a white hare-witch!"

"As it was mine, too. But things change, Ursula, and mostly it is for the right reasons. You will know when the sun-turn comes."

"Then I shall simply vroosh whoever it is away!"

Her mahpa smiled. "You will to begin with. But he will return, many times, despite all your vrooshing. And to begin with, you will feel quite happy to watch him pid-pad away."

"Indeed, I will, Mahpa. Peffa-happy."

"But then will come the one sun-turn when he *doesn't* come for you, Ursula. And for the first time in your life you will feel quite strange. Your heart will feel sad and you will begin to get eyesplashy…"

"Never!" Ursula vilishly protested, knowing full well that she had never cried in her life – over anything.

"Oh, but you will," her mahpa griffled. "And when the tears begin to roll down those cheeks of yours, you must put them in this oidy potion bottle and keep them safe."

"Collect my tears?" Ursula's gasped, pulling a face and frowning. "I *really* don't think so, Mahpa. This is all most peffa-un-tzorkly! Completely un-tzorkly! I think you are drinking too much grimwagel wine and your griffles have become quite shloffelled."

But Ursula's mahpa shook her head. "When that sun-turn comes you *will* be eyeplashy, Ursula. Your white wizard-hare suddenly won't be there, and what's more, he will never come back to you willingly again. If your heart is broken, you will fill the bottle with tears. If it isn't broken, the bottle will remain empty and you will forget all about him until the right wizard-hare arrives."

Ursula still shook her head defiantly. "I will never shed a single tear for any wizard!"

"And I thought the peffa-same thing about your pahpa."

"I'm going out on my broom now," Ursula declared, pid-padding straight to the front-creaker.

Ursula's mahpa watched her leave, shuddering as the door slammed, knowing that for all Ursula's stubborn resistance and her willingness to embrace the solitary lifestyle, whichever white wizard-hare finally got to wear her tear-filled potion bottle around his neck and ride on the back of her broom, would *really* have earned the right. In some senses, she already felt quite sorry for him…

And, of course, as is so often the way of these things, the wizard-hare that came for Ursula turned out to be Ledel Gulbrandsen, the very same hare she'd loathed and despised as a leveret. Although, to be fair (while Ursula herself would have been the peffa-*last* to admit it) perhaps her raging, splurked anger towards him was actually more to do with a slight jealousy and deeply hidden admiration that she'd never griffled even the oidiest griffle to anyone about – including herself.

Jealous? The peffa-tzorkly and self-contained, solitary Ursula Brifthaven Stoltz? Surely not? Just what was it that she had to be jealous about? Surely it wasn't Ledel's popularity in the valley?

Surely it wasn't the fact that he was acknowledged by so many to be the next great wizard-hare, such was his majickal-proficiency at the white-arts? Surely not his home, then, three times bigger and far more impressive than the small cottage she lived in with her own mahpa and pahpa? On reflection, perhaps there were quite a snutch of reasons to be jealous...

But, of course, the one thing Ledel Gulbrandsen couldn't do, was fly. Only witches could take to the lid on their roaring vroffa-brooms. So Ursula set out with ganticus determination to be the peffa-briftest flyer in the valley, soon able to outsmart and better even her own mahpa at manoeuvres of such aerobatic daring that they had others on the ground gasping as she swooped, looped and tore through the lid, day or night, rain or shine, finding her own total bliss and contentment simply to be up and away from everything – and, most importantly, the peffa-splurked Ledel Gulbrandsen and his fawning admirers.

But – ineviatably – and just as her mother had predicted, there came the sun-turn when Ledel turned up at her creaker, a bunch of fruffel-drops wilting from the three-hour journey in his paw. Ursula didn't even bother to open it.

The following sun-turn, he returned. And the next. And the next, always knocking politely, calling her name, even though she had her paws pressed hard to her long white ears most of the time.

Gradually, the sun-turns began to get shorter as the long winter nights set in. By now, Ursula had taken to absentmindedly checking through the windows, occasionally glancing to see if she saw Ledel's swinging lantern approaching through the dark, snowy distance. One even'up, she caught herself doing this, and was so russisculoffed that she resolved that this time she would finally open the creaker to him, but only to give him a peffa-splurked piece of her mind and to vroosh the bottom of his wizard's robes on fire.

"That should see you home safely!" she griffled, after the fiery deed was done. "Now be away, Gulbrandsen, and leave me alone!"

But instead of turning, Ledel simply smiled and looked into her eyes.

"Your robe is burning really quite badly," Ursula observed.

Ledel just nodded.

By now, Ursula had taken to absentmindedly checking through the windows, occasionally glancing to see if she saw Ledel's swinging lantern approaching through the dark, snowy distance.

Ursula frowned. "And now I smell that your fur is smouldering, too. Either that, or you really, really need a bath." She slammed the creaker in his face, watching through the window as he rolled in the snow to put out his burning robes, happily chickling as he pid-padded away with his lantern, doing the occasional jig in the deep, dark night.

All through the winter, Ursula's solitary isolation was broken every day by Ledel's inevitable arrival. She'd lost count of the amount of his robes she must have burnt, save for the fact that the whole business had become nothing less than really rather tedious. He arrived – she opened the door – harangued him – set him on fire – then slammed the door. A routine that had grown so wearisome, it bored her rigid.

So, one even'up, she gave the matter some peffa-serious thought. Surely it couldn't go on like this? That night, as she lay in bed thinking about Ledel making his way slowly back home with just a flickering lantern and scorched robes, she reached a decision – the next time she saw him coming, she would open her bedroom window when he was still quite some distance away and see if she could vroosh him on fire at long range. Yes – she resolved to herself, Ledel Gulbrandsen would make excellent, if not tzorkly, target practise.

The following even'up she was ready, waiting by her open window, ignoring the cold filling her bedroom, eyes keenly scanning the snowy horizon for the first glowing glimmers of an unsuspecting peffa-splurked hare making his way to her house. She was really quite pleased with herself for coming up with such an entertaining diversion with which to pass the long even'ups, and hoped that by the coming spring, she'd be expert enough to light Ledel up from the peffa-first moment she spied his splurked ears appearing over the distant horizon.

However, this was also the peffa-same even'up that Ledel Gulbrandsen *didn't* pid-pad through the snow to her cottage. All night she waited, paw tensely gripped around her wand, eyes keenly peering into the black, searching for just the oidiest sign.

But nothing. Ledel hadn't made the journey.

Which was when it happened. Gradually, the pure peffa-russis-culoffed rage that had been boiling up inside her, garrumbloomed into angry howls. How could he? How *dare* he? Just where was he, when she'd gone to all this ganticus amount of trouble to try and vroosh him on fire from the comfort of her own bedroom?

The back of her throat began to tighten, her eyes suddenly widening with the beginnings of a new and most unpleasant sensation. She was about to cry…which, of course, enraged her even more, as she remembered her mother's griffles and began angrily collecting the hot tears in the small leather potion bottle around her neck – filling it slowly throughout the rest of the night, hating herself for being so weak, for her mother's griffles coming true, for not being able to set Ledel on fire…just loathing everything…and resolving as she defiantly put the stopper in the bottle, that her life as a solitary white-hare witch would be *truly* peffa-tzorkly from that moment on – she would 'rise-above' everything, including any other hare's expectations of who she was, or what she should be. Ursula Brifthaven Stoltz, she resolved, had cried her last tear.

The following morn'up, she took to the lid, flying across three valleys to her old home, there to be greeted by her mahpa with a ganticus smile across her face.

"Ursula, you have returned!"

"Indeed, just as you knew I would one sun-turn," Ursula sourly griffled, being smothered in a hare's hug and having to endure several minutes of fussing as her mahpa tutted about the state of her dress and how she looked like she wasn't feeding herself enough.

"I'm fine, Mahpa," Ursula eventually managed to griffle after they'd settled down for a hot guzzilda-brew in the small kitchen. "I'm managing just fine."

Her mahpa couldn't conceal her excrimbly joy. "And I know *exactly* why you have come to me. You have filled your bottle with tears for a white wizard-hare, haven't you? I can tell by the look on your face – you look radiant!"

"Splurked nonsense. It's the cold wind. I was simply flying too vilishly again."

Ursula's mahpa lowered her voice to a whispgriffle. "Everyone's been griffling about it, Ursula. All of us, here in the valley. How Ledel Gulbrandsen has been pid-padding to your cottage every even'up." She could barely contain her joy. "Oh, Ursula your pahpa and I are so proud! Just think, with you and Ledel together, we'll have the Gulbrandsens as our new friends! We'll be able to go to their house! Your pahpa will drink krullwort with Ledel's pahpa, and I will finally be able to see the size of his mahpa's new cauldron. It's the talk of the valley, you know. It's supposed to be ganticus! She might even let me stir it." She squeezed both her paws together and closed her eyes. "Oh, this is just so excrimbly and peffa-tzorkly!"

"Mahpa," Ursula slowly asked. "Do you remember what it was like to be solitary; before Pahpa came for you?"

"Oh, yes, I do. And if I'm really honest, then I have to say that it was peffa-boring and most splurked. All that time on your own, collecting herbs and stirring a cauldron, waiting for a wizard-hare to arrive. I mean, it's all very well to be solitary for a while, but mostly it's a peffa-ganticus waste of a hare-witch's time."

Urusla found it hard to believe the griffles. "But all my life you've bought me up to be solitary," she protested. "Yet now, I'm thinking the whole thing was simply a splurked spuddle to make me leave home and find a wizard-hare."

"And Ledel really is a peffa-tzorkly one, isn't he?"

"He is nothing of the kind!" Ursula snapped. "He is a peffa-clottabussed splurk, and that's all!"

Ursula's mahpa laughed. "But you filled your bottle with eyesplashers for him when he no longer came for you, Ursula. Your heart wept for him. You may think he's a splurk, but Ledel will be a saztaculously tzorkly match for you. I know his own mahpa will be relieved, as she has grown quite juzzpapped from having to make new robes every time you vroosh his on fire."

Ursula narrowed her eyes. "Mahpa," she calmly griffled. "I do not care for Ledel's mahpa, or her ganticus cauldron, just as I do not care for Ledel. Yes, I filled this bottle with eyesplashy, but they were tears of..."

Her mahpa danced around the room clapping her paws without waiting to hear more. "Oh, but this is *such* peffa-excrimbly news!" She gave Ursula a long hare's hug. "Now you must fly straight to their ganticus cottage, present yourself at their creaker and beg for his forgiveness. If he accepts, you give him your bottle of tears for his safekeeping as a symbol of your trust that with Ledel by your side, you will have cried the last of your lonely eyesplashers, and all will be truly tzorkly for the rest of your lives together."

"*Beg?*" Ursula gasped, vilishly shaking her head. "I will do no such thing!"

Her mahpa eagerly ushered Ursula to the front-creaker and her waiting vroffa-broom. "Hurry, Ursula! Go to him, for he won't ever come to you ever again! Give him the bottle, before it's too late!"

Ursula knew it would be useless to argue. Her mahpa was too excrimbly, her white hare's face too full of the ganticus possibilities that a new life as a friend of the Gulbrandsens would offer. Narrowing her eyes, she mounted her broom and set off back into the lid, its branches roaring red as she flew straight to the Gulbrandsens' impressive cottage amongst a lush pine-forest, deep on the other side of the valley.

"Ledel Gulbrandsen, you splurk!" she called out, hovering on her broom just a short distance away. "Come out and show yourself! I have something for you! Something you want from me! An oidy potion-bottle of my tears!"

Nothing happened for a snutch of moments, the only noise the gentle splutting of Ursula's broom echoing amongst the trees.

Next, the front-creaker opened and a white hare-witch emerged, pid-padding her way towards Ursula, beckoning her down. "I'm Ledel's mahpa," she griffled, frowning. "I think the point you're missing, Ursula, is that he has to be *begged* to come and take your bottle. Then you must allow him onto your broomstick for the 'vroffa-blinksnap'. Didn't your own mahpa griffle to you about this? I'm truly shocked. I mean, everyone knows that your cottage is quite oidy compared to ours, and that you are peffa, peffa-lucky that my Ledel has been pid-padding to you – but I would have thought your own mahpa would have schooled you correctly."

Ursula narrowed her eyes. "Get Ledel, now. If he's not here in the next few blinksnaps, then I will leave. He'll never see me again."

"And that may not be such a bad thing," Ledel's mahpa quietly griffled, hurrying back to the house.

Ledel, when he came, didn't appear either happy or excrimbly. Instead, he simply pid-padded to where Ursula hovered, her long red shoes just a few inches from the ground. "You wish to give me your tears?" he quietly griffled.

Ursula silently took the oidy leather potion bottle from her neck and threw it at his feet. "I never beg for anyone."

He looked down at it for a snutch of moments, softly chickling to himself. "I imagined it all so differently," he griffled, reaching down and putting the bottle in his robe-pocket. "Tradition dictates that I wear this around my neck, but I won't do that for you, Ursula." He took a long hare's breath in the still, silent forest. "You don't have to be a white wizard-hare to feel that those tears are eyesplashers of rage – not love."

Ursula shifted uneasily on the broom.

"I didn't stop coming to your house because I wanted you to fly to me. I stopped because I finally realised just what a clottabussed splurk I was being. You despise me." He shrugged. "I'm not sure how many times a wizard-hare needs to be set on fire before he gets the message, but I'm fairly certain it shouldn't have taken as many times as it did."

Ursula managed to smile just the oidiest smile. "Perhaps I am being a little sorry for that."

"Don't be, I'm just glad I came to my tzorkly-senses in the end." He smiled at her. "I was even beginning to have splurked nightmares about you trying to vroosh me on fire from your bedroom window."

"Oh, to think that I would stoop so low!" Ursula protested, awkwardly clearing her throat and feeling the sudden need to change the griffversation. "Nice woods you have here."

"You *would* have done, wouldn't you!" Ledel laughed. "You would have vrooshed me on fire from your window, simply to make you chickle!"

"Nonsense!" Ursula snapped back. "I was bored, and you would have made peffa-perfect target practise. Quite a different and more practical matter, Ledel."

He stopped laughing, his face suddenly shocked, whiskers twitching.

"What is it?" Ursula griffled, looking around. "You sense danger?"

"No," he quietly griffled. "You just called me by my name. You called me 'Ledel' – and there were no 'splurked' or 'clottabussed' griffles, either."

Ursula frowned. "It's time for me to go. I have been here too long already. I must return to my mahpa and pahpa and griffle to them that we are not to be betrothed."

Ledel smiled. "Personally, I think my mahpa will be peffa-relieved."

"I'm not so sure about mine," Ursula griffled. "She was so excrimbly at the thought of seeing the size of your mahpa's cauldron."

At which point, to their ganticus susprise, they both burst out in chickles at the thought of the ganticus cauldron and its strange lure for Ursula's mahpa, their excrimbly laughter echoing deep into the woods for all the forest creatures to hear. Ursula was quite unable to stop herself chickling, and then, to her even greater surprise, felt another tear begin to roll down her cheeks. "Quickly!" she managed to cry out between chickles, rocking on her broom, "Fetch an oidy bottle from your potionary! I am having eyesplashers again!"

Ledel, also chickling uncontrollably, stumble-padded back into the house, bringing out another oidy leather bottle, watching as Ursula filled it with her tears of laughter, before finally, managing to secure the stopper.

"That," she panted, wide-eyed. "has *never* happened to me before. I have chickled at many things, Ledel, but never enough to eyesplash. Never."

He nodded, as if reading her every thought, and knowing in that one blinksnap it would *only* be the life of a solitary hare-witch that Ursula would always value above everything else, with its isolation and fierce independence from all other creatures. "I must go," he quietly griffled. "But before I do, will you promise me one thing?"

"I do not make promises," she griffled. "But I will listen to your griffles."

He cleared his throat, trying his briftest not to let her know how glopped he really felt. "I will keep your tears of rage and russisculoftulation with me – always. Perhaps, from time to time, I shall pid-pad over to your valley for you to try some vrooshing target practise. But I want you to know that those tears you just cried – your chickling eyesplashers – those are your *true* feelings, Ursula Brifthaven Stoltz – that's the real, tzorkly *you*. And I think that it might not be so splurked to sometimes let them show. So take them with you. Wear them around your own own neck. Let them always be a reminder of who you really are, just who you can be." He smiled at her. "I'll take your bottle of rage, you keep your bottle of chickling eyesplashers."

Ursula suddenly gunned the vroffa-broom, its loud garrum-blooming filling the woods.

Ledel struggled to hear, watching confused as Ursula beckoned him with a delicate white paw and helped him on to the back of the broom.

"Just for one trip, then off you get," she griffled. "And do not think for a moment that this is a 'vroffa-blinksnap', you splurk!"

She gripped the handle and together they roared up through the trees and away into the clear blue lid, Ledel clinging onto her robes and gasping for breath with the sheer force of the flight. She flew straight up, almost vertical, heading higher and higher, before suddenly and expertly lurching the broom sideways, then doubling straight back down at truly terrifying speed, only stopping at the last possible blinksnap to arrive at exactly same spot they'd left.

"You can open your eyes and get off now," she calmly griffled. "And let there be no more of your splurked griffles about what is 'the real me' from now on."

Ledel fell from the broom, lying on the ground, gasping for breath. "But you'll still vroosh me on fire if I pid-pad over to your cottage?"

"Only if I can be bothered," Ursula griffled, before roaring back into the lid, leaving a breathless, bewildered, yet quietly smiling wizard-hare on the ground below.

Over the next few moon-turns, Ledel did indeed sometimes make the long pid-pad over to Ursula's cottage, dutifully stopping at the end of his journey to be vrooshed on fire at long distance, before rolling in the snow and making his smouldering way to the front-creaker, which (if she could be bothered) Ursula would sometimes open for him, when they might, on occasion, share a glass or two of her homemade juhpel-fruit wine, griffling and chickling about the chaos they had caused amongst all the white hare-witches and wizards when it was discovered that although Ursula Brifthaven Stoltz had given Ledel Gulbrandsen her tears *and* let him ride on her broom – neither of them had the oideist intention of ever getting betrothed. Much had been made of it in the valley, the Gulbrandsens understandably relieved for themselves and their son; Urusla's own Mahpa and Pahpa continually shaking their heads in peffa-confused astonishment, unable to accept their daughter's decision, and with it the end of their dreams to befriend the Gulbrandsens – which, the Gulbrandsens, being the sorts of Arctic white-hares they were, were also peffa-relieved about, although Ledel's mahpa never quite understood the hilarity over the size of her beloved cauldron.

For Ursula's part, she mostly tolerated Ledel's occasional appearances, but quickly grew to realise that really, she had very little in common with him at all. As a solitary white hare-witch, she knew nothing of the other hare-witches or wizards he liked to griffle about, and further, didn't much care to know about them, either. She was quite simply utterly happy with her solitary life, giving her the freedom to do exactly what she liked, when she liked. She could, she thought, ask for nothing more…

So it was with these tzorkly thoughts in mind that she finally crossed the Icy Seas that night after the long journey back from Matlock's crumlush cottage garden, swooping low over the valleys and snow-capped mountain ranges to eventually glimpse her cottage in the distance, a sight she found suddenly alarming when she noticed a flickering, glowing light from within.

Someone was inside and had already lit the piff-tosh…

She quietly landed her broom by the front-creaker and, wand in paw, ready to vroosh and stroff whatever unfortunate creature lurked inside, burst in.

"Ledel!" she cried. "What in Oramus' name are you doing here, you splurk?"

He leapt from the chair by the piff-tosh. "I pid-padded to see you, but you weren't here. So I made a fire to welcome you. Aren't you pleased to see me?"

Ursula yawned. It had been a long flight from Winchett Dale and she was really quite juzzpapped. "No, not really," she griffled, slumping into her favourite armchair, then lazily setting his robes on fire with a half hearted vroosh of her wand.

Yelping, Ledel vilishly pid-padded outside to painfully roll in

Someone was inside and had already lit the piff-tosh...

a small patch of snow. When he was sure he was extinguished, he ventured back inside.

"The fact that I am not being here," Ursula explained to him, warming her cold paws on the splutting piff-tosh, which – if she was ever really, *really* pressed – she might *just* admit wasn't the most splurked thing to arrive home to, "does *not* give you the right to come into my cottage. I wish you to leave, and not return for a long time. I'm most disappointed in you, Ledel."

But he stayed put. "Where have you been?"

She narrowed her large, brown eyes. "To see a friend and help him with something. And what is this to you, Ledel?"

Ledel nodded, silent for a snutch of moments. "I have been griffling to some members of *The League of Lid-Curving Witchery*."

"Really?" Ursula, answered, unimpressed. "I would have thought you would have had better things to do with your time. Like learning your wizard-spells?"

"I wanted to know what they thought about you."

She clicked her tongue. "Tcha! They are mostly covern-witches. I rarely associate with them."

Ledel took his time, carefully measuring his griffles. "They tell me you rode with them to The Vroffa-Tree Inn."

"As I do every year to change the branches on my broom, yes. Ledel, what is all this?"

He cleared his throat. "And you met a hare there. A majickal-hare. His name is Matlock. The entire league saw, all the witches, Ursula – they all saw you eating niff-soup with him."

She narrowed her eyes. "So what if I did? He was just another hare, a clottabussed majickal-hare from Winchett Dale trying to complete his first Most Majelicus task. We had soup, so what?"

Ledel grimaced, flared his nostrils slightly, nodding to himself. "And since then you've been helping him in this task?"

She nodded. "A little. When I want to. It is my right, my choice to do so." She looked at him. "You have problems with this? Because if you do, I can easily be vrooshing you on fire again."

Ledel's jaw flexed and tightened. "Yes, I do, Ursula." He reached into his robe and produced his own twisting wand, its tip already beginning to fizz bright blue sparks. "You're not wearing the potion bottle around your neck. The one with your chickling tears. You gave it to him, didn't you? You gave it to Matlock – a peffa-clottabussed hare from Winchett Dale."

"Because it was mine to give," Ursula slowly griffled, holding his eyes and levelling her own wand. "Now leave, or I will set you alight."

"Just try," Ledel griffled. "Go on. Try."

"Oh, this is so splurked!"

"Go on. Try to vroosh me on fire."

"You really want me to?"

He nodded. "I do. Go on. What are you waiting for, Ursula? Are you twizzly?"

Which, of course, was all the encouragement and goading she needed. Juzzpapped from the journey and russisculoffed by Ledel's invasion of her home, she let fly with a fire-vroosher right at his robes…except – this time – it didn't hit…

Ledel, with little more than a contemptuous flick of his own wand, effortlessly repelled the vroosher straight into the piff-tosh. "I've always been able to do that," he griffled, as Ursula gasped in shock. "From the first moment I pid-padded here. Repelling a fire-vroosher is one of the easiest things a wizard-hare can do, one of the first things he learns. I simply let you think you could better me, that's all."

Ursula was still staring into the piff-tosh, quite unable to believe what she'd just seen. "It…didn't happen," she griffled, frowning in confusion. "You can't do that."

"It did, and I can. I have studied the white majickal-arts every sun-turn since I was a leveret. Everyone griffled that I was to be a most tzorkly wizard-hare, and that's what I've become. But you never noticed, Ursula, you never saw, you never even thought to ask."

Still frowning, Ursula tried again, sending out another vroosher, watching in dismay as Ledel once again easily deflected it into the piff-tosh.

"We could do this all night," he calmly griffled. "But it would be quite splurked and clottabussed. Besides, I must leave. I have a journey to make along Trefflepugga Path in order to get to Winchett Dale tomorrow morn'up."

Ursula stiffened at the mention of the name. "Winchett Dale? Why?"

"You haven't heard?" Ledel griffled, smiling and expertly tossing his wand from paw to paw. "It's the Dale Vrooshfest, Ursula. At this very moment majickal-hares from all the dales are pid-padding their way to Winchett Dale to see who can conjure the most peffa-saztaculous vroosher and be crowned *Briftest Majickal-Hare of All the Dales*." He paused, looking at her for a snutch of moments. "But this time, I have an oidy feeling that the honour might well go to a white wizard-hare from across the Icy Seas."

"You're going to Winchett Dale?" she griffled, feeling suddenly unexpectedly twizzly at the thought.

"Indeed," Ledel griffled. "And then I'll be able to meet this Matlock myself, won't I? I daresay he will be favourite to lift the trophy in his own dale, but he hasn't come up against me yet; Ledel Gulbrandsen the first Arctic wizard-hare to win the Dale Vrooshfest." He put away his wand. "And, of course, I shall be expecting your support, Ursula. You could even do me the courtesy of offering me a lift back to Winchett Dale on your broom. After all, it would be quicker than taking Trefflepugga Path – and I'm sure you know the journey well enough by now."

"What's happened to you, Ledel?" she griffled. "Why are you so cold to me? We used to chickle together as good friends."

He half-smiled. "You gave this Matlock splurk your potion bottle. Willingly, too, I suspect. Why?"

"It's no business of yours," Ursula snapped. "Not the oidiest, oidiest bit."

Ledel shrugged. "Then I will leave, as it is a long journey, and I assume you won't be offering me a lift."

Ursula said nothing, her back towards him, still watching the fire, its flickering splutting flames throwing golden dancing light around the room. She took a deep breath, unable to turn and face him. "Ledel," she quietly griffled, "there's something that is peffa-important for you to be understanding. Really, *really* peffa-important. I shall *always* be a solitary white hare-witch, nothing will change that. I gave Matlock my tears for reasons you'll never understand. You assume that I have feelings for him – I don't, just as I have none for you. He is simply another splurked hare. Matlock wears my potion-bottle around his neck for reasons even he doesn't understand, and I hope never discovers." She rubbed her face with her paws, slowly turning to Ledel and taking a peffa-deep breath. "The real reason I gave Matlock the bottle is…"

But Ledel had already left without hearing a single one of her griffles. The room was empty, save for Ursula and just the oideist, lingering smell of burnt wizard's robes…

It had taken Serraptomus a long time to eventually find Proftulous. Time that Winchett Dale's most officious krate would have much preferred to spend on an oidy bit of whittling and carpentry before settling down to some well-earned nifferduggles. However, with the truly glubbstooled revelation that he'd completely forgotten the Dale Vrooshfest, it seemed to Serraptomus that there was little choice but to resign himself to a nifferduggleless night, trying his briftest to at least try and sort out some arrangements for the hoards of imminently arriving creatures. Which, of course, if you were ever to meet Serraptomus, you would know to be almost impossible, for the only thing he's truly officious and peffa-efficient at is his admirable ability *not to* sort anything out properly at all. All of which suits the residents of Winchett Dale peffa-perfectly, as they aren't really the kinds of creatures to waste their time making – or keeping to – any kinds of arrangements, either. As such, it's a system that has stood the tests of time across the generations, rightly earning Winchett Dale the reputation of 'the most peffa-glopped of all the dales' – a worthy and undisputed title which the clottabussed creatures take to their hearts with immense pride, as and when they can really be bothered.

Therefore, hosting the looming Dale Vrooshfest, with all its grillions of expected and peffa-complicated arrangements, represented no worries to the rest of Winchett Dale at all. They would simply glopp-up, it would all go peffa-glubbstooled and everyone would go, leaving the dale's precious reputation vividly intact. And it has to be remembered, that for most of the imminent visitors, this would be their first, and perhaps only trip to Winchett Dale. As such, they would surely *expect* the vrooshfest to be the most saztaculous gobflopp. So, by trying to actually do anything bar moving twelve chairs and a table from the inn up onto the High Plateau in preparation, would only be to disappoint grillions of visitors who wanted nothing more than to have a shindinculous sun-turn chickling at how glubbstooled Winchett Dale really was. Therefore, it had been decided that once the dismally small collection of table and chairs had been taken to the High Plateau, there really wasn't much need to arrange anything else, and they could all go to bed.

However, for Serraptomus, deep in Wand Wood on Matlock's secret errand to find Proftulous and deliver his whispgriffled message, a dreadful vrooshfest would have quite a different significance. Even though he had mostly forgotten what had been griffled to him by the *Dale Vrooshfest Selection Committee*, one thing had crept back into his mind – that such is the importance of the vrooshfest that if it is considered a success by the committee, then the leading most-officious krate of the hosting dale is swiftly and amply rewarded with promotion to the hallowed ranks of *Most Officious District Krate*, a rank entitling the proud bearer to oversee all krating activities in several dales at the same time, whilst mostly indulging in large feasts with other equally peffa-important creatures and doing peffa-little else besides.

Such a tempting, committee-based lifestyle, Serraptomus now remembered, was the main reason he had griffled so keenly to the *Dale Vrooshfest Selection Committee* in the first place, eagerly trying to assure them that Winchett Dale would really work peffa-hard to prepare for the saztaculous event, despite its infamous reputation for glopping-up.

"The sun-turns of glopping in Winchett Dale are peffa-definitely over," he had confidently explained to the astonished committee. "By making us host dale, all visiting creatures will be treated to a most rigorously prepared and saztaculous sun-turn."

"Are you sure?" Lord Garrick, chaircreature of the committee had griffled, frowning. "I mean, is this the same Winchett Dale that once threw a pie at a tree to see what noise it would make?"

"Indeed it is," Serraptomus proudly replied. "And it was sort of a 'thwupp'."

"What was?"

"The noise the pie made. Mostly. We did try it on other trees, but by then it was mostly glopped bits and pieces and just sort of 'gliffed', instead."

Lord Garrick sighed. "Serraptomus, please tell me you have other forms of entertainment planned rather than simply throwing pies at trees?"

Serraptomus scratched thoughtfully at his chin with a stubby paw, looking at the impressive ceiling and surroundings of the ornate committee-room, wondering if one sun-turn it wouldn't be his own officious portrait hanging from the same walls.

"Serraptomus!" a committee member had hissed at him. "We're waiting. What other entertainment do you intend to provide?"

Jolted back to the paw-sweating reality of the griffversation, Serraptomus thought it best under the circumstances to simply begin making things up, a tactic he'd tried numerous times in the past without a great deal of success, but at that moment, with his krate's back to the wall, he really saw no reason not to give it another go. "Well," he griffled, his limited, officious-imagination racing, "let me see now. We'll be having a visit from the most ganticus todel-bear in all the dales, and…"

"A what?" Lord Garrick frowned, clearly confused.

"A todel-bear," Serraptomus replied. "All peffa-ganticus and todelling. Saztaculous it'll be. Really todelly, I can promise you that."

There was a long pause. "And what exactly *is* a 'todel-bear'?"

Serraptomus, who hadn't really anticipated this question, began to scatch the back of his neck quite noisily.

"You just made it up, didn't you?" another committee member griffled. "You made it up to impress us. I've never heard of a todel-bear, ever." He turned to the rest of the committee who were equally at a loss.

"Well…" Serraptomus griffled, his mind now racing more vilishly than a long-legged tweazle being chased by a pack of hungry dworps, "then that's precisely why you'll all *have* to come to Winchett Dale for the vrooshfest! So you can see the most ganticus todel-bear! It really is the most saztaculous sight, and…"

Garrick raised his hand, sighing. "Serraptomus, please just stop griffling." He turned to the other members. "I'm really quite hungry, and would like to feast now. Perhaps we all vote and it can be decided?"

The rest of the committee nodded, also peffa-hungry themselves and more than ready to pid-pad into the next, even more saztaculous room where their ganticus and elaborate feast awaited.

"All in favour of Winchett Dale hosting the next Dale Vrooshfest – raise your paws, talons, wings, or whatever."

Which they all did, except for a bright orange sazpent at the end of the table, who cast his vote with a forked-tongue, before slithering after the others who were already piling next door for food.

"If Winchett Dale hosts a successful vrooshfest," Garrick had confided to Serraptomus, "then you too could be joining us, Serraptomus; having feasts and enjoying the most splendidly crumlushed time doing little or nothing of any consequence for the rest of your sun-turns. But if it goes wrong…"

"Oh, nothing will go wrong, Your Lordship," Serraptomus assured him, vastly excrimbly at the thought of long years of committee membership and lazy feasting.

Garrick smiled one of the thinnest smiles Serraptomus had ever seen. "Get it wrong and I will personally see to it that you are removed from office and spend the rest of your sun-turns right here, washing-up in the basement kitchens." He licked his lips. "And believe me, with all this eating and feasting – the washing-up never, *ever* ends."

All thoughts which swirled through Serraptomus' officious, rather oidy brain as he made his way into Wand Wood, calling for Proftulous, anxious he griffle to him as soon as possible before he forgot the message Matlock had whispgriffled to him in the village square.

So it was with ganticus relief that he finally spotted a distant glow of a lantern through the trees, and the familiar bulky figure of Proftulous bending over the entrance to a tweazle-mound, his arm already thrust deep inside, straining to pull one of the unfortunate creatures out.

"Proftulous!" he called over. "Thank-goodness I've finally found you!"

Proftulous turned, withdrew his arm, a wriggling tweazle in

his ganticus paw. "Hush!" he griffled at it. "I's be thinking that someone's been calling my name."

The tweazle stopped struggling and squinted into the gloomy undergrowth. "It be Serraptomus," it griffled. "Though what he be out in the woods at this time of night for, I've not the oidest idea."

"Serraptomus?" Proftulous griffled, confused. "You be sure of this?"

"Absolutely," the tweazle replied. "I can hear all his wheezing and officious pid-pads."

Sure enough, a snutch of moments later, Serraptomus burst into the clearing, puffing heavily.

Proftulous turned to the tweazle. "Well, bless my drifflejubbs, you be right! 'Tis Serraptomus, looking just as peffa-glopped and glubbstooled as always." He stroked the tweazle on its oidy furry head. "I s'pose you want me to be letting you go and not stroff you because you've been all nice and helpful?"

The tweazle frowned, half closing its small black eyes as it considered this. Finally, it shrugged. "But you'd only come back and get me another time, wouldn't you?"

Proftulous nodded, trying to think of a helpful suggestion. "But I s'pose, you could be escaping and making it peffa-difficult for me to be finding you?"

Again, the tweazle mulled it over. "But, inevitably, sooner or later, you'd find me, stroff me, pop me in your leather tweazle pouch and turn me into a pie, wouldn't you? I mean, it's simply a matter of time, really, isn't it?"

Proftulous nodded.

The tweazle sighed. "Then I suppose it may as well be now. I've nothing peffa-special planned, and I've had a pretty good life up til now."

"Fair enough," Proftulous griffled. "You just be shutting your eyes for a snutch of blinksnaps, and it'll all be over…"

The tweazle vilishy held up an oidy paw. "Whoa! Mr Dworp, before you do, can you just tell me…"

"It won't be hurtin' none, I promise," Proftulous assured him. "It'll be over in a blinksnap. I's real good at it."

"No," the tweazle insisted, "I was just wondering…"

Serraptomus, his breath finally returning, loudly cleared his throat. "Will that tweazle please shut up! I've peffa-officious and important griffles to relay! Proftulous, just stroff it, so we can get on with things."

"Now hang about just a snutch of blinksnaps," the tweazle griffled to him, shocked by the officious outburst. "I don't want to get russisculoffed with anyone – never have done, never will. But this is *my* stroffing we're griffling about here, Serraptomus, and as such, it's quite an important moment in my long tweazle-life, and I feel one that at least demands a certain air of dignity – officious or not." He turned to Proftulous, who was nodding in earnest agreement. "I was just wondering – what it's going to be like – you know – after I'm stroffed?"

"Oh, good grief!" Serraptomus exploded. "Who cares? Who *actually* cares? You're just…a tweazle, for Oramus' sake! Just an oidy, pointless – and frankly rather irritating – tweazle! You were born to be pie-filling from the first moment you opened your eyes! Now just shut them, let Proftulous do what he has to do, so we can get on with what's really peffa-important!"

But Proftulous was simply looking at the confused creature in his paw. "What be your name, Mr Tweazle?" he asked.

"Kiffel," it griffled.

Proftulous nodded. "Well let me griffle to you, good Kiffel, that I haven't the oidiest idea what the place I send you to will be like, exceptin' that I knows it to be crumlush."

At his side, Serraptomus snorted. "And what would *you* know about it?" he griffled. "You, a mere dworp?"

Proftulous slowly turned to the officious krate, his voice low, steady and peffa-serious. "Because," he calmly griffled, "I do."

Kiffel shifted slightly in his paw. "Right," he griffled. "I think I be ready now. All ready for the off. Just be promising me one thing, will you?"

"Of course," Proftulous griffled.

"Just don't be putting any niffs in the pie with me, will you? I never could stand the things."

"A promise is a promise, good Kiffel," Proftulous griffled, before shaking the oidy tweazle's paw one final time. "Now, you be closing your eyes and it'll all be over in a blinksnap."

At which point Serraptomus – unable to watch – turned away, only turning back when Proftulous had placed the stroffed creature respectfully in the leather tweazle-pouch around his waist.

"So," Proftulous griffled, turning to the slightly ashen krate, "what be these peffa-important and officious griffles you has to be griffling to me?"

Serraptomus, blew out his cheeks, shaking his head, shocked at the speed of what had just happened.

"You be forgetting them?" Proftulous asked.

"No. It's just…"

"It just be what?"

"Well, I…er…"

"You griffled that you had something peffa-important to tell me," Proftulous reminded him.

Serraptomus nodded, still trying to forget about the stroffed tweazle. "I do," he croaked, "it's just…"

"What?"

"Well," he griffled, officiously clearing his krate's throat. "Don't you…you know…*feel* anything for them?"

Proftulous looked down at the bulging tweazle-pouch, patting it gently with his paw and smiling. "They all be in a better place now, Serraptomus," he griffled. "A place that be even more crumlush than Winchett Dale. And I get's meself a most slurpilicious tweazle-pie into the bargain. So the way Proftulous be seeing it is this – both me and Kiffel now be feeling a right lot more fuzzcheck than we did just a snutch of blinksnaps ago."

Serraptomus tried to nod, looking away from the bulging leather pouch.

"I's been eating tweazles for all my time in Winchett Dale, and there's not been one of 'em that's been objecting," Proftulous griffled. "'Tis just how it is, that's all." He reached out and patted the confused krate on his shoulder. "Now, what's these griffles you need to be telling me? They be about Matlock and how he's going to be all winning the Dale Vrooshfest tomorrow morn'up?"

Serraptomus, thankfully reminded of the whispgriffled message, shook his head. "Matlock isn't going to be at the vrooshfest,

Proftulous. He's been called away to complete his second Most Majelicus task. He's left the dale with the snoffibs in a ganticus lid-machine. He seemed quite peffa-twizzly to me."

Proftulous narrowed his eyes. "He be gone? On the second task? Without me – his briftest friend?"

Serraptomus nodded. "Up and away into the lid, he went. But before he did, he whispgriffled to me that he wants you to take his place in the vrooshfest."

"*Me*?" Proftulous gasped. "To be competing with all the majickal-hares?" His jaw hung open. "But I can't be doing any of the saztaculous vrooshing, can I? It's one of the most clottabussed suggestions Matlock has ever been making, and he's certainly been making enough of them in his time."

"Indeed," Serraptomus griffled. "But he also told me that you had a wand."

Proftulous thought for a snutch of blinknaps.

"A wand that his dripple gave you just this even'up?"

The confused dworp suddenly remembered. "He be right! Ayaani did give me a wand – a peffa-oidy one!" He reached into the leather pouch, his paw finding its glopped-up way through stroffed tweazles to the very bottom, before he pulled out the oideist twig Serraptomus had ever seen.

"That's...a wand?"

Proftulous nodded. "Indeed. It just be oidy, that's all. But Ayaani be griffling to me that it be peffa-powerful and ganticussly majickal."

Serraptomus shook his head. "Well, all that Matlock would griffle was that you were to take his place in the vrooshfest, and to use that wand."

"But I don't even be looking like a majickal-hare," Proftulous objected. "I'll be looking like a right clottabus, lining up next to all the saztaculous majickal-hares from all the dales."

Serraptomus simply shrugged. "Quite probably, but really, it's not my problem, is it? I simply had to deliver Matlock's message. A task, which I believe I completed with a fair degree of saztaculous officiousness." He turned to leave. "And, really, if you think *you've* got glubbstooled problems, then believe me, they're oidy compared to mine. If tomorrow goes all peffa-glopped..."

"Which it will," Proftulous unhelpfully griffled.

"...then I'll be spending the rest of my sun-turns washing-up in a basement kitchen."

Proftulous watched the officious krate pid-pad away into the forest, wondering just what on earth to do. If Matlock had asked him to take his place at the Dale Vrooshfest, then as his briftest friend, he had to, even if it meant becoming a chickling-stock in front of every creature in all the majickal dales. But what worried him far more was the thought of Matlock himself, alone as he faced the second Most Majelicus task.

Proftulous urgently needed to griffle with someone he could trust to find out just what in Oramus' name was going on. He closed his eyes, waiting for the intuitive extrapluff to tell him what to do. A snutch of blinksnaps later, he was lump-thumping away, wiping an oidy mirrit from his shoulder, determined to find Laffrohn, landlady and keeper of The Vroffa-Tree Inn, deep beneath Winchett Dale. For if there was one thing that was ever certain in all the majikcal-dales, it was that Laffrohn always seemed to know just about everything that was going on.

But in order to get there, Proftulous would have to use the mirrit-tunnels...

4.

Laffrohn, Alvestra and the Vroffa-Tree Inn

No one quite knows just when the first mirrit first began tunnelling under the dales – except that it was most probably a peffa-long time ago.

If you were ever to find yourself in the position of being trained as a majickal-hare (which although unlikely, perhaps the one thing that Winchett Dale does teach us is that sometimes, *anything* is just the oidiest, oidiest bit possible) you would find yourself confronted by a series of majickal books – or 'driftolubbs' as they're commonly referred to – volumes of ancient majickal wisdom and dalelore which have to be read, scrutinised and thoroughly absorbed, in order that you're be able to master many saztaculous vrooshers to use with your trusted hawthorn wand. And there, in the slimmest and oidiest of all the majickal driftolubbs – the rather unadventurously entitled *Majickal Dalelore – Volume 68 (revised edition)* – you'd discover a brief section about mirrits. Further, if you were to then sit down and actually read it, (a practice most apprentice majickal-hares describe as 'peffa-boring') you'd soon uncover many powerful and important majickal-secrets that so many others miss, as most apprentices wrongly assume there's far more saztaculous stuff to be found in the much larger, more vroosher-friendly volumes in the series.

But, to mirrits…

Absolutely oidy, with even oidier legs, mirrits look to all intents and purposes like a scrittling maggot. Born whenever a majickal-creature has an intuitively extrapluffy thought, the blind mirrit will almost immediately appear somewhere on the creature's robes or fur, before dropping to the ground and making its way slowly towards the nearest mirrit tunnel, a journey that may take several sun-turns, there to finally join grillions of other mirrits, all about their principle business of extending the tunnelling network by eating into the soil deep under the dales. The fruits of all this chomping, munching and subterranean scrittling are a saztaculous collection of tunnels, there to be accessed only by Most Majelicus creatures, as short-cuts and a much needed underground route to avoid the necessity of ever having to pid-pad, lump-thump or scrittle along the peffa-twizzly and often-dangerous Trefflepugga Path.

And what of these 'other' Most Majelicus creatures, you may well wonder? Surely the right is reserved solely for majickal-hares? And here, you'd be wrong. Whilst the majickal-hare is the only creature that has to complete three Most Majelicus tasks in order to wear red-robes – other creatures are simply born Most Majelicus, spending the quiet majority of their lives simply doing Most Majelicus things in and around the dales without many other creatures ever really realising. There are Most Majelicus trees, too, and plants, and even rumours of an entire Most Majelicus forest, hidden deep and fantastic in a far and distant dale – although it's also worth remembering that most dale rumours of this type should be taken with a peffa-large pinch of heffel-salt.

Amongst this strange menagerie of Most Majelicus creatures is, of course, Proftulous the Dworp – the only dworp in all dworping history to have ever been given the honour. Having once eaten a peffa-ganticus tweazle pie cooked by the licking flames of Matlock's own set of majickal-driftolubbs, Proftulous inadvertently ingested their contents alongside the pie itself, making him quite the most extraordinary dworp of all. And ever since his ganticus feast, he'd been able to lump-thump along the many mirrit-tunnels with as much right and impunity as any other Most Majelicus creature – although a fair few he met down in the peffa-dark confines of the narrow tunnels did sometimes give him quite the strangest looks.

Right at the centre of this mirrit-eaten catacomb, deep beneath the ever-changing landscape of Trefflepugga Path, is a most saztaculous and ganticus torchlit cavern, and there, floating on a shindinculous blue lake is the one place where all Most Majelicus creatures are forever welcome – The Vroffa-Tree Inn, surrounded by vroffa-trees and run by its crumlush landlady, Laffrohn, known to all for her enthusiastic welcome, guzzworts, roaring log fires and most slurpilicious food. Indeed, some Most Majelicus creatures simply use the mirrit tunnels to go and have a guzzwort and a meal at The Vroffa-Tree Inn, and for no other reason. Others treat it as a welcome break in their journey to have a good griffle and a chickle at what's been going on back up on the surface, before setting on their way again. Only once in every year does The Vroffa-Tree Inn shut its large oaken creakers to Most Majelicus creatures, the one even'up when it rises from the lake, up through the ground to float just above Trefflepugga Path, there to await the arrival of *The League of Lid Curving Witchery*, all anxious to fly down and replace the vroffa-branches on their brooms with the tzorkliest pick of this year's crop. A truly saztaculous spectacle, but one best to witness from *inside* the inn, rather than outside of it.

Proftulous, although a frequent visitor to the inn, and good friend of Laffron, had never witnessed the glopped-up chaos of the visiting witches, but had spent some moon-turns there as a guest, tending the vroffa-trees in the inn's crumlush garden as he waited for Matlock to solve the riddle of Trefflepugga Path.

So it was to Laffrohn that Proftulous went on the night Matlock began his quest to solve the puzzle of the Tillian Wand, hoping that she of all creatures would be able to griffle to him exactly what was going on. For in her time as landlady to so many Most Majelicus creatures, she had both been told and overheard a grillion majickal things that most would never, ever hear, and if anyone knew what Proftulous should do, it would surely be Laffrohn.

His mind made up, he made his way straight to the very heart of Wand Wood to the Last Great Elm, standing at the base of the trunk and looking up into the branches. "Zhava!" he urgently whispgriffled in the darkness. "Stop those nifferduggles and be all waking up! I need to be using the tunnels, and it be a twizzly emergency!"

The tree shifted a little, slowly opening its eyes and looking down. "Proftulous?" she griffled, yawning. "What in Oramus' sake are you doing out here so late?"

"I be needing to lump-thump to The Vroffa-Tree Inn," he explained. "Matlock's gone away, and I have to be him in a vrooshing contest, and I need to be seeing Laffrohn and…"

Zhava held an elderly branch against his yechus mouth, silencing him. "All this is very well, Proftulous. But have you any idea how much an old tree like me needs her nifferduggles?"

"I be right sorry about that, Zhava, it's just that…"

"And," Zhava insisted, "you haven't even had the manners to griffle 'sorry' to me!"

Proftulous blinked. "But I did. I be griffling that just now."

"When?"

"Right before you griffled to me that I hadn't griffled 'sorry' to you, I'd already griffled it."

"Then I'm really confused," Zhava admitted.

"That's because you be quite peffa-old," Proftulous griffled.

"But I did be griffling 'sorry' to you, I really did."

Zhava considered this. "Then I would have heard it, wouldn't I?" She leant right over, closely scrutinising his face, her branches brushing the top of his head. "I don't suppose you're telling spuddles to old Zhava, are you, Proftulous? Just because she's getting old and can't be hearing too good anymore?"

But before Proftulous could even begin to answer the confused tree, the whole of Zhava's trunk was suddenly pushed backwards, revealing a large hole in the ground, and a series of strange creatures dressed in various shades of red and carrying torches emerged in a line from the open mirrit-tunnel beneath her roots.

"Even'up," one of them cheerfully griffled to Proftulous. "We're here for the Dale Vrooshfest tomorrow morn'up. We are in the right place, aren't we – Winchett Dale?"

"Indeed, you be that," Proftulous griffled, realising that now was his briftest chance to slip past the eager Most Majelicus crowd of visitors and lump-thump down into the open tunnel before Zhava could get any more russisculoffed. "You's all here in Winchett Dale."

Another Most Majelicus creature, possible the thinnest Proftulous had ever seen, let out a sigh of relief. "Thank Oramus

A series of strange creatures dressed in various shades of red and carrying torches emerged in a line from the open mirrit-tunnel beneath her roots.

for that," she griffled. "Only we weren't completely sure of the way. We just sort of looked for the most glopped-up mirrit tunnel and followed it, hoping it would lead us here." She looked at Proftulous. "Now can you be most awfully kind and show us to our seats? Only we want to get settled in nice and early to get the briftest possible view before the others arrive."

"What *others*?" Zhava cried from over her shoulder, still almost bent double. "There's more of you?"

"Oh, more than a ganticus plenty!" a third Most Majelicus creature griffled. "I'd stay there, if I was you, otherwise you'll be up and down until morn'up."

Sure enough, every time Proftulous tried to enter the mirrit tunnel, he'd lump-thump straight into another party of Most Majelicus creatures on their way out, all peffa-keen to go and find their seats before the Dale Vrooshfest began. It got so bad that eventually there were at least three-hundred of them aimlessly standing around Zhava, waiting for instructions, mistakenly assuming that Proftulous had been sent as part of an official reception and welcoming committee to greet their arrival. Some even began wondering if there weren't going to be complimentary guzzworts and bowls of niff-soup, citing other vrooshfests when they'd received similar preferential treatment. Others thought that perhaps they'd get presents, new robes or free wands to mark their arrival, believing that the longer they waited, and the more that gathered in the increasingly cramped space, the more saztaculous and crumlush their rewards and gifts would be.

"There has to be something *truly* peffa-shindinculous about to happen," one griffled to another. "Otherwise the dworp wouldn't keep us waiting all this time."

Proftulous, still trying his briftest to lump-thump down the tunnel before being pushed back by yet more Most Majelicus arrivals, was getting increasingly russisculoffed with the whole glopped-up situation. It just didn't seem possible to him that there could ever be that many Most Majelicus creatures in all the majickal-dales. And yet, still they came, pid-padding, lump-thumping, scrittling, slithering, flapping and some even throzzing; Zhava complaining bitterly all the while and demanding just when the cheerful invasion would possibly stop.

Eventually, thwarted for the final time, Proftulous re-emerged from the tunnel, bellowing and roaring loudly for silence – the sudden noise quietening everyone.

He cleared his throat. "Right, all you Most Majelicussy folk has got to be listening to my griffles, as they be most peffa-important."

"Is it about our special-visitor gifts?" one asked, before being vilishly hushed by the others.

Proftulous tried to think as hard as he could, a difficult task at the briftest of times. "Er…no, it not be about rewards…"

"Well, what is it?" another demanded, as the mood began to turn just the oidiest bit yechus.

"It be…" Proftulous struggled, desperate for anything that might help him finally get down into the tunnel and on his way to The Vroffa-Tree Inn, "…it be about Winchett Dale."

"Well, what about it?" a creature asked.

Proftulous cleared his throat, suddenly extrapluffing a vision of exactly what he must do – no matter how glubbstooled it sounded. He wiped the mirrit from his hairy shoulder. "Well, when some of you's first arrived, I may have griffled to you that this was Winchett Dale."

"Yee-ess?" a Most Majelicus sazpent hissed.

"Well, the thing is that now I've realised I was mishearing things."

"Misss-hearing?" the sazpent griffled.

"Indeed," Proftulous nodded. "What I was really meaning to griffle is that this place is *Binchett Vale*. Not Winchett Dale – Binchett Vale. A different place entirely."

"Binchett Vale?" a Most Majelicus cottle-shrubb cried out, shaking its red leaves in confusion. "Are you absolutely peffa-sure, dworp? Only I've never heard of such a place in all my sun-turns."

"Doubly sure," Proftulous griffled. "Cross my softulous and hope to stroff if I be making it up and telling you spuddles about it." He desperately looked to Zhava for support.

"Will I be able to get my old trunk upright and have a night's peace?" she whispgriffled to him.

Proftulous nodded.

She took a deep breath, raising herself slowly with a series of loud and painful creaks. "The dworp is right," she imperiously announced. "This *is* Binchett Vale, and *not* Winchett Dale. I'm afraid you've all gone and fetched up in quite the wrong place."

Some of the creatures were getting suspicious, murmuring amongst themselves.

"You see," Proftulous went on, eager to press the point, crossing the fingers on his ganticus paws behind his hairy back, "if this *was* Winchett Dale, then we'd have got all sorts of lovely welcoming guzzworts, slurpilicious treats and fuzzcheck rewards ready and waiting for you, wouldn't we? After all, we would have been peffa-hard at work preparing for the Dale Vrooshfest for many years. We wouldn't just be leaving you all wandering around and uncertain in a glopped-up dark wood, now would we?"

The sazpent slithered forward. "Not so, dworp!" it hissed. "Because that's *exactly* the sort of thing we *would* expect from Winchett Dale. A ganticus glopp-up, from the first moment we arrived." He turned to the others, their torchlit faces nodding in agreement. "Something that certainly hasn't disappointed us so far."

Proftulous frowned, realising that perhaps he had been bettered by the sazpent. But then another thought suddenly struck him "Aha!" he griffled, raising a paw, quite excrimbly. "But what you've forgotten, Mr Sazpent, is this – because Winchett Dale always glopps-up, then surely it follows that the one time you *would* be expectin' it to be glopping up, then it *wouldn't* – would it? For Winchett Dale be so peffa-clottabussed and glubbstooled that it would peffa-definitely also glopp-up at being glopped-up!"

A few Most Majelicus heads slowly nodded as they began to follow the train of Proftulous' vilishly improvised logic. Gradually one or two began heading back towards the entrance of the mirrit tunnel.

"The way I sees it," Proftulous went on, gently pushing others towards the base of Zhava's trunk, "the more vilishly you's can all be getting back down and finding the right tunnel to Winchett Dale, the less of their saztaculous welcoming gifts and rewards you'll be missing."

"Indeed!" Zhava heartily agreed, creaking slowly back over to open the tunnel entrance once more. "And on behalf of all Great Elms everywhere, I bid you farewell, good-bye, and have a safe journey from Binchett Vale."

Commotion ensued, as suddenly some three hundred Most Majelicus creatures of every description all headed back down into the narrow tunnel, pushing and scrumming, desperate to get to the 'real' Winchett Dale as quickly as possible without missing any free guzzworts, slurpilicious treats or welcoming gifts of any kind.

Proftulous waited at the very back, thanking Zhava profusely, then finally setting off into the crowded darkness himself, lump-thumping into the tunnel and pushing the Most Majelicus battering ram of excrimbly creatures as hard as he could from the back, knowing there wasn't a single creature in all the dales that could possibly stop the greedy momentum of the hurtling wall of creatures in front. The tunnel walls shook with so much pid-padding and stampeding lump-thumping. The noise was almost deafening, a ganticus, rumbling garrumbloom as they headed deeper down into the depths.

"You needs to be turning up that way!" he suddenly cried out from the back, the message quickly spreading to the front as the entire hoard veered into an ajoining tunnel on the left. "Winchett Dale be up there!"

Thankfully, in a snutch of blinksnaps they were gone, leaving just their echoing cries and garrumblooming pid-pads. Next, Proftulous' Most Majelicus eyes majickally adjusted themselves to the darkness, and taking a deep dworp's breath, he finally set off for the familiar cavern that was the home of The Vroffa-Tree Inn.

On the way, he passed several more Most Majelicus creatures journeying to the Dale Vrooshfest, but here the tunnels were wider, allowing them to fortunately pass without incident, a good thing, as Proftulous noticed that they seemed to be clearly the worse for wear after too many guzzworts – a sure sign he was lump-thumping ever closer to the inn.

Gradually, the tunnel began to slope down, Proftulous looking ahead, surprised to make out what looked like dozens of wet footprints on the ground. He stopped, bent down and ran a paw along the damp earth, frowning. In all his journeys through the tunnels, he'd never known them to be wet before.

He lump-thumped further down the slope, seeing the familiar torchlit glow from around the corner that signalled the entrance to the ganticus cavern, realising that he was now lump-thumping and splashing in cold water up to his ankles. He turned the corner, astonished to see just how far the vast cavern-lake had risen since his last visit. The oidy wooden bridge was almost underwater, the floating inn with its crumlush garden of vroffa-trees higher than he'd ever seen it. Undeterred, he waded in, up to his knees, before lump-thumping across the bridge to the safety of the garden, vilishly making his way up to the heavy oak creaker and pushing it open.

"Laffrohn!" he called, searching the empty inn, its tables full of recently finished guzzwort jugs, wooden tankards and half-eaten plates of food. Behind him, the roaring piff-tosh splutted and hissed, as if somehow disapproving of his presence. "Laffrohn, where be you? I need's to be griffling to you about something most peffa-important!"

"We're over here," a crumlush voice he instantly recognised called back. "In the corner, Proftulous."

Proftulous lump-thumped around the corner, ducking his ganticus head to avoid a large beam, finally seeing Laffrohn and Chatsworth sat at a small candlelit table, sharing a large jug of guzzwort. "Chatsworth?" Proftulous griffled. "What you be doing here?"

The elderly red-robed Most Majelicus hare slightly raised his eyes. "Enjoying a quiet guzzwort, Proftulous. That much, I would have thought, would have been immediately obvious to even the most clottabussed dworp."

Laffrohn smiled, pulled up a stool for Proftulous to settle his ganticus bulk on and poured him a guzzwort. "It's been a peffa-long night," she griffled, "what with everyone stopping in before they go to the vrooshfest in Winchett Dale. Is everything prepared and ready up there?"

Proftulous finished his guzzwort in one gulp before pouring himself another. "No, it not be, Laffrohn," he griffled. "It not be at all ready, not the oidiest bit."

Laffrohn smiled. "Well you's not to be worrying your dworp's head about all that, Proftulous. Everyone expects it to be a saztaculous glopp-up, and I'm sure Winchett Dale won't be disappointing them come the morn'up."

"But Matlock's gone," he griffled, wiping his lips as he finished his second guzzwort, unable to stop the panicked griffles tumbling from his mouth. "He's all gone away and is trying to complete his second Most Majelicussy task, and I don't know where he is, and he wants me to be him at the vrooshfest, and I be so worried about him and all twizzly, and…"

"And methinks you're always griffling far too much, far too vlishly," Laffrohn griffled, lightly patting the top of his heavy paw, then asking him to explain all that had happened as slowly and clearly as possible as she and Chatsworth listened.

"And so you see," Proftulous finally told them both, "there's no way I could ever be passing for any kind of majickal-hare, is there? I'll be all lining up with the rest of them, looking like a peffa-clottabus and not being able to do a single vroosher. And all the time I'll be worried to my crimple about what Matlock be up to."

Chatsworth lightly drummed his elderly claws on the table. "Proftulous, there's something you need to understand. There is much happening all around us – even as we sit here – that seeks to change everything and anything that we know and love. All that we hold dear will soon be in twizzly-peril, as surely as the waters of the lake are now rising to swallow up this saztaculous inn."

Proftulous looked to Laffrohn, who merely nodded, putting a paw to her lips to hush his griffles and questions.

Chatsworth shifted slightly, grimacing with the effort, rubbing his wrinkled brow, trying to find the right griffles that the confused dworp might somehow understand. "I know you're briftest friends with Matlock…"

"I be that," Proftulous vilishly griffled, earning a light bliff around the ears from Laffrohn as another warning to keep quiet.

"…but the facts of the matter are these," Chatsworth continued. "Matlock has been sent on an almost impossible task – to find the Tillian Wand. It is the most dangerous of all three Most Majelicus tasks, and I'm afraid, nearly all majickal-hares who attempt it, fail."

"Well, he can be trying again, can't he?" Proftulous griffled, unable to stop himself, earning a swift kick under the table from Laffrohn.

Chatsworth looked him in the eye. "I'm afraid it's not quite as peffa-simple as that, Proftulous. Fail to find the wand, and the majickal-hare is stroffed." He took a deep hare's breath. "There are, I'm afraid, no second chances."

Proftulous sat in silence, jaw slowly dropping, hanging on every griffle.

"Proftulous," Chatsworth continued, "both Laffrohn and I know that you are just a dworp – and frankly, a peffa-clottabussed one at that. I realised this the first moment I saw you. I'd never known a dworp quite so completely clottabussed as you. Nevertheless, as I trained Matlock, I made sure the two of you became briftest friends, knowing that having a faithful dworp was a sure sign that one day he would grow into a majickal-hare that I would feel peffa-confident in nominating to undertake the three tasks. Much has been engineered and prepared here, Proftulous, just for this one peffa-important sun-turn; the sun-turn Matlock undertakes the second task."

Proftulous blinked, trying to follow the elderly hare's griffles.

Chatsworth lowered his voice as the whole inn and its floating gardens suddenly lurched a little, the rising waters slapping against the side of the ganticus cavern walls outside. "Quite soon," he slowly griffled, "I am to be taken to the Majickal Elders, there to stand trial for my interference in Matlock's progress. There are some who disapprove, Proftulous, and peffa-powerful creatures they are, too."

Proftulous eye's widened. "So you're going to...you be going to..."

"Stroff?" Chatsworth finished for him, half smiling. "Yes. It is my time. Matlock knows. I've already told him."

Proftulous looked to Laffrohn, his yechus face becoming quite twizzled. "It not be true," he griffled. "Chatsworth, you can't be getting all stroffed and be leaving us?"

Laffrohn tried to smile. "Just listen, Proftulous. We really don't be have much time. Already, the waters are rising. They have come sooner than we think, much peffa-sooner. The great sun-turn is suddenly upon us, and you needs to be listening peffa-hard to what Chatsworth has to griffle."

Chatsworth nodded at Proftulous. "Matlock has to complete the task by this time tomorrow. It is all the time he has. However, it may well run out sooner, we have no way of knowing. He will need to find the Tillian Wand and bring it back to Wand Woods in order to give it to Jericho and Lily Krettle – keepers of the second task. If he fails, they will stroff him. Wherever he is when the sands of his time run out, he will be majickally bought back to their peffa-twizzly tower and be made into hare soupy-soupy."

Proftulous' eyes suddenly widened in twizzly shock. He swallowed hard. "Hare…hare soupy-soupy?"

Laffrohn gently squeezed his paw. "'Tis what be happening to most of them what be taking the task, Proftulous," she griffled. "There not be many that even *see* the Tillian Wand, let alone bring it back. 'Tis only the most peffa-majickal of hares that can be doing that."

"But…but…" Proftulous griffled, searching both their faces imploringly, "I don't want Matlock being stroffed."

Chatsworth held his dworp's eyes for a long moment. "Proftulous," he slowly griffled. "I'm afraid that's what's going to happen. That's *exactly* what's going to happen. It's what *must* happen – for the sake of all of us, and all the majickal dales. " He lowered his head. "Matlock must be seen to fail the task. There really is no other way. I'm sorry."

Proftulous sat stunned at what he'd just heard, not believing a griffle of it, yet knowing that because Chatsworth and Laffrohn were amongst his briftest friends, somehow it *had* to be true. He cleared his throat, making a yechus noise as Laffrohn gently reached up and wrapped her arm around his shoulders. "He…has to be stroffed?" he whispgriffled, awkwardly rubbing his paws together. "Matlock, my briftest friend, the briftest friend any dworp could have in all the majickal dales – has to be stroffed?

Laffrohn let out a slow breath. "'Tis the only way, Proftulous."

He turned to her, indignant. "But there *has* to be being another way! There has to! None of this be right at all!" He stood and lump-thumped around the empty inn, suddenly turning to them. "You's both be peffa-majical and Most Majelicussy!" he angrily griffled. "You can be saving him! You can't just be letting Matlock be stroffed! You *can't!*"

Laffrohn shook her head. "There's nothing we can do, Proftulous, nothing. If Matlock is seen to complete the task, then

Jericho and Lily Krettle will inform the Majickal Elders. They are already watching us, Proftulous. Things will get so much more peffa-glopped than you could ever imagine in a grillion, grillion sun-turns."

"But how?" Proftulous griffled, his yechus voice starting to shake a little. "I just not be understanding any of it!"

"Because," Chatsworth suddenly griffled, becoming russisculoffed, "you're not *meant* to understand any of it! You're just… a dworp, for Oramus' sake!"

Laffrohn tried to reach for the elderly hare. "Chatsworth, I don't think now's be the time to be…"

"Time?" he vilishly shot back, eyes ablaze. "What would Proftulous ever know about 'time'? Except, of course, when he wants to fill his ganticus crimple full of tweazle-pies? He's just a dworp, Laffrohn!" He pointed a shaking paw at Proftulous. "Your 'task' is to do exactly as Matlock told you to do – take his place in the vrooshfest, and nothing else!"

"But I don't know how!" Proftulous moaned.

"You're Most Majelicus, for Oramus' sake! Just do something Most Majelicus!" he angrily pid-padded towards the leaded windows, pointing outside. "Look out there, Proftulous, just look! Can't you see it? The waters are rising, and a ganticus moon-tide is on the way. Its power is immeasurable. Already the lower mirrit-tunnels are mostly flooded. Soon this entire cavern will be under water, and even this inn itself will sink far below into the glopped-up depths." He turned, his face as intent as the force of his griffles. "There is no 'time', Proftulous; not for me, for you, for Laffrohn, for Matlock – for any of us! All the while, as grillions of creatures gather for the Dale Vrooshfest, the constellation of The Great Broom is changing, realigning, right above their heads and threatening to bring peffa-terrible things." He stopped, taking seveal deep hare's breaths and closing his eyes, before reaching out for Proftulous' paw, taking it in his own and slowly opening his eyes once more. "Do as Matlock asked you, my friend. That's all I can griffle to you. Leave now. Go back to Winchett Dale before any other of the tunnels are flooded. When you get there, tell the whole woods what is happening. Get the trees, plants and rocks to move and block the entrance, anything you can think of. Then go to Matlock's cottage, find one of his green robes and caps, put them on, and wait for the morn'up, then join the others up on the High Pleateau. Hopefully you'll all be safe, and the tunnel entrance will hold throughout the tidal-surge." He slowly shook Proftulous' ganticus paw. "I've only been hard on you because I lost my own dworp," he quietly griffled. "I think that was wrong of me at times, and for that, I'm truly sorry."

Laffrohn pid-padded to the window, anxiously looking outside at the rising, chopping waters. "Now's the time for you both to be pid-padding and lump-thumping away while you still can," she griffled. "It's getting much more glopped out there."

"What about you?" Chatsworth asked her.

She paused for snutch of moments then smiled, slightly chickling to herself. "Oh, I think I might just stop for one last guzzwort, Chatsworth. Say a proper 'good-bye' to the old place. After all, I've been having some crumlush times in here – right peffa-crumlush."

"And I did, too," Chatsworth griffled, giving her a long hug. "And at the end of the sun-turn, perhaps that's the main thing, isn't it?"

"The most *peffa*-main thing," Laffrohn agreed. "Always has been, and always will, methinks. I wish you well on your journey, Chatsworth."

He nodded, then pid-padded outside, Laffrohn and Proftulous watching him cross the bridge, then wade through waist-deep murky waters until finally reaching a ladder and slowly climbing up towards one of the highest mirrit-tunnels.

"Now you, Proftulous," Laffrohn instructed. "Off you be lump-thumping back to Winchett Dale while there's still time."

Together they walked outside and through the crumlush garden bordered by sleeping vroffa-trees, all oblivious to the dangers around them.

"Why they all be nifferduggling?" Proftulous asked.

"T'isn't time for them to be waking up, yet," Laffrohn griffled, lightly stroking the trunk of the nearest one. "They only be waking up on the sun-turn that *The League of Lid-Curving Witchery* comes for their new flight branches for their brooms. Then they all starts to get excrimbly, waving and thrashing, and next thing you know, they're flying this whole inn right up through the earth and onto Trefflepugga Path."

Proftulous suddenly had an idea. "So's if we wakes 'em all up now, they'd fly us both out of here, and The Vroffa-Tree Inn would be all safe forever?"

Laffrohn smiled, slowly shaking her head. "'Tis a crumlush idea, Proftulous."

"And it be a right clever one for a clottabussed, Dworp, too!"

She nodded. "It be that, Proftulous. But I'm afraid nothing can be waking these trees when they're nifferduggling – nothing. There's a full six sun-turns before they be due to be waking up, but by then it'll all be too late."

Dismayed, Proftulous looked at the rising waters, hearing a sudden fizz as a flaming torch on the far side of the ganticus cavern was quickly swallowed by the flood.

"'You must go," Laffrohn urged, pushing Proftulous onto the oidy wooden bridge. "You leaves it any longer, and these waters will be over that yechus head of yours."

But Proftulous wasn't listening, instead carefully looking at the many tunnel entrances, some as high as the ganticus cavern roof itself. Another torch fizzed out nearby. "I not be lump-thumping anywhere," he griffled, turning to Laffrohn, his face set. "I think it would be rather crumlush to be keeping you company over that last guzzwort of yours."

"No, Proftulous, you must go."

Proftulous smiled at her, wrapping a ganticus arm over her shoulders and gently steering her back towards the creaker. "Let's have no more of your griffles, Laffrohn. What say you see if there's one last tweazle-pie to be cooked in this saztaculous old inn of yours, shall we? I'll be sorting out the guzzworts, and you be putting the pie on the piff-tosh. I really can't think of a brifter way to celebrate the last of this shindinculous place."

Laffron gave him a long look. "You be peffa-serious? You'll stay with me until the end?"

"Never more so," he griffled. "Now lets get ourselves guzzworted and feasted."

And so it was that with these griffles – and Laffrohn knowing that once Proftulous' clottabussed mind was made up, there wasn't really the oidiest thing she could do about it – that the two of them sat down to guzzworts and the inn's final tweazle-pie as the waters rose, lifting the floating gardens higher and higher towards the cold stone roof of the ganticus caven, its flaming torches gradually fizzing out, until just one remained, flickering in the near darkness, beside the entrance to the last mirrit-tunnel.

Proftulous had just finished a yechus mouthful of tweazle-pie as a ganticus garrumblooming crack echoed from outside, lurching the entire inn and gardens. He looked up, as another shook the inn. "'Tis the vroffa-trees," he calmly explained to Laffrohn, wiping glopped-up drool from his mouth. "They all be breaking on the cavern roof as we be rising up."

Laffrohn nodded. "It be so sad, Proftulous. They've been here as long as I have."

"Be there any more tweazle-pie? Only I be supposin' we've still got time before the inn be all drowned to the bottom?"

Laffrohn smiled. "Is that all you *really* think about, Proftulous?"

"Mostly, yes," he griffled.

Laffrohn nodded, realising in that blinksnap that for all the imminent danger, and the rising, churning, peffa-twizzly inevitability of what has about to happen – there was really no one else in all the majickal-dales she would have wanted to share her last guzzworts with than Proftulous. Something about him just resonated calm, be it his endless tweazle-pie griffversations, his ganticus dark-brown eyes, or simply the predictable sounds of his satisfied, rumbling crimple – Proftulous, Laffrohn decided, was probably one of the briftest creatures she had ever known in all her peffa-many years.

Another tree cracked and broke outside, the roof of the inn now scraping against hard stone, sending guzzwort jugs and plates tumbling. Proftulous stood and went to the window, peering into the gloom, seeing the final torch just inches away from being snuffed out.

He turned to Laffrohn. "Well, I be thinking that this be the right time."

"For what?"

He reached into his tweazle bag, bringing out and brandishing his peffa-oidy twig-wand. "For me to be trying this."

Laffrohn frowned as the first waters made their way over the garden edge, running along the pathways and under the inn's creaker, vilishly beginning to pool around the slate floor. "And what be that, for Oramus' sake?"

Proftulous puffed out his chest. "It be my very own majickal-wand," he proudly griffled. "Given to me by Ayaani, so that I can be all majickal. And now we're going to be trying it out."

"But Proftulous," Laffrohn griffled, a powerful surge of water flooding in, knocking over tables and chairs and instantly putting out the roaring piff-tosh in a ganticus spluttering hiss. "It just be a twig! And I don't be thinking Ayaani be liking you that much, anyway!"

Undeterred, with the pouring water already up to his waist, Proftulous swept her into his arms and waded towards the creaker as the entire inn listed dangerously, sending floating tables crashing into the walls. "Well, methinks this is where we'll be finding out, won't we?" he griffled to her. "Let's you and I be seeing just how much Ayaani really likes old Proftulous."

Struggling against the surging current, he was just able to find a gap just large enough to wade outside into the garden, the oak creaker slamming behind them, water pouring through the broken windows.

"Proftulous!" Laffrohn cried out in the gloom. "I did have a plan, you know! I wasn't simply going to drown and be stroffed!"

"And what be that then?" Proftulous griffled feeling the ground beneath slip away under his feet.

Laffrohn clung on tightly to his neck, trying to disguise the rising twizzlyness in her griffles. "I was going to use one of the empty guzzwort barrels to be all floating away in."

Proftulous chickled out loud. "Escaping in a guzzwort barrel?" he griffled. "Laffrohn, I may be clottabussed, but I can griffle you this – there be no way that would have worked, just no way at all!"

She gasped from the cold water, realising they were now both floating, the roof of the cavern just a few feet above their heads and the inn sinking vilishly below the swirling waters, making its unstop-pable way slowly – almost calmly – deep into the cold, inky back.

"So what be *your* plan, then?" she griffled, watching the last of the stone chimney slip below.

"Plan?" Proftulous griffled, treading water, shifting her onto his back, and swimming to the nearest piece of broken floating vroffa-tree. "This not be a 'plan', Laffrohn – this be one of my saztaculous extrapluffs!"

"Then Oramus be helping us!" Laffrohn cried, as the final mirrit-tunnel began to flood with water, threatening to snuff out the flaming torch at its entrance.

"We not be needing Oramus," Proftulous spluttered, heaving Laffrohn onto the snapped vroffa-trunk. "All we needs to be doing is be waking this nifferduggling tree up!" One arm around the trunk, the other brandishing the oidy twig-wand, barely able to keep his ganticus head above the water, he took a peffa-yechus deep dworp's breath and cried out, "By the majickal-lore of all the dales, be waking this tree up so we's can be flying away from here!"

Nothing happened.

"I really think I was much preferring my barrel idea," Laffrohn moaned.

"Just be paddling us to the tunnel!" Proftulous roared. "If we gets close enough, the water will take us right inside!"

"To drown and then stroff in a mirrit-tunnel," Laffrohn muttered under her breath, trying as briftest as she could to kick and paddle. "A twig-wand, indeed! I always knew Ayaani be hating you."

Behind, Proftulous quickly swam to the mess of tangled branches that had once been the top of the splendid vroffa-tree, trying to push with all his might and guide it towards the tunnel entrance, frantically griffling any majickal vrooshers his clottabussed mind could think of, desperate for the nifferduggling tree to wake.

"We're not going to make it, Proftulous!" Laffrohn cried, the cavern roof now just inches from the top of her head, vroffa-branches scraping and snapping against it.

"There be no such griffle as 'not'!" Proftulous spluttered. "Not for Proftulous, anyway!"

"There do be!" Laffrohn cried, bending her head as low as she could. "You just be griffling it just then, you ganticus clottabus!"

Proftulous let out a pained roar as he bliffed his head against the cavern roof, repeatedly thrashing his oidy twig-wand against the sleeping vroffa-tree and urgently commanding it to wake up. "You's gots to be waking up!" he cried as they neared the tunnel, the water now lapping less than a mirrit's leg from the flaming torch. "Please! Or we'll be all drowned!"

Laffrohn struggled to guide the trunk, reaching down into the flood and frantically paddling with her paws "Use the last torch!" she shouted. "Light the ends of the branches before it goes out!"

Gasping and heaving, Proftulous bent the nearest branch with all his might, trying desperately to find a dry spot to hold over the flame, praying to Oramus that he hadn't indeed eaten his last ever tweazle-pie. "You be all catching fire," he urged, water soaking his face, as suddenly, to his ganticus relief, the end of the branch suddenly fizzed bright red at the peffa-same blinksnap the cavern was plunged into darkness.

"Now get on behind and hold on tight!" Laffrohn cried out. "I's be thinking that this is going to be one peffa-russisculoffed vroffa-tree!"

Sure enough, the snapped trunk of the rudely awakened tree began thrashing in the water like a russisculoffed sazpent; coughing, spluttering and roaring, before suddenly straightening and vilishly flying away down the fast-flooding mirrit-tunnel, hurtling into the black, Laffrohn and Proftulous desperately hanging on as they flew through the labyrinthine network of tunnels, heading closer to the surface, before finally bursting back out onto the surface, each branch of the panicked tree glowing bright red as they screamed high into the twinkling-lid before finally – thankfully – it began to slow, panting from its efforts, Laffrohn trying her briftest to level it.

"Use your ganticus, glopped-up knees!" she shouted to Proftulous as they headed straight into a cloud. "Steer it with your knees!"

Proftulous tried, whooping with excrimbly joy as the vroffa-tree responded. Pushing with his left knee turned it to the right; pressure with his right wheeled it to the left. "But how do we get down from here and be landing all safely?" he cried from the back.

"Like this!" Laffrohn griffled, leaning down on the trunk and causing it to suddenly dip and descend. "When we get near to the ground, lean right back!"

Proftulolus let another excrimbly whoop of joy as they began picking up speed, diving back through the clouds. "Now this," he griffled, both cheeks flapping in the roaring wind, "be a *grillion* times better than floating away in a glubbstooled old guzzwort barrel, Laffrohn! I be liking this muchly, I really peffa-do!"

"Now get on behind and hold on tight!" Laffrohn cried out. *"I's be thinking that this is going to be one peffa-russisculoffed vroffa-tree!"*

"Lean back, you ganticus clottabus!" Laffrohn cried over her shoulder. "We'll be stroffed as those tweazles in your pouch if we hits the ground this fast!"

Proftulous leant back and the tree began to slow, levelling itself as the ground rose up to meet them, finally slowing just enough to land in an undignified scramble, Proftulous and Laffrohn rolling on the ground, crying out in excrimbly joy to have landed safely and escaped the flood.

Immediately, the russisculoffed vroffa-tree tried to stand, pushing itself up on its branches, but with the rest of its trunk and roots deep beneath the cavern lake, the briftest it could manage was to topple straight over, outrage in its griffles. "What in Oramus' name has been going on?" it demanded, staring at them both. "Laffrohn, where am I? Why have I been woken? And, if you wouldn't mind, please griffle where the rest of me is!"

Laffrohn stood, padding herself down in the moonlight. "It be a peffa-long story, good tree," she griffled. "But thanks to you, we're still alive."

"Indeed," the irate tree observed. "But I see that both of you have legs. Something I seem to be lacking. Would you mind griffling to me just what happened to my roots?"

Laffrohn made Proftulous help the tree upright as she explained all that had happened. The tree listened, trying to understand, Proftulous' huge arms wrapped around its trunk to stop it falling.

"So," the irate tree slowly griffled, "you're griffling to me that I'm the only vroffa-tree left? That the inn has gone, and all my brother and sister trees are somewhere at the bottom of the lake?"

Laffrohn nodded, looking up at the still smouldering flight branches, their tips glowing red against the twinkling-lid above. "Tis true," she quietly griffled, patting the bark of its trunk. "And I be most peffa-sorry. There be nothing I could be doing to save them."

Proftulous, trying to think of something that would make the tree feel less glopped-up, cleared his throat. "But be thinking of it this way," he griffled, "if Laffrohn had had her way, then we wouldn't have even been griffling to you right now, because her ganticus plan was to use a barrel and…"

"Enough, Proftulous!" Laffrohn hissed, silencing him and looking all round, her nose ears and whiskers twitching, as if suddenly recognising something in the unfamiliar landscape.

"You be being here before?" Proftulous asked her.

She half-closed her eyes, momentarily lost in thought. "Once," she quietly griffled. "A peffa, peffa-long time ago. Too long ago."

Proftulous gently lowered the tree back onto the ground. 'So you know where we are?"

She nodded, shivering in the moonlit breeze. "Somewhere that I always knew that I would return to one sun-turn."

"Why?" Proftulous griffled.

Laffrohn looked back into the twinkling-lid, wrapping her short arms around herself. "This place was the last time I ever saw my sister," she griffled, shaking her head. "A most peffa-glopped sun-turn, Proftulous. Peffa, peffa-glopped."

Proftulous raised an eyebrow, surprised. "I not be knowing that you has a family, Laffrohn. I always be thinking that you be like me, with no mahapa, pahpa, brothers or sisters."

She turned to him. "You has them, Proftulous, it's just that you don't be remembering them. You were already a roaming dworp when Chatsworth found you and named you Proftulous."

Proftulous nodded keenly. "S'right," he proudly griffled. "I be named Proftulous – after the star what be closest to the moon." He pointed a ganticus paw into the twinkling-lid, aiming it at an oidy pin-prick of light almost touching the full moon. "That be me up there, that be, Laffrohn. That be the star of Proftulous. Chatsworth once told me about it, how it looks peffa-oidy, but really it be the most ganticus star of all – 'tis simply that it be so peffa-far away."

She half-smiled. "'Tis true," she griffled. "Sometimes the oidiest, oidiest things can really be the most ganticus."

"What be happening to your sister?" he asked.

Her face clouded a little. "She stroffed."

Proftulous lowered his head. "I be peffa-sorry about that."

Laffrohn shook hers. "'Tisn't for you to be sorry, Proftulous. You be having nothing to do with it. T'was simply how it was, that's all." She tried her briftest to smile. "And besides, it be far too long ago to be all worrying us now, far too peffa-long."

"What happened?"

Laffrohn took a deep breath, slowly sitting on the trunk of the vroffa-tree, Proftulous joining her in the moonlight. "We were both young, but she was older, more crumlush than me. Always turning heads and chickling. There were plenty of creatures that wanted to be her sweetheart, but there was one she loved above all others, the one that she be completely devoted to." She turned to Proftulous. "They be getting married, and be going to live in a most saztaculous castle not too many pid-pads from here. I would sometimes go visiting, and we would go and pick truppleberries together, or watch the sun go down, and she would tell me about how happy she was, and all the plans she had."

"Please," the vroffa-tree griffled underneath them, "is this going to take long? Only you're both quite heavy. Especially the dworp."

Proftulous lightly bliffed the trunk with his heel.

Laffrohn cleared her throat. "What you has to be remembering, Proftulous, is that this was all a peffa-long time ago. Things in the majickal-dales weren't as they are now. There were many twizzly dangers everywhere. Long, long-nosed krellits hadn't even been banned onto Trefflepugga Path, there were no officious krates to keep order, and creatures such as you'd never be imagining were all lump-thumping around, just waiting to stroff and eat you."

Proftulous eyes widened. "It be sounding most twizzly."

Laffrohn nodded. "One sun-turn, my sister and I came pid-padding back to her castle to discover a peffa-bad witch had glopped it all up. Her name be Alvestra, and she was truly yechus and twizzly, Proftulous. So there she be, waiting for us to return, standing with her broom in her long clawed hand, her sharp and pointed teeth all spinning around in her mouth, the worst rage in her peffa-glopped eyes you ever did see, the most twizzly shrieking echoing all over this valley. Everyone feared Alvestra, everyone knew she would stop at nothing to find what she could of a wand she believed to be hers – the Tillian Wand, Proftulous. The same wand Matlock be out there searching for right now."

Proftulous began to get more anxious. "But," he griffled, "this is terrible news! Most glubbstooled and gobflopped. This peffa-yechus

Alvestra witch will be all stroffing him!"

Laffrohn shook her head. "No, Alvestra already be stroffed, Proftulous. She stroffed that very same sun-turn. When we saw her outside the castle, my sister ran inside and up to the tallest tower, where her husband was waiting in a peffa-twizzled panic. Alvestra followed, convinced my sister was hiding the wand. A peffa-terrible vrooshing battle ensued, but my sister's majick was no match for Alvestra's, who raised the whole tower up, and downside-upsied it, smashing it into the ground below."

Proftulous put a ganticus paw to his mouth.

"I simply had to watch, Proftulous, knowing that all three of them would be stroffed inside. I was too young, my majick was too useless, too oidy. There was nothing I could be doing to be helping. It was the last I ever saw of my sister Lily, and her husband, Jericho. They were stroffed for a wand they didn't ever have, for reasons they never knew." She took a long deep breath. "Like I griffle, they were peffa-different times, back then. And we must all be grateful for that."

"It be a most sad and twizzly tale," Proftulous griffled. "I's be feeling an oidy bit eye-splashy for you."

Laffrohn stood, stretched. "Don't be," she griffled. "My sister and her husband be happy now, as keepers of the second Most Majelicus task, elected by the Majickal Elders to be overseeing that everything's done properly. From what I be hearing, they be properly enjoying it, and be right reliable. There's not a single hare that fails the task that they don't be boiling up and making into soupy-soupy. Been doing it for far too long now, they have."

"But," Proftulous asked, completey befuddled, "how can your sister once be all crumlush and nice, but now be all twizzly and yechus?"

"As she is *now*," Laffrohn griffled. "Her and Jerocho, both. The stroffing changed them. Each now has an oidy part of Alvestra in them. Their teeth are razor sharp and spin just like hers did, and their majick is far more powerful than any Most Majelicus creature's will ever be. As they all stroffed together, so three became two. Alvestra's body was never found, but now she helps guard the task she herself never completed – the finding of the Tillian Wand."

Proftulous pulled a murp-worm from his ear, trying not to look too scared, but his paw was shaking so much the fortunate creature wriggled free and dropped to the ground, peffa-relieved it hadn't been eaten. "It all be making me most afraid, Laffrohn," he griffled. "I not's be liking this Alvestra, or your sister, or her husband. They all sound peffa-glopped." He shook his dworp's head. "And the Majickal Elders, too. They be making it all wrong, having a Most Majelicus task where majickal-hares gets turned into soupy-soupy." He took a breath, frowning. "Sometimes, it seems that it *all* be going wrong, Laffrohn, everything."

Laffrohn nodded. "Tis what Baselott, Chatsworth's Most Majelicus master, first noticed, many years ago, Proftulous. Things were wrong, and peffa-strange. When Chatsworth himself became Most Majelicus, he noticed it, too, and began to see the unfairness of things. But when he taught Matlock as an apprentice, he saw something different in him, something he'd never seen in any other apprentice." She turned to Proftulous. "And he also saw that same thing in *you*, Proftulous – something peffa-special that made him think that perhaps you and Matlock were destined for much higher things. 'Tis why he has broken so many rules so far – in order to give both of you as much help as he could. And now, he has to face the trial of the Majickal Elders. 'Tis the reason why Matlock must be seen to fail this task, Proftulous, 'tis the reason he must be made all stroffed and soupy-soupy."

Proftulous shook his head. "I still don't be understanding any of this. Why does Matlock have to be stroffed?" He smashed a ganticus paw against his knee. "It *not* be right – any of it!"

Laffrohn hushed him, taking hold of his paw. "Proftulous, be stopping all that whining and moaning. Right now, we must be finding our way back to Winchett Dale and be warning as many creatures as possible about the rising waters. It be the only thing we *can* do right now, Proftulous – the only pid-pads and lump-thumps we can take."

"I not be happy about any of this," Proftulous bitterly complained.

"Then that just be the way it is," Laffrohn firmly replied. She gently awoke the vroffa-tree who had fallen back into nifferduggles, politely asking if it would be so peffa-kind as to take to the lid again, but this time a little more slowly. "We'll head towards Trefflepugga Path," she griffled. "Look for all the torches making their way towards Winchett Dale for the vrooshfest. They'll guide us there."

Proftulous, without really knowing what else it was that he could do, silently took his place on the back of the trunk, holding on tight as they set off high into the twinkling-lid on what was perhaps one of the most ganticus vroffa-brooms ever seen in all the majickal-dales.

And yet, for all Proftulous' concerns, worries and twizzly fears about Matlock, if he'd only chosen to glance across and see the distant pin-prick of yellow light drifting in the dark blue lid, he'd have realised in that precise blinknsap just how close he really was to his briftest and most majickal friend.

5.

Grik, Baselott and the Nullitts

Matlock came awake in the lid-machine, slowly remembering where he was, as a large snoffib's face came into focus, its scaly hand lightly shaking his shoulder.

"Wake up," Spig griffled. "We're almost at Snoffib Dale."

Matlock raised himself up as a ganticus sploink of rain dropped onto his face. "I must have been peffa-juzzpapped," he griffled. "I don't even remember falling into nifferduggles." He suddenly remembered the hourglass, the rising sands of his heartbeats, trying not to imagine what it must look like, how full the top bowl already was, how much time he had left…

"You'll need this," Spig griffled as more rain began to fall, passing Matlock the widest brimmed hat he'd ever seen. "The lidsplashy is especially heavy over Snoffib Dale. In fact it hasn't stopped raining ever since we made our thinking-machine. I've made holes in it, so you can poke your ears through."

"I have to put my ears inside the thinking-machine?"

"No," Spig quietly chickled. "The hat. The holes are in the hat."

Matlock put it on, Spig helping his long hare's ears through two holes in the brim.

"And now," the young snoffib announced, flourishing a pair of socks, "I simply put one of these over each of your ears to keep them peffa-dry as well."

"Are you sure?" Matlock griffled, anxious not to offend, but not terribly keen on the thought of someone else's socks over his ears. "I can simply pull the hood up on my robe."

"You could," Spig agreed. "But frankly, you've probably never known rain like we have in Snoffib Dale. It's really peffa, peffa-heavy."

"But," Matlock griffled, "it's not going to be a problem, is it? We can always shelter in your cottage and…"

"I don't have a cottage," Spig griffled.

"Well someone else's cottage then?" Matlock suggested as the rain did indeed appear to be getting suddenly much heavier, bouncing off the ganticus rim of his hat and quite stinging his long bare, ears. "Dr Klazon, or Dr Crumble – they'll surely let us stay in their homes until the lidsplashy passes?"

"They don't have cottages either."

"They don't?"

"None of us do," Spig replied quite calmly. "But we have hats and a thinking-machine. You get used to it."

Matlock tried to make sense of the youg snoffib's griffles. "But *someone* must have a cottage in Snoffib Dale, surely?"

Spig shook his four-eyed snoffib's head.

"Not even…a cave, or something?"

"We have no caves. Or trees, or mountains, or lakes…or anywhere, really," Spig griffled.

It was raining heavily now and even under the protection of the ganticus yellow balloon, great heavy drops flew in, quickly soaking all the chairs, carpets and furniture in the large basket. Crumble, sporting his own wide-brimmed hat had taken the sail-wheel while Klaxon peered over the side, guiding the descent through the deluge and the darkness.

"It rains like this all the time?" Matlock griffled to Spig, reluctantly taking the socks and pulling them over his long wet ears.

"Absolutely," Spig replied. "Day and night, ever since we made the thinking-machine, right across the whole of Snoffib Dale."

Matlock shook the brim of his hat, accidentally soaking Ayaani who had been quite contentedly nifferduggling in his hood until that point. "And you haven't thought about building shelters?"

Spig shrugged. "The thinking-machine would be angry with us," he griffled. "It would be a most glopped-up waste of time when we could be sitting around it in our hats learning answers to peffa-difficult questions."

Matlock blinked, shocked. "It…gets *russisculoffed* with you? I thought it was a machine?"

"You'll find out peffa-soon enough," Spig griffled as the balloon suddenly bumped down into a ganticus puddle. "We need to leave now before it all collapses down on us."

Matlock followed Klaxon and Crumble out onto a sea of mud, leaving Spig to vilishly put out the fire before escaping the fast deflating canopy as it fell and draped itself over the basket with a heavy, wet flop.

"So," Klaxon griffled to Matlock through the pounding rain, the brim of his own ganticus hat running like a waterfall, "welcome to Snoffib Dale!"

"I don't like it!" Ayaani quietly moaned, slipping down into the relative safety of one of Matlock's robe pockets. "It's far too peffa-wet!"

Matlock tried to make out as much as he could in the darkness. Dawn was just beginning to break on the horizon, revealing possibly the flattest landscape he had ever seen, bordered with just a distant mountain range, far, far away. He couldn't quite believe his eyes. Just as Spig had described, the whole dale was completely deserted, barren and empty, and seemed to stretch for a grillion pidpads.

And yet, slowly, as more sunlight found its way down, Matlock began to realise that his surroundings were actually peffa-different to what he had first thought, the orange dawn light gradually revealing the endless horizon simply to be a wooden fence surrounding them on all four sides. Indeed, as far as he could make out, what they were really all standing in was just a small glopped-up, rain-sodden field. He shook the brim of his hat, tried to wipe some of the lid-splashy from his face and whiskers, before pid-padding to the fence and peering over, shocked to discover that there wasn't a single oidy drop of rain to be seen on the other side. Everything was quiet, lush and saztaculously green. He could see trees, vales and smoke lazily rising from distant chimneys. If anything, it looked just as crumlush and peffa-shindinculous as Winchett Dale did most morn'ups.

He turned as Klaxon approached, the rain driving back into his face again.

"Awful place!" the snoffib announced.

"Indeed," Matlock agreed. "It's truly terrible in here! I don't know how you stand it."

Klaxon frowned. "Not Snoffib Dale!" He angrily pointed back over the fence. "There! What you see over there! Nullitt Dale! That's the truly awful place!"

"Really?" Matlock griffled. "But Nullitt Dale looks so nice and crumlush and dry and…"

"*They* don't have a thinking-machine," Klaxon sternly interrupted. "The nullitts know nothing, therefore they have nothing, so they *are* nothing. That's why they're nullitts."

Matlock frowned. "But they have the most crumlush place to live in, don't they? While you live in this fenced-off glopp-up."

Klaxon jerked his head, heavy rain pouring into all four eyes. "And that's why you live in Winchett Dale, Matlock," he griffled. "Because your griffles are as confused and clottabussed as your opinions."

"But this is just dreadful in here!" Matlock griffled, reaching into his robe and drawing out his Most Majelicus wand. "Let me vroosh the fence away. You'll be able to get out. You'll be free, and able to join them, away from all this mud and rain."

Klaxon angrily grabbed Matlock's paw. "You'll do no such thing!" he warned. "You vroosh that fence, and the nullitts will get in! Grillions of them, Matlock, all peffa-desperate to be here and gain our knowledge and facts and peffa-valuable answers! The fence doesn't keep us in, Matlock – it keeps the nullitts out!"

Matlock was quite simply stuck for griffles. He shook his head, the true reality of the snoffib's real existence literally coming to light with each ray of the slowly climbing sun fighting its way through the heavy rain. He turned to Klaxon. "There's only the three of you, isn't there? Just you, Dr Crumble and Spig, all of you living here in this oidy, glubbstooled field. There aren't any other snoffibs, are there? It's just you three."

Klaxon flushed russisculoffed red under his soaking wide-brimmed hat. "No, Matlock, once again, you are quite, quite wrong."

"So where are all the others, then?"

"I'll show you," Klaxon briskly griffled, turning into the pounding rain. "Follow me and you'll find out."

Matlock reluctantly pid-padded after the irate snoffib towards the middle of the field, where if anything, it seemed to be raining even harder. "Where are we going?" he cried out, the lidsplashy pounding and thundering onto his hat.

"To meet Dr Forticus Grik!" Klaxon called back.

Soaked through, his long purple shoes uttely glopped with oozing mud, Matlock wondered how much more of this he could stand, although to be fair to Spig, he was now rather glad to be wearing a pair of old socks over his ears.

"This way!" Klaxon urged. "We're nearly there."

Matlock could just about make out Spig and Dr Crumble up ahead; already sitting in a puddle around what looked like a small iron stove belching out thick black smoke in the very centre of the field.

"Sit down," Klaxon instructed.

"I'd prefer to stand, really," Matlock griffled.

Klaxon shook his head, all four eyes blinking intensively. "You want to be solving the puzzle don't you? Your puzzle of the Tillian Wand?" He grandly motioned to the smoking machine, splutting and hissing as rain hit its peffa-hot surface. "*This* is our thinking-machine."

Matlock wiped rain from his face, trying not to frown. "That?"

Klaxon nodded. "A thing of sheer and most shindinculous beauty, isn't it?"

"But it's just a stove," Matlock insisted. "I've got one like it in my cottage. It doesn't 'think' – I just roast niffs in it."

Sensing Klaxon was about to explode with rage, Dr Crumble, obediently sitting in the mud at Matlock's feet, tugged at his robes. "Perhaps if you were to ask it a question," he griffled, "you'd see that this is no ordinary stove, Matlock."

"But you must sit down in the mud first!" Klaxon ordered.

"Oh, for Oramus' sake! Why?" Matlock asked him.

"Because that's what we *always* do."

Sighing, and not really knowing what else to do in the peffa-glopped circumstances, Matlock slowly and peffa-cautiously began to crouch down.

"That's not sitting!" Klaxon barked at him. "Get that hare's backside right down in that puddle! Just like this. Watch, you can do it!"

Matlock watched as Klaxon sat down heavily in the mud, soaking Spig and Crumble in thick, black water.

"Your turn!" he griffled to Matlock. "Come on, we haven't got all sun-turn!"

Matlock reached into his robe pocket, waking up a protesting Ayaani and moving her into his hood, before sitting down as gently as he could, screwing up his hare's face as he felt the mud, rain and gloop soak into his robes, legs and backside.

"Now you can ask it a question," Crumble helpfully griffled, wiping splashed mud from his face. "Go on, anything you like."

"Is it *really* necessary to have to sit down, though?"

Crumble smiled, his lizardy hand pointing to the machine which seemed to now be vibrating. Another thick cloud of smoke spluttered from the blackened stovepipe chimney, as if it was clearing its throat. "It's a peffa-good question, hare," it suddenly griffled to Matlock. "Just give me a snutch of moments, and I'll see if I can find out. There must be an answer around here somewhere. Hang on."

"You mean you don't *know* the answer?" Matlock griffled, getting increasingly russisculoffed in the heavy rain.

"Not as yet, no," the machine griffled, in what sounded to Matlock uncannily like the voice of another snoffib. He screwed up his hare's eyes and peered at the bottom of the machine, seeing a chink of warm, orange light from below, and making out four eyes looking straight back at him through a grill.

Again, the machine griffled. "There'll be a book down here about sitting, probably. I'll just try and find it."

"*Down here*?" Matlock griffled. "What do you mean – 'down here'? I take it you're Dr Forticus Grik?"

The four eyes blinked. "Indeed, good hare. I'd offer to come out and shake your paw, but as it's so lid-splashy and yechus out there, I'd much rather stay in here, frankly."

Matlock turned to the others in astonishment. "He lives under the machine?"

They all nodded.

"In the dry? And the warmth?"

They nodded again.

"Without ganticus hats, or muddy robes, or endless rain?"

"Listen," Klaxon griffled, 'It's not easy for Dr Grik, you know. He has to keep the thinking-machine stoked with wood."

"But why?" Matlock insisted, wanting to shake the indignant snoffib by the shoulders. "It's not a machine, you ganticus clottabus! It doesn't 'think'! It's just a plain old boring stove in a peffa-glopped field!" He angrily withdrew his wand and aimed it at the soot-covered, smoke-belching stove, sending a bright red vroosh straight at it, toppling it over and shooting a shower of sparks and embers hissing into muddy puddles; Spig, Klaxon and Crumble all shrieking in horror.

"Right!" Matlock griffled, marching over to the small hole directly beneath where the stove had stood. "Let's see where this leads, shall we?"

"You…you…can't do that!" Klaxon cried, panicking. "Only Dr Grik is allowed into the hole! There's not enough room, and it's really, really peffa-glopped down there! In fact, he's told us that he suffers far more than we do in our eternal quest for facts and knowledge. Far, far more!"

"Really?" Matlock griffled, the rain still pounding all around. "And how far has it got you – this 'eternal-quest' of yours?"

Klaxon frowned, flushing all colours of the rainbow, trying to think.

Crumble stood awkwardly. "Well, we did get to Winchett Dale and win the question even'up," he quietly griffled. "It's not all bad news."

"That's right!" Klaxon cried, seizing on it. "We did, didn't we? We won the question even'up in Winchett Dale, which proves we must be the peffa-cleverest creatures in all the majickal-dales!"

Matlock ignored him, instead peering into the hole and glimpsing the familiar four-eyed head of a twizzly snoffib trying to hide behind what looked like a comfy armchair. "I'm coming down," he shouted.

"Do you really have to?" Dr Forticus Grik answered. "I mean, you'll make everything wet, muddy and glopped. Only, I've kept this place tidy for years, and now I'll get your yechus pid-pads all over my saztaculous carpets."

Matlock made out a small ladder at the side of the hole, using it to quickly climb down into what was quite the most crumlushed underground living room he'd seen. A flickering piff-tosh illiumnated exotic furniture and priceless ornaments on shelves, and in the middle was a table set with fine food and guzzworts.

"Forgive me," Grik nervously griffled to him. "I was just about to eat when you arrived." He tried to chickle. "And frankly, the last thing I expected to see was a majickal-hare."

Matlock looked around the homely burrow, removing his hat and wet socks from his ears. "Who made all this?" he asked, genuinely surprised and wanting to know. "How did it get here?"

Grik coloured slightly, clearing his throat. "I…er…I just sort of found it, really." He pulled back a curtain to reveal a second, much larger room cut into the earth, full of books of every size, shape and description. "We used to have much bigger lands," he griffled, "many, many moon-turns ago. We lived easily alongside the nullits, even though they would mostly chickle at our desire for answers. Then one sun-turn, I went out for a pid-pad and stumbled on this place. I scrambled away the grass and found an oidy trapdoor. Everything you see around you is exactly as I found it that very same sun-turn."

Behind, the others were now silently making their way down the ladder, looking round in stunned silence, quite unable to believe what they were seeing with their four eyes.

Matlock turned to Grik. "And then you kept it quiet, I suppose? You saw a chance to live down here on your own, all crumlush and safe?" He pointed to the books. "Those gave you all the 'answers' you needed, didn't they?" He shook his head, turning to the others. "How many years has he been doing this?"

Spig slowly removed his hat. "Three," he quietly griffled. "It's been so long that I can't really remember what it was like before the rain, the field, the fence and the thinking-machine."

"And all this time, you thought Dr Grik was having the worst of it?"

Spig nodded. "That's what he always told us." He thought for a snutch of moments. "Why would he lie?"

Klaxon, his voice beginning to shake, turned to Forticus Grik. "Indeed. Why *did* you lie to us and tell us all those spuddles about our lives being so much brifter than yours? When all the time you were really living like this?" He angrily threw his ganticus hat onto the pristeen carpet and began vilishly stamping his muddy feet all over it.

Grik, enraged, yelped and quite unexpectedly pushed Klaxon right over, picking up the soaking hat and angrily hurling it back outside through the muddy hole, before dropping to his knees and frantically trying to wipe the mud from his carpet. "Everything has to be clean!" he protested. "Clean and crumlush! Answers cannot be kept in a glopped-up burrow!"

The others stood in shocked silence as he glared at them all, breathing heavily. "How *dare* you all stand there and accuse *me* of taking advantage, when I gave you everything you needed! Answers! So many grillions of answers to anything your glopped-up minds would think to ask! How easy do you think that is, eh, having to listen to your endless boring, purile questions, then try and find the answers? And then, just a blinksnap later, you'd ask another one! On and on it went, sun-turn after sun-turn; one stupid, peffa-clottabussed question after another. How tall is the tallest puffshroom? What's the most glopped-up thing a krate ever did with a pencil? Where are the cheapest neffle-hammers made?" He turned to Matlock, almost pleading. "Honestly, it's enough to send you mad! I have all this *proper* knowledge, really peffa-important answers, right here in these books, and all these clottabusses ever want to ask is 'Who has the biggest nose in Alfisc Dale?'"

"I think it's Frubble the Unwashable," Klaxon griffled, slowly standing back up. "At least that's what you said."

"I made it up, you fool!" Grik barked at him. "Frubble the Unwashable doesn't even exist!"

Klaxon flushed complete white, barely able to say the griffles. "You...you...made it up?"

"I made it *all* up!" Grik griffled. "All those grillions of useless answers – *especially* yours, Klaxon – I just made them up!"

Klaxon had gone into shock. "So…so…you're saying that the dale's most ganticus eater *isn't* Fleevil Osser from Juffle Dale, who once ate nineteen whulp-truffles in just one sitting?"

Grik sneered. "I wouldn't even know a whulp-truffle if it came in here and shook my hand, you clottabus."

"But that was my favourite fact!" Klaxon roared. "My peffa-favourite! I've been waiting to be asked that for years, desperate to give the answer!"

Crumble awkwardly cleared his throat. "I must say, I did always think the answer to that one was an oidy bit glopped."

Klaxon turned on him, still outraged by the revelation. "Oh, you *did*, did you? *Now* you tell me, Crumble, do you? Now? Because it's all very well, isn't it, now that I look like a complete clottabus in front of everyone! But I didn't notice you griffling anything of the sort at the time!" He poked Crumble hard in the ribs. "Not a single griffle from you then, was there, Crumble, eh? You just sat in that puddle, right next to me in the rain for all those years and you never once griffled anything to me about Fleevil Osser being made up!"

Crumble hung his snoffib-head in shame. "Only because it was your peffa-favourite fact," he quietly griffled. "I just didn't want to see you disappointed, that's all."

Matlock, whose mind was on peffa-more urgent matters, turned to Forticus Grik. "The books that you have? You say they have *real* knowledge, real answers?"

"Of course," Grik griffled. "If only anyone could be bothered to ask me some real questions."

"I'm here to find the Tillian Wand."

Grik glanced around then shook his head. "I'm pretty sure it's not here. I'd have noticed by now."

Matlock gently let out a breath. "Are you just as clottabussed as the others?"

Grik shrugged. "Possibly. It's not been easy for me, recently."

"I was referring to your *books*," Matlock tried. "I need to find as much information as possible about the Tillian Wand in your books."

Grik stared blankly back, stuck.

Matlock sighed as the truth suddenly hit him. "You can't even read, can you?"

"Not a griffle," Grik sheepishly admitted. "Tried a few times, just couldn't make head nor lizard's tail of it. Just a peffa-lot of glubbstooled squiggles and lines."

"Show me the books," Matlock ordered. "I don't have a lot of time."

"Of course," Grik replied, leading Matlock into the next room, then watching him vilishly searching the many shelves for any of the ancient volumes that looked as though they might have even the oidiest scrap of information about the Tillian Wand.

"Help me!" Matlock called to the others. "You don't have to be able to read. Some of these books have pictures, if you see one of a wand, show me. I can't do this by myself, there's just too many."

Forgetting their bickering and differences for a moment, all four snoffibs joined Matlock pulling out dusty books and leafing through them, looking for anything that might resemble a picture of a wand, before passing them over to Matlock.

Ayaani, all too glad to be out of the rain, scrittled over the shelves, using her oidy paws to flick through pages. "I think," she griffled to Matlock, a small brown leather-bound diary in her paw, "that perhaps the finding of the Tillian Wand isn't the question you should be asking."

"Well, it's the one I need to be asking right now," Matlock replied, throwing another book aside. "Unless I want to be ending up as hare soupy-soupy, that is."

"I think you're wrong," Ayaani griffled. "I think the question you should be asking is, 'How did all these books get here in the first place?' Look around you, it's a burrow full of books. The snoffib only chanced upon it by accident. He can't even read. It used to belong to someone else. A secret burrow, where a creature could live undisturbed and unseen, perhaps for many years."

Matlock turned to her, frowning. "Well?"

"How many creatures do we know that can read?" she griffled, passing Matlock the diary. "And more importantly, how many do we know that can actually *write*?"

Matlock took the diary, opening it, his eyes slowly reading the handwritten griffles on the first heavy parchment page:

Here be the griffle-diary of Baselott,
Most Majelicus Hare of Nullitt Dale.

Matlock almost jumped in shock. The hairs on the back of his hare's neck stood on end. "Baselott?" he softly whispgriffled. "Baselott lived here?"

"It is a most crumlushed place," Ayaani griffled. "And peffa-similar to your own cottage."

Matlock re-read the griffles, unable to believe his hare's eyes. "But why was he here, underground? Majickal-hares live in cottages, not burrows."

Ayaani nodded. "True. Unless, of course, they be hiding from something..."

Matlock turned the page with a trembling paw, reading the old griffles from his master's master, imagining Baselott writing them by candlelight in his red Most Majelicus robes, a quill in his paw, hidden deep underground.

> I have thought long and hard about whether to write these griffles. Much of me simply wants to pid-pad away from all that has happened and pretend that none of it occurred. It would be quite the peffa-simplest thing to do, perhaps the most obvious thing. But I cannot. This sun-turn has been coming for a peffa-long time, and the writing can no longer be avoided. So I must set to and try and explain as much as I can with what little time I have left...
>
> As with all Most Majelicus hares, I was born out in The Great Beyond, there to be found by my master, a great and saztaculous Most Majelicus hare called Trommel. As dalelore and tradition dictate, he bought me back along Trefflepugga Path, allowing the path itself to decide my new home and the place where I would start my apprenticeship to one day become a majickjal-hare. I remember peffa-little of these times in Currick Dale, just occasional glimpses of myself practising a vroosher under Trommel's expert tuition and stumbling as I painfully learnt to walk on hind legs.
>
> Yet, when the sun-turn came and he considered me ready

"I think you're wrong," Ayaani griffled. *"I think the question you should be asking is, 'How did all these books get here in the first place?'"*

enough, Trommel presented me with my very own dripple.

"Treat it with respect," Trommel warned me as he was leaving. "It will be your briftest friend and familiar from now on. It won't ever griffle, it won't ever make even the oidiest noise, yet it will keep your house tidy, make you brews and niff-soup, and ride in the hood of your robe for company. But be warned – a majickal-hare and his dripple always stroff on the very same sun-turn. So it is up to you both to keep each other safe and well at all times."

And for a while, we were exactly that; safe and well. I remember those happy times as majickal-hare of Currick Dale with great fondness. I tended to the ceatures needs, dispensed potions and vrooshers, did all the things expected of me, my faithful dripple forever by my side. And when I wasn't out and around in the dale, I was reading – reading voraciously, and as much as I could. I read the entire set of majickal-driftolubbs two or three times over, and anything else I could lay my paws on. Griffles fascinated me, books were storeworlds of knowledge and experience. Yet disturbingly, the more I studied majickal-dalelore, the more I also began to question it... I became aware that I was fast developing a different, more enquiring mind; scientific, rational, logical. It didn't matter to me that I could vroosh a leaning-jutter's leg better with a mere flick from my wand – what mattered was *why* I could do that.

The spells and majickal incantations I had studied and learnt were simply griffles to me, just sounds, which when combined with a piece of shaped hawthorn, somehow made majick happen. I wasn't convinced of any of it, and set about to explain it all with logic – reasoning that whilst the growth of an oidy acorn into ganticus oak tree might appear truly majickal, it could also be explained as simply the base alchemy of all life. Nature appears majickal, yet of course we know it isn't. It's simply the way of all things, and to griffle it as anything else, I found to be increasingly clottabussed.

Of course, I had to hold such thoughts deeply to myself. To even question the wisdom and teachings of the Majickal Elders is peffa, peffa-dangerous, as I discovered all too soon...

"Matlock!" Klaxon griffled, his excrimbly voice suddenly cutting across Matlock's thoughts. "Come see! It's stopped raining outside. It's sunny, and really quite crumlush!"

Matlock put down the diary, pid-padding to the hole and climbing the ladder. Sure enough the muddy field that was the whole of Snoffib Dale was now bathed in warm sunlight. "It was the thinking-machine," he griffled. "The yechus smoke caused all the rain."

Klaxon looked at him. "So all this glopped-up lid-splashy – that was Dr Grik's fault, too?"

"There's no other explanation, is there?" Matlock griffled. He pointed at the fallen stove. "The machine is glubbstooled and doesn't work any more, so the rain has stopped. Grik wanted to stay warm, dry and safe in the burrow, but in doing so, he made it eternally rain for the rest of you."

Grik awkwardly cleared his throat, aware all eyes were on him, be they in sets of two, or four. "Well, I didn't want to get cold," he weakly offered. "You wouldn't have wanted me to get cold, would you?" He turned to Matlock, all four eyes imploring. "And it kept all the books warm and dry, didn't it?"

Matlock turned away as yet another row broke out, knowing he had better things to do than stand in a glopped-up field listening to four snoffibs arguing. He vilishly descended back into the burrow, picked up Baselott's diary and continued reading…

> Inevitably, the sun-turn came when Trommel came to visit me in my cottage, griffling that he had nominated me to undertake the three tasks to becoming Most Majelicus. I accepted and easily completed each one – not by majick – but by using science, reason and the power of logic. Trefflepugga Path, for all its perilous twists and turns, was easy for me to solve. Likewise, the puzzle of the Tillian Wand, using what I had learnt from books to be able to predict precsisely the moment when it would appear. The third and final task I found the peffa-easiest of all. I had triumphed in all three, without using even the oidiest vroosher or potion along the way.
>
> Naturally, as tradition dictates, Trommel had to present me

with my red Most Majelicus robes of office. As he did so, he griffled to me how proud he was to have been my master, that I would now be able to use the mirrit-tunnels quite freely and it would be my duty from now on to use them to venture out into The Great Beyond and find my own apprentice majickal-hare to bring back and train in the ways of majickal-dalelore.

I griffled to him that I was sorry but it would be a waste of my time. I tried to tell him of my real interest – understanding majick through science and my experiments. He was outraged and peffa-russisculoffed with me, griffling that I should do no such thing, and to interfere with majickal-dalelore would be peffa-dangerous to every living creature. He made me promise to stop my researches. I promised, of course, but broke it the moment he left. Nothing would stop me from my quest. If I could master and explain majick then I could surely teach it to *any* creature, not simply just a hare from The Great Beyond? All creatures would benefit and soon be able to vroosh themselves better with new spells that I would devise. I saw a brifter future for everyone, and if breaking a promise was to be the price – then so be it.

However, one sun-turn, as I was completely absorbed in my potionary trying to replicate a peffa-elementary vroosher to turn skroff-daisies into wilting reeds, I was suddenly aware of a noise I hadn't heard before. Imagine my surprise when I realised it had come from my silent, nameless dripple! I could barely contain my peffa-excrimblyness, and set about using scientific methods to see if I could teach it how to griffle. Many moon-turns passed and eventually my dripple was able to say a snutch of griffles. However, the more griffles my dripple learnt, the more it also began to sicken. I began worrying for my own safety, knowing that if my dripple was to to stroff, then inevitably – as majickal-dalelore decrees – I would stroff at the very same blinksnap.

No amount of potions could keep my dripple alive. It stroffed – and yet here is the most saztaculous thing – I didn't! Not only had I taught my dripple some griffles, but I had also outlived it! Majickal-dalelore meant nothing to me from that sun-turn forth. Saddened as I was by my faithful dripple's passing, I also knew that my scientific studies were the only way. My dripple's all too short life had proved this to me. It had griffled, it had stroffed, and I had lived. Something was wrong with the fabric of majick – and I was determined to find out exactly what it was.

Heartened, I threw myself into reading and questioning everything I could, using the mirrit tunnels to make frequent visits to libraries across the dales, spending long sun-turns eagerly reading as much as I could, trying to find any answers or clues to help in my researches. On my way back, I would often stop at The Vroffa-Tree Inn, deep beneath Trefflepugga Path, griffling with Laffrohn and all the other most-majelicus creatures, trying to learn whatever I could without arousing their suspicions as to my true intentions.

Back home in Currick Dale, creatures were beginning to wonder why I spent so much time away when I should have been caring for them as their majickal-hare. They wondered where my dripple was, leading to many excuses as I tried to persuade them it was simply out on a chore. Realising I needed to be seen acting like a normal Most Majelicus hare, I resolved that I would indeed go to The Great Beyond to find myself an apprentice – not to train in the ways of majickal-dalelore; but in the ways of science...

I used the tunnels, eventually finding a hare. Not that bringing it back was easy. Far from it. I wasn't bothered what hare it was, simply that I could take it – a task that I thought would be far easier than it was. Not wanting to waste precious time when I could have been at work on my experiments, I grabbed the nearest leveret I could find; its mahpa, pahpa and family all thumping and growling at me, desperate to protect it. Fearing for my life, I turned and fled for the safety of the mirrit-tunnel, knowing none could follow me down, holding the wildly bucking leveret by the ears, trying not to be bitten.

However, it was at this point that something peffa, peffa-glopped happened. Something terrible, that still haunts me after all these moon-turns. The leveret's mahpa, determined to save her young son, followed us into the tunnel, screaming with rage. I pid-padded as vilishly as I could, but still she came, bounding down, her leveret crying out in utter, twizzly-terror.

And then, just as suddenly, it stopped. I turned to see her stroffed body on the floor. Only Most Majelicus creatures, or those being taken by Most Majelicus creatures can survive the tunnels. She hadn't stood a chance. I remember being quite still, alone in the darkness with just a struggling leveret, not knowing what to do, covering its eyes and trying to calm it, my own heart beating more vilishly than it had ever done, watching in despair as the tunnel floor slowly sucked its poor stroffed mahpa down into the depths.

It was a long pid-pad back to my cottage potionary in Currick Dale, the hare eventually falling into nifferduggles. I called it Chatsworth, and hoped it would soon learn to forget just what it had seen in the tunnels.

Matlock paused, wiping his brow, imagining Baselott in the burrow, writing the griffles. He remembered their only meeting when he had seen Baselott in his blue robes of a Majickal Elder at the Currick Dale Dripple Fair, the one sun-turn in the year he was allowed to return to the dales to complete the duties of dripple-selection for majickal-hares. Matlock remembered the baskets full of dripples all silently waiting to be chosen, Baselott's warm smile, his calm griffles – but also his final chilling warning to Matlock, that when they met the next time it would be under 'very different, more glopped-up circumstances'.

He also thought of Chatsworth, his master, wondering why he hadn't ever griffled about what had happened to his mahpa in the mirrit-tunnels. But then, Matlock was forced to admit, Chatsworth had rarely griffled about his own life, ever. He had simply done what he was supposed to do; become Most Majelicus, then trained other hares to be majickal, too. As far as Matlock knew, the rest of Chatsworth's life was a mystery.

He felt strange and twizzly reading the griffles, as if somehow he was intruding. He looked over his shoulder, seeing Ayyani perched there, her face quizzical.

"Are there any clues?" she asked. "To help us find the wand?"

Matlock shook his head. "No. It's just about Baselott," he griffled. "And Chatsworth."

"Is that why you look so sad?" she asked. "Because there are no clues?"

He took her in his paw and set her next to the book. "No, it's not that," he quietly griffled.

"What then?"

"Ayaani, have you ever thought you've really known someone, then discovered that really, you never knew anything about them at all? And perhaps that it's just too late to find out what you should have known all along?"

She stared blankly back.

He pointed to the diary. "These griffles," he griffled, "make an oidy sort of sense, but then no sense at all."

Ayaani angrily stamped her foot. "Then stop reading them! We've got to find the Tillian Wand."

Matlock turned the pages, eyes flicking to where the griffles finally stopped. "I can't stop, Ayaani," he explained, scanning the lines and seeing his own name suddenly jump out at him like a twizzled dilva-beetle from a bunch of russisculoffed moondasies. "This is about me, too."

He read on…

Training Chatsworth as an apprentice was far harder than I thought. I tried to think back and remember how Trommel had trained me with care, rewards, encouragement and discipline. But I didn't have the patience for it. Chatsworth only responded to discipline; rewards meant nothing to him. He was a peffa-slow learner, too, preferring to spend his time playing with his glopped-up dworp. I would sometimes watch them from my potionary window, knowing that when the time came and Chatsworth had to undertake the first Most Majelicus task of solving the riddle of Trefflepugga Path, his dworp would be lost to him forever, just as every majickal-hare's is. I occasionally wondered how he would cope with this loss, as I would sometimes still have to scold him for becoming eyesplashy when he thought of his own mahpa, and what had happened in the mirrit-tunnel. I soon began to realise that of all the hares I had chosen, perhaps Chatsworth was least suited to the life of a majickal-hare.

Should I have returned him to The Great Beyond? It is a question I have asked myself many, many times. But having Chatsworth with me allowed me to get on with my real purpose – my scientific experiments. Whenever Trommel came to the cottage, he was relieved, assuming I had abandoned them in order to train Chatsworth – which of course, was a lie. But Trommel was happy. Old as he was, and nearing the end of his pid-pads upon these majickal-dales, at least he was convinced that I had finally turned my back on science...

The time eventually came for Chatsworth to undertake the three Most Majelicus tasks. He was worried, peffa-twizzly and anxious, yet, to my regret and disappointment, I still made him set out to try and solve the riddle of Trefflepugga Path. He barely survived, peffa-lucky not to have stroffed and perished on the path. The vrooshers he had learnt from the majickal-driftolubbs were virtually useless. As a consequence, I was worried for his safety on the second task – the finding of the Tillian Wand – so went to find Trommel to try and persuade him that Chatsworth simply wasn't ready.

It took two sun-turns for me to eventually track Trommel down to The Vroffa-Tree Inn, where he was enjoying a guzzwort with Laffrohn. We griffled long into the night, Trommel still insisting that Chatsworth should undertake all three tasks, despite the risks and my protests. Eventually, my master went upstairs to his last and final nifferduggles.

The next morn'up, Laffrohn woke me, Trommel's red Most Majelicus robes over her arm. "He has been taken into Oramus' most eternal care," she griffled to me. "It was his time, and he knew that. He is on his way to becoming a Majickal Elder. Take these robes and give them to Chatsworth. The robes themselves will give him Most Majelicus powers. This way, he won't have to complete the other two tasks."

So it was that Chatsworth, my useless apprentice, became the only Most Majelicus hare never to complete the three tasks. I presented him with the stolen red robes, swearing him to absolute secrecy over what Laffrohn had done, griffling to him that we must hide, knowing that when Trommel became

154

a Majickal Elder he would soon griffle to the others about what had happened, and Chatsworth, Laffrohn and I would all be in ganticus danger.

We had no choice, we left Currick Dale and came here, to this place, an old burrow I found that could hide us both. We stayed hidden for as long as we could, and I told Chatsworth all that I knew about the ways of majick and science. He learnt about his dworp and the sacrifice it had made for him, even though he now had no memory of it. The revelation seemed to unsettle and anger him. He became quite eyesplashy, demanding to know more about the unfortunate creature.

"It was my friend?" he griffled. "My briftest friend?"

I nodded.

"And I will never see it again?"

"It is the way of the first task," I told him. "Just as I have no memory of my own dworp, so you will never have a memory of yours, either."

"But I want to find it again!" he griffled, bliffing the table with his paw. "It gave everything for me! What's its name? Where is it?"

He asked, and asked, but I couldn't ever tell him. I needed him at my side, not on some glopped mission to find a dworp called Marellus. So, to distract him, I gave him chores, trying to occupy his every waking moment, hoping he would soon forget about Marellus. I never knew if he ever did.

"Marellus," Matlock whispgriffled, turning to Ayaani. "Chatsworth's dworp was called Marellus."

Ayaani sniffed. "So? They all have names. Yours is called Proftulous, and what a glopp-up he is."

"Yes, but Chatsworth never knew," Matlock griffled to her. "Since Baselott stroffed, Chatsworth has spent much of his time looking for a dworp that was once his briftest friend. He didn't even know its name, still doesn't to this very sun-turn. But it was called Marellus."

"Which proves one thing, I suppose," Ayaani griffled. "Chatsworth can't have ever read this diary, can he?"

155

"It's stranger than that," Matlock griffled. "Chatsworth never became Most Majelicus, either. He only ever completed the first task of solving the riddle of Trefflepugga Path. Baselott knew he would stroff trying to find the Tillian Wand."

Ayaani frowned. "But he wears the red Most Majelicus robes."

"Because Laffrohn and Baselott gave them to him. They're not Chatsworth's. They belonged to Baselott's old master, Trommel."

Ayaani scratched the side of her head with an oidy paw. "Methinks this makes no sense whatsoever."

"It's all in these pages," Matlock griffled. "So many things that I never even knew, never suspected for even the oidiest blinksnap."

"Then perhaps you should read the rest," Ayaani griffled.

Matlock slowly nodded, before turning his attention back to the diary one final time…

Whenever I left the safety of this burrow, it was mostly to see Laffrohn at The Vroffa-Tree Inn, and there we would griffle in utmost secrecy, wondering just what it was that was making everything so peffa-glopped. Majick and dalelore just didn't seem to be working as it had before. Things had changed, my griffling dripple had proved it beyond all doubt. I had created vrooshers of great power, then trained Chatsworth in them, vrooshers which I should never have even been able to even contemplate. The most powerful of these I called the Mutato Corpore – a changing spell that for a period of time allows its user to assume any living form it likes. Thus were Chatsworth and I able to become the oidiest, most unseen creatures, keenly listening to griffles of officious krates and other Most Majelicus hares to secretly discover if anyone had begun to suspect the same peffa-terrible thing that I was becoming more and more convinced of.

We discovered little else, but knew all too well that we were still in peffa-twizzly danger. Our investigations and frequent late-night visits to The Vroffa-Tree Inn would surely be noticed all too peffa-soon. Laffrohn and I resolved that we needed another, a hare that could never be suspected of ever doing something as glopped as to question majickal-dalelore and the wisdom of the Majickal Elders. Chatsworth would go out into The Great Beyond and fetch a hare to be his first apprentice, and Laffrohn and I would do our peffa-best to ensure he went to Winchett Dale, the most peffa-clottabussed of all the dales. Chatsworth did exactly that – bringing back a peffa-ordinary hare he called Matlock, training him to be a majickal-hare exactly according to dalelore. When Chatsworth was done, he would leave Matlock in Winchett Dale, Laffrohn and I both knowing that when the time came and Matlock undertook the three Most Majelicus tasks, we would be able to use him as we saw fit.

The more we griffled about this, the more it became apparent what must happen. Laffrohn and I made a ganticus plan. Matlock would complete the first task and, with our help, solve the riddle of Trefflepugga Path. All would look well with the Majickal Elders. However, it would also be peffa-important that he was seen to fail the second task and that Jericho and Lily Krettle stroff him and make him into hare soupy-soupy. His failure would be the only way to satisfy the Majickal Elders that Laffrohn and I couldn't ever be seen as any sort of threat to their power – as between us, we hadn't even trained a hare that could be remotely considered to be Most Majelicus. They would no doubt chickle long and hard over our foolhardiness in ever nominating a majickal-hare from Winchett Dale. They would no longer be interested in us.

All is going to plan as I write these griffles. Chatsworth is training young Matlock to be a majickal-hare, and really he is quite the most clottabussed hare there is, almost peffa-perfectly suited to Winchett Dale. He has a dworp friend called Proftulous, a ganticus tweazle-eating glopped-up fool of a creature. In just a few moon-turns, Matlock will wear the green robes of his rank, and Chatsworth will leave him in Winchett Dale, there to stay until Laffrohn and Chatsworth decide that it's time to nominate him for the three Most Majelicus tasks.

As I sit here contemplating my last few sun-turns in these dales, I am filled with both twizzlyness and excrimblyness; twizzly that once in Oramus' most eternal care I shall once again meet Trommel, who I am hoping has been so distracted by his duties as a blue-robed Majickal Elder that he hasn't been able to keep too much of a hare's eye on what I've been up to; and excrimblyness in finally being able to wear the blue robes myself and quietly continue my investigations into what it is that is going so badly glopped. I am determined to find the truth, and I am convinced that the real answers lie with the Majickal Elders, rather than here in the dales.

My final act will be to write a large revision to the driftolubb 'Majickal Dalelore – Volume 68'. In it, I shall not only detail my experiences with my dripple, but also just what I suspect is *really* happening amongst the Majickal Elders. It is too dangerous to even mention here, far too peffa-ganticus a thing to even begin to contemplate. But if I am right, there will be some who will never wish to see it either read or published. Its omission will be ominous, and further proof that perhaps I have been right all along about my own private theory – not a single griffle of which I have ever dared to breathe to either Chatsworth or Laffrohn, as I feared they would think me quite ganticussly clottabussed.

Only time itself, will tell.

"Master," Ayaani griffled. "What's wrong? You look quite peffa-glopped."

Matlock turned to her, still trying to digest it all. "You know you don't read?"

She nodded.

"Sometimes I wish I'd never learnt to, either."

Her oidy black eyes blinked in confusion. "What did it say? You griffled that it mentioned you."

Matlock shut the diary. "It did," he griffled, looking at her and knowing he just didn't have the hare's heart to tell her the truth – that they were both expected to fail, that it was somehow important that they did, and in doing so they would both be stroffed. It seemed just too peffa-awful and glubbstooled to even contemplate. He cleared his throat, trying his briftest to sound unconcerned. "It was just a load of nonsense, really. I think Baselott must have gone an oidy bit clottabussed in his old age."

"And there was nothing about the Tillian Wand?" Ayaani asked. "We're still no nearer to finding it?"

"No," he quietly griffled, opening the diary once more, noticing there was one final page at the very back that he'd missed the first time, "there wasn't."

Ayaani blew out her cheeks and frowned. "Then I will go and ask the snoffibs if they know anything," she griffled, scrittling away to climb the ladder. "We've got to do something peffa-soon. This is all getting far too peffa-glopped and confusing, and frankly the way I see it, we don't have a lot of time left."

"I'll be out in a couple of blinksnaps," Matlock griffled. "I just need to check something."

"Just be peffa-vilish," Ayaani griffled, scrittling outside. "We're wasting time we really don't have."

Matlock made sure she was gone before turning to the final page, disappointed to find that it was just blank, faded yellow parchment.

Until a quill suddenly jumped from a nearby shelf and began frantically scratching at the paper, vilishly forming griffles before his astonished hare's eyes...

Matlock, I know you are reading this!

"Baselott?" he gasped. "Is that you?" The quill went to work once more...

These griffles were never intended for your eyes! Only great harm will come from you reading them!

"But you wrote them!" Matlock insisted, feeling his fearful heart thumping heavily in his chest. "You wrote them to be read by someone!"

The quill urgently scratched again...

Not by you! Never by you!

"Then who?" Matlock demanded to know. "Who are they for, if not me?"

The quill suddenly rose into the air and turned, its needle-sharp end hovering directly in front of his face, opening to reveal an oidy set of vilishly swivelling, yechus teeth.

"Get away!" Matlock cried out, peffa-twizzled. "Get away from me!"

On the table, the diary cracksploded into flame. He leapt back, reaching into his pocket for his wand, trying desperately to swipe the yechus quill away, sending bright red vrooshers flying around the burrow; books and shelves bursting into flame all, as a pair of lizard's hands suddenly grabbed him from behind and began urgently pulling him towards the ladder.

"You first!" Forticus Grik cried, pushing Matlock. "Up you go! I'll be fine! Go on, go!"

Matlock climbed, gratefully reaching for the outstretched hands of Spig, Klaxon and Crumble, the yechus quill still following and flying around his face, snapping and biting.

Together, they hauled him up onto the wet mud, thick black choking smoke now beginning to pour from the open burrow, Matlock managing to catch the hissing quill in his paw, its teeth still vilishly spinning in rage. "Who are you?" he shouted at it. "Baselott? Jericho Krettle? Lily? Who?"

The quill chickled. "All of them! And none of them! And so much more than them! So much more than *you*, Matlock the majickal-hare!" It twisted violently in his paw. "Such excrimbly fun, isn't it? How vilishly does that peffa-glopped heart of yours beat now, Matlock? How many grains of sand do you think you have left?"

He yelped in pain as it bit right into his paw, chickling and wriggling free, flying into the smoke before making the most yechus cackling scream he had ever heard; Grik, Klaxon and Crumble all covering their ears, their snoffib bodies flushing pure white with twizzliness as a ganticus plume of thick black smoke shot from the burning burrow, shaping itself into a yechus swirling witch before their terrified eyes, the flames licking at its feet, smoke trails gradually forming ripped robes and a long, pointed black hat, its yechus face staring down at them.

"You dare to seek the thing I never found?" it shrieked, two bright red eyes flashing. "You dare to find what's rightfully mine? You will fail, Matlock, because that is your destiny, that has *always* been your destiny – and now you have seen it written!"

Matlock held out his wand, taking a deep hare's breath and

sending a vroosher straight at the swirling apparition.

"What?" it chickled, vilishly gliding right down to his face, its burning, choking breath making his eyes smart and stream. "Are you so afraid of smoke, Matlock, that you have to vroosh it with your pathetic wand?" It half-closed its yechus eyes, inspecting the wand more closely, tutting mockingly. "Ah, and I see you have a Most Majelicus wand. I'm not sure those are even allowed to be used by majickal-hares, are they?"

"It may not be allowed," Matlock griffled, fighting for breath, "but it won't stop me using it!" He sent out another vroosher, watching helplessly as it merely passed through the yechus creature, sailing harmlessly into the clear blue sky beyond.

"I'd say the wand-thing isn't really working," it griffled. "I could stroff you now, Matlock, right here in this peffa-glopped-up field. But really, I so much prefer to watch when a majickal-hare gets all boiled into hare soupy-soupy."

"Who are you?" Matlock spluttered, wiping eyesplashers from his smoke-blackened face.

"Someone you will see again, Matlock!" it screamed, letting out another yechus screaming cackle, before finally becoming just a single plume again, leaving everyone peffa-twizzly and shaken at what they'd just seen.

Ayaani scrittled over, climbing up Matlock's blackened robes, darting gratefully into his hood, paws on his shoulders "It was right about one thing, though," she griffled.

"What's that?"

"The wand. It really wasn't working."

"Thanks for that."

"Your robes need cleaning. They smell yechus."

"You see," Matlock griffled, "I'm really wondering just how you think you're helping, right now?"

She shrugged. "Just griffling to distract you, that's all. I find it often helps if we've just gone through yet another peffa-twizzly situation."

"I think I preferred you when you were just my silent faithful dripple familiar."

A sudden coughing and spluttering from behind made them all

turn as **Dr Forticus Grik's** head appeared from the smoking burrow. "If it's not to much of an inconvenience," he griffled, "I'd quite like an oidy bit of help getting out. Frightfully hot, you know, down here."

Together they hauled **Grik** out onto the wet mud, helping him shakily to his feet as he beamed a ganticus snoffib smile and presented **Matlock** with a small blue book, still smouldering at the edges. "I stayed because I needed to find this," he panted. "I knew it would be somewhere."

Matlock vilishly ushered them all away from the burrow entrance as it began to garrumbloom, flames now openly bursting from the concealed entrance, drawing rain clouds over the fields once more. He turned the book in his paw as the first drops fell, reading the leatherbound cover: *The Orders of Celestial Constellations.*

"It's always been one of my favourites," **Grik** explained. "Not that I ever read it of course, but the pictures are quite saztaculous. Used to stare at them for hours. But I have a feeling you'll need it **Matlock**, if you're to stand the oidiest chance of finding that **Tillian Wand** of yours." He shrugged. "Felt like one of those extrapluff things you majickal-hares have, just griffling to me that I had to get it for you."

"Thank you," **Matlock** griffled, flicking through the pages at diagrams of dozens of different star constellations.

Klaxon, still looking russisculoffed and thoroughly miserable, pid-padded over. "So what now, **Grik**?" he demanded. "It's raining again, and we haven't even got our hats anymore! They're all burning down in your secret-burrow!"

"Perhaps," **Crumble** suggested. "We should get **Dr Grik** to go back down and fetch them for us? After all, it isn't very nice out here without our hats."

Matlock, wet through, bitten, muddy, juzzpapped, smelling of smoke, had had enough. He put the book in his pocket, got out his wand and sent a powerful red vroosher right at the fence, the force of it almost knocking him off his feet into yet another muddy puddle.

The fence instantly cracksploded, sending broken, splintered wood everywhere.

He turned to the four horrified snoffibs. "Right," he griffled, grinding his hare's teeth. "*This* is what's going to happen. You're all going to leave this glopped-up place. You're going to go through the hole in that fence to Nullitt Dale and learn to get on with them as friends and live a normal life. They'll be no more secret-burrows, or thinking-machines, or lid-machines, or question even'ups…"

"Or big hats?" Spig asked disappointedly. "Only I quite liked mine."

Matlock sighed. "Look, you can wear a big-hat if you really want to. All I'm griffling is that it's gobflopped to be standing here in the pouring lidsplashy when its crumlush just over there! Now follow me, for Oramus sake, all of you!"

Matlock marched to the burning fence, followed by a miserable trail of soaked, chastened snoffibs looking around the muddy field for the last time.

"Can we take the lid-machine?" Grik asked, pointing to the balloon.

"No," Matlock firmly griffled. "You want to get around, you use Trefflepugga Path like everyone else."

Ayaani chickled into Matlock's long ear. "Never seen you like this before," she griffled. "Quite a bossy majickal-hare if you want to be, aren't you?"

"Believe me," he griffled to her. "This is just the beginning. We're going to find that wand, Ayaani. We're going to do what Chatsworth never did. We're going to complete this task without anymore smoke twizzliness, or witches, or spinning teeth, or stroffing, or hare soupy-soupy – any of it. Why? Because I choose not to have any more of it, Ayaani. There, I've griffled it – *I choose not to*. It's just a wand, that's all – and we're going to find it. It's really that simple."

"I just wish it was," she quietly whispgriffled.

At the gap in the fence, Matlock ordered the hesitant snoffibs to pid-pad through to the crumlush land of Nullitt Dale, taking off his sodden purple shoes and smiling his familiar curved hare's smile as he finally felt warm grass under his feet and the morning sun beaming down from high in the bright blue lid.

"So this is it," he griffled to Grik, Klaxon, Crumble and Spig. "Your new home. I suggest you get to know the locals. I've never heard of nullitts, but they don't sound too twizzly to me."

Ayaani tugged down on Matlock's long ear, whispgriffling into it. "I wouldn't be so sure about that. Methinks there's a reception committee on the way, and by the looks of things, they look quite russisculoffed."

Matlock turned, astonished to see a hoard of what clearly looked like snoffibs approaching in the sunlight. There must have been over a hundred, some chickling and pointing, all led by the largest snoffib Matlock had ever seen.

"Oh, by the eyesplashers of Balfastulous!" Grik moaned at his side. "'Tis the wife."

"Your *wife?*" Matlock griffled, open jawed.

Grik nodded, his face ashen. "I married a nullitt. Worst thing I could ever do. Peffa-glopped."

"But…" Matlock griffled, at a genuine loss, "she's a snoffib. They're *all* snoffibs – just like you!"

Grik vilishly shook his head. "Never!" he griffled. "They're nullitts – we're the only snoffibs around here. Just us; me, Dr Crumble and young Spig."

"And me," Klaxon insisted, hurt. "I've always been a snoffib, too. You told me so, Grik. You told me I wasn't a nullitt."

The crowd drew closer, stopping just a snutch of pid-pads away. The large female stepped forward. "So, Forticus," she boomed, all four eyes blazing. "you've finally decided to come home, have you?"

Grik cringed as the crowd chickled. "Karla, I can explain everything, peffa-honestly I can."

"And just where is my stove?" she asked. "The one you took from the kitchen *three* years ago, when you first decided to set up this peffa-glopped question even'up team? It's been missing ever since!"

Matlock simply watched, not really having the oidiest clue what was going on.

Grik pid-padded over to her, trying to kiss her cheek, but being bliffed sharply around the head as the rest of the nullitts all cheered.

"Three years," Karla Grik griffled, "you've had my stove, Forticus. You took it from the kitchen and I haven't seen it since. When I came back to get it, you and your peffa-glopped friends had put this glubbstooled fence up!"

"You only had to ask me for it, my love," Grik weakly griffled. "I would have given it to you."

Karla narrowed all four eyes. "I couldn't *ask* because it was always pouring with rain! I could barely even see you!"

Klaxon stepped forward, anxious to disassociate himself from the others. "And I would just like to add, Karla, that it was truly and completely peffa-glopped in there. Permanently lid-splashy, all the time. Crumble, Spig and I were forced to wear ganticus hats, but your husband had a crumlush burrow underneath the stove and…"

Grik wheeled on him. "It wasn't a stove, you clottabus! It was a thinking-machine!"

Matlock held up a paw to silence the chickling spectators. "Hello, everyone,'" he griffled. "I don't know who you all are, but…"

"Who are you, then?" a nullitt griffled.

"My name's Matlock. I'm a majickal-hare from Winchett Dale and…"

"What's one of them, then?" another asked.

"Well, it's a hare."

"Fairly obvious."

Matlock nodded, "That does majick, I suppose."

Karla Grik pid-padded over, carefully looking Matlock up and down, all four eyes frowning. "You looked peffa-glopped and muddy just like the rest of them," she suspiciously griffled. "I take it you're part of my clottabussed husband's glopped-up plan to train the cleverest question even'up team in all the dales?"

"Not really," Matlock griffled. "I only met him this morn'up. I'm searching for the Tillian Wand, really."

She looked at Matlock for a long time, frowning and nodding to herself, before finally reaching out to gently stroke Ayaani on her soft dripple's head. "I believe you, Matlock. I've heard of majickal-hares, and I suspect the last thing they want to do is waste their time with a bunch of gobfloppers like my husband and his clottabussed friends." She lowered her voice. "It's not the first time he's done this, by the way. The last time he was gone for two years with just a saucepan. He got six other nullitts to go with him into the forest to try and become 'brippults' – whatever they were supposed to be. This time it was 'snoffibs'. Honestly, I try and griffle to him, time and time again – Forticus, you're a nullitt, you always have been, you always will be – but he just never seems to accept it. Took a mixing bowl once, was gone for seven moon-turns trying to become a 'whapdorf'." She winked at Matlock with the outside two of her four eyes. "I've had a lock put on the kitchen creaker since he's been gone, so hopefully it'll put an end to it."

Matlock nodded. "Probably the briftest thing," He turned to Grik. " So I'm guessing you're not really a doctor, either?"

Grik silently shook his head.

"Why not just be a nullitt?" he asked him. "They seem like quite a fuzzcheck bunch of folk."

Grik slowly looked into Matlock's orange hare's eyes. "Because they don't know anything," he quietly griffled.

His wife threw up her lizardy hands. "Oh, Forticus, not this again!" She turned to Matlock. "The thing about us nullitts is that we don't know anything about things that we don't *need* to know about. We know lots of other things, though. We know about growing and harvesting, and cooking and looking after our cottages and…"

Klaxon sensing a saztaculous opportunity to finally dispense his favourite fact, impressively cleared his throat. "Aha!" he griffled to them all, seizing on the chance. "But do you know that the dale's most ganticus eater is Fleevil Osser from Juffle Dale, who once ate nineteen whulp-truffles in just one sitting? Bet you didn't know *that*, eh?"

There was a long confused silence, before Matlock gently whispgriffled in his ear. "If I remember rightly, I think that was something that Grik made up."

Klaxon flushed every colour in russisculoffed embarrassment as the nullits all laughed. "Oh, yes!" he cried out accusingly above the happy commotion. "You all go ahead and mock! Go on, have a right good chickle at us! But I want you to know that last even'up we attended and won the ganticus question even'up at the Winchett Dale Inn!" He nodded his head triumphantly. "That's right! Us! Me, Crumble and Spig – we're all winners!"

"Where was Grik, then?" someone asked.

"Probably hiding under his wife's stove because it was raining!" another added, as laughter rang out once more.

"And what, exactly, did you win?" Karla Grik asked.

Crumble proudly stepped forward. "Three plates of tweazle-sandwiches."

"*After three years?*" she griffled. "That's all you've got to show for it? Just three plates of tweazle-sandwiches?"

Crumble shifted awkwardly. "Well, not really no. You see...you see...the problem was...that a dworp had already eaten them."

"My dworp, actually," Matlock added. "Proftulous. He loves tweazles in anything. But Klaxon's right, they did win the question even'up, even though they don't have a trophy to show for it – and despite the fact that my dworp was in the lead for most of the time."

"Your *dworp?*" Karla griffled, vilishly turning to her husband. "Is that true? A tweazle-eating dworp from the most clottabussed dale of all the majickal-dales was actually beating your highly-trained question even'up team?"

"Only because they didn't ask the right questions," Klaxon tried, vilishly pointing to Crumble. "And he was completely peffa-glopped! Didn't answer a single one of them."

It took a while for the crowd's laughter to subside, after which Matlock held up a paw for silence. "Listen," he griffled. "I don't have a lot of time. But before I go, I just want to griffle this. Whatever you may think of Forticus Grik and his clottabussed ambitions, to my mind, he's also a hero. For just now, when I was in peffa-twizzly danger he saved me from a fire, risking being stroffed himself in order to bring me this book." He reached into his gown and held it aloft. "And that alone makes him a snoffib for me, because when the right time came – he *did* have the right answer and knew exactly what to do."

"Let me see that book," a female nullit suddenly called out, pid-padding through the crowd to take it from Matlock's paw, opening the pages with her lizardy hands and nodding. "*The Orders of Celestial Constellations.* I haven't seen this for many a moon-turn."

"You can read?" Matlock asked.

"Indeed," she griffled, her long fingers tracing the griffles. "Though I'm a lot better with my spectacles on." She passed the book back. "As a nullitt, I only know what I need to know. And as a lidgazer, I needed to know how to read." She pointed to the fence, the thick plume of smoke still rising through the rain behind it. "Two of your kind lived there once, although they both wore red robes, not green like yours. One sun-turn, as a young nullitt out exploring, I stumbled upon them quite by chance. The older one was keen to see if a nullitt could ever be taught how to read as an experiment. In exchange for my secrecy, he taught me."

"They were Baselott and Chatsworth, my old master," Matlock griffled as the crowd of snoffibs began wandering away, still chickling and laughing happily. Only Spig remained. "Chatsworth taught me to read, too."

"Then that's something else we have in common," she griffled, smiling brightly.

"Something else?"

"I see that you already know my son."

Matlock turned as Spig stepped forward.

"Hello, Mahpa."

She gave her son a hug, all four eyes closed in quiet delight "Hello, Spig. Did you have a truly saztaculous adventure?"

Spig tried to wriggle free. "I got to drive the lid-machine," he griffled. "And wear a big hat."

His mahpa smiled. "Oh, to be young again. All four eyes keenly filled with the imminent vision of adventure!"

"Not really, Mahpa," Spig mumbled. "I was mostly sat in a puddle in a peffa-glopped lidsplashy field."

She shrugged. "Young nullitts these days – they want everything, don't they? You had a hat, what more did you need?" She reached out for Matlock's paw. "I'm Estrella, and what you were griffling about the Tillian Wand interests me greatly. And the name of your dworp, too – Proftulous. It's all peffa-interesting. Come, you must follow me, I think I just might be able to help you." She peered over Matlock's shoulder. "By the way, what's that creature in your hood?"

"My dripple," Matlock griffled. "She's quite tame."

Estrella reached out and stroked Ayaani's head. "Baslelott would sometimes griffle of these dripple things, too. I think he had one, once."

"He did."

"Shame," she griffled. "From the way he used to describe his,

I always thought dripples would be far more crumlush than that." She turned, indicating Matlock should follow. "But perhaps you just got a peffa-glopped one."

Matlock, Estrella and young Spig made their way across the lush grasslands towards a distant cluster of small round stone cottages, their chimneys idly trailing in the clear morn'up. As they pid-padded, Matlock griffled of his quest, feeling strangely easy telling her as much as he knew, Estrella occasionally asking questions, or simply nodding to herself as she listened.

"So you see," Matlock griffled, anxious to quicken the pace to wherever it was they were going. "I don't really have a lot of time to find the wand and…"

Estrella stopped, turning to Matlock and pointing at the grass. "But if you were to find it here, Matlock, right here, at this very blinksnap, then you *would* have time, wouldn't you? All the time in the world."

Matlock looked down. "But it's not here, is it?"

"That's not what I meant," she griffled. "Three years ago, Forticus Grik came to me griffling that he was thinking about becoming a snoffib. Of course, everyone thought he was being even more clottabussed than usual. But then, that's how we all know him – always wanting to be something he isn't. And perhaps that's what really makes him who he is. Anyway, I griffled to my Spig about it and asked him if he wanted to go on an adventure. He told me that he would. So I decided to tell Forticus about the secret burrow of books, then showed him exactly where it was. I knew my Spig would be safe as he was only a short distance away, and perhaps more than that, he would have the time to have an adventure – something peffa-different from simply living with his boring, old lidgazer mahpa." She smiled. "Three long years. But it was the *time* that he needed, Matlock. It was also the time that Forticus, Klaxon and Crumble needed, too. So you see, perhaps time isn't just about how it passes, it's what it gives you, what it shows you." She looked at Matlock long and hard. "And if this really *is* to be your final sun-turn on these dales, Matlock, then who's to say that you wouldn't find the Tillian Wand right at your feet? For wouldn't it just be in the most peffa-perfect place?"

"Perhaps," Matlock agreed, smiling.

"So let's not think about time," Estrella griffled. "Let's think about finding, instead."

They pid-padded on, the grass slowly giving way to a path leading into a small village of round stone houses, all busy with nullitts about their chores. Estrella led Matlock to the tallest one, pointing to the top where a large telescope protruded from an open window.

"'Tis my lidservatory," she proudly griffled, opening the front creaker and showing Matlock up a long, curved wooden staircase. "I spend most of my time here. Especially at night. It's why Spig gets bored, I suppose."

"But it was Spig that also won the question even'up in Winchett dale," Matlock griffled. "All down to him."

"My Spig?" she smiled.

"Indeed. He answered a question about spuddles and the constellations."

Estrella beamed with pride. "Well, I wish I'd been there to see that." She opened a small wooden-creaker at the top of the staircase, pointing to the ganticus telescope inside. "Mind you, if I had this trained on Winchett Dale, I most probably wouldn't have missed a single moment."

Matlock's eyes widened at the size of the machine, respendant in highly polished metals, its gears, cogs and levers covering the central wooden cylinder inset with the cleanest disc of pure glass he'd ever seen. "It's saztaculous."

"It was a gift from my great gand-pahpa," Estrella griffled, turning the cogs and lining the telescope up to the full moon. "Take a look, Matlock. At this time of the year, the moon and the sun are both visible in the same sky."

Matlock put his hare's eye to the end of the telescope, seeing just a mass of light grey holes.

"Craters on the surface," Estrella explained.

"They're ganticus," Matlock gasped, unable to believe what he was seeing.

Estrella nodded. "It is the largest full-moon the dales have seen for many years. Already the tides will be higher, the seas will be rising."

She wound the cogs, and the telescope moved to focus on the very edge of the moon's surface where it met the clear blue morning sky.

"Look closely, what do you see?"

Matlock squinted. "Just the moon and the sky."

"Look closer. Right next to the surface, an oidy speck of light. You see it?"

Matlock nodded, just making out a tiny star, perhaps the oidiest he had ever seen, so oidy he would never have noticed it without the telescope.

"It's more visible at night," Estrella griffled. "'Tis the star of Proftulous, the peffa-same name as your tweazle-sandwich eating dworp. The first star in the constellation of The Great Broom."

Matlock watched as she went to a nearby table and unrolled a large parchment map, pointing to a constellation of stars forming the shape of a witch's broom flying directly away from the moon.

"There are four stars in all," she carefully explained. "Proftulous, Marellus and Flavius form the vroffa-branches. And at the other end, the lone star of Xavios forms the very front of the broom."

Matlock followed the lines, seeing the shape emerge. "Marellus was the name of Chatsworth's dworp," he quietly griffled.

Estrella raised her four eyes. "Was it, now? All peffa-interesting, Matlock. Peffa-interesting indeed. Pass me my spectacles."

Matlock followed her lizardy finger to a nearby shelf, passing Estrella the four-lensed glasses, listening as she put them on and began flicking through the blue book Forticus Grik has rescued from the fiery burrow.

"Look here," she griffled, pointing to a similar diagram on the smoke-blackened page. "Again, the same constellation, The Great Broom. But what do you notice that's different?"

Matlock looked, trying to find something, feeling rather out of his depth. "Erm...I'm not really sure that I..."

"The gaps, Matlock," Estrella griffled, her voice becoming excrimbly. "The gaps between the stars of Proftulous, Marellus and Flavius. See how much wider they are compared to the ones on my map?"

Matlock looked more closely. "Well, I suppose so, but it was probably drawn by someone else, and perhaps it isn't as accurate, and..."

Matlock watched as she went to a nearby table and unrolled a large parchment map, pointing to a constellation of stars forming the shape of a witch's broom flying directly away from the moon.

She took off her spectacles, giving him quite the longest, hardest look. "Lidgazers like myself, Matlock, *never* get our observations wrong. Accuracy is the very foundation of our art and science. What you are seeing here is an constellational map drawn a long time before the one on the table." She put her spectacles back on. "And in that time, the stars themselves have moved. The ends of The Great Broom almost appear to be coming together."

"What does it mean?" Matlock asked.

She considered this for a while, silently comparing the chart and the book. "What do you know of the spuddles of the constellations, Matlock?"

Matlock couldn't lie. "Not much, I'm afraid."

"Why?" Estrella asked, surprised, pointing to shelves around the outside of the lidservatory heaving with books. "So many griffles have been written about them. I thought all you majickal-hares did was read. Baselott was peffa-keen to read everything that he could."

Matlock shifted slightly. "I suppose I'm more what you might griffle to be a 'paws-on' sort of majickal-hare, really."

She frowned. "Oh dear. Such as shame, methinks." She pid-padded over to the shelves and reached for a book wedged tightly between the others, bringing it back to the table and blowing dust from its cover, then opening it with great ceremony. "I prefer a much more 'eyes-on' approach, myself."

"Well you certainly have enough of them," Ayaani quietly griffled from Matlock's hood.

Estrella leafed through the old, heavy pages, humming contentedly until she found the right one. "Aha!" she griffled. "Here we are – the spuddle of The Great Broom." She passed him the book, and Matlock read the handwritten griffles.

> Rumoured to be a broom of Alvestra, defeated in her battle with Tillian to gain his mythical wand, the four stars of Proftulous, Marellus, Flavius and Xavios form the constellation of a witch's broom, seen flying away from the moon, as if Alvestra herself is twizzly to leave Oramus' influence. The ancient spuddle of the Tillian Wand griffles that one sun-turn, the four stars of The Great Wand will come together in just one line, which when seen

with the moon, will take the shape of a ganticus glowing wand – the Tillian Wand of majickal-dalelore, and sought after during the second Most Mjajelicus task by all majickal-hares.

Matlock took a breath, re-reading the griffles.

"Interesting, isn't it?" Estrella griffled. "Not that I believe a single griffle of ancient spuddles about peffa-yechus witches called Alvestra."

"Well perhaps you should, Mahpa," came a voice from the doorway. "I stood in the field with Matlock. I saw the peffa-glopped witch with my own four eyes."

"Spig!" Estrella griffled. "How long have you been listening?"

"Not long Mahpa, I was looking to see if you had any big hats and I…"

"Quiet!" Matlock griffled, his mind churning with possibilities. "When I took the task, there was a puzzle in creeping green ivy on the outside of the Krettle's peffa-glopped tower." He pointed to the chart. "This constellation of The Great Broom, the stars, everything – it's all in the puzzle." He closed his eyes in concentration, recalling and reciting the ivy-griffles out loud:

Look to the lid, the sand and the sea,
And there reflected in your sands of time,
Four dworps linked in all eternity,
A wand from a broom to make a Tillian shine,
There to be grasped, and taken by paw,
According to Most Majelicus dalelore.

"Don't you see?" he griffled. "The spuddles, the maps the stars, the 'four dworps linked in all eternity'? Proftulous is a dworp, Marellus was a dworp, and I'm willing to bet Flavius and Xavios were, too." He turned to Estrella, beaming widly. "Here it is! It's telling me everything. Right here on these charts – the Tillian Wand that aligns itself from a witch's broom!" He gave her a big-hug. "That's what the Tillian Wand *is*, Estrella. The Tillian Wand is a witch's broom! Now, all I have to do is find the right one."

The Dale Vrooshfest...

# 6.

Goole, Garrick and the Ripped-Robes

As the sun gently rose over Winchett Dale the following morn'up, it was to greet the sight of thousands of excrimbly creatures of every description making their way down from the ganticus stone archway that stands at the entrance to Trefflepugga Path at the northern-most tip of the dale.

Some had already arrived overnight and were deeper down the dale, mostly wandering around, bemused and bewildered as to why it was that nothing seemed to be prepared or even vaguely readied for this most peffa-special of sun-turns.

An insistent few had gone further, right into the nifferduggling village of Winchett Dale itself, unable to comprehend why not a single inhabitant appeared to be awake or the least bit ready to welcome them in any capacity, whatsoever.

One or two of the even bolder visitors had eventually taken to knocking on doors, there to be met by bleary-eyed Winchett Dale folk, wondering just what it was that was so important to have woken them from their precious nifferduggles. When reminded that it was the sun-turn of the Dale Vrooshfest, most seemed to be either confused and had forgotten entirely, or had just gone back to bed, wishing the visitors a saztaculous sun-turn, before shutting the creaker in their shocked faces.

All, that is, except for one industrious, opportunistic, attention-seeking, one-legged, one-eyed, tricorn hat and eye-patch wearing, singing kraark by the name of Goole. Sensing a fabulous chance to showcase his skills in front of what he assumed would be a peffa-eager audience, Goole vilishly scrittled off to a small patch of damp grass in Chiming Meadows, eagerly waking up four nifferduggling ploffshrooms.

"Up we get, me hearties!" he griffled, his long black beak and flaxen wings shining in the morning sun. "Goole's been thinking we have a show to be putting on!"

The four oidy-ploffshrooms gradually came awake; stretching, yawning and wondering just what all the fuss was about.

"There be grillions of strangers all over the dale," Goole griffled, his one good eye glinting under his hat. "And they not be knowing what to do with themselves. A crowd's gathering in the village-square – and where there be a crowd, Goole knows there's always an opportunity for a saztaculous showstopper!"

All four ploffshrooms groaned.

"But don't you see?" Goole griffled. "This could be our peffa-lucky break!"

"*Your* peffa-lucky break," the eldest ploffshroom corrected him. "If you want to put on a showstopper at this time in the morn'up, Goole, then it's up to you."

"But you're my band!" he insisted, theatrically flapping his wings, the jangling rings on each of his flight feathers tinkling across the meadow. "You're the most saztaculous and fuzzcheck ploffshroom rhythm-combo in all the dales!"

"True," the ploffshroom agreed. "But we also be needing our nifferduggles, Goole. We can't just be launching into all our crumlush musical business first thing in the morn'up."

Goole dropped to his one good knee. "Listen, good shroom-folk, 'tisn't often you'll see old Goole begging like this…"

"Thank Oramus for that," another ploffshroom griffled, yawning. "It's making me feel quite ill, frankly."

"…but if begging is what it takes, then that's how far I'm prepared to 'umble and 'umiliate meself in front of you all." He whipped off his tricorn hat and lifted his black eye-patch with a flourish. "Just look into me milky-white eye – go on – see the genuine beggingness in there. Go on."

"Please, Goole, put it away," the third ploffshroom grimaced. "And I've never been so close to the bindings on a wooden-leg before, either. The whole glubbstooled sight of you is just too much."

The fourth ploffshroom nodded. "Goole," it griffled. "How about if you promised *not* to beg?"

Goole uneasily stood back up on his one good leg. "Well if that's what it takes to get you lazy lot to play along to me showstopper, then that's what I'll be doing. No more begging from this kraark, I can promise you that." He popped his hat back on, flipping down the eye-patch with a loud snap. "So are you with me, my faithful band of musical brothers? Are we ready to hit the road and deliver a ganticus Goole-sized portion of peffa-fuzzchecked showstopping for the visiting strangers?"

The four ploffshroms cursed and mumbled, slowly reaching for their oidy instruments. "I suppose so," their leader reluctantly griffled. "Only it's hardly a 'road' is it? More like an oidy path through the meadow."

"Oh, it might be just a path at the moment," Goole enthusiastically agreed as he set off back to the village, "but peffa-soon it could be our road to ganticus success! Follow me, good ploffshrooms, there's not a blinksnap to lose!"

Lazily readying themselves, the four yawning ploffshrooms trailed after Goole with their instruments, trying to find some sort of consolation in the fact that they'd never have to witness the glopped-up sight of him begging again.

In hindsight, perhaps they should have heeded the calls in their Sisteraculous telling them to head straight back to the meadow, particularly the oidiest one, who was soon accidentally stepped on and stroffed as they entered the crowded village square, now more or less packed with confused and irate creatures, all demanding to know just when the formalities of the vrooshfest would begin. Goole, realising that the ganticus moment he had dreamt of for so long was finally upon him, picked up the three remaining ploffshrooms with his wing and pushed himself to the centre of the square, his long black beak grinning.

"Good creatures and fair visitors to this dale!" he cried, a circle breaking around him as he set the ploffshrooms gently on the ground to let them half heartedly launch into a lazy cabaret-rhythm that really suffered due to the recent unexpected loss of the poppy-shaker. "I bid you welcome to Winchett Dale! My name is Goole and…"

"When's the vrooshfest starting?" a peffa-russisculoffed long-tongued fropple called out.

Goole blinked in slight confusion with his one good beady eye. "The what?"

"The vrooshfest! The Dale Vrooshfest!" the fropple replied "That's what we're all here for, you great clottabussed flapper!"

"A vrooshfest?" Goole griffled, urging the ploffshrooms at his feet to keep playing, anxious not to lose the crowd. "Never heard of it, personally."

A large groan broke out as news slowly filtered over the square that the glopped-up kraark wasn't, in fact, part of the sun-turn's highly-planned events. Instead, a tall, officious creature dressed in quite saztaculous blue and yellow robes, with a long and pointed black nose, parted the crowds to stand next to Goole, towering over him.

"And who exactly are you?" it griffled imperiously, the disgruntled crowd slowly hushing.

Goole awkwardly tried an oidy jig, tipping the side of his tricorn hat and beaming his best smile. "Goole's the name – and crowd-pleasing's the game." He held out a wing to shake. "At your service to entertain all you good folk with the absolute peffa-briftest that Winchett Dale can offer."

The officious creature ignored the proffered wing. "And are you part of the opening ceremony for today's saztaculous vrooshfest?"

Goole cunningly narrowed his one good eye. "Does it mean I can sing?"

"Presumably," the creature replied.

Relieved, Goole pumped up his chest. "Then I most *peffa-definitely* be a part of your vrooshfest thing! Abso-peffa-lutely!"

"Well, I suggest you griffle to us exactly what's going on! Why are we all stuck here with no one to show us to our seats? Where are all the flags, the food, the many guzzwort tents, marching bands and so much more?"

Goole nodded towards the ground. "Well, there's these ploff-shrooms," he griffled. "I mean, they're peffa-glopped at marching because they've only just woken up, and…"

"Only just *woken up*?" the officious creature gasped. "Just what in Balfastulous' name is going on here, kraark?"

"Search me," Goole shrugged, still genuinely befudddled. "I just turned up to give you a showstopper and now you're being all russisculoffed with me. Doin' this out of the goodness of me own heart, I am. Already lost the poppy-shaker, we have, so some of the close harmonies'll suffer."

"Where's Serraptomus?" the creature officiously barked, searching the square. "He should be here, where is he?"

"In bed nifferduggling, I expect," Goole griffled. "Rarely gets his softulous out of bed before most afternoon'ups, does Serraptomus."

Disturbed from his heavy slumbers by the increasing commotion outside, Serraptomus, perhaps unwisely, cautiously chose that precise moment to open his bedroom window and peer bleary-eyed at the ganticus crowd packing the square below. "Oh, my driffle-jubs," he quietly moaned, before being spotted by the long-nosed creature now making his way stridently through the crowd to stand under the window.

"Serraptomus!" it bellowed. "Get down here, now!"

"Morn'up, Lord Garrick," Serraptomus feebly offered, feeling suddenly glopped to his crimple.

"Don't you *dare* 'morn'up' me!" Garrick fired back in a blinksnap. "I told you when you came before the selection committee that if this Dale Vrooshfest turns out to be an almighty gobflopper, then I would hold you *personally* responsible! You assured me that you would have everything ready, that it would be a peffa-ganticus success and an excrimbly and memorable sun-turn for everyone! But so far, all that's seemed to have happened is that we've all blundered in here after a peffa-long journey to be greeted with nothing more than a singing kraark!"

Serraptomus winced. "It's not Goole, is it? Has it got a wooden leg and just one eye?"

Garrick nodded.

"I'll be down in a snutch of blinksnaps!" Serraptomus griffled.

"Just don't let him sing, whatever you do, he's completely glubbstool at it!"

Vilishy dressing in his tattered tweed jacket, Serraptomus made it into the square, wheezing nervously. "So peffa-sorry, Your Lordship," he apologised, unwisely offering his paw for an officious handshake. "You see, we had an oidy bit of an emergency here in the dale last even'up, so things haven't *quite* gone to plan and…"

Garrick held up a paw. "Where is our reception committee? Our gifts? Our breakfasts? Our brews and guzzworts? Our tents, chairs and tables from which to enjoy the vrooshfest?"

Serraptomus, probably under the most intense pressure he had ever been under to think up a viable excuse, frowned heavily, looking up into the bright morning sunlight for any sort of inspiration.

"Well, Serraptomus?"

He blew out his officious cheeks. Twice.

"Serraptomus! We're waiting."

"It's all up on the High-Plateau!" he suddenly blurted out, trying to smile. "Everything! It's all there, ready and waiting for you! The lot! Saztaculous breakfasts, guzzwort tents, tables, chairs, flags, bunting – all sorts of simply crumlush things! All up on the High Plateau!"

Lord Garrick frowned suspiciously. "And the ganticus todel-bear, Serraptomus? The one you *specifically* promised would be here for the vrooshfest?"

Serraptomus swallowed hard, beginning to wonder if now wasn't the time to confess to Garrick that absolutely nothing – barring twelve chairs and a table from the inn – had been prepared, and simply begin his long pid-pad to the committee's kitchens and start washing-up.

"Serraptomus!" Garrick pressed. "The ganticus todel-bear – will it be up on your High Pleateau?"

"Er…"

"Oh, just answer me, for Oramus sake!"

"Of course it's there!" Serraptomus griffled, trying to chickle at the same time. "The todel-bear is in position and all peffa-ready to be…er…todelling throughout the whole sun-turn. Saztaculous, it is! You have to see it. No peffa-problems."

"Good," Garrick replied. "Then take us there now. Let there be a ganticus opening ceremony with much feasting – then let the contest begin!"

Serraptomus, sensing that he had really gobflopped peffa-spectacularly this time, simply began to whine.

"Stop that ridiculous noise at once!" Garrick ordered. "Lead us to your High Plateau!"

Goole scrittled across to the distressed krate, whispgriffling in his ear. "I'm thinking that now might be a peffa-perfect time for me to be putting on a showstopper of perhaps seventy verses, or so?"

Serraptomus looked at his kraark friend, relief flooding over him. "The absolutely most peffa-perfect time," he whispgriffled. "Keep them all here as long as you can while I try and sort something out." He turned to the crowd, clearing his throat, trying to sound as upbeat as possible. "Ladies and gentlecreatures!" he boomed. "We shall shortly be pid-padding to the High Plateau for the beginnings of the Dale Vrooshfest…"

A rousing cheer broke around the square.

"…but before we do, in order to start the festivities according to Winchett Dale tradition, Goole will now regale you with one of his saztaculous showstoppers!"

"But why can't we just go now?" someone shouted. "It's really peffa-cramped in here, and there's more arriving at the back every blinksnap!"

"It won't take long," Serraptomus assured them. "And it is our tradition, after all. What sort of officious krate would I be if I didn't arrange a typical Winchett Dale style showstopping welcome for you all, eh?"

"Well, you'd have gone up a lot in my estimation," Lord Garrick muttered, tutting heavily, as Goole began once again trying to work the crowd, pathetically lifting his wings and encouraging them all to clap along.

"So peffa-happy to be with you all this saztaculous morn'up!" he griffled, beginning a glopped jig as the three remaining ploffshrooms did their briftest to try and conjure some rhythmical majick from the ground by his feet. "My name's Goole and here's an oidy showstopper all about my eye. It goes like this:

I…I…I…I…have got an milky-white eye!
I…I…I…I…bet you want to know why!
I…I…I…I…can't even fly!
It's be-eeee-cause – of my milky-white eye!"

Much to the crowd's horror, Goole then eagerly scrittled forwards, proudly, but ill advisedly lifting his eye-patch and gleefully showing the peffa-glopped eye in question. However, the ensuing gasps of horror did allow Serraptomus to slip quietly away from the chaos, hoping in his officious heart that his singing friend could buy him enough time to try and organise something vaguely approaching a Dale Vrooshfest up on the High Pleateau.

Though quite how we was going to produce a ganticus todel-bear out of thin air, he hadn't the oidiest idea…

"Down there!" Proftulous pointed, as he and Laffrohn flew high above the village square on the broken vroffa-tree. "There be grillions of creatures!"

Laffrohn looked down. "What they all be doing in the square?" she cried. "They should be up at the High Plateau!"

"You be forgetting that in Winchett Dale everything always gobflops," Proftulous griffled. "It looks like they be listening to one of Goole's showstoppers."

Laffrohn shook her head. "Nothing ever changes in Winchett Dale, does it?"

"And that's what we all be liking about it," Proftulous smiled, watching Goole's tiny figure terrifying the shocked crowd with his eye. "After all, we are the briftest gloppers in all the dales!"

They flew out, away from the village and high over Wand Wood, alighting in Matlock's walled cottage garden on the edge of the trees.

"So," Laffrohn griffled. "Here we be. Lump-thump inside and get a set of Matlock's robes."

Proftulous frowned. "I not be feeling at all happy about this, Laffrohn," he griffled. "After all, I just be a clottabussed dworp. I'm not sure any creature-folk will really be believing that I be a majickal-hare, even with Matlock's robes on."

Laffrohn narrowed her eyes. "Matlock griffled that he wanted you to take his place at the vrooshfest, Proftulous, and that's exactly what you're going to do."

Knowing she was too forceful to argue with, Proftulous reluctantly lump-thumped into the cottage, appearing a snutch of blinksnaps later with a set of green robes over his arm. "Was strange in there, Laffrohn," he griffled. "It not be seeming right without Matlock doing all his majicky-business."

"We can't be worrying about Matlock now," Laffrohn griffled. "We has too big a job to do saving all the creatures before the mirrit-tunnels flood and all of Winchett Dale be under water." She tried putting the robes over Proftulous' ganticus head, ripping them as she did so. "Matlock will be busy doing the briftest that he can do – now we has to find the courage to be doing the same."

Proftulous forced himself into the torn material, ripping it even more, until really, he was simply a ganticus, clottabused dworp in a green, velvet vest that stopped somewhere short of his waist. "But I's don't want Matlock to stroff and be turned into hare soupy-soupy," he griffled.

Laffrohn tried her briftest to try and make him look presentable. "None of us *wants* that, Proftulous," she explained. "'Tis simply what might happen."

"Laffrohn," he quietly asked, "what does your Sisteraculous be griffling to you about Matlock and the task?"

Laffrohn paused, lightly scratching her head. "The curious thing is," she griffled, "there be times that I don't think I even have one."

Proftulous' eyes widened. "But everyone has a Sisteraculous," he griffled. "Every creature, every tree, every plant – everything."

She frowned slightly. "Well, I not be so sure about that. Sometimes, when I hear folk griffling about what their Sisteraculous be telling them to do, I must confess that I don't understand a single griffle of it."

"But 'tis like an extrapluff," Proftulous explained, "except that it's there all the time, not just when you really be needing it."

Laffrohn smiled at him. "Oh, I know full well what the Sisteraculous *is*, you clottabus. 'Tis simply that I haven't heard mine griffling to me, ever." She shrugged. "Sometimes, I tell folk that my Sisteraculous has been griffling to me – but really, it's not true, Proftulous." She adjusted some hanging green threads over his shoulders. "Makes me wonder if I wasn't the only creature ever born in these dales without one."

"'Tis peffa-odd," Proftulous agreed. He thought about it for a snutch of moments. "But p'raps it's because you're the only creature that never really *needed* one, Laffrohn. P'raps you already be so saztaculous that you know exactly what to do all of the time, anyway. Apart from the barrel idea, though – that be a right gobflopper."

She reached up and lightly bliffed the end of his ganticus nose, then turned as she heard something approaching through the woods. "If my ears don't deceive me, I do believe that a krate is about to be finding us."

"You see?" Proftulous griffled. "You have got a Sisteraculous, Laffrohn! It just griffled to you."

"Not really," she griffled, watching as Serraptomus blundered through the garden gate, "I just heard his officious wheezing, that's all."

Serraptomus raced down the path, a ganticus smile spreading over his puffing face. "Matlock!" he griffled, looking Proftulous up and down. "You're back! Hurrah! The vrooshfest is saved! You'll make it all saztaculous for everyone, and I'll not be washing-up for the rest of my sun-turns!"

Proftulous frowned. "I not be Matlock."

"Nonsense, you're wearing Matlock's robes. You must be Matlock."

Laffrohn lightly tapped Serraptomus on the shoulder with her crumlush paw. "Take a long look, Mr Krate, a peffa-long look. Does it *really* look like Matlock to you?"

Serraptomus wrinkled up his nose, peering very closely. "I'm not quite sure," he griffled. "But if it isn't Matlock, then why is it wearing his robes?"

"Because you griffled to me that Matlock told you I had to!" Proftulous griffled. "Remember, the message you gave me last even'up when you found me stroffing tweazles?"

Gradually, Serraptomus' face began to change as the truth slowly dawned. "Well, I'll be a fluff-thropp's uncle! It's *you*, Proftulous! All dressed up in Matlock's robes!"

Laffrohn sighed heavily. "We need to get everyone up to the High Plateau for the vrooshfest as vilishly as possible. There's a peffa-terrible flood on its way." She turned to Proftulous. "Where be the mirrit-tunnel entrance in Winchett Dale?"

"Under Zhava," he griffled. "The Last Great Elm of Wand Wood."

"Good. Then that's where we'll go first. The tunnel entrance must be blocked as firmly as possible. Hopefully, it'll hold back the waters for a while."

"Everyone wait a snutch of blinksnaps," Serraptomus griffled, officiously holding up a paw and turning to Laffrohn. "Just who are *you*, anyway? I'm the only creature allowed to give the orders in Winchett Dale."

"I be Laffrohn," she griffled to him. "Landlady of The Vroffa-Tree Inn, and right now the one creature who might just be able to make your vrooshfest the briftest there ever was."

For Ledel Gulbrandsen, the long overnight trip along Trefflepugga Path to Winchett Dale had thankfully been an uneventful one, the path granting him safe passage across the Icy Seas via a long series of majickal, floating stepping stones, before leading him through a series of continually moving, twisting valleys, until at last he spotted a distant line of flickering torches held by other creatures making their way to the Dale Vrooshfest.

By morn'up he'd arrived, eager to griffle with Matlock before the contest started, setting off away from the excrimbly crowds and into Wand Wood, looking for any tell-tale smoke trails rising from a majickal-hare's cottage, keen to meet the rival of his affections for Ursula and give him a peffa-tzorkly piece of his mind.

Indeed, this whole business of Matlock the Hare seemed to Ledel to be most peffa-splurked. Whilst fully realising that Ursula didn't want to be his match, Ledel simply couldn't – *wouldn't* – understand how she, as a solitary Arctic white hare-witch, would *ever* want to give the oidy potion bottle of her tears to a mere brown-haired majickal-hare. Especially one from Winchett Dale. After all, he knew his own deep white Arctic fur to be quite crumlush, his dark whiskers thick and strong, his nose to be possibly one of the finest twitching sights in all the dales, and his smile to curve just that bit more spectacularly than any other hares he had ever met. Admittedly, one of his white, black-tipped ears was just the oidiest bit smaller than the other, but most creatures overlooked this, awed as they were from the general saztaculousness of the rest of him. A finer looking hare than Ledel Gulbrandsen, it was often griffled, would be peffa-difficult to find.

So it seemed to Ledel absolutely and totally peffa-splurked that Ursula Brifthaven Stoltz could ever have passed him over in favour of a glopped majicjkal-hare. Even their robes were quite glubbstooled compared to his; theirs a sort of predictable dark-green, his a glowing white, studded with gems and threaded with exotic silvers. Whatever it was that this Matlock the Hare had done to gain such affections in Ursula's favour, Ledel was determined to find out.

So it came as something of a surprise to him when he eventually spotted a small cottage on the far edge of the woods, and there, emerging from a side gate, was what he could only describe as quite the ugliest, most ganticus, peffa-splurked majickal-hare he'd ever seen. Its ears weren't the least bit long and pointed, it wore no shoes, and its tiny robes hung ripped and torn on its hairy softulous. Beside it were two smaller creatures, all three of them pid-padding and lump-thumping towards him. Ledel took a breath, drawing his wand from his robe pocket and commanding the peffa-strange trio to stop.

"Matlock the Hare!" he called out, his voice echoing from nearby trees. "Stay right where you are! Don't take another lump-thump!" He levelled the wand. "My name is Ledel Gulbrandsen, and I have travelled across the Icy Seas to defeat you in vrooshing combat!"

Proftulous, standing some twenty lump-thumps away, and having difficulty hearing since Laffrohn had rammed Matlock's green cap on his head, asked Ledel to repeat himself.

Ledel did so, frowning.

Proftulous pointed to the strange white hare. "I's never be seeing one like that before."

"He be a wizard-hare," Laffrohn griffled. "One of Ursula's kind." Proftulous bucked up at this. "He be knowing Ursula? Then p'raps he be knowing all about Matlock, too!" He unwisely took a lump-thump closer, a cracksploding vroosher from Ledel's wand instantly garrumblooming into the ground at his feet.

"Stay right where you are!" Ledel cried. "No more lump-thumps!"

Serraptomus, seizing a saztaculous chance to be officious, slowly pid-padded towards the aggravated wizard-hare, having a quiet griffversation with it as Laffrohn and Proftulous watched, before pid-padding back. "He says that his name is Ledel Gulbrandsen."

"We got that bit," Laffrohn observed. "And?"

"Well, here be the peffa-curious thing," Serraptomus griffled. "He seems to think that Proftulous is in fact, Matlock."

"And, of course, no-one else has ever been doing that, has they?" Laffrohn scowled. "What does he want?"

Serraptomus lowered his voice to a whispgriffle. "Well, he seems to have rather a neffle-flea in his hare's bonnet about...er...Matlock seeking the attentions of a peffa-good hare-witch friend of his."

"Ursula," she nodded.

"Something about an oidy potion bottle, too? Couldn't really understand a griffle of it. I told him Matlock will go over and have a good griffle with him, sort it all out."

"Matlock? You mean Proftulous, surely?"

"Aah," Serraptomus griffled, shifting awkwardly, "the thing was he just looked *so* peffa-saztaculous that..." He tailed off.

"That you didn't actually tell him it was Proftulous, did you?"

Serraptomus, caught, began to whistle for no reason.

Laffrohn threw her short arms in the air. "Oh, for Oramus sake! You're a complete clottabus!" She took a pid-pad forwards. "I'll griffle him the truth, though why it always has to be me that's sorting everything out, I'll never know."

She didn't get another pid-pad before another vroosher cracksploded at her feet.

"Just Matlock!" Ledel called over, the end of his wand smoking. "No more griffles or pid-pads from anyone else! Just Matlock! Come to me now. I need to see the face of Matlock the Hare!"

"I think," Proftulous slowly griffled, "that he means me." He cautiously lump-thumped over to stand in front of the wand-wielding hare.

"Let me see your wand!" Ledel commanded.

Proftulous reached under the ripped robes for his tweazle pouch, squirming a ganticus hand through a gloop of stroffed tweazles, finally finding his peffa-oidy wand. "Here it be."

"That's your wand?" Ledel griffled, astonished. "It looks more like a twig, it's so oidy."

"True. But it do be my wand," Proftulous confirmed.

Ledel took a long look at the creature in front of him. "Oh, my griffles," he gasped. "You're even more glopped and splurked close-up than you are from a distance." He pulled a face. "And your breath…it's truly yechus!"

"It be all the tweazle-pies," Proftulous admitted, smothering a ganticus belch. "Bits can be getting stuck in my teeth for quite a while." He narrowed his eyes, concentrating, suddenly fascinated by something above Ledel's head. "Sorry for me being rude, but is one of your ears being shorter than the other?"

Ledel instinctively brushed a protective paw through both ears. "Absolutely not!" he griffled. "They are both *exactly* the same size, and quite the most saztaculous hare's ears in all the majickal-dales."

"Even though one be shorter than the other one?"

"Look, there's nothing wrong with my ears."

"I never griffled that there was," Proftulous griffled. He scratched at his chin thoughtfully. "I just be trying to work out if one be shorter than the other – or if the other be longer than the shorter one. 'Tis most vexing."

Ledel pulled a face. "*Vexing*? What on earth does that griffle even mean?"

"It means to be confused and an oidy bit glopped about things. Matlock often uses it when he be getting all vexed."

"But *you're* Matlock!"

"See, now *you're* getting all muchly vexed," Proftulous calmly explained to him. "Because I be Proftulous, Matlock's briftest friend."

It took a peffa-long moment before the obvious truth finally sank in. "You're…not Matlock?"

Proftulous reached under the ripped robes for his tweazle pouch, squirming a ganticus hand through a gloop of stroffed tweazles, finally finding his peffa-oidy wand. "Here it be."

"It be the robes," Proftulous helpfully griffled. "It seems they be making everyone most vexed when they see me in them. I just be a peffa-clottabussed dworp, really."

Ledel narrowed his eyes, looking Proftulous up and down. "Well," he cautiously griffled, "I suppose you do look a bit too ganticus…"

"And yechus, too," Proftulous eagerly added. "Don't be forgetting that bit. Whereas Matlock be all brown and furry and crumlush. And both his ears be just the peffa-perfect length, too."

"Look, can we please stop griffling about my ears?"

"I not be griffling about *your* ears, I be griffling about Matlock's."

"Well, can we just stop griffling about *any* sort of ears, then?"

Proftulous nodded, shrugging. "How about noses?"

"Why in Oramus' name would we even *want* to griffle about noses?"

"Well, they not be ears."

Ledel lowered his frizzing wand. "Are you *really* Matlock's briftest friend?"

"Indeed," Proftulous proudly griffled, "I be that. Most peffa-certainly I am."

Ledel shook his wizard-hare's head in quiet confusion, almost at a loss for griffles. In all his years, he couldn't remember ever encountering such a clottabussed glopp-up as the grinning dworp that stood before him. He took a breath, trying for a more reasonable tone. "Then perhaps you would be able to griffle to me precisely where he is?"

Proftulous shook his head.

"You can't, or won't?"

Proftulous thought about this. "Well I could," he tentatively griffled, "if I be knowing where he was. Only I not be."

"His briftest friend doesn't even know where he is? On the sun-turn of the Dale Vrooshfest? Oh, for Oramus' sake, you *must* know!" Ledel looked all round, narrowing his eyes and searching the trees. "He'll be out in these woods somewhere, won't he? Practising his saztaculous vroosher that he thinks will win him the contest. Or perhaps he's shaking like a coward in his cottage, hiding from me. Which would explain precisely why he sent his briftest friend dressed in a set of his robes to try and fool me." Ledel threw back his head and laughed. "As if such a splurked plan would ever work on me – the great and saztaculous Ledel Gulbrandsen!"

"Who also has one ear bigger than the other," Proftulous reminded him.

Ledel raised his wand again. "Look, you don't even have a proper wand so you can leave my ears right out of it!"

"It does be a proper wand," Proftulous protested. "It just be peffa-oidy, and not be working too well. But it definitely be a proper wand."

"Prove it," Ledel sneered.

"I will," Proftulous replied, "when I be taking Matlock's place in the vrooshfest."

Ledel screwed up his face, completely unable to believe what he'd just heard. "*You?*" he griffled. "In the Dale Vrooshfest – with just a twig for a wand?"

Proftulous nodded, furtively looking around for any eavesdroppers. "Matlock not be here," he whispgriffled. "He be away on a Most Majelicus task, trying to find himself a Tillian Wand. So now I has to be him in the vrooshfest. And not only that, we has to get everyone up to the High Plateau peffa-quickly before the mirrit- tunnels become all flooded and it all goes even more gobflopped than usual and Serraptomus ends up washing-up for the rest of his sunturns." He took a breath. "It all be peffa-complicated, really it be."

Ledel frowned. "Is a single griffle of that *actually* true?"

"Every griffle," Proftulous earnestly nodded. "I's never been known to be lying to anyone because I be too clottabussed to be making anything up in the first place."

Ledel considered this. "And he's really gone? Matlock's not here?"

Proftulous frowned, trying to understand the question. "I don't suppose he be a 'here' because he be a hare, not a 'here'. But he do be a hare that not be here, I be knowing that much. Matlock peffa-definitely be a hare that could be anywhere, other than a hare what could be here."

Ledel blew out his cheeks. "Right, I'm not having any more of this splurked nonsense!" He beckoned to the others, calling Laffrohn and Serraptomus over, Laffrohn doing her briftest to explain things as clearly as possible – a task even she found difficult in the circumstances.

"So, you see," she finally concluded, "we needs to be blocking the mirrit-tunnel entrance as vilishly as possible, then be moving the creatures up to the safety of the High Plateau so the contest can begin and everyone will be distracted and not be thinking any peffa-twizzly thoughts about the ganticus flood." She looked at Ledel's immaculate white robes. "I take it you'll be taking part?"

"It's why I came," he griffled. "To beat this splurked Matlock the Hare and win the contest – the only Arctic wizard-hare ever to do so." He lowered his voice, whispgriffling in Laffrohn's ear. "He wears the potion bottle of a tzorkly white hare-witch around his neck. It's all most peffa-splurked."

"I know," she whispgriffled back, quietly leading him a few pid-pads away. "I be the landlady of the inn where they first met. But if I were you, Ledel, I wouldn't be worrying myself twizzly with thoughts of Ursula losing her heart to Matlock. After all, she be far too solitary and tzorkly – and as for Matlock, well," she nodded over at Serraptomus and Proftulous, "you only have to be looking at his friends to realise just what a clottabus he is."

Ledel glanced at the confused dworp and tweed-jacketed krate. "I'm beginning to get the picture," he quietly griffled. "But won't it be obvious to everyone that the dworp isn't Matlock?"

"But you thought that he was," Laffrohn smiled. "Sometimes, methinks, it isn't what folk actually see, 'tis what they *want* to be seeing that really counts." She winked. "We simply need to make them want to see Matlock, that's all."

Serraptomus pid-padded over, nervously raising a paw. "Erm… good and saztaculous Arctic wizard-hare fellow, I don't suppose you have a vroosher in your repertoire that could conjure a ganticus todel-bear, do you?"

"A todel-bear?" Ledel griffled.

"Indeed," Serraptomus earnestly nodded. "And a really peffa-ganticus one, too."

Ledel narrowed his eyes. "I think I'm getting the hang of this, now. Has this got anything to do with you washing-up for the rest of your life?"

Serraptomus nodded miserably.

"And I'm also suspecting that you have about as much an idea of what a ganticus todel-bear actually is as I do, yes?"

Another sombre nod from Serraptomus.

"You really have *no* idea, do you?"

Serraptomus swallowed hard. "Not even the oidiest," he mumbled. "I just made it up to impress the committee."

Ledel turned to Laffrohn, ignoring the clottabussed griffles. "We need to block a tunnel?"

Laffrohn nodded. "As vilishly as possible."

"Well, I suggest we go and do that, instead of griffling about todel-bears."

Surprisingly, it didn't take them long to make a huge pile of protesting colley-rocks around Zhava's roots, despite her constant demands to know exactly what was going on. Proftulous was dispatched to find as many of the small griffling boulders as he could, bringing them back for Ledel to vroosh into position under Laffrohn's careful scrutiny, slowly building the pile, while Serraptomus did his utmost officious best to try and look as though he was somehow in charge of the whole operation.

"Excellent teamwork!" he griffled after the job was done, the pile of protesting colley-rocks now as high as his head and shoulders right around Zhava's trunk. "See? All it took was some most peffa-saztaculous krate organisation, and all was easily achieved."

The others ignored his griffles, as Laffrohn sent him away into the village to begin bringing the other creatures up to the safety of the High Plateau.

"We'll meet you there," she told him. "Fetch them all, but be sure you don't griffle a single griffle about the rising flood. The last thing we be needing at the moment is a peffa-twizzly panic."

Serraptomus nodded. "But before I go," he griffled to them all, "can I just ask one final time – does *anyone* know of a saztaculous vroosher that could majick a ganticus todel-bear?"

The silence was deafening.

"Tell me," Ledel eventually griffled, "will they give you a brush for the washing-up, or will you simply have to use your paws?"

7.

Luck, Flutebeaks and Soriah

Matlock's discovery that the Tillian Wand was, in fact, a witch's broom had filled him with peffa-excrimblyness. He tried to level his vilishly beating heart, all too aware of each grain of sand with every thump in his chest. He wondered just how many beats he had left, daring to imagine the ganticus hourglass for just a twizzly blinksnap, seeing Jericho and Lily Krettle's razor-sharp teeth drooling and spinning in eager anticipation, a splutting cauldron boiling in readiness beside them…

It's time, he told himself, to be as calm as possible, recalling his master's griffles as Chatsworth had explained the true nature of the task – to be able to control his fears no matter how peffa-twizzly the situation became. And yet, the more Matlock thought about it – the more he had learnt about his master – the more he questioned him. Chatsworth, Matlock now knew, hadn't even undertaken the second task, saved from the fate of doing so by Baselott, a hare who had rejected the ways of majickal-dalelore in favour of science and experiments.

Matlock remembered the griffles he'd read in the secret burrow, wondering just what it was that Baselott suspected was *'really happening amongst the Majickal Elders.'* The same thing that was somehow *'too dangerous to even mention here, far too peffa-ganticus a thing to even begin to contemplate.'* Whatever it was, Matlock knew the secret would most likely only be discovered in Baselott's final revisions that he had submitted to *Majickal Dalelore – Volume 68* shortly before he stroffed, written on thirteen pages of parchment that were never, ever published. The key to everything, he knew, would be somewhere amongst the griffles on those pages – every extrapluff in Matlock's softulous told him so, whilst his Sisteraculous practically screamed it in his long hare's ears. He knew that somehow he must find those pages for the real mysteries to be solved.

Sitting alone in Estrella's lidservatory, he tried to make some sort of sense of it all. As far as he could gather, he'd been sent to find a wand, a task he was expected to fail at and be turned into hare soupy-soupy. Even Laffrohn, one of his most trusted friends seemed to already know of his intended fate, spending long hours griffling with Baselott deep underground at The Vroffa-Tree Inn. It seemed incomprehensible and most peffa-glopped that Laffrohn would have wanted him to fail. After all, she'd been so willing to help him solve the riddle of Trefflepugga Path. Whatever it was the two of them had griffled about on so many occasions, whatever it was that Baselott truly suspected was going on – Laffrohn had never griffled a single griffle about any of it.

Everything, it seemed to Matlock, was just peffa, peffa-glopped, with more and more revelations to discover at every twist and turn. His hare's brain almost ached with it all.

And yet there was one thing, he realised, that seemed to bond all the peffa-strangeness together – *him*. Somehow, Matlock knew, reluctant as he was to admit it, he was a ganticus part of things. But as for how ganticus, he hadn't the oidiest idea.

But first, there was the small matter of finding a witch's broom...

Which was why, the longer he thought about things in the quiet of the lidservatory, the more he realised the real 'puzzle' wasn't about a wand at all. It was more to do with him; what he was, who he was, *why* it was that he was somehow central to so many peffa-ganticus and secret things he knew so little about.

Behind him, the door opened, and Estrella set down two brottle-leaf brews on the charting table. "Looks like you've got the weight of the dales on those majickal-shoulders of yours."

Matlock half-smiled. "Sometimes, it feels like that. Life was just so much easier back in Winchett Dale before all this Most Majelicus business, it really was." He took a grateful sip of the warm brew. "I never wanted to do the tasks in the first place."

"So why do them?" Estrella asked. "It be most glopped to be all stressing with doing things if you don't have to do them."

"Because my master nominated me," he griffled. "I didn't really have a choice."

"And if you were to become Most Majelicus," she asked him, "what would your life be like then?"

Matlock tried to answer the question as best as he could. "Well, I'd have to wear red robes, then spend the rest of my sun-turns going out into The Great Beyond to find hares I could bring back and train as my own apprentices."

She pulled a face. "It doesn't sound all that saztaculous to me. Not the oidiest bit Most Majelicus."

"Nor me, neither," he quietly admitted.

"So that's all you'd do? Just teach apprentices?"

"As far as I know, yes."

"And you'd miss the life you had before, I be guessing?"

Matlock nodded, not really knowing what else to griffle.

"And if you don't complete all three tasks?"

"Then I'll stroff," he griffled, trying to smile and make light of it. "Many majickal-hares do. Or, if I'm peffa-lucky I might be returned to The Great Beyond, never to remember anything of my time in the dales."

Estrella scratched the side of her head, all four eyes frowning slightly. "Well, far be it for a nullitt to griffle as much, but I be thinking that it's all peffa-glopped. Not only that, but you have to keep one of those yechus dripple things with you all the time, too."

Matlock smiled as Ayaani tutted in his hood.

Estrella hesitated slightly. "Matlock, do you ever wish that you were still out in The Great Beyond?"

"I don't know," he griffled. "There's so very little that I can really remember about it."

"I've heard of it," she griffled. "I've often tried to imagine it. I suppose what I'm griffling is that perhaps it be a place where things aren't quite so peffa-glopped as they are here. A place where things are always crumlush, where creatures don't waste their time finding glopped-up things from thinking-machines, or having to pretend they're something they're not." She softly chickled. "I've even heard that we have a dale somewhere where creatures use oidy pebbles as a way of paying for things, and the more that you have, the more saztaculous you feel."

"There is," Matlock griffled. "It's called Alfisc Dale. I've been there."

"So it's true?" she griffled, all four eyes widening. "They use pebbles?"

Matlock nodded. "They call them drutts."

Estrella shook her head. "Just sounds so completely glubbstooled to me." She went to the telescope, peering through. "I suppose that's why I love the stars, Matlock. They're simply there, constant, above us all the while. And no matter how peffa-glopped things become, I can always look at them floating in the lid, looking down on us all, making me feel just the oidiest part of something so saztaculous, so special, so peffa-shindinculous that it is a privilege for me to be amongst them." She turned to Matlock. "I'm hoping The Great Beyond is like that."

Matlock smiled, briefly daring to imagine a world without officious-krates, glopped-up tasks, drutts, long, long-nosed krellits, twizzly smoke-witches and all the other things that made his life in the majickal-dales quite glubbstooled at times. "But right now I have to be finding a witch's broom."

Estrella thought about this. "Strange, because of all the sun-turns you could have chosen, perhaps this is the most peffa-perfect one to be finding brooms."

"How so?"

"Where will all the dale-creatures be this morn'up?"

Matlock thought about it, suddenly remembering what he'd quite forgotten in all the twizzly events of the last few hours. "The Dale Vrooshfest?"

Estrella held up a lizardy-finger. "All except for two types of creature," she griffled. "Us nullitts, who think the whole thing to be a ganticus waste of time and effort – and *The League of Lid-Curving Witchery*, who frankly, aren't impressed by the spectacle of a few majickal-hares trying out vrooshers to impress one another on a distant hillside. It's all most un-tzorkly and splurked to them."

"I can imagine," Matlock griffled. "I have a friend who's a solitary white hare-witch. There's peffa-little she's ever impressed by."

Estrella chickled. "I've heard the solitary ones are the worst. Still, if you want to have the briftest chance of finding more witches brooms than you ever realised, I'd pid-pad out of here and follow the river that runs through this dale. In time it joins another, then another – before finally meeting the Icy Seas. There, on the banks, you'll find the most ganticus gathering of witches of every description as *The league of Lid-Curving Witchery* meets for the ganticus Estuary Festival, their very own celebration of peffa-splurked, tzorkly-witch madness, held on the exact same sun-turn as the Dale Vrooshfest." She dug Matlock lightly in the ribs. "I've been to both in my time, and frankly found the Estuary Festival to be far more fun – providing you don't get stroffed, that is."

"But I've never even heard of this Estuary Festival," Matlock griffled. "Then again, I hadn't heard of the Dale Vrooshfest, either."

"Trust me," Estrella griffled, leading him back down the stairs and to the front creaker, "if it's a witch's broom you're after, the Estuary Festival's the place to go." She reached out and stroked Ayaani's frowning head in his hood. "Look after him, won't you?" she whispgriffled. "Only he doesn't seem all that peffa-clever to me."

"I still haven't forgotten your earlier remarks," Ayaani griffled.

They said their goodbyes, Spig coming to the creaker to wish them well, waving alongside his mahpa as Matlock and Ayaani vilishly set off for the river at the edge of the village, briskly following the gently flowing water along the lush grassy bank.

It was, had it been any other sun-turn, quite the most saztaculous morn'up. The sun was high in the lid, and a light autumnal breeze played around the riverbank. Meadowbuzzers and brightly coloured lifflewings danced in the air as the first few leaves began lightly falling, drifting to the ground, relieved perhaps, that their spring and summer duties were over.

At the end of the dale, the river turned sharply, beginning to chop and swell over rocks and boulders, picking up speed as it flowed steadily into a larger river beyond.

"How much further?" Ayaani griffled.

"To griffle you the truth I've no idea," Matlock griffled. "All Estrella would tell me is that the rivers meet and eventually become the estuary that runs into the sea."

"But we could waste so much time just pid-padding like this," Ayaani moaned. "There has to be another way. Use your wand, make a boat or something."

"A boat?"

"Seems like the right thing to do."

"So now you're going to griffle to me that there's a vroosher you just 'happen' to know that can majick a boat?"

"Why would I know that?" she griffled, offended. "You're the majickal-hare. You've got the Most Majelicus wand." She thought for a snutch of moments. "Didn't you once use it to fly up into the lid on Trefflepugga Path?"

"I did," Matlock agreed. "Though it mostly did all the flying stuff by itself. I just hung on as best as I could. Only Oramus knows where we'd both end up if I tried that again."

"How about you give it a clear instruction this time?" Ayaani suggested. "Just griffle it to fly us to the Estuary Festival."

"You think that'll work?" Matlock asked.

"It worked when you needed to save the lid-machine, didn't it?"

Matlock nodded, remembering how the red-vroosher had freed the trapped balloon back in Winchett Dale. He reached into his robe, slowly drawing out the Most Majelicus wand, its end already frizzing and glowing bright red.

"Well go on," Ayaani encouraged. "Griffle to it!"

"I would do," Matlock gasped. "But you're holding onto my neck too peffa-tightly."

Ayaani relaxed her grip as Matlock tried to clear his mind and think of what might possibly pass as a spell for a Most Majelicus flying-vroosher. He closed his orange hare's eyes, concentrating.

"Anytime soon would be a peffa-good thing, methinks," Ayaani griffled.

Matlock opened them. "The thing about this wand," he slowly griffled, turning it in his paw, "is that it always seems to do what it thinks is necessary at the time."

"Well, I think it's peffa-necessary we get to the Estuary Festival to find the Tillian Wand as vilishly as possible."

Matlock held the wand aloft. "Ayaani, I'm not sure it works like that." He cleared his throat, before griffling to the wand in what he hoped would be his most confident, majickal voice. "Most Majelicus wand! Take us to the place where you think we need to be!"

Instantly, the wand began to shake and splutt in his paw, fiercely directing itself at the ground and letting out a garrumblooming red-vroosher that powered them both suddenly and shockingly high into the air.

"It's working!" Ayaani cried, clinging to Matlock's neck once more as his long ears flapped all about her face. "We're on our way!"

However, to their dismay, just a snutch of blinksnaps later, they plummeted straight back down, landing with a heavy thump at the exact same spot on the bank they'd started from.

"I'd consider that to be somewhat less than a total success," Ayaani sourly observed.

"Maybe not," Matlock griffled, looking around. "Perhaps this is precisely the place that we *should* be."

"Here? By a river? Doing nothing?"

"Not necessarily nothing, as such," Matlock griffled, noticing a vilishly approaching dust-trail from the far side of the dale. "I think perhaps we're meant to be waiting to see just what – or who – that is."

Ayaani turned to the trail, squinting with her oidy black eyes. "Are you sure?"

Matlock put the wand back in his robe. "Not really. But in truth, I'm an oidy bit short on other ideas at the moment."

As the trail got nearer they were able to make out quite the most curious creature pid-padding towards them as vilishly as possible. Twice the size of Proftulous, and almost as yechus, with large webbed feet, green fur, a long pointed snout and branches growing from the place on its head where its ears should be, it stopped just in front of them, panting desperately, dropping a large heavy sack onto the ground.

"Hello?" Matlock griffled, as Ayaani cowered in his hood. "Can we help you?"

...with large webbed feet, green fur, a long pointed snout and branches growing from the place on its head where its ears should be, it stopped just in front of them, panting desperately, dropping a large heavy sack onto the ground.

The curious creature bent over, still fighting for breath, holding up a paw with six claws at its end. "More a case…" it puffed, "…of what I…can do for you." It stood upright, taking another ganticus breath. "'Tis the worst thing about this job, the timing." It held out a paw. "I'm Luck, by the way. Or, As-Luck-Would-Have-It, to give me my full name."

"You're luck?" Matlock griffled, taking in the full sight of the peffa-glopped, green creature.

"That's me," it nodded. "Some creatures think I'm simply an abstract concept, but really when you think about it – and obviously in this job, I have a lot of time to do just that – if I really was abstract, then I would surely cease to function as an actual real or imagined fortune-based concept of reality. Which would, of course, be unlucky for me – thereby proving the existence of luck in the first place, as it's surely impossible to have one without the other."

Neither Matlock or Ayaani could griffle a griffle.

"Like I say," Luck griffled, "I've probably had too much time to think about it."

"You're *really* luck?" Matlock griffled.

Luck pulled a face, quite annoyed. "Oh, I see. I get it now. You're one of these 'unbelievers', are you? Despite the fact that I'm stood here right in front of you, just when you most need me to give you some luck." He pulled a superior face. "Well, if that's your frankly grossly offensive attitude, then I shall be forced to ply my fortune-based vocation where it would be better appreciated. I know for a fact that there's a long-legged ruffle nearby who needs a ganticus dollop of luck. Dreadful time of it, recently, he's had."

"What in Oramus' name is he griffling about?" Ayaani whisp-griffled in Matlock's ear.

"Not sure," Matlock griffled. "But I think he's about to go."

"Good," Ayaani griffled. "He's even more clottabussed and glopped-up than Proftulous, which is really griffling something."

Luck threw the sack over his shoulder. "So I take it you won't be needing your one piece of luck then, hare? Fine, I'll just give it to someone else."

"There's luck in that sack?" Matlock asked.

"Pretty much," Luck griffled. "Plus a few old sandwiches.

Spend a lot of time out and about, you see."

Matlock frowned. "My luck is in *there*?"

Luck shrugged. "Everyone's is. It's how the system works." He set the sack back down, opening it for Matlock to peer inside, showing him grillions of floating green lights swirling around in the darkness. "Behold," he griffled, "all the luck in the world."

Matlock couldn't take his eyes off the peffa-curious sight. "But who made it? Where does it all come from?"

"Don't know," Luck griffled. "Not my job to ask – just to give the stuff out. And really, if you want to get abstract and metaphyisical about it, then we could also ask ourselves where does *anything* come from, thereby invoking age-old debates about time-continuums and the very nature of existences right across the…"

"Yes, we could," Matlock interrupted him. "But I didn't actually ask that, did I?"

Luck raised both eyebrows. "Sorry. Like I say, too much time on my paws to be thinking about all this stuff." He lowered his voice to a confidential whispgriffle. "To be peffa-honest with you hare, there's been griffles up there," he discreetly pointed to the clear blue sky, "amongst the Majickal Elders, that really I'm not cut out for this job anymore because I spend too much time worrying about non-luck related issues. There've even been complaints that some creatures aren't getting their luck when they most need it."

"Which presumably is unlucky," Matlock griffled, trying to follow the thread.

"Oh yes," Luck agreed, his green face suddenly clouding and frowning, the leaves on his branches shaking in russisculoftulation. "Unlucky, he's *always* there! Blooming apple of the Elders' eye, he is. The moment I'm late for giving out some luck, he's right in, dishing out unluckiness, great big grin on his face, mocking me. If I hadn't got to you in time – whoosh! – he'd have been straight here, you mark my griffles, and then you'd have been the unluckiest hare in all the dales."

"Well, I'm glad you got here first," Matlock griffled.

"Oh, don't be," Luck smiled. "Just a matter of luck really."

"I think," Ayaani whispgriffled to Matlock, "now would be a good time to ask him for our luck and leave."

"The peffa-perfect time," Matlock agreed, looking up at the ganticus green creature. "Er…Mr Luck, I was just wondering if you wouldn't mind giving me my piece of luck? Only I really could do with it."

Luck reached right to the bottom of the sack, bringing out a tattered book, its pages curling, opening it quite deliberately slowly.

"You griffle that you've met the Majickal Elders?" Matlock asked him.

Luck nodded, flicking through the book, eyes scanning the lists on each page. "Of course. As an abstract entity, it's all too peffa-easy for me to cross between the ethereal layers of what we purport to be our separate but conjoined existences."

"I didn't understand a single griffle of that," Matlock admitted.

"I meant that 'yes', I've met them. It's part of the job, you see. All us abstract concepts are called to meetings with the Elders; myself, Unlucky, Love, Greed, Ambition, Guilt, Happiness, Unhappiness – there's quite a few of us when we all get together. Some of us spend most of their time out in The Great Beyond. For instance, I haven't seen Empathy for many a moon-turn. Apparently, she has quite a time of it out there. It's s'posed to be the most peffa-glopped of all the abstract jobs, that one. The creatures just don't seem to be able to understand her – which some would say is an oidy bit ironic in itself."

"What are the Majickal Elders like?" Matlock asked.

"Mostly like yourself," he griffled. "Hares, but all dressed in blue robes, thinking they're superior and spending a ganticus muchness of their time pontificating."

"Pontificating?"

Luck nodded. "It's a sort of a committee griffle for 'not doing very much'."

"Oh," Matlock griffled, a little disappointed. "I thought it would be different to that."

"Don't get me wrong," Luck griffled. "The place is nice enough. Lots of lovely, crumlush buildings and places to pid-pad around, all immaculately clean and saztaculous, but really, there doesn't seem to be an awful lot going on up there. I just get summoned, told I'm glubbstool at what I'm doing, then have to make my way back here and try and do better."

"It all sounds quite…"

"Dull?" Luck nodded. "You'd be right there, Mr Hare." He licked at a claw with his long tongue, turning over the pages in the book. "Now, let's get you your oidy piece of luck shall we? Name?"

"Matlock the Hare."

Luck scanned the pages. "Right. There it is. I've got you now. Says here you're entitled to one piece of luck in your lifetime, and you'll most be needing it when you're stood on a riverbank trying to get to the Estuary Festival to find a witch's broom that you assume to be the Tillian Wand while you're on the second Most Majelicus task, that if you fail, will result in you being turned into hare soupy-soupy."

"It says all that in there?"

"See for yourself," Luck griffled, showing Matlock the tattered page. "Destiny does most of my notes for me, and she's usually pretty thorough."

"Destiny?" Matlock griffled. "As in, the things in my life?"

Luck nodded.

"So…she knows everything that will happen to me?"

Luck pulled a slight face. "Not *strictly* everything, no. It's sort of shared between her and Fortune. Then Irony has a look-in – always has to stick his ganticus nose in, he does – and of course the whole thing has to be approved by Fate, who only puts his signature on it after adding a few details depending on what sort of mood he's in. Then it's off to Oramus for the final seal of approval. After that, it's pretty much done."

"This is all *true*?" Matlock asked, shocked.

Luck chickled, nodding as one or two leaves fell from his branches. "I've heard that out in The Great Beyond there are creatures that spend the whole of their lives griffling and arguing about the nature of predetermined existence and the right of the individual to shape their own destiny, when really, it's mostly decided by what mood us abstracts are in at the time."

"But this is so wrong," Matlock frowned. "You can't just shape lives like that."

"Wrong it may be," Luck agreed, "but that's how it's done at the moment. And until the sub-committee of the *Internal Fates and*

Destinies Commission reports back with findings to the *Majickal-Elders Review Committee on Rights and Justices* – that's how it'll continue to be done."

"And how long will that take?" Matlock asked, aghast at what he was hearing.

Luck quickly put a ganticus paw over Matlock's mouth. "Hush! And if anyone ever asks, then I wasn't the one that told you any of this, alright?"

Matlock nodded from behind the hand, relieved when Luck finally took it away.

"Now let's get you your one piece of luck, then I can be on my way." He held open the sack, concentrating hard, eyes closed, Matlock watching in amazement as the branches on either side of his head carefully reached down inside and slowly pulled out two bright green lights, holding them in front of Luck's face. "Is this the luck of Matlock?" he asked, opening his eyes.

The branches nodded up and down.

Luck pulled a confused face. "But it clearly states in the book that he's only entitled to *one* oidy piece of luck in his life, not two."

Again, the branches nodded, but this time also came together, shaping and moulding the two lights into just one single bright green glow.

"I see," Luck nodded frowning and muttering to himself, checking his book and flicking through the pages. "Well this is most irregular and peffa-glopped." He turned to Matlock. "In all my years I've never come across this. All I can think of is that your luck is somehow perfectly intertwined and matched with the luck of another, and that you both need your combined luck at this precise moment in time." He checked the book again, frantically reading names and making furious comparisons. "It *has* to be here. The name of the other creature has to be in here."

"Well, I'm travelling with my dripple," Matlock suggested, trying to help. "She needs luck too. Our destinies are entwined."

Luck shook his head dismissively. "Dripples aren't entitled to any luck. It's in the rules. No, it has to be someone else, another creature entirely."

"Proftulous?" Matlock tried. "He's my dworp. He's trying to be me at the Dale Vrooshfest at the moment. He probably needs some luck more than anyone and…"

"Just stop griffling!" Luck suddenly shouted. "Stop giving me names! Dworps aren't even *in* the book, they're so peffa-clottabussed!" He turned back to the pages, vilishly scanning them. "The other name must be here! The system has never been wrong before. That's why it's a system, for Oramus' sake. System's don't go wrong, they *can't* go wrong!"

"If I could perhaps just take my oidy piece of luck and leave?" Matlock cautiously griffled, reaching out for the temping green light. "Only, I'm not really bothered about the other name at the moment, really."

Luck vilishly caught his paw and screwed up his eyes, studying Matlock's face closely. "It's *you*, isn't it?" he slowly griffled, the menace suddenly thick and heavy in his voice. "You're the one who's messed up my system, aren't you?"

"Absolutely not," Matlock tried to reassure him, watching the branches on Luck's head begin to twitch and turn towards him.

"You're the one who's been confusing me and asking too many questions!" Luck roared, his reaching branches suddenly wrapping themselves around Matlock's face.

"No!" Matlock protested as the branches tightened, curling like russisculoffed sazpents around his neck. "I was just standing here and you came along!"

"Your sneaky tricks and distracting griffling have ruined my system! You're nothing but a bad-luck hare, Matlock! And as such, your luck has well and truly run out!" He vilishly opened the sack, his branches forcing Matlock and Ayaani inside, bundling them both into the black choking depths, bright green luck flashing all around them "You'll be peffa-peffa sorry you ever messed with me, hare!"

"What are you going to do?" Matlock cried out from inside.

"Stroff you, of course!" Luck replied. "You're a mistake in the system!"

Matlock felt the bag being lifted and roughly slung over Luck's shoulder, both he and Ayaani being jolted and thrown from side to side as Luck began pid-padding away, starting to pick up speed. He reached into his robe pocket for his wand, but couldn't get his paws on it. "Ayaani!" he urgently griffled. "My wand! Vilish!"

"I can't," she squeaked. "I'm stuck in your hood! Move over, let me out!"

But such was the bouncing and buffeting inside the sack that neither could move without being tumbled over the other. It was hopeless.

"I really don't think ending up in a sack is anywhere approaching good luck," Ayaani moaned as Matlock was flung against her once again. "How can we possibly be stroffed surrounded by all the luck in the world? It's just so totally glubbstooled!"

But at that moment, the two bonded green luck lights suddenly crackspoded, dazzling Matlock with their blinding intensity. He heard a deafening roar and a series of vrooshers, then the sound of Luck roaring in pain, before finally dropping the sack with a painful thump.

And next, the most welcoming sound – the distinctive, tzorkly and formidable voice of Ursula Brifthaven Stoltz.

"Well, that was lucky," Matlock heard her griffle. "I needed some new branches for my broom. I'll just take those ones from your head, thank you."

Matlock desperately called to her from inside the sack, but as far as he could gather, she was too busy breaking Luck's branches to hear.

"Oh, do stop all this useless protesting!" she griffled over Luck's pained cries. "They'll grow back again!"

Gasping, Matlock finally managed to finally open the sack, pushing out his head and ears, watching Ursula send bright blue-vrooshers straight at a fast-retreating Luck, both branches now lying on the ground at her feet. "Ursula?"

Instantly she turned, raising the wand and levelling it at him. "Matlock, you ganticus splurk! What are you doing in a sack?"

"It's a bit of a long story," he griffled. "I'll tell you if you put the wand away."

"I have no time for long stories – especially yours, Matlock." She turned to Luck, now little more than an oidy dust-trail in the distance. "Who's your peffa-splurked, green friend with the ridiculous flappy feet?"

"Luck, if you'd believe it."

She narrowed her eyes. "Frankly, not a griffle." She pid-padded over, putting away the wand and reluctantly helped Matlock out of the sack. "But then again, nothing surprises me with you."

Matlock straightened his robes checking that Ayaani was still safe in his hood.

"What's inside the sack?" Ursula asked.

"All the luck in the world," he griffled. "Except the oidy bit I probably used when you came along just now."

Ursula inspected the sack, watching as it shifted and moved, briefly looking inside and letting out a low whistle. "All those green things – they're luck?"

Matlock nodded.

"Good," she griffled. "Then I can sell them. Tie it up, they must not escape."

"Sell them?"

"At the Estuary Festival. I was on my way when my vroffa-branches began to give up on my broom. I spotted your friend had some on his head and swooped down to get them." She turned to the branches. "Presumably," she slowly griffled, "if your friend is who you say, then those are peffa-lucky branches, too?"

"I'm not sure," Matlock griffled. "He didn't seem that lucky to me." He watched as she crouched down and began expertly tying and weaving the branches into her broom.

"I take it," she griffled, "that you are not at the Dale Vrooshfest because you have already met Ledel Gulbrandsen?"

"Who?"

She tutted. "Ledel Gulbrandsen. The white Arctic wizard-hare who will win the contest with his peffa-tzorkly vrooshing, thereby humiliating you in the process. I assume you met him, then hid in your splurked friend's sack in order to be secretly smuggled from Winchett Dale."

"It's not *quite* like that, no," Matlock griffled, going on to griffle to her just what had happened to him in the few short hours since she had last flown away from his cottage garden the previous even'up.

"So," she griffled when he'd finished. "your second Most Majelicus task has already started and you need to find a witch's broom that is also somehow a wand? At least you can griffle that your life is never dull, Matlock."

211

"But that's the whole point," he quietly griffled. "I rather liked it being dull."

"Which is why you are such a ganticus splurk." She gave him a long, hard look.

"What's that for?" he asked.

"Hush! I'm making my mind up."

He watched as she slowly paced around her broom, counting and reasoning things out on her long, elegant white paws, occasionally stopping to turn and look at the potion bottle of her eyesplashers still tied around his neck, weighing up what was clearly a peffa-important and most tzorkly decision.

"Fine," she finally griffled, nodding. "If you have to find this Tillian Wand, I will help you. But you must do exactly as I griffle. We shall go to the Estuary Festival and sell the luck in this sack. It will cause a great commotion amongst the other witches, and give us the chance to see all their brooms." She gave him another look. "And you're *totally* sure this wand of yours is a witch's broom?"

"Convinced of it," Matlock assured her. "It's written in the stars and in the puzzle of the creeping-green. It all makes peffa-perfect sense. It has to be a broom."

"Very well," she griffled. "And I suppose that if it all goes splurked then at least I'll have sold enough luck to buy myself a peffa-tzorkly set of new robes." She fired up the broom, its deafening roar once again filling the small valley. "What are you waiting for? Get on, you splurk! There's an Estuary Festival full of witches and brooms waiting for us this very blinksnap!"

Many years ago, in a moment of idle boredom, a long-winged flutebeak from Sveag Dale decided it would try and compile a list of local attractions and places of interest for any potential visitors to the majickal-dales *not* to visit – indeed, to be avoided at all costs – a bold enterprise that was glopped from the start for the following three reasons:

1. Despite his ability to fly from dale to dale, the flutebeak hadn't really travelled too far from his own dimble-tree, and therefore had very little actual, practical knowledge

that would have been of interest to potential visitors.
2. As he could neither read nor write, any aspirations the flutebeak may have had for his list to be genuinely helpful was completely reliant upon visitors personally seeking him out and griffling to him directly, therefore rather limiting its overall efficacy.
3. As there are so peffa-few visitors to the dales (most who accidentally stumble upon an entrance to Trefflepugga Path are pretty much 'disposed of' by waiting long, long-nosed krellits) one had to question both the need and demand for such a gobflopped list in the first place.

And yet, as is so often the way with clottabussed ideas, none of these reasons were thought to be sufficient enough by the flutebeak to put him off. So he set to, convinced that he could compile a saztaculous list, despite his lack of any real experience in either list-building, or the intended subject-matter.

It was a long afternoon'up's work, and the flutebeak worked furiously, intently scouring its oidy mind for any sort of memorable, peffa-glopped experiences he could pass on to more or less non-existent visitors. Other flutebeaks, outraged that he had stumbled upon something with which to counter the almost continual boredom of simply being a flutebeak, were all too vilish to scoff and criticise, damning his pathetic efforts and chickling loudly.

However, the flutebeak was made of stronger, more clottabussed stuff than his winged companions, and stuck to the task, sitting quite still in his dimble-tree, eyes closed in concentration, his beak moving slowly from time to time as he considered the importance of his task.

Ranking was the thing he found hardest. Rating the experiences from simply 'an oidy bit glopped' all the way through to 'Most ganticussly peffa-glubbstooled – to be avoided at ALL costs!' was proving trickier than he imagined. Originally, he had intended to put 'making a list' on his list, as the process was causing him quite a headache in his oidy bird brain. But then he realised that at least he wasn't bored anymore, which put the experience into a whole new light, necessitating him removing it from his list before it had ever been on it in the first place.

Such dilemmas soon began to pepper every suggestion the flutebeak could muster, as he slowly drew the conclusion that for every peffa-glopped place or experience, there was also an unexpected upside. Pid-padding along Trefflepugga Path? Yes, you could get stroffed, but sometimes the ever-changing path threw up some truly saztaculous scenery. Griffling with a slow-jarrock? Yes, it could well turn out to be most tedious experience of your life, but very occasionally it might have something interesting to say. Eating cloff-beetles of an even'up? Indeed, they were truly yechus, but nearby dilva-beetles would be peffa-pleased they weren't on the menu.

So it was that at the end of all his thinking, the juzzpapped flutebeak could only really think of one truly accurate thing that could – without any dispute – take its rightful place on his completely useless list:

> Never, under ANY circumstances, even think of being tempted to EVER visit the Estuary Festival!

Satisfied that this was the only occasion that truly merited inclusion, the flutebeak then drifted into peffa-contented nifferduggles high in his dimble-tree, knowing that for an all too brief afternoon'up he had at least found something to beat the almost constant boredom in his flutebeaked life.

And what solid evidence did he have to draw such a conclusion about what appeared to be simply a harmless festival of riverside-based fun for some witches? Well, perhaps the first griffle to take issue with is 'some'. For the Estuary Festival plays host to *all* the witches in *all* the dales; witches of every size, description, shape and colour, from the peffa-oidiest to the most ganticus, flying in on complete vroffa-trees, screaming and cackling high in the air as they send down cracksploding vrooshers onto unfortunates below.

The next griffle would, of course, be 'fun'. And although one creature's definition of 'fun' might very well differ from another's – there was absolutely no way one could ever imagine any of what the witches got up to at the festival as 'fun', as it is a peffa-rare Estuary Festival that doesn't end in vengeful witch-rivalry played out over numerous vroosher-fights, especially when fuelled by ganticus amounts of grimwagel wine and guzzwort. Brooms and hats are frequently stolen, petty jealousies ending in spectacular spells and stroffing, hoards of other witches all eagerly egging the feuding participants on.

With such peffa-glopped things happening, a terrified and peffa-twizzly visitor might well wonder just why it is that the Estuary Festival is allowed to continue in the first place. Surely the officious authorities of the majickal-dales could close it down and ensure not another witch is ever allowed to behave in such a way? And to understand why they don't, it's important to remember the Estuary Festival's *real* purpose – to ensure that not a single witch will ever make her way over to the far more civilised, family fun-based celebrations of the Dale Vrooshfest. Just the thought of an unexpected appearance by *The League of Lid-Curving Witchery* was enough to make the *Dale Vrooshfest Committee* twizzly enough to ruin their feasting – a situation considered so peffa-serious by its chaircreature, Lord Garrick, that he quickly sanctioned the setting up of the Estuary Festival – entrusting the running of it to his own son who had just finished a three-year course on 'Management and Committee Ethics – the Saztaculous Importance of Family, Bribes and Feasting'.

Many thought that the setting up of the Estuary Festival was one of Lord Garrick's finest masterstrokes, and any suggestions from other disgruntled committee members that he should have at least declared that his own brother also ran a reasonably large tent-hire and guzzwort business were quickly squashed. Literally – he had a ganticussly fat whupple sit on any objectors. Thus, any further whispgrifflings about Garrick and his vast family-fortune were kept peffa-quiet, most creatures realising it would be better to turn a blind-eye, rather than be sat on.

And yet, regardless of whatever glopped and greedy dealings may have led to the Estuary Festival, a casual observer couldn't help but observe the unintended irony that such dealings merely underpinned what was a fairly glopped and greedy festival in the first place. Which perhaps, made everything peffa-perfect and right in its own glubbstooled way…

For Matlock, however, clinging onto Ursula's robes with one paw, the other trying not to drop a sack full of all the remaining luck in the world as they roared through the lid on her newly branched vroffa-broom, ironies were the last thing on his mind. He looked down, seeing the rivers merging and swelling below, flowing out towards the distant shoreline of the Icy Seas.

"How much further?" he managed to griffle, the wind almost taking his breath away.

In front, Ursula tutted, then took one arm off the broom to point at the looming banks where three rivers met, spume and froth tumbling over nearby boulders. "Next thing you'll be asking is 'Are we there, yet?' Just be quiet, I'm trying to concentrate!"

Matlock didn't dare griffle another griffle, instead beginning to make out what looked like grillions of flies hovering and darting over the banks, then hearing the familiar roar of witches' brooms, watching as they gleefully vrooshed each other, some falling straight into the churning rapids below.

"Looks like the fun's already started!' Ursula cried over her shoulder. "Hold on. I'm landing!"

Matlock clung tightly as the broom suddenly lurched down towards a large collection of ganticus tents on the far estuary bank, the ground rushing up so vilishly that he had to shut his eyes, his crimple turning.

"Right," Ursula announced, once they were safely on the ground, "Give me the sack and I'll find somewhere we can sell it."

An oidy witch no more than waist-high unwisely chose that moment to come too close, Ursula effortlessly vrooshing it with her wand, sending it clean off its feet and crashing into the side of a nearby tent. "You go and fetch the drinks."

"Me?" Matlock griffled, aware his throat was suddenly rather dry. "Are you sure? I mean, if it's alright with you, I'd much rather stay here and…"

"Pffft!" Ursula griffled. "If you think I am going to stay here and help you find a witch's broom without a ganticus glass of grimwagel wine, then you are *very* much mistaken." She pointed to the largest tent, its roof adorned with ripped black flags, a peffa-glopped commotion of screaming and cackling coming from inside. "That's the wine and guzzwort tent. Now go. And make sure I have a clean glass."

Matlock's mouth hung open. "You're honestly griffling that you want me to pid-pad in there to get you a drink?"

"What's wrong with that?" she snapped. "Ledel Gulbrandsen would have no problems with it. In fact, he would've already done it before I had to waste my time asking him. *And* he would have bought me back *two* glasses by now, not just one. So go. Stop standing there with your mouth all glopped open like a great, clottabussed splurk."

Matlock swallowed hard. "But surely it's too dangerous and twizzly for a majickal-hare?"

"Probably, yes," Ursula agreed. "But if you are to be stroffed because you cannot be finding this Tillian Wand of yours, then really, what's your worry? This way, at least you will be stroffed trying to bring me wine, a far more noble finding task."

"Basically, either way I stroff."

"Well, I was hoping it would be in the hare soupy-soupy *after* you've bought me my wine."

"You're too kind."

"Not really."

"I was being sarcastic."

Ursula frowned. "Sarcastic? I have never even heard of that griffle."

"Which doesn't surprise me."

"You are being sarcastic now?"

"No."

"Good, then go and get my wine."

Matlock watched as she pid-padded away between cackling witches, confidently vrooshing them out of her way, the sack of luck and her broom thrown expertly over her shoulder. "Well," he griffled to Ayaani, "I'm not sure this isn't all going to go peffa-glopped."

"Oh, I think it'll go saztaculously," she replied from his hood. "After all, all we have to do is fight our way into a huge tent full of clottabussed witches, somehow get a glass of wine, then bring it back to Ursula who will be selling all the luck in the world, while we try and find a broom that is, in fact, the Tillian Wand. I mean, really, what could be peffa-simpler?"

217

"Now you're being sarcastic?"

"My master is a genius," Ayaani sighed. "Let's just try and get this done. Methinks it might be time for you to take one of those deep hare's breaths of yours."

Matlock tried to smile, aware there was now a growing crowd of witches beginning to surround them. Some were dressed in ripped rags and dresses, some crawled on all fours. Some had tails, some had horns, some had long thin legs and arms on ganticussly fat bodies. Some had long noses, some had snouts, some were quite bald, others had long glopped hair falling down to their feet. But whatever sort of creature they were, however they snarled or cackled, whatever the colour of their twizzly eyes or yechus, rotting teeth – they all wore a black witch's hat.

"Morn'up, good lady witch-creatures!" Matlock griffled, trying his briftest not to sound as twizzly as he felt. "I wonder if you'd be so good as to let me through to the guzzwort tent?"

A horrible cackling and snarling broke out.

"Only, I rather need to get a good friend of mine a glass of wine," he tried to explain.

The most yechus of the witches vilishly held up a clawed hand. "What 'friend', hare?" it asked suspiciously. "Majickal-hares don't have any friends – apart from clottabussed dworps and splurked dripples, that is."

A smaller witch drew out her wand, pointing it straight at Matlock's head. "Can I be vrooshing and stroffing it?" she asked. "Only I's never stroffed a hare before. I hear their ears be good for grinding up and making into potions."

The larger witch bliffed the smaller one, sending it piling into the others, who chickled, cheered and cackled. "You heard me, hare! Just who is your friend?"

"Ursula," Matlock managed to griffle. "Ursula Brifthaven Stoltz."

The cackling commotion stopped, replaced by low, urgent whispgriffles.

"Ursula Brifthaven Stoltz?" the large witch griffled, her pure black eyes staring intently. "Are you sure, hare?"

"Peffa sure. We've just arrived. We flew in on her broom."

The witch crept forward, suddenly reaching out to pull at the oidy-leather potion bottle tied around his neck, inspecting it closely, her nostrils flaring. "And she also gave you this bottle of her tears? The most peffa-tzorkly and precious thing a solitary white-hare witch can ever give to another?"

Matlock nodded, swallowing hard, aware the crowd was becoming bigger with every passing blinksnap.

The witch closed her eyes in thought, chewing on her bottom lip with one long and yechussly rotten tooth. "I have heard of Ursula Brifthaven Stoltz. We all have. The only hare I know that she would do such a thing to is the saztaculously brilliant and fully-gruppled Ledel Gulbrandsen." She poked Matlock hard in the ribs. "And you, hare, are clearly *not* him."

"Oh yes he is, you yechus old splurk!" Ayaani suddenly griffled, running up onto Matlock's shoulder.

The witch's black eyes widened as she took several pid-pads backwards. "You…you have…a griffling dripple? It's not possible! No dripple *ever* griffles!"

"Well, Ledel Gulbrandsen's does," Ayaani defiantly griffled. "And he also has a Most Majelicus wand, too! So stand back all of you, unless you want to be vrooshed right back to whatever glopped-up, splurked caves and hovels you came from!"

"A…Most Majelicus wand?" she gasped.

"Show them, master," Ayaani griffled as Matlock duly brandished the wand, its bright-red end already frizzing and splutting.

A peffa-oidy witch, no bigger than Matlock's paw, flew close on her broom, circling him twice and hovering right in front of his face. "Pardon me for asking," she griffled, "but aren't Arctic wizard-hares supposed to be white?"

"Erm…" Matlock griffled, trying to think of something, "…we're really only white in the winter. We tend to go brown in the summer."

"Really?" she griffled. "I never knew that. But what about your robes? Aren't they supposed to be white and inlaid with crumlush gems and silver thread? Yours just look – and really, I don't mean to be rude – but they're just, well…green and splurked."

"Ah. Yes," he nodded. "The robes." He beckoned her in closer, lowering his voice. "The thing is that sometimes being Ledel

Gulbrandsen can be – how can I griffle this? – an oidy bit glubstooled at times with so many witches recognising me and wanting to see my saztaculous vrooshers. So sometimes I dress as a clottabussed majickal-hare to avoid them."

The oidy witch smiled. "So it's a disguise?" she whispgriffled.

Matlock tapped the side of his nose twice and winked at her. "Just our secret though, eh?"

She nodded. "Would you be so kind as to do one thing for me?"

"It depends what it is."

She held out an oidy hand. "A kiss is all I ask."

"Of course," Matlock griffled, lightly kissing the back of her hand, then watching as she chickled and flew in three circles before returning to the others and griffling to them that she was now completely convinced that the glopped hare was, in fact, Ledel Gulbrandsen, a revelation that quickly spread through the excrimbly crowd, pressing in, anxious to glimpse the legendary and saztaculous hare from across the Icy Seas.

"Stay back!" Ayaani warned them from Matlock's shoulder. "Or my master will stroff you with his Most Majelicus wand!"

"But I really wouldn't mind being stroffed by Ledel Gulbrandsen," one witch griffled. "After all, he is so saztaculously-tzorkly!"

"Please everyone," Matlock tried, as the peffa-glopped circle closed in. "I really have to be going to the guzzwort tent. Ursula will be wanting her wine and…"

He got no further, gasping as he was suddenly lifted right off his feet and held aloft by the crowd, passing him above their heads from one to another through dozens of reaching, scrabbling hands, all gradually moving him towards the ganticus guzzwort tent.

"Well," Matlock griffled to Ayaani, as she clung to his chest, "at least we're not stroffed."

"Not yet," she muttered, reaching down to grab a witch's hat and fling it as far as she could while its shocked owner shrieked in rage. "But let's face it, we haven't even got the wine, yet."

In the next few chaotic moments they were carried inside the tent to be greeted by a ganticus roar from hundreds of witches. Some flew in circles above their heads, narrowly missing each other, swooping down to take a look at the two unexpected visitors. The air was thick with cheers, cackles and screams, mixed with a heady fog of burning incense, fumes from splutting cauldrons, guzzwort barrels and grimwagel wine vats.

A powerful bright green vroosher shot into the roof, instantly downing a flying witch who crashed behind the bar to yet another ganticus cheer.

"Silence!" a voice commanded from the far side of the tent, Matlock breathing a peffa-grateful sigh of relief as he was finally set back down on his feet, the hushed witches now backing away, leaving him alone in the very centre.

"Just who are you?" the booming voice asked.

Matlock turned to see a small raised platform where three witches in saztaculous green and golden robes watched intently from ornately carved wooden thrones. The witch in the centre repeated her question, beckoning him closer with her smoking green wand.

Before he could even answer, a tall thin witch rushed forward. "Please, Your Tzorkliness, this be Ledel Gulbrandsen, the most saztaculous wizard-hare in all the majickal dales!"

The throned-witch softly chickled then levelled her wand, sending out another bright green vroosher that vilishly knocked the unfortunate witch clean out of the whole tent.

This time, no one cackled or cheered.

"I shall ask you one last time," she icily griffled to Matlock. "Just who are you?"

Matlock swallowed hard, the silence as thick and heavy as the muggy atmosphere. "I'm Matlock the Hare," he quietly replied, watching the tip of her frizzing wand, eyes slightly closed, waiting for his turn to be vrooshed. "Not Ledel Gulbrandsen. I've never even met him. I don't know who he is. I'm just plain old Matlock the Hare from Winchett Dale."

A sharp intake of collectively yechus breath greeted the shock announcement.

"Then at least I applaud you for your honesty," the witch griffled, nodding slightly. "If you had continued with your ridiculous lie that you were in any way connected to Ledel Gulbrandsen, I would have stroffed you where you stood."

Matlock tried to smile, but his whiskers were trembling too much.

"You!" she suddenly cried to the others. "Be about your guzzworting and feasting! There is nothing more to see!" She pointed to Matlock. "Approach."

She clapped her hands and instantly the cacophony resumed, the witches returning the tent to its peffa-glopped chaos in what seemed like less than a blinksnap. Matlock took a deep hare's breath and pid-padded to the wooden thrones, watching as the other two witches were dismissed and stepped down from the platform, scowling as they passed him by.

"Sit," she instructed, indicating the empty throne on her left.

Matlock sat, amazed to discover that the moment he did, the only noise he could really hear was just the sound of her voice. It was if, he thought, he was suddenly sitting in some kind of invisible bubble. He could see the peffa-glopped chaos around them, but heard almost none of it.

"I'm Soriah Kherflahdle," she griffled. "Grand High Priestess of the Tzorkly Order of *The League of Lid-Curving Witchery*. It's a most splurked mouthful, so I'll not mind if you call me Soriah. Not that the favour is granted to everyone, mind. Most have to call me 'Your Tzorkliness', but frankly even that becomes a saztaculous bore after a while."

"Of course," Matlock griffled, trying to be polite and not look too closely at her red and black eyes. Her snout reminded him of a kruvel-wolf's, and he also noticed she had hooves for feet. "It must be peffa…boring for you."

She smiled, a bright green tongue suddenly darting out and licking her red eye. "So," she griffled, pointing at the potion bottle around his neck. "The rumours are true. Ursula Brifthaven Stoltz has indeed given you her eye-splashers?"

Matlock somehow found the strength to nod.

"You are twizzly because of how I look?"

"An oidy bit," he confessed.

She smiled. "The thing about having ganticus power, Matlock, is that it removes you from other creatures. They see in you what they want to see – what their fears tell them to see." She pointed at the

She smiled, a bright green tongue suddenly darting out and licking her red eye.

silent chaos in the tent. "And in exactly the same way, I simply hear what I want to hear. Each of these witches will see me differently; some as a peffa-splurked mess, some as the most beautiful and crumlushed witch they have ever known. Very few will ever see the real Soriah Kherflahdle, but Ursula is one who does. That is why she is so very special to me. She alone is truly-tzorkly, a genuine solitary hare-witch, just as I was many years ago."

"You were a white hare-witch?" Matlock frowned.

"And *still am*," she griffled, "to those of true enough hearts to actually see it. Look at me, Matlock, look peffa-closely into my eye. What do you see?"

Matlock did as she asked, trying his briftest to ignore the yechus feelings in his crimple, leaning closer and staring deep into her one red eye, putting a paw to his mouth in shock as he gradually made out a tiny figure of a white-hare in green and golden robes staring back at him. "That's really you?" he griffled. "You're trapped?"

"It's the price of power," Soriah griffled. "Creatures see you for *what* you are, not *who* you are."

Ayaani cautiously crept from Matlock's hood to stand on his shoulder, seeing Soriah for the first time. "Ursula?" she griffled. "Is that you? Nice robes. Big improvement, methinks."

Soriah reached out a clawed hand, Ayaani stepping effortlessly on, completely calm and without a single twizzle. "You see me as I truly am," Soriah griffled, nuzzling Ayaani under her chin. "But then again, Ayaani, you were always going to be the special one, weren't you?"

Matlock watched in astonishment as Ayaani happily rolled, tumbled and played around the yechus creature. "I…I still can't see you as anything other than yechus," he quietly griffled.

"It doesn't surprise me," Soriah griffled, passing Ayaani back. "Trommel was just the same in the beginning."

"Trommel?" Matlock griffled.

"The majickal-hare I once gave my own bottle of feelings to," she explained. "He saw me as just a peffa-glopped witch, but gradually came to see the real truth of what I was."

"You knew Trommel?" Matlock asked, shocked. "Baselott's master?"

"The very same," she griffled. "And not a finer majickal-hare could you find in all the dales. His only mistake was to bring that splurked hare Baselott back from The Great Beyond as his apprentice. It wasn't Trommel's fault, but it was then that the majickal order of all things began to go quite splurked. Baselott changed everything."

"He was my master's master," Matlock griffled, wondering if for just the oidiest blinksnap he'd glimpsed a long pair of white hare's ears sticking through the golden brim of her witch's hat. "He taught Chatsworth everything he knew, then Chatsworth taught me."

"I know," Soriah griffled. "I know so much about you, Matlock, things you thought no creature would ever know."

"How?"

"Once fully developed, a solitary white hare-witch's powers are the most tzorkly and majickal of them all, Matlock – but *only* if she remains solitary to her craft. If she is spends too much time with others, her powers fade. It was why I could no longer be with Trommel. I had given my feelings to him, and that was enough. His use to me was over. It is just the same for you and Ursula. Just like her, I helped Trommel complete the three tasks to become Most Majelicus, and in so doing gained great and important majickal wisdom. But once he had completed them, I never saw him again, leaving to concentrate on my own solitary studies, already knowing that one sun-turn, I would be called to the very same throne I now sit upon." She looked him straight in his hare's eyes. "The three tasks, Matlock, are simply part of the ganticus journey for a solitary white hare-witch. Beyond that, they serve no real purpose, save for you to one day become a lowly teacher to wide-eyed apprentices from The Great Beyond. It is what the *witch* learns that is so vitally important. The three tasks have peffa-little to do with the majickal-hare that is foolish enough to undertake them." She smiled at him. "After all, why do you think that so many hares stroff during the tasks? Their deaths, Matlock, are simply there to teach true solitary witches harsh lessons and majickal truths, without ever having to endanger themselves."

Matlock tried not to believe what he was hearing. "So…so I'm doing all this purely for Ursula's sake?"

"Not that she knows it yet," Soriah griffled. "She is still too young, too headstrong. But she will come to realise it in time, Matlock."

"But I could get stroffed!" Matlock objected, angrily bliffing the arm of the throne. "And for what? So that one sun-turn, Ursula can sit on a wooden-throne in a glopped-up guzzwort tent, looking all glubbstooled and yechus like you?"

Soriah chickled. "You have spirit, Matlock, I'll give you that. Many have been stroffed for griffling a lot less, believe me."

"And what about all the dripples?" he insisted. "Because if I stroff, then Ayaani stroffs, too."

"There are many things that even I don't understand, or can't begin to answer," she griffled. "Like you, for example."

"Me?"

She nodded. "You have a Most Majelicus wand and your dripple clearly griffles. None of this is right, Matlock. It's almost as if…" she thoughtfully scratched at her snout, "…almost as if…"

"What?"

She looked at him long and hard, then finally shook her head. "But no, that could never happen."

"*What* couldn't?" he pressed.

"The thing that couldn't happen," she simply griffled. "Because it couldn't. Because it would be far too peffa-splurked to even begin with."

"What 'thing'?"

She didn't answer, instead clapping her hands and summoning a distant wine-glass and bottle, Matlock watching as they sailed elegantly through the air, threading delicately between cackling witches, before finally the bottle obediently poured itself into the glass without spilling a drop. "Take us to Ursula," Soriah ordered, indicating Matlock should follow, rising from the throne and following the floating glass, pid-padding out of the tent into the mid-morning sunshine, the crowds of witches parting and bowing reverently as they passed.

"Impressive," Matlock muttered.

"Just a tzorkly parlour trick," Soriah griffled. "Nothing more."

They pid-padded on, following the wineglass past rows of

smaller tents, the occupants all vilishly rushing out to bow and curtsey, some even removing their hats.

"Sometimes," Soriah observed, "it's easy for me to believe that witches spend their lives continually fawning like this. After all, I see very little else from them."

"They clearly respect you," Matlock griffled.

"Splurked nonsense!" she bit back. "They either fear me, or want to please me to gain something for themselves."

"So you don't have a familiar, like a dripple or a dworp that you can just be friends with?"

She stopped, turned, looked at him. "I had a snupple when I was younger. It was very much like your dripple, but white, and couldn't griffle. I got rid of it."

"Why?" Matlock asked, shocked.

"Because I couldn't *trust* it," she calmly replied. "And trust is everything to a solitary white hare-witch. Everything. When I became High Priestess I knew that from that moment I would be truly solitary – without anyone, or anything I could ever trust again."

"It all sounds quite lonely, really," Matlock griffled.

She frowned. "That's because you know nothing. After all, what will *your* life be like if you ever complete your tasks and become Most Majelicus? How exciting will that be for you, Matlock, to be simply wandering around in The Great Beyond, looking for hares to train as your apprentices? Because at the end of the sun-turn, Matlock, you're just a peffa-splurked majickal-hare with a ganticus glopp-up of clottabussed friends from Winchett Dale, whom I'm assuming are making a typical gobflopped mess of running the Dale Vrooshfest at this very moment."

Matlock couldn't help but smile at the thought of it. "I'm sure they are. They're peffa-good at gobflopping. But the last thing you can griffle about them is that they're ever lonely."

"It doesn't make them any less of the joke of all the dales, though, does it?"

"No," he agreed. "But perhaps it simply makes them a happier one."

She shook her head, tutting, and they pid-padded on, passing more tents and rows of stalls selling all manner of wands, brooms, cauldrons, hats, robes, spells and quite the strangest things Matlock had ever seen. There were creatures in cages, bottles of ground chemicals, shrubs and potions being bartered and shouted over by groups of haggling witches, all eager for a bargain and the peffa-latest, tzorkly items.

But much as there was to see, Matlock's mind furiously churned with Soriah's griffles. He still couldn't believe that somehow the three Most Majelicus tasks existed simply for the benefit of solitary hare-witches – although part of him did accept that were he ever to finish them, then the prospect of actually being Most Majelicus wasn't one of the most attractive ones he'd ever encountered. He thought of Chatsworth, his master, nearing the last of his sun-turns in the dales, a hare who had devoted much of his time to simply pid-padding around in red robes, training other apprentices. It all seemed so completely dull and glubbstooled, regardless of the fact that Chatsworth hadn't even completed the tasks in the first place.

A thought occurred to him and he tugged gently at Soriah's robes. "Did Trommel have a dworp?" he asked.

She turned. "Of course."

"What was it called?"

"Xavios," she griffled.

Matlock nodded, thinking of the constellation chart he'd seen in Estrella's lidservatory, more pieces of the puzzle tumbling into his mind. "And I'm assuming that Baselott's dworp was called Flavius?"

A smile slowly spread over her face. "And now," she griffled, lightly bliffing his ears, "that splurked hare's brain of yours is finally beginning to *think*." She pointed up into the clear blue lid. "Somewhere up there are the four stars of The Great Broom – Proftulous, Marellus, Flavius and Xavios – the same names of four dworps all directly connected to you." She suddenly dropped down to his eyeline. "But the ganticus question for you, Matlock – *the peffa-ganticus one* – is *who* names dworps?"

"Chatsworth named mine when I was just his apprentice," Matlock griffled. "He called it Proftulous, after the star that's nearest to the moon."

"Indeed, he did," Soriah agreed. "But who would have *told* him to name it Proftulous? Think about it. It's just too much of a coincidence that four generations of majickal-hares also name their dworps from the same four stars in the only witch's constellation in the whole of the twinkling-lid." She leant down and whispgriffled into his ear. "I'm thinking there's a reason, Matlock, it may be tzorkly, it may be majickjal, but perhaps the *real* thing you should be looking for is the name of the hare that first decided that Trommel's dworp would be called Xavios. Because after that, it seems that everyone else simply followed suit, almost to instructions, until all four dworps were duly named – finally finishing with you and Proftulous." She looked around. "It's as if whatever was started four generations ago, whatever happened, whatever it was about – it was *always* going to end with you. You, Matlock, are perhaps the only inevitability in all of this."

"So who was Trommel's master?" Matlock griffled, desperate to know. "Because he would have started it, wouldn't he?"

"And that," Soriah griffled, "is something that *even I* don't know. Trommel was already a majickal-hare when I met him, trying to solve the riddle of Trefflepugga Path, just like when you met Ursula. We griffled of many things, but he never told me the name of his master, ever."

"You didn't ask?"

"Why would I? I was as Ursula is now; young and solitary. He was just a splurked majickal-hare that I felt sorry for. I had no interest in his life or history."

"But you gave him the potion bottle of your feelings," Matlock reminded her. "You must have felt something for him?"

She reached out a long thin hand, idly flicking and playing at the oidy leather potion bottle around Matlock's neck. "Do you really know what's inside this bottle?"

"Probably not," he quietly admitted. "I tend to get most things glopped. The more I think I know about this whole business – the whole of my life, even – the less I actually seem know about *any* of it. It's all most vexing."

"But isn't that also the most saztaculous and tzorkly thing about life – the *not* knowing?"

"Perhaps," he griffled, "provided you aren't the one being vexed. Tell me about the bottle."

She nodded. "Some witches give away their feelings to a match she knows she can spend the rest of her sun-turns with. The bottle is full of tears she has cried at the thought of never seeing her truelove again. It doesn't happen often. Most of us are quite content with each other's company, living in coverns, and going about our tzorkly business."

"But I suppose solitary white-hare witches are different?" Matlock griffled, not knowing if he really wanted to hear the answer.

"Only the *true* solitary ones," she replied. "Witches like Ursula, and many years ago, myself." She clapped her paws and glass moved on, the two of them following just a short distance behind, the crowd still parting and bowing. "We give our feelings away for very different reasons, Matlock. The bottle around your neck contains the eyeplashers of a true and tzorkly white hare-witch who will one day become High Priestess of *The League of Lid-Curving Witchery*. As such, their purpose is peffa-different. They aren't the tears of young love, and you mustn't ever confuse them as such. Ursula's tears are there to absorb your feelings, Matlock, as you undertake the tasks."

"*My* feelings?" he griffled, completely stunned.

She nodded. "Whether you are twizzly, excrimbly, fuzzcheck, glopped-up, juzzpapped, sad, lonely, russisculoffed; all those feelings will be trapped inside that bottle. One sun-turn, if you complete the three tasks, Ursula will ask for it back, then make a potion in her cauldron, mixing the eyeplashers with some grimwagel wine, before drinking it and making all your experiences a living part of her – a peffa-necessary and tzorkly part of her. It will be as if she herself pid-padded every pid-pad of the way with you. She will feel and re-live all those experiences, and they will only add to her true tzorkliness. That is the real purpose of the bottle around your neck Matlock. It serves no other."

Ayaani crept onto Matlock's shoulder, whispgriffling in his ear. "Methinks all this makes the question even'up seem like a peffa-long time ago – and frankly, far more preferable."

Matlock nodded, reaching round to lightly stoke her soft dripple's ears. He cleared his throat. "Soriah, griffle me this. What happens if I stroff during the tasks? The bottle becomes useless, doesn't it?"

The High Priestess wheeled round, flicking out her green tongue. "Far from it. To stroff is perhaps *the* most essential experience the tears can absorb. Trommel lived, and perhaps, in some ways, I regret that. I sometimes imagine how much sweeter my wine-potion would have tasted if he had indeed stroffed."

"Well, doesn't this just get brifter and brifter?" Ayaani griffled. "Now it turns out we're simply waiting to get poured into a witch's wine glass."

Soriah narrowed her eyes. "You have quite a splurked sense of humour, dripple."

"You'd get used to it," Ayaani griffled, "if you stuck around long enough, which believe me, I hope you don't. And while we're on the subject of things going glopped and glubbstooled, is there anything else we might need to know – like, we're just about to be stroffed and eaten by long, long-nosed krellits, or a mountain's going to garrumbloom and cracksplode, burying us forever, or..."

Soriah vilishly drew out her wand, its bright green end frizzing. "Enough of your griffles, you oidy splurk, or I shall vroosh and stroff you both where you stand!"

Much to her confusion, Matlock simply chickled. "And we really wouldn't stop you for a blinksnap," he griffled. "Quite frankly, after the things we've discovered, the sun-turn we've had, all the peffa-glopped and twizzly things that have happened, it might even be a relief. That way we wouldn't have to waste any more time searching for a wand that doesn't exist, worrying about being turned into wine and soupy-soupy, or wondering about why it is that somehow we're the peffa-last link in something we never even started in the first place." He turned, looked at Ayaani, who nodded at him, before both of them simply lay down on the grass, arms neatly crossed over their chests, eyes closed, smiles on their faces. "So please vroosh us. But don't be too long. I'm sure there's much brifter things a peffa-important yechus old witch like you should be doing than stroffing a mere glopped-up majickal-hare and his dripple."

Not a single watching witch dared breathe.

"Get up," Soriah quietly ordered. "Both of you."

"It's okay. We're fine down here, thanks," Matlock jovially griffled, Ayaani nodding alongside him. "Two new ones on their way to Oramus' most eternal care – here we come!"

"I ordered you to get up!" she commanded.

"Heard you the first time," Matlock griffled. "They may be long, my ears, but they do work."

"And mine," Ayaani chirped. "We're waiting and ready to go. Let's get on with it."

"If you don't get up immediately, I *will* vroosh and stroff you both!" Soriah fumed.

"Are we there, yet?" Ayaani griffled.

Two green vrooshers instantly shot from Soriah's wand, cracksploding into the ground just above their heads.

"Missed," Matlock griffled. "Please try again."

Soriah frowned, slowly putting away the wand, reluctantly reaching for Matlock's paw and pulling him to his feet. "I see why Ursula chose you," she quietly griffled. "On the one paw you are completely clottabussed and splurked, yet on the other, you have what could be ganticus courage."

"I think the two run very much paw in paw," Matlock griffled as Ayaani scrittled up his robes and back in his hood. "Now, what else do I need to know to find the Tillian Wand?"

The three of them moved off, pid-padding after the floating wineglass, the other witches returning to their tents and stalls, griffling of what they'd just seen – the splurked majickal-hare and his griffling dripple bettering their High Priestess.

And strangely, the longer they walked, the more Matlock began to see Soriah changing before his hare's eyes; her hooves gradually disappearing to be replaced by long red shoes, her hands becoming white paws, the long white ears he had glimpsed earlier now proudly jutting through the wide brim of her green and golden hat.

"I see you now," he told her. "I see you as you really are."

She turned to him, an arctic white hare-witch with normal brown eyes. "You're disappointed?"

"Relieved," he replied. "Although, because you now also look so much like Ursula, you still make me an oidy bit twizzly if I'm honest."

She smiled.

"I'm looking for a broom," he griffled. "A witch's broom that's the Tillian Wand."

"I know," Soriah griffled. "And now you want me to simply griffle to you which one of all these grillions it might be?"

He nodded.

"You *honestly* think the second task would be as easy as this? Simply to find a witch's broom?" She looked away for a snutch of moments, remembering, lost in her thoughts. "It was the one task Trommel almost stroffed on. When I drank the potion of my tears, I saw and felt all of it; his panic, his twizzliness, his confusion and sheer russisculoffedness. There were just thirteen grains of sand left when he finally bought it back to the Krettles' splurked tower. The cauldron was already boiling. Another few blinksnaps and he'd have been hare soupy-soupy."

"Where did he find it?" Matlock asked.

"It doesn't matter," she griffled. "Yours will be in quite another place entirely. And the spirit of Alvestra, the most esteemed of all witches, will always be trying to find it first. Your chances are as oidy and splurked as your dripple's nose."

"*Please*," Matlock implored her. "Just tell me which one of the brooms it is."

She just looked straight at him, not griffling a griffle, letting him work it out for himself.

"It *isn't* a witch's broom?" he slowly griffled, a sinking feeling growing in his crimple.

Soriah idly played with her whiskers as if making up her mind, then nodded at the floating wineglass. "Deliver yourself to Ursula," she griffled, clapping her paws and turning to Matlock. "Follow me."

He pid-padded after her as they made their way through another long row of stalls and tents, leaving the festival behind and making their way down to the water's edge. There, they both stood in silence for a snutch of blinksnaps, feeling the sea-breeze on their faces, watching the ganticus estuary flowing into the Icy Seas, listening to its slapping and frothing, the dulled, echoing chaos of the festival far behind them. The full moon hung silvered in the blue autumnal lid, high above their heads.

"When we witches stroff," Soriah began, "we don't pass into Oramus' most eternal care as other creatures do. We stay here, right in these majickal dales, our sprits becoming part of the landscape that surrounds us all. I myself have my hare's eyes on a distant mountain I would like to be one sun-turn. For us, there is no Oramus, or Majickal Elders, or committees, or any of the splurked things dale-creatures have. We worship nothing, save for the land and the spirit that exists in all living things. We celebrate each moment, and live within it, giving thanks merely to time and nature itself. For beyond the moment and the now, Matlock, there is nothing. We accept the order of our lives and the way things are. Yes, we have fun and sometimes drink too much wine and guzzwort. Yes, sometimes our sun-turns are splurked and sometimes they are peffa-tzorkly, but mostly it is the peffa-simplest act of just being which grounds us, regardless of how high we fly on our brooms."

"And this is what makes you 'tzorkly' is it?" Matlock asked.

She slowly nodded. "Tzorkly – in your griffles it means 'to rise above'. And so we are both tzorkly and grounded at the same time. These two essential principles shape our life and beliefs. We call it 'as above, so below', the two halves of all life itself – and this is the real secret to understanding the puzzle of Tillian Wand."

Matlock listened, watching the waves breaking on the shoreline. The tide was turning, he could sense it, already the estuary beginning to churn and froth as it met the surge of the incoming sea. "As above, so below," he griffled. "Just like the Tillian Wand. Half was thrown up into the twinkling-lid, the other half deep into the sea."

"But it is only when the two come together that you will ever find it, Matlock." She pointed up into the lid. "The moon and tides are intricately linked. Tonight's full moon will bring a ganticus tide, just as it did when Alvestra finally beat Tillian and he was washed onto the shore. Already the estuary fills and rises too fast. The seas have been flooding caves and tunnels for many sun-turns. Shortly, I shall order my witches to leave, it will be too dangerous to stay here. The festival will be washed away, the waters will run inland, every creature will have to find a place of safety."

Matlock stared at the estuary, noticing the middle now beginning to flow back on itself, the sea creeping closer, bringing bigger and bigger waves. "How glopped is it going to get?" he griffled, concerned for friends in Winchett Dale.

She turned to him, her white-hare's face deadly serious. "Matlock, we witches live in the moment. As yet, we have no spell that can griffle the future. None in all the dales."

"Then this could be most peffa-glopped," he griffled, mind racing. "If the water gets into the mirrit-tunnels then anything could happen."

Soriah nodded. "Some griffle that it has been made much worse by The Great Beyond, that they have grillions of thinking-machines that have made endless rain. Others griffle that it is all Oramus' fault, that he has left his home in the moon and does not care for them anymore. A few griffle that is merely the natural order of things, and that ganticus tides have always been a part of everything since the oidiest beginnings of time itself. But whoever is right or wrong, whatever has caused this to happen, there is nothing tzorkly or majickal we can do to stop it."

Ayaani hopped up onto Matlock's shoulder. "Right," she griffled, her oidy black eyes staring from the moon to the sea, "both of you stop griffling and just let me think." She made a series of clicks with her tongue, concentrating intently.

"No one's *ever* told me to stop griffling before," Soriah whisp-griffled to Matlock.

"It's probably better we're both quiet," he replied. "She can get quite russisculoffed if she wants to. She once put gofflelions in Proftulous' tea, and he couldn't sit down for a week."

Soriah winced.

"It seems to me," Ayaani griffled to them both, "that everything has come to this one point, this one moment, this one sun-turn. And regardless of who started what, why they did it, and what for, there are currently four stars re-aligning themselves in the twinkling-lid to form the shape of a wand with the moon as its frizzing tip, right at this ganticus high-tide. If that's true, and we can believe the ancient spuddle, then we have only found half the wand – the other still lies somewhere deep in those seas. But perhaps there's just the oidiest chance that if we can actually find it and somehow join it with the stars in the lid, then there could be just the peffa-oidiest, oidiest chance that we might just stop the glubbstooled flood from glopping up all the dales."

"Why didn't I think of that?" Matlock griffled.

Ayaani sighed. "Because you're a clottabussed glopp-up?"

Soriah was still looking far out to sea. "But it's so ganticus," she griffled. "How could you possibly search the entire Icy Seas?"

"Look," Ayaani calmly explained, "I just try and stick to the real, the rational, the here and now. It's not my job to come up with the majickal stuff." She disappeared back inside Matlock's hood. "I'll leave that to the experts."

Matlock looked towards the horizon, noticing distant storm clouds gathering, tumbling their way closer, their ganticus dark shapes casting looming shadows over the grey, chopping water. "Soriah," he griffled. "There's something you should know about Trommel."

"What of him?"

"After he stroffed, Baselott took his Most Majelicus robes and gave them to Chatsworth, my master. They lived together in a hidden burrow in Nullitt Dale, planning something. I read Baselott's diary. He talked of Trommel and how they had argued. He thought he had discovered something peffa-ganticus that he wouldn't tell anyone about. He turned his back on majick, choosing science and experiments, instead."

Soriah slowly closed her eyes, smiling. "A secret burrow, you say? And Trommel's stolen robes worn by your master?" She took a deep breath, exhaling slowly. "So much of this is *finally* beginning to make sense to me now."

"And there's another thing. I think that Laffrohn from The Vroffa-Tree Inn is involved and…"

He got no further, interrupted by a distant burst of loud, raucous cheers from behind. Screams followed, then another ganticussly loud cheer.

"Follow me," Soriah griffled. "Something's going on back there, and I don't like the sound of it. Not one splurked bit."

Before he could protest, she was pid-padding vilishly back to the festival, heading past rows of tents towards a large crowd of excrimbly witches, Matlock following as she bliffed and vrooshed her way to the front, the crowd solemnly parting to reveal Ursula stood behind a table with the stolen sack of luck.

Silence descended and Ursula awkwardly bowed, frowning as

She giggled in a way that Matlock thought was just the oidiest bit crumlush. "Well, you see, I got so bored with waiting that when the glass finally did come..." She smothered a hic-cup. "...I drank it and sent it straight back."

she realised Matlock was standing at Soriah's side.

"Ursula Brifthaven Stoltz," Soriah griffled. "Would you mind griffling to me *exactly* what's going on?"

Ursula took a large swig of her wine. "Well, at the moment," Ursula griffled, slurring, "I'm griffling to you, and you're looking all sort of splurked."

Soriah narrowed her white hare-witch's eyes. "Just how many grimwagel wines have you had, Ursula?"

She giggled in a way that Matlock thought was just the oidiest bit crumlush. "Well, you see, I got so bored with waiting that when the glass finally did come…" She smothered a hic-cup. "…I drank it and sent it straight back."

"Twice!" a voice griffled from the crowd. "That's her third she's on!"

Soriah frowned. "You should be ashamed, Ursula! This is no way for a true tzorkly white hare-witch to behave, no way at all."

"Why should I care?" Ursula griffled, trying a pirouette and falling against the side of the table. "After all, I have all the remaining luck in the world." She righted herself, lifting the heavy sack and dangerously swinging it twice round her head before clumping it back onto the table with a loud crash.

Soriah turned to the nearest witch. "What in Alvestra's name is she griffling about?"

"It be true, Your Tzorkliness," the witch griffled, pointing at the sack with a long, clawed finger. "There be all bits of green floaty luck in there. And she has a book with our names on, so you can be buying your own bit of luck, right out of the sack."

"And do you honestly believe that?"

The witch nodded, her eyes already excrimbly at the prospect.

Soriah turned to Ursula. "So what were all the screams I heard just now?"

Ursula chickled. "From witches who didn't think it was true."

She turned to the crowd. "Does *everyone* believe in this splurked nonsense?"

An oidy witch, no bigger than Matlock's knees broke through. "Not me!" it angrily griffled. "I don't believe a single griffle of it! The whole concept that somehow your luck can be carried about then sold from a sack is quite simply, utterly splur…"

A large boulder fell from the sky, crushing the witch instantly.

"Ooh," Ursula slurred, "now that *is* peffa-unlucky." She spread her arms. "So, who's for buying a bit of their luck, eh? Come on, if you've got a name, it'll be in the sack. Or buy someone else's, then sell it back to them for more than you paid! Don't delay, ladies – once it's gone, it's gone!"

"No!" Soriah commanded as the witches rushed forward, sending out a bright green vroosher that lassoed the sack and bought it straight into her outstretched paw. "If anyone needs all the remaining luck in the world then it's Matlock the Hare. Everyone else – this festival is now over! The tide is too strong and the river rising too fast. Be away on your brooms, head for the hills until the flood is over." She turned to Matlock, handing him the sack as the rest of the witches quickly dispersed to find their brooms. "I hope it helps."

He tried to appear grateful.

"What's wrong?"

"I'll tell you what's wrong," Ursula griffled, pid-padding over unsteadily. "He only ever had one piece of luck in the sack, and he's already used it. So it really doesn't matter *how* much luck there is in there, he's never going to get another piece in his mis…his mis… his mis'rable, clottabussed, safe, boring…little life!" She dropped to her knees and began chickling. "Just look at him, Your Tzorkliness – he's…he's…he's such a splurked dumfelwurbler!"

"Dummfelwurbler?" Matlock asked, turning to Soriah.

"Trust me," she griffled, "you don't want to know." She snapped her paws three times and a large wooden tankard full of a milky-green liquid flew right in front of Ursula's face. "Stop that un-tzorkly chickling and drink it!" she ordered. "You're a disgrace, and your drunken behaviour has splurked the reputation of *The League of Lid-Curving Witchery*. Think yourself lucky that you still have your hat and your wand."

Ayaani, watching from Matlock's shoulder, whispgriffled into his ear. "Methinks I rather like Ursula when she's all wine-glopped."

Matlock watched Ursula take sips from the tankard and pull the most yechus face. In a snutch of moments she began shaking her head, moaning and standing back up, suddenly seeing Soriah and Matlock as if for the first time and instantly dropping back down onto one knee and bowing, a look of embarrassed horror on her face.

"I'm so peffa-sorry, Your Tzorkliness," she griffled, the sound of roaring filling the sky as the first of the witches left the festival. "I just don't know what came over me."

"Three ganticus glasses of grimwagel wine, I suspect," Soriah coldly observed. "Enough for anyone, I would assume."

Again, Ursula apologised.

Soriah told her to stand. "I'm going to take this bag of luck to the Dale Vrooshfest in Winchett Dale," she griffled, "then try to give it to as many creatures as I can. A ganticus flood is coming. They'll need to be in the highest place possible."

Ursula nodded. "And what am I going to do, Your Tzorkliness?"

"You?" Soriah replied, smiling. "You're going to stay right here and find a tzorkly way for Matlock to search the Icy Seas. He still has a wand to find, and the way things are going, it's far more peffa-important than any of us realise."

8.

Kringle, Fellic and Drutted-Secrets

Held once every seven years, vast amounts of effort, drutts and determination go into organising each Dale Vrooshfest, the hosting dale all too aware that its reputation has never been more at stake, and that the least glopp-up will be griffled about for years to come. Careers and fortunes have been made and lost with just the oidiest success or gobflopp, resulting in sleepless nights for all concerned for many moon-turns prior to the actual vrooshfest itself.

But come the actual sun-turn, and the hosting dale nervously welcomes creatures from all other majickal-dales, all agree it's the most crumlushed spectacle to see and be a part of. A lifetime's memories can be made at just one vrooshfest as creatures regale their young with tales of contests they have seen between legendary majickal-hares, all equally determined to conjure the most saztaculous vroosher and be crowned *Briftest Majickal-Hare of All the Dales*.

And as for the prized trophy itself, a great pressure exists for the majickal-hare from the hosting dale to lift it. Much is expected of him to conjure a most ganticus, saztaculous vroosher of extraordinary complexity, colour, height and overall majikalness. Contestants are scored by a panel comprising of previous winners, Most Majelicus hares and one lone scrambling-jillott, whose job is to mostly keep the judge's niff-soup and guzzwort replenished throughout proceedings. Should there ever be a tie or dispute of any kind, then Lord Garrick, as Official Chaircreature of *The Dale Vrooshfest Committee* kindly makes himself available to be openly bribed before choosing the overall winner – a situation that has curiously occurred in each of the last four vrooshfests since he became chaircreature.

So it was with all these thoughts in his officious mind that Serraptomus set off back to the village, wheezing through Wand Wood, knowing the situation was rather unlikely to have improved since he had left Goole the singing kraark regaling a reluctant audience with one of his legendary, glubbstooled showstoppers.

He wondered just what in Oramus' name he could do to put the inevitable off much longer, how quickly Lord Garrick would come to the obvious conclusion that nothing had either been prepared or planned at all. His moans slowly became a high-pitched whine as he neared the village outskirts, the ill-tempered crowd now openly booing, hissing and jeering. Closest to him, a large group of red-robed Most Majelicus creatures were complaining of having been deliberately misdirected down the mirrit-tunnels by a clottabussed dworp, resulting in a long and unnecessary detour along Trefflepugga Path before they'd finally arrived.

Serraptomus swallowed hard, trying not to be noticed, a task he achieved reasonably successfully for the next two blinksnaps. However, on the third, he was spotted.

"It's the clottabussed krate!" someone shouted, the crowd turning and bearing down, demanding to know what was going on.

He backed away, holding up his paws, trying not to stumble. "Have...have you all enjoyed the singing?"

A fresh chorus of boos and complaints rained in as the crowd parted and Lord Garrick, a face like garrumblooming, cracksploding thunder, strode forward. "Stop right where you are, Serraptomus!" he boomed. "Explain yourself this instant!"

His mind completely panicked and glopped, Serraptomus frantically looked for an escape, then suddenly ran as vilishly as he could right through the crowd to the centre of the square to join Goole, still somehow managing to sing from under a large pile of rotten fruit.

"Goole!" he hissed. "Help me, please!"

Garrick roughly seized Serraptomus by the frayed tweed lapels of his jacket. "This has gone far enough!" he hissed. "Take us to the High Plateau right now!"

Goole poked his head through the pile of fruit. "You want another song?"

"No!" Garrick barked, bliffing the tricorn hat from the flinching kraark's head. "We've all heard more than enough!"

"Pity," Gooled mumbled. "Had a lovely one lined up all about me wooden leg. Only done it once, and it bought the house down, it did."

"Just shut that beak of yours!" Garrick snarled, turning to Serraptomus who had started to openly whine again. "I think it's about time we all went to the vrooshfest, don't you, Serraptomus?" He dropped the shaking krate onto the floor. "Lead us there, right now!"

Serraptomus stood, taking deep breaths and brushing himself down, slowly picking up Goole's hat and giving it to his friend, then holding out a paw for the grateful kraark to hold in his own wing. "Shall we?"

"Do you know?" Goole griffled. "I think we just shall."

Wing in paw, looking every inch like the strangest and most clottabussed married couple, the two friends made their way slowly back through parting crowds, Garrick insistently pid-padding behind.

"It's not often that I can griffle that the whole crowd's behind me," Goole observed, smiling. "Quite a novelty, really." He looked up at Serraptomus. "Cheer up. You look like it's your last sun-turn in the dale."

"It probably will be," Serraptomus griffled, going on to quietly explain his vrooshfest dilemma.

"Washing-up for the rest of your sun-turns in some glubbstooled committee kitchens?" Goole griffled, shocked. "It'll never happen. Winchett Dale won't let it happen. Matlock won't let it happen. He'll make everything majickally saztaculous again, you'll see."

"Slight problem," Serraptomus confessed. "Matlock's not here. He left with some snoffibs last even'up in a lid-machine. He's asked Proftulous to take his place."

"Proftulous?" Goole griffled, shaking his head. "In that case we really are glopped."

The long procession continued out of the village, the three ploffshrooms racing in front, trying their plucky best to add some jollity to proceedings as thousands of irate spectators snaked their way up to the High Plateau, anxiously awaiting the many tents and the saztaculous vrooshfest arena from which to finally settle down and enjoy the ganticus opening ceremony.

Serraptomus tried not to think about the lone table and chairs from the Winchett Dale Inn. "Where's everyone else from the village?" he discreetly asked Goole.

"Most of 'em left the moment I opened me beak," the singing kraark griffled. "I could see 'em all pid-padding away as vilishy as possible. Don't think there was a single one of 'em left by the time I got to the first chorus."

"Well, they can't be blamed for that," Serraptomus griffled. "Most of them are music lovers, after all."

They continued on, across the wooden footbridge that crossed Grifflop Marshes and began the slow ascent up onto the High Plateau, spirits amongst the ganticus crowd beginning to rise as they realised they were at last nearing the vrooshfest.

"I take it we're nearly there, Serraptomus?" Garrick called from behind. "I can't help but think it would have been much easier to have directed everyone up here in the first place."

"What with?" Serraptomus asked over his shoulder, trying to buy some time.

"Signs."

"Slight problem with that, Your Lordship. None of us can read and write, so I'm not sure how we would have made them in the first place."

"How about signs with arrows pointing the way?"

"What's an arrow, then?"

"What's an arrow?" Garrick gasped. "You clottabus! It's a sharp, pointy thing you fire from a bow to stroff things."

"Aah," Serraptomus nodded. "That's probably why we've not heard of them here in Winchett Dale, then."

The path grew steeper as it neared the flat grassy edge of the High Plateau, and there, waiting to welcome them – to Serraptomus' surprised and most ganticus relief – was Laffrohn, together with what had to be all the other creatures of the village, big crumlush smiles on each of their faces.

"What's going on?" he muttered to her.

"What's going on?" she griffled. "It be the Dale Vrooshfest, of course – in all its saztaculous and spectacular glory! There be guzzwort and feasting tents and crumlush seating and stalls and rides and all sorts of everything majickal." She pointed at the green plateau, empty save for just the lone table and chairs at the very far side. "Just look at it, Serraptomus! See the ganticus flags and bunting of many colours? See how lavish it all is? We've been sorting everything out, don't you be worrying about that."

Serraptomus squinted, trying to make out anything that could remotely be considered lavish, but just seeing a wide, empty expanse of grass. "Are you sure?" he mumbled, confused, rubbing his eyes.

Behind him, the rest of the crowd was making its way up onto the plateau, equally bewildered. "Where's the guzzwort tent?" one demanded.

The tall figure of Slivert Jutt, alone in the middle-distance, called over. "Just over here, good visitor-folk! One at a time, now. No needs to be rushing."

"But there's nothing there!" another creature cried out. "You're just stood on some grass pretending to pull a pint of guzzwort!"

Silvert was outraged by the suggestion. "I'll have none of your glopped-up griffling in my guzzwort tent!" he cried back, passing the pretend guzzwort to a Winchett Dale resident who really made a show of smacking his lips and savouring every mouthful. "You can be considering yourself last in line!"

Garrick strode purposefully over, the confused crowd following behind. "Are you the landlord of this invisible tent?"

"Indeed, I be that," Slivert replied, still pretending to pull pints and giving them to more of his Winchett Dale regulars. "But I'd be careful with your griffles if I was you. For this be no 'invisible' guzzwort establishment. Take a *good* look round. Us Winchett Dale folk can all see it, and we be from the most peffa-clottabussed of all the dales. So if you *can't* be seeing it, then that would surely make you even more clottabussed than us, wouldn't it?" He passed a pretend guzzwort to Laffrohn who sipped at it, wincing slightly.

"Slivert," she asked, passing it back, "does this be tasting an oidy bit too guzzworty to you?"

"Ooh, I not be knowing," Slivert replied, smiling as he offered it to Garrick. "Perhaps this here important and peffa-clever creature could be having a taste of it and deciding?"

"This is ridiculous!" Garrick griffled. "There's nothing there!"

"But we so very much value your opinion," Laffrohn pressed him. "And just think how peffa-glopped you'd feel to know that everyone saw you being even more clottabussed than Winchett Dale because you couldn't even see a guzzwort that be right in front of your eyes. I'd just take a sip, if I were you, and tell us what you think."

Everyone watched as Garrick slowly took a cautious sip from the non-existent guzzwort in his cupped, empty hand.

"Well?" Slivert griffled. "It be good or bad guzzwort? Only, if it be glopped, then I'd have to be closing the guzzwort tent for the whole vrooshfest."

A gasp of horror from the thirsty crowd greeted the announcement.

Garrick took a deep breath. "No," he quietly griffled. "It's… fine." He turned to Laffron, ignoring the cheers from the visitors as they quickly stampeded to the invisible bar; desperate for guzzworts to prove they weren't more clottabussed than anyone from Winchett Dale. "I take it this is your doing?"

"How so?" she griffled, pretending to be shocked.

"Because that gobflopper Serraptomus doesn't have the brains to think this one up."

Serraptomus, immensely relieved and beaming widely, appeared by his side, knocking back an invisible guzzwort in one go, before wiping his lips and slapping Garrick on the back. "Gosh," he griffled. "Really needed that! Going peffa-well so far, don't you think?"

"Let's not have a debate with me about thinking," Garrick hissed. "You've just managed to convince yourself that you've drunk a guzzwort that doesn't even exist!"

"Have I?" Serraptomus frowned, staring down at his empty paw. "Tasted slurplicioius to me. Though I sort of agree with Laffrohn, it was an oidy bit on the guzzworty-side. Still, I expect it's because it's a peffa-special guzzwort Slivert has brewed just for the vrooshfest."

Garrick ignored him, turning to Laffrohn. "And I take it all the food tents will all be exactly like this, 'conveniently invisible' to anyone who just happens to be more clottabussed than creatures from Winchett Dale?"

Laffrohn cast her eyes around the empty plateau. "I see them," she griffled. "I see all of them. And methinks they all be seeing 'em, too." She pointed towards the crowd, now beginning to go and explore the many non-existent tents and stalls, hands cupped with nothing but thin air where a guzzwort should be. Winchett Dale villagers were now happily directing visitors to the non-existent breakfast tent, where a queue was already forming, waiting for pretend bowls of niff-soup and rolls. "It'd be such a shame," Laffrohn griffled to him, "if you were the only one who couldn't see any of it."

"Oh, for Oramus' sake, this is absolutely peffa-ridiculous!" Garrick snorted, suddenly being tugged on his robes by an excrimbly fellow committee member.

"Come and see the saztaculous table and ganticus thrones they have prepared for us, Lord Garrick!" it griffled. "The legs are made of solid silver, and its top pure gold, and it has upon it the most slurpilicious and ganticus feast piled high, just waiting for us to start!"

Garrick turned to Laffrohn, sighing. "I take it this is the glopped table and chairs I saw just now?"

"Not if you're cleverer than Winchett Dale folk," she griffled, smiling sweetly.

Together, they slowly pid-padded through the excrimbly crowds to the lone table and chairs, the committee already standing behind them, ready for Garrick to take his place, pointing and drooling at all the imaginary food. Urged by Laffrohn, he reluctantly sat, looking distastefully down at the table, then pointed to some scratched griffles in it. "It says here 'Proftulous is a glopp-up!'. And it smells of guzzwort. This is clearly a table from your inn."

Laffrohn closely inspected the griffles. "*If* it did say that, then that'd be Matlock, as he's the only one from Winchett Dale that can be reading and writing, as he be their majickal-hare. But as it be a solid gold and silver table laden with saztaculous and slurpilicious food, then it really *can't* be saying that, can it?"

"You," Garrick commanded, poking the committee member on his left hard in the ribs. "Read these griffles! What does it say?"

"What griffles?"

"The griffles right here!" Garrick barked, stabbing his finger at them.

"You'll have to move that plate of culhacken-pies, first" the committee member griffled, "only I can't see a thing."

Another committee member at the far end of the table suddenly piped-up, "Culhacken-pies? Saztaculous! Pass them over here!"

Garrick watched in complete dismay as the rest of the committee squabbled over the pies, arguing over who had the biggest one and threatening each other with invisible spoons, all eagerly agreeing that it was most peffa-certainly the briftest Dale Vrooshfest breakfast feast, ever. In fact, they were so unanimous in their verdict that Laffrohn could sense the whole business was beginning to get to Garrick, who was now slowly beginning to watch invisible plates being passed back and forth, following them with his eyes, and once or twice had even licked his lips.

"Everything be to your liking?" she asked him.

He ushered her in close, whispgriffling in her ear, his voice quite confused. "Can they...can they *really* see it?"

"Can't you?" she griffled.

"I...I'm not sure."

She frowned at him, clearly not prepared to accept the least uncertainty. "Well, methinks you *have* to be sure, Your Lordship. Only you wouldn't want this committee to be realising that their chairperson be more clottabussed than Serraptomus, would you? And the longer you be taking to be making up your mind, the more folk'll begin griffling the most glopped-up things about you. So I'd be tucking in and enjoying this saztaculous feast, if I be you." She flourished a paw over the completely empty table. "See, there still be plenty left."

Garrick stared at the scratched wooden surface, drumming his long fingernails and swallowing several times before gingerly reaching out a hand and taking an invisible sandwich from a nearby plate, slowly lifting it to his mouth and taking a bite.

"There," Laffrohn griffled, satisfied. "I always knew you weren't one of the clottabussed types. Now, if you be excusing me, we have a saztaculous opening ceremony to be putting on." She happily pidpadded away, telling the rest of the Winchett Dale creatures to get everyone ready and settled at the edge of the plateau.

"How d'you think it all be going?" a long-haired disidula asked. "Is we all be fooling them well enough?"

"It be going saztaculously well, thank-you, Fragus," she griffled. "Just keep doing what I be telling you and we might just get away with it."

"It be strange to think they all be more clottabussed than us, though," Fragus griffled. "Even the Most Majelicus ones have been griffling about what a saztaculous breakfast they've all had."

"Well sometimes, Fragus," Laffrohn griffled, "'tis the creatures that you most expect to be all clever and shindinculous who turn out to be the most clottabussed. Now, did you find me that grifflelot?"

"Indeed, I be doing that," Fragus assured her, pushing forward a young creature whose entire head seemed to consist of just a ganticus hornbeak with two orange and black eyes set above it. "He be called Kringle and he be quite shy."

Laffrohn looked at the odd creature. "Shy? That's not a good thing for a grifflelot. Not a good thing at all, Fragus."

"He still be working alright, though," Fragus insisted. "Go on, give him a try."

Laffrohn reached down for one of the grifflelot's long thin arms, clasping its paw to her mouth, before turning to face the crowd, her griffles suddenly booming and ringing out over the entire High Plateau, the grifflelot's ganticus beak opening and closing in perfect time with each of her griffles. "Good creatures of all the dales! Please be taking your places for our ganticus opening ceremony which will be starting in just a snutch of moments!"

Loud cheers rang out. Laffrohn lowered Kringle's paw from her mouth. "Seems you be working pretty well, good Kringle."

"If you need me louder, just move my paw closer," he griffled. "Let's get ourselves out there and start announcing things."

"Good creatures of all the dales! Please be taking your places for our ganticus opening ceremony which will be starting in just a snutch of moments!"

A distant garrumbloom of thunder echoed far away, Laffrohn looking to the lid and noticing a dark line of threatening cloud building on the distant horizon just beginning to rise and clip the bottom of the moon. She shuddered slightly, wondering just how glopped the flood would be, how high it would come, hoping that everyone would indeed be safe up on the plateau.

"What's your name?" Kringle asked her.

She looked down at the grifflelot. "Laffrohn."

"Why are you looking all worried and twizzly?"

She tried to smile. "Just an oidy bit of nerves," she griffled. "After all, it isn't every sun-turn that I get to be the announcer of the Dale Vrooshfest." She turned to Fragus and the others, recomposing herself and issuing more instructions. Next, she took hold of Kringle's paw and pid-padded purposefully into the centre of the plateau, trying not to think how many grillions of creatures' eyes were upon her, knowing the vital and most peffa-important thing was that none of them should panic – everything must appear to be exactly the same as any other normal vrooshfest.

Which, to be fair, up until that point, had gone rather better than even she could have wished. The idea had been simple, based on Serraptomus' and Ledel's complete inability to see Proftulous for who he really was when dressed in Matlock's robes. It had occurred to her that perhaps this was the way to give everyone a saztaculous vrooshfest from nothing. And when coupled with the fact that no one ever wanted to be thought of as a peffa-glopped and clottabussed as anyone from Winchett Dale – her idea of the invisible vrooshfest was born.

It was as if she was working purely on instinct, intuition guiding her every griffle and pid-pad of the way. If she'd ever suspected that she didn't have a Sisteraculous before – now she couldn't be in any doubt. She'd lost The Vroffa-Tree Inn to the flood but was determined no one would lose anything else.

She stopped in the very centre of the plateau, looking towards the sea of expectant faces. Some sat, some kneeled, some perched, some stood in rows up to thirty-deep, creatures of every description, all keenly waiting for her griffles. She closed her eyes, griffled a short, silent prayer to Oramus then slowly put Kringle's paw to her lips, his ganticus-beak already opening in readiness.

"Majickal and most crumlushed creatures," she griffled, her voice echoing around the nearby mountains and cliffs. "I think you'll all agree that you've just witnessed the most saztaculous opening ceremony in the entire history of all the Dale Vrooshfests!"

Stunned silence greeted the announcement until the creatures of Winchett Dale began to gradually clap and cheer, stamping their feet, whooping and whistling, urging those nearest to do the same, griffling excitedly about the many and wondrous things that had just appeared in the opening ceremony that never was.

"Did you see it?" a welted spottle asked his confused neighbours. "Absolutely saztaculous! The fluff-thropp pryamid must have been the most ganticus ever!"

"How about the lid-boomers?" a disidula added. "The most ganticus and peffa-splendid I've ever seen!"

Gradually, from confused group to group, fantastic tales began to emerge as creatures tried to outdo one another with what they'd seen and what others had missed, all desperate not to appear clottabussed in any way, whatsoever.

"The singing whulp-trees were quite shindinculous!"

"That parade of leaping pond-blaarpers fair took my breath away!"

"Ah, but did you see the flying trogglewings making their ganticus griffles in the lid? Now they really were saztaculous!"

All of which – of course – never happened. But such was the state of the crowd, their desire to 'see' what wasn't there, that by the time everyone had finally finished griffling about it, all were more than satisfied they had indeed witnessed the briftest opening ceremony to a Dale Vrooshfest, ever.

Laffrohn put Kringle's paw to her lips once more. "And now," she announced, "as is tradition, will you please welcome the competing majickal-hares from all the majickal-dales!"

The three ploffshrooms dutifully scrittled over, Kringle dropping his other paw onto the grass, his beak soon amplifying their crazy rhythms right around the plateau as the crowd began to clap along, looking towards the far side where Slivert Jutt and Fragus the disidula were making a predictable mess of lining up the majickal-hares in any kind of peffa-glopped order.

A committee member rushed over to Laffrohn, a crude list in his paw. "The names of all the hares," he griffled, panting slightly. "Just read them out when they come in."

Laffrohn put on her spectacles, casting her eyes over the long list of names, stopping at one halfway down. "Why has Felic from Ceedius Dale got 'winner' written next to it?"

"Ah," he admitted, looking slightly uncomfortable. "Perhaps not read that bit out. It's Lord Garrick's favourite. Ceedius Dale have promised him a ganticus amount of drutts if Felic wins."

Laffrohn frowned.

"Saztaculous show so far!" the committee member griffled, hastily backing away. "Loved the dancing chillups! Never seen so many before in my life!"

Laffrohn shook her head, watching him leave, before signalling to Slivert and Fragus to begin the procession, a ganticus roar from the thousands of excrimbly onlookers greeting the entrance of the majickal-hares into the grassed arena, each one dressed immaculately in their green-robes, long shoes and caps, waving their wands at their own supporters, beaming broadly, their dripples all sitting proudly to attention in their hoods.

Laffrohn tried her briftest to read out the names, but such was the noise from the crowd that it was almost impossible for her to be heard, so she dropped Kringle's paw and simply watched the grand parade, part of her really wishing Matlock was amongst them, wondering just how saztaculous he would have looked, how much Ayaani would have chickled and waved, how much they would have enjoyed pid-padding amongst such distinguished, majickal company.

The hares slowly circled the entire arena, gradually lining up in the middle, facing Garrick's table. He stood and then tried to make an announcement that no one could hear. He tried again, getting whistles and boos for his efforts, as Laffrohn pid-padded over, Kringle by her side, whispgriffling to him just how to use the ganticus beaked grifflelot. Together they awkwardly lifted Kringle onto the table to face the nervously waiting majickal-hares, Garrick putting the paw against his mouth.

"I say!" a russisculoffed committee-member gasped, staring in shock at the table. "That splurked little chap has just stepped in the sandwiches!"

"Careful, Your Lordship," another anxiously griffled. "If it takes another pid-pad, it's right in the cakes!"

"And have you seen those feet?" another hissed. "They're enough to put anyone off their feast!"

"Look!" Garrick exploded, pushed to his limits. "I've had just about enough of this! There is no feast! There are no pies or cakes, or sandwiches or any sorts of *anything* on this table!" He banged it with his fist. "See? It's just a glopped-up table from their inn! It's not gold, or silver, and we're not sitting on thrones…"

Garrick stopped, as Laffrohn gently removed Kringle's paw from his mouth, the entire crowd now beginning to laugh at him, chickling uncontrollably and pointing, a loud chant of 'Garrick's more clottabussed than all of Winchett Dale!' echoing around the plateau. Hearing it, the three ploffshrooms set to, vilishly giving it a slow backing-rhythm. He turned to Laffrohn, his face quite pale. "They heard every griffle of that, didn't they?"

She nodded. "Perhaps just try sticking to introducing the contest?"

He swallowed hard, trying to think of a way out the mess, cautiously raising Kringle's paw to his mouth once more. "Creatures of all the majickal-dales!" he griffled, trying to sound as upbeat as possible. "So glad you all enjoyed my joke! But the thing about a joke is that if it goes on too long – an oidy bit like this chanting – then it can become rather peffa-glopped and boring."

The chant merely rose in volume.

He frowned, confused. "Is this working?" he asked Kringle, urgently tapping at the paw. "Only they can't seem to hear me."

Kringle shook his head.

"Please make it work," Garrick begged, as one or two of the committee now gleefully began taking up the chant themselves.

"Not until you griffle that I have the most crumlush feet in all the dales." Kringle demanded.

"What?" Garrick griffled, aghast, looking down in horror at the offending feet.

At his side, Laffrohn nodded. "Griffle to everyone that Kringle's feet be crumlush, and he'll get his ganticus beak all working again, you'll see."

Garrick hesitated, horribly caught between the ridiculous feet and the increasingly raucous crowd, several of whom were now even beginning to throw invisible bread rolls at him. "Alright, alright!" he griffled, putting the paw back to his mouth, his griffles once again booming over the plateau. "Er...please be quiet. That's it, we've all had our joke now, and I'm peffa-pleased that you all enjoyed it. But before I go on, I'd just like to griffle that..." He swallowed hard as finally the crowd settled, keenly waiting on his next announcement.

"Get on with it!" a voice called out.

Garrick tried to be as upbeat as possible. "Er...I'd just like to griffle that...that this creature has the most crumlushed feet in all the dales."

"Well, you would griffle that!" someone called out. "You're even more clottabussed than everyone in Winchett Dale!"

Garrick tried to nod in the most dignified way possible as everyone chickled at him, before beckoning the smirking creature from the crowd to the table. "What's your name?" he asked it.

"Drup," it griffled, another cheer braking from its friends.

Garrick frowned, griffling into the paw. "Well, Drup, I've no idea what you are..."

"I'm a leaning-jutter from Trollitt Dale!" Drup griffled, turning to his cheering supporters and raising a peffa-hairy fist in the air.

Garrick grimaced. "Well, I think even *you'll* agree that this creature's feet are truly crumlush and possibly the briftest feet you've ever laid your jutter's eyes on?"

Drup leant over, closely inspecting Kringle below the knee for a long moment. "Oh, that's peffa-bad luck," he finally griffled, pointing at the table. "It's only gone and stepped in all your sandwiches, hasn't it?"

At which point, deafened by the cheer, defeated by the utter clottabussedness of everything, Garrick wearily sat back down, passing the paw back to Laffrohn and scowling at his fellow committee members.

Laffrohn waited until a hushed silence finally descended. "So," she griffled into Kringle's outstretched paw, "we now come to the main event of the sun-turn – the competition to decide just who really is *Briftest Majickal-Hare of All the Dales*." She looked across at Slivert Jutt, nodding as he showed Proftulous and Ledel Gulbrandsen into the arena. "And it gives me the utmost pleasure to introduce our very own majickal-hare from Winchett Dale – Matlock the Hare!"

A ganticus roar greeted Proftulous' ragged arrival as he waved at the crowd, slowly lump-thumping over to join the rest of the majickal-hares, proudly holding his oidy twig-wand high in the air, twirling and flourishing it for all to see.

"And also," Laffrohn continued, "I would like you all to give a most crumlushed welcome to a peffa-tzorkly wizard-hare from across the Icy Seas – M*iiii*ster Ledel Gulbrandsen!"

Kringle looked up as another roar greeted Ledel's entrance. "You're quite good at this, Laffrohn. Really, I should know. I've had to griffle at some really gobflopped do's in my time."

"Thank you," she quietly griffled. "Once a landlady, always a landlady."

Ledel and Proftulous took their places at the end of the line, the other majickal-hares eyeing them suspiciously. Proftulous shifted awkwardly from ganticus foot to ganticus foot, all too aware how much bigger he was.

A hare further down the line narrowed his eyes. "Methinks you look rather like a dworp, Matlock." The hare puffed out his chest as proudly as he could. "I be Felic, from Ceedius Dale."

"Ooh," another hare griffled in admiring tones. "I've heard you're the one to beat. Do you have a truly saztaculous vroosher prepared?"

"Indeed," Felic sniffed. "And t'will be so much more than your mere ordinary vrooshers. My vroosher will be peffa-shindinculously saztaculous. A vroosher to end all vrooshers." He looked back across at Proftulous, frowning. "Are you *sure* you're not a dworp?"

"Not really," Proftulous honestly replied. "But I do be wearing the robes of a majickal-hare, don't I?"

The other hares looked across, nodding and conferring, seemingly satisfied.

Ledel stepped dramatically from behind Proftulous' bulk.

"Whilst I am wearing the robes of an Arctic wizard-hare – the first wizard-hare ever to win the Dale Vrooshfest!"

Felic pulled a face, looking Ledel up and down. "Is this allowed?" he griffled. "Artic wizard-hares at a vrooshfest?"

"There's nothing in the rules to prevent it," Ledel calmly griffled. "And perhaps it's about time a wizard-hare ruined your splurked vrooshfest, anyway."

"And what sort of wand are you using?" Felic asked suspiciously.

Ledel brandished it with a practised, expert flourish, the others all flinching slightly. "A wand made from the fallen branch of an Arctic gezzelder, thought to be the most majickal of all trees."

A low, impressed murmur greeted the announcement.

"Whereas I just be using an oidy twig," Proftulous griffled. "Only I don't think it be working all that properly. I tried it once and right gobflopped at it."

Stunned shock greeted his griffles, none of the other majickal-hares quite knowing what to even begin thinking of the ganticus hare with quite the most yechus, grinning face, proudly holding aloft what was obviously little more than a useless twig.

Moments later, Laffrohn ordered them all to wait on the edge of the plateau as the competition began in earnest, with each majickal-hare being required to pid-pad to the centre, announce his intended vroosher, then perform it as everyone watched, before finally being awarded a series of scores.

Serraptomus busied himself with officiously relaying scores from the judges to Laffrohn, trying his briftest not to forget them, repeating them over and over until he could finally griffle them into Kringle's outstretched paw. One or two, of course, he got hopelessly wrong, or forgot entirely, necessitating another wheezing trip back to Garrick's table as the waiting crowd jeered and booed.

"I told you it was fifty-three!" Garrick would hiss at him. "Fifty-three. Five and three. What in Oramus' name could be more difficult than that?"

At which point Serraptomus would only get more confused. "Making a ganticus boat out of pastry?"

"*What?*"

"It'd be more difficult than trying to remember the scores," he'd griffle. "Much more difficult. I mean, how would you cook that much pastry in the first place? The mast would be all snappy. And if you got hungry you might eat a hole in it and sink."

And then Garrick would scowl at him, resorting to bliffing the score the actual number of times on Serraptomus' head in order to get him to remember it.

However, the first few hares, it was unanimously agreed by both judges and the crowd, fell someway short of being saztaculous. As younger hares, it seemed that nerves and inexperience glopped their efforts in sometimes unintentionally spectacular style, leaving them to pid-pad miserably from the arena, trying to hold back eyesplashers and burying their heads in their waiting masters' Most Majelicus red-robes, all dreams of being named *Briftest Majickal-Hare of All the Dales* quite quashed.

The second drove, however, were clearly more experienced. As a result, the crowd dutifully 'whoo'ed' and 'aaah'ed' their superior vrooshers, breaking into appreciative pawplause for the more saztaculolus efforts. The majickal-hare from Bibble Dale managed to vroosh the entire green grassy plateau a deep shade of crimson red; the contestant from Fortwell Dale made his ears grow over ten pid-pads high by sending up a yellow vroosher that he expertly caught on his own head. However, the majickal-hare from Possolg Dale outdid them both with a vroosher that left his wand and formed the shape of a ganticus bowl of niff-soup high in the lid, floating right over the crowd, before turning to a grillion fluttering leaves and petals drifting gently down on their awed heads.

From the side, Proftulous watched nervously. He turned to Ledel. "What are you going to be vrooshing?"

Ledel put his paw to his lips. "It's a secret. What about you?"

Proftulous looked down at his twig-wand. "I don't be having any idea," he quietly griffled. "This wand is supposed to be all majickal, but I not be sure that it won't go all gobfloppy again."

Ledel took it. "Well, it *is* just an oidy twig."

Proftulous nodded, hoping in his dworp's heart that somehow Matlock had some sort of plan for all this, that he'd known exactly what would happen before he'd set off to find the Tillian Wand, and that somehow everything would be all fuzzcheck and happy for everyone in the end. Because, Proftulous reminded himself, that was how it always *had* been, regardless of how twizzly things got – somehow everything always ended up fuzzcheck, with he and Matlock enjoying brottle-leaf brews in his crumlush cottage garden, chickling about their latest peffa-glopped adventure and griffling of tweazle-pies. So this sun-turn had to be no different – it *couldn't* end up with Matlock being stroffed – it just couldn't...

"What are you thinking?" Ledel asked him.

"About tweazle-pies and happy endings," Proftulous griffled. "But I'm just not sure about this one, Ledel. It all used to be so simple and fuzzcheck, but now it all be peffa-serious and..."

Ledel reached up and put a paw around his shoulders. "Remember, we have a job to do here, Proftulous. The waters will rise and we must look after everybody."

"But why must the waters come?" Proftulous asked him. "And why can't Matlock be here? Why does he even have to be doing these glubbstooled Most Majelicus tasks? Why is *any* of this happening?"

"Tis a question for Oramus, not us," Ledel quietly replied, turning towards the heavy full moon in the clouding lid.

Proftulous looked up. "Perhaps *He* had somewhere brifter to go," he softly griffled.

"Felic from Ceedius Dale!" Laffrohn suddenly called from the centre of the plateau. "Be kindly pid-padding over and introducing your saztaculous vroosher!"

The confident hare pushed through the others, stopping by Ledel and Proftulous. "I do believe this competition already has my name written all over it," he smugly smiled.

"Really?" Proftulous griffled. "I not be realising your name was 'Dale Vrooshfest'."

Felic frowned, turning to Ledel and swirling his wand in front of the Arctic wizard-hare's face. "Shall I tell you the difference between wizard-hares and majickal-hares?"

"We're so much better looking than you?"

Felic's smile was icy-cold. "Majickal-hares have a purpose, a structure. We are chosen from The Great Beyond. We have masters and Mjaickal Elders. We have rules, majickal-systems, dworps, dripples, crumlush cottages, driftolubbs and a community of peffa-grateful creatures that respect us utterly, knowing our place in the history of their dales is so much more majickal than theirs will ever be. We are the backbone of these dales, Ledel Gulbrandsen, whereas you wizard-hares are little more than an occasional amusement that live in barren icy-wastelands amongst peffa-glopped witches, snow and little else."

"But they also be wearing saztaculous robes," Proftulous griffled, pointing at Ledel. "Just look at his, compared to yours. They're right crumlush."

Felic scowled as Proftulous and Ledel cheerfully waved him away, watching him pid-pad into the middle of the plateau and thrust Kringle's paw to his mouth. "Good creatures of this saztaculous Dale Vrooshfest," he brightly announced, all smiles. "I be Felic from Ceedius Dale, and I will be perfoming my very own saztaculous vroosher that I call 'the peffa-garrumbloomer!'"

"Whooo!" the crowd good-naturedly gasped.

"Now I need you all to be standing well back, as when this vroosher goes off, it really is peffa-ganticus!"

"Is this safe?" Laffrohn asked him, becoming concerned. "We're not about to all be cracksploded and stroffed, are we?"

Felic slowly turned, looking at her as though she was something glopped he'd just stepped in. "I do beg your pardon? Do you even *know* who I am?"

Laffrohn raised her eyebrows, tutting as she led Kringle to safety.

Felic, it should be griffled at this point, had always been annoyed that Trefflepugga Path hadn't chosen Svaeg Dale for his home, complete with its many lavish halls and outdoor arenas, the peffa-perfect dale for a hare of what he clearly thought were his saztaculous abilities. For Ceedius Dale, while being a mostly harmless dale, just didn't quite have the same amount of 'fuzzchecked-pezazz' for a hare like Felic, who had recently taken to trying to stage great shows for all the residents, complete with saztaculous vrooshers and solo dance routines that he combined into what was probably one of the first majickal-spectaculars of its time – primarily consisting of some glopped-dancing, woeful vrooshers and a loose storyline featuring himself as hero. And whilst the creatures of Ceedius Dale had become understandably bored of Felic's shows, he knew all too well that a truly spectacular performance and the coveted crown of *Briftest Majickal-Hare of All the Dales* would be enough to secure him a permanent spot in one of the larger outdoor arenas in Svaeg Dale, the ultimate home for any creature with even the oidiest showbusiness ambitions.

However, as he proudly stood before the silent, expectant crowd, the one thing Felic *didn't* know was that he had only been made favourite to win because the residents of Ceedius Dale had secretly promised Lord Garrick a substantial pile of drutts to ensure he did, all too peffa-keen that Felic leave their dale forever, desperately hoping their bribe was suitably ganticus enough so they'd never have to endure another of his gobflopped, majickal-saztaculars ever again.

All of which had now placed Garrick in a rather awkward position. Well used to receiving huge bribes for favours granted, the matter of deciding the winner of the Dale Vrooshfest was sometimes an oidy bit trickier to fiddle, something he quickly realised as soon as he saw Felic in the centre of the plateau doing what could only be remotely described a some sort of elaborate dance that frankly, all felt dreadfully embarrassing.

He beckoned Laffrohn over. "Are you sure this is Felic from Ceedius Dale?" he quietly asked, frowning as he discreetly looked at his list.

She nodded. "The peffa-same. The one that you wrote 'winner' next to."

Garrick looked back over at the glopped-jigging figure, blew out his cheeks and sighed. A slow paw-clap had begun around the arena, with several creatures already beginning to openly heckle.

"You be alright, Your Lordship?" Laffrohn asked. "Only you've been gone awfully glopped and pale."

"I foolishly wondered just how much worse this sun-turn could get," he griffled miserably, watching as Felic began turning cartwheels that clearly needed a lot more practice. "I think I know, now." He turned to her, his eyes almost pleading. "What am I going to do? He's absolutely peffa-awful! The crowd hate him. How can I *possibly* make him the winner?"

Laffrohn watched Felic for a snutch of moments, frowning,

she too wondering just what it was the badly-dancing hare was even trying to do. "Perhaps," she quietly griffled, "you should be thinking about giving the bribe back?"

"But I can't," Garrick moaned. "I gave it to my cousin to buy a ganticus guzzwort tent for the Estuary Festival. I don't have the drutts any more."

Laffrohn looked towards the increasingly threatening skies. "Then I be guessing that in a short while you won't be having the tent, either. There's a ganticus flood coming that'll start at the estuary. It'll all be washed away and gone."

"A ganticus flood?" Garrick whispgriffled, getting twizzly. "Will we be safe?"

"As long as we all stay here on higher ground," she replied, "and no one gets twizzly. We all simply has to be calm until it rides out."

Garrick was lost for griffles, looking from the distant dark clouds, then up into the clear blue lid above, muttering to himself. "This is true?"

She nodded.

He stood. "We need to find somewhere to griffle."

She led him from the table and through the jeering crowd, all increasingly unimpressed with Felic's frantic efforts.

Garrick spotted a small tent, away from the others, holding the heavy canvas open, just the two of them slipping inside. "What are you laughing at?" he griffled, confused. "This is clearly a peffa-serious situation."

"You," she griffled, chickling. "Holding a tent like that, when clearly it just be thin air – there's nothing here."

He threw up both arms, looking round and seeing just the nearby crowd and sky. "It's been a long and most confusing sun-turn."

"And it be far from over yet," Laffrohn griffled.

He studied her closely. "Just *who* are you, anyway? You're clearly not from Winchett Dale."

She took his arm, pid-padding by his side, away from the arena towards the very edge of the plateau where it looked out over the rest of Winchett Dale. "I be Laffrohn, landlady of The Vroffa-Tree Inn."

He raised his eyebrows. "I've heard of it. A secret inn that exists deep below the ground, floating on a lake and only used by Most Majelicus creatures. I've always thought it was some kind of a spuddle. But it really exists?"

Laffrohn took her own moment to reflect. "Not any more," she griffled. "The waters rose too fast. Now she lies at the bottom of the lake and the mirrit-tunnels underneath us are vilishly flooding."

Garrick looked around. "It's so hard to believe. It's all so peaceful up here."

"'Tis a peffa-different story down below," she griffled. "Do you even know what mirrit-tunnels are?"

He shrugged helplessly. "I'm just the chaircreature of a glopped-up committee. I might have been told at some point, but frankly, I probably wouldn't have been listening."

Laffrohn nodded, well able to believe his griffles. "Mirrits are born from the extrapluffs of majickal-hares, said to be given to them as moments of majickal inspiration by Oramus *Himself*. Mirrits themselves are peffa-oidy, and most glopped, with all yellow, magotty bodies and just the oidiest, oidiest legs. Once born however, they make their way to the nearest tunnel entrance, there to join the others, scrittling deep down inside and eating away at the earth, making the tunnels bigger and bigger." She pointed out over the crumlushed green landscape. "There be tunnels everywhere, some as old as time, interconnecting and extending right under all the majickal dales, and only able to be used by Most Majelicus creatures. Some folk griffle that the tunnels were Oramus' way of ensuring that rich veins of majickal goodness run right through the heart of all the majickal dales. But with them flooding so fast, 'tis almost like all that goodness is going, too."

"What are we to do?" Garrick asked.

Laffrohn took a breath. "This sun-turn has been coming for a peffa, peffa-long time. Many years ago, a Most Majelicus hare called Baselott stumbled upon it, by the way of all his science and reading researches. He came to me at The Vroffa-Tree Inn, and we griffled long into the night, wondering just what we could do to avoid the peffa-glopped tragedy. He had studied the stars and the moon, lidgazed at the possibilities, consulted his tidal charts and was able to predict the precise sun-turn the flood would occur and the ganticus tide would sweep everything away."

"And it's today?" Garrick weakly griffled.

Laffrohn nodded. "We needed a plan – a truly peffa-ganticus one – to somehow be ensuring everyone was safe. And this is where Oramus must have helped us, as we realised the date would fall on the exact same sun-turn as the Dale Vrooshfest, the one occasion where nearly every creature gathers in the same dale. Baselott checked and rechecked his calculations to be absolutely certain.

"Next, we had to be finding a dale that could host so many creatures in a high and safe enough place. We travelled all over, using the mirrit-tunnels, visiting each dale in turn – until we came here, Winchett Dale, and saw this High Plateau, knowing that at last we had found it, the safest place for such a ganticus number of creatures." She smiled at him. "After that, it was simply a matter of making sure the committee chose Winchett Dale to host the vrooshfest. Which of course, you did."

Garrick frowned. "I…I was *forced* to chose Winchett Dale?" he asked, shocked. "You majicked me in some way?" He remembered Serraptomus standing in front of him, making his peffa-glopped boasts about todel-bears, the entire committee shocked that Winchett Dale would even consider themselves a suitable host, let alone send their krate along to present their case.

He looked at Laffrohn. "Did you know that Winchett Dale once threw a pie at a tree simply to see what noise it made? That's how truly clottabussed they are."

She smiled. "But *you* still chose them, didn't you, Garrick – even though you knew it was a completely glopped decision and the entire vrooshfest would be one enormous gobflopper."

Garrick coloured slightly, clearing his throat. "I seem to remember," he quietly griffled, "that we were all bored and hungry. Serraptomus promised all would be saztaculous, so we gave him a chance and retired to our feasting."

Laffrohn narrowed her eyes. "And you *honestly* expect me to believe that? You may be greedy, but you be far from clottabussed like the rest of your glubbstooled committee. You already knew you were going to award the vrooshfest to Winchett Dale before Serraptomus even puffed and wheezed his way into that room. And

I'm willing to be betting that a truly ganticus bribe lies at the heart of it."

Garrick said nothing, trying his briftest to look shocked and innocent.

"So what I be looking for right now," Laffrohn slowly griffled, her voice deadly serious, "is a name. Who was it? Who bribed you to choose Winchett Dale?"

Garrick swallowed hard.

Laffrohn sighed. "Of course, I could be making this peffa-simpler, and simply be pid-padding back into the arena and be griffling to everyone just what a greedy glopp-up you are."

"You wouldn't do that," Garrick griffled, getting twizzly. "Would you?"

She merely nodded, her face stone.

He rubbed at his face then began scratching his palms for no reason.

"I could be counting to five," Laffrohn griffled, turning to go, "but frankly, it would be a muchly waste of my time. Methinks I'll just pid-pad over there now and let Kringle's paw do the rest."

"No! Wait!" Garrick called, lowering his voice to an urgent whispgriffle. "I'll griffle you the name, just...just please don't griffle to *anyone* that I told you."

She looked into his greedy, pleading eyes, nodding slowly.

"It was Baselott," he quietly griffled, the fight gone. "The Most Majelicus hare you griffled of earlier."

Laffrohn nodded, betraying nothing.

Garrick swallowed. "He came to me some years ago, griffling to me that Winchett Dale would have to host the next vrooshfest. Well, I laughed at him, didn't I – chickled right in his hare's face. The idea was just so...peffa-clottabussed."

"But then he offered you a ganticus pile of drutts, and you suddenly be changing your mind?"

He let out a breath, nodding slightly, steepling his fingers either side of his long nose. "It was truly ganticus, Laffrohn – *peffa*-ganticus – more drutts than I'd ever know what to ever do with. I'd be the richest creature in all the dales." He looked at her. "Why are you chickling at me?"

"Because drutts are just oidy pebbles. They're not worth anything. Baselott played you for the greedy fool you are – and won."

He narrowed his eyes at her. "But this is where you're so wrong, Laffrohn, despite your chickling."

"Go on."

"Because I had so many drutts – they *became* worth something, don't you see? I was able to flood them into other dales and places where they'd never even heard of drutts – I was able to change things. When creatures wanted more drutts, they came to me and did whatever I asked of them. I went from being a humble chairperson of a glopped-committee into one of the most powerful creatures in all the dales."

Laffrohn tutted, shaking her head. "And because of these pebbles, you chose Winchett Dale?"

"It was peffa-easy," he admitted. "The rest of the committee are fools! You've seen them, eating invisible feasts and drinking pretend guzzworts, all because you've convinced them that somehow they're real." He suddenly reached into his robe, pulling out a small round pebble. "You see this drutt? It's *exactly* the same trick, Laffrohn. To you or me, it's just an oidy pebble – but to them," he pointed towards the baying crowd, "to those glubbstooled gobflopps – they're *drutts*; things they must have, things they cherish and desire."

Laffrohn needed to know more from the greedy chaircreature. "And what else did Baselott ask you to do?"

He swallowed again, caught. "What else?"

"'Tis a ganticus amount of drutts, simply to be awarding the vrooshfest to Winchett Dale. Remember, of all the dale creatures, I knew Baselott better than most. And while I know he wanted us all to be safe from the flood – that reason alone isn't enough. You're clottabussed and greedy, you would have awarded the vrooshfest to Winchett Dale for a tenth of the amount. Baselott was scientific, he thought *everything* through. There was always more than one reason for anything that he did." She looked Garrick hard in the eye. "What else did he ask you to do for him? What was his *real* reason for visiting you that sun-turn and giving you all those drutts?"

"It...it...was just something peffa-oidy," Garrick stumbled.

"Something...peffa-ordinary and quite insignificant."

"What was it?" Laffrohn growled.

Garrick swallowed hard. "He griffled to me..."

"Get on with it!" she barked, making him jump. "Remember, I be a landlady for far longer than you've been taking bribes, so if you want to be seeing just how I deal with a ganticus creature who's been having too many guzzworts in my inn – go ahead and try me! Either that – or get griffling!"

Garrick yelped. "It was just some oidy papers!" he cried, anxiously looking round and dropping his voice. "Thirteen pieces of parchment. He griffled to me that they would be delivered to me after he had stroffed, and I was to look after them, safely under lock and key."

"The revisions," Laffrohn whispgriffled, taking a slow breath. "His revisions to *Majickal Dalelore – Volume 68*."

"I've no idea what they are," Garrick griffled. "They're still rolled and sealed, just as they were when the other Most Majelicus hare first gave them to me."

Laffrohn nodded, deep in thought, trying to understand, dissecting each new bit of information, weighing it against those she already knew, some she suspected, and others that always been just the darkest, most distant possibilities. "He was Most Majelicus, this other hare? Are you sure?"

"He wore the red robes. He griffled that his name was Charlesworth, or something."

"Chatsworth," Laffrohn quietly nodded, another ganticus piece of the puzzle dropping into place.

"You're...you're not going to griffle about this to anyone, are you?" Garrick begged.

She looked at him, her mind made up. "Not if you be doing two things."

"What are they?"

"Firstly, you be griffling to me exactly where the thirteen pages are."

"Locked in my desk," he griffled. "In my study. Still untouched, from the even'up I put them there."

"Where be the key?"

He frowned, reaching back into his long robe pocket, bringing out a large bunch of blackened iron keys jangling on a thick, round ring…

He frowned, reaching back into his long robe pocket, bringing out a large bunch of blackened iron keys jangling on a thick, round ring, taking her slowly through them, one by one, griffling which doors they opened. "And this," he griffled, holding the oidiest one, "is the key to my desk. The drawer is underneath. The rolled-up papers are inside."

Laffrohn nodded, satisfied, taking the keys.

"And the second thing I've got to do?" he griffled.

She looked back at the ganticus circle of jeering creatures. "For once in your life, you're going to be acting like a chaircreature of *The Dale Vrooshfest Committee*. You're going to be getting off that greedy, bribed, well-feasted backside of yours and make sure that no one gets twizzly when the floods all be coming."

"Me?" he griffled, horrified, going quite pale. "What, you mean – actually *do* something? On my own?"

She put a paw on his shoulder, smiling sweetly. "Oh, I think you can be managing, I really do. Just think how the history-books will play this out." She bliffed him lightly in the ribs. "You never know, Garrick, you might just turn out to be a hero in the making – one that simply lost his way for a while chasing piles of worthless pebbles."

"And what will you be doing?" he sourly asked.

"Me?" she griffled. "I'm about to take the last remaining vroffa-tree and ride it like the wind to find those thirteen missing pages. Because if I be right, there's a peffa-injustice about to be done – one that I might have even played a part in, myself. And as sure as my name be Laffrohn, landlady of The Vroffa-Tree Inn, then right at this very blinksnap there's an ordinary, glopped-up majickal-hare named Matlock that needs all the help I can be getting him."

She pid-paded away, then stopped and suddenly turned, calling back. "Because if he does be finding the Tillian Wand, it might just save the sun-turn for all of us!"

9.

Ayaani, Eyesplashers and Garrick's Castle

"The way I see it," Ayaani griffled, sitting in the middle of the three thrones in the Estuary Festival's abandoned guzzwort tent, "if these really *are* to be my last few hours in the dales, then there'd be worse places to spend them." She looked at Matlock and Ursula's sullen faces on either side. "Mind you, I could think of some brifter company to share them with."

Matlock turned to her. "We may be sat in thrones, but we're hardly feeling as regal as you, Ayaani."

She stood, but instead of scrambling into Matlock's hood, climbed down and scrittled across the glopped-grass. "Methinks you two need to do some griffling," she announced, "while I try and think us a way out of this peffa-glubbstooled mess." She scrittled outside, the first heavy drops of rain already beginning to fall, the full waters of the estuary rising dangerously higher on the bank with every blinksnap.

Inside the empty tent, Matlock decided to break the silence, not really knowing what to griffle, yet sensing in his Sisteraculous that Ayaani, in her usual dripple'd way, was all too right; things needed to be griffled about, grievances aired, explanations given. "Listen, Ursula…"

He got no further as she rounded on him, staring across the empty throne between them. "How could you? How *could* you?" She pointed a white paw accusingly. "I send you to do one thing for me – just *one* peffa-oidy thing – but could you do it? Oh no! Instead of bringing me a glass of grimwagel wine, you – the peffa-splurked Matlock the clottabussed hare from Winchett Dale – *you* decide to bring back *The Grand High Priestess of the Tzorkly Order of The League of Lid-Curving Witchery!*" She narrowed her eyes. "I have *never* been so embarrassed in all my life!"

"I didn't intend to," Matlock griffled, shocked at the force of the outburst. "I went to get the wine, then Soriah and I got griffling, and…"

Ursula's eyes widened. "*Soriah?*" She shook her head. "You're on first-name terms with the most peffa-powerful and tzorkly witch in all the majickal-dales?"

He shrugged. "I suppose so. She said it would be quicker than addressing her by her full title. She seems quite fuzzcheck once you get to know her."

"Quite fuzzcheck?" Ursula gasped, outraged. "*The Grand High Priestess of the Tzorkly Order of The League of Lid-Curving Witchery* is now 'quite fuzzcheck'?"

"Reasonably," Matlock griffled. He folded his arms across his chest. "She told me a lot of interesting things," He nodded at the empty throne beside them. "For instance, that one sun-turn, you'll be sat right here."

Ursula threw back her head and tutted. "I can assure you there will be no such thing happening."

"She's a solitary white-hare witch, just like you. She sees something in you and thinks you'll be the next Grand High Priestess."

"Tchoh! That is splurked nonsense!"

Matlock tutted. "You would call her a liar?"

Ursula rounded on him. "No! I call *you* a liar, Matlock, for making it all up!"

Matlock drummed his paws on the arm of the throne. "Bet you'd like to sit in it, though, wouldn't you? See how it's going to feel?"

"I will do no such thing," she insisted. "It would be most disrespectful and peffa-splurked."

"Ayaani did," Matlock calmly griffled.

"Yes, and that is because she is just as splurked and disrespectful as you are!"

Matlock knew he shouldn't get too russisculoffed. He wanted to, but losing his temper would only use up more of his peffa-valuable and vilishly disappearing heartbeats. And after all he'd learned about the true nature of the oidy-leather potion bottle, the last creature he was going to waste any of his precious heartbeats on was Ursula Brifthaven Stoltz.

Instead, he slowly walked to the middle of the empty tent, composing his thoughts, then turned, noticing she had indeed quickly changed thrones and was now sitting in the middle, running her paws along its arms, eyes closed, an oidy contented smile on her face. "I remember when we first met," he griffled, "and you pid-padded into The Vroffa-Tree Inn as I began my journey to solve the riddle of Trefflepugga Path."

She slowly opened her eyes. "So?"

He half-smiled, quietly chickling to himself.

"What is so funny?"

"You," he griffled. "And me."

She leant forward. "There is no 'you and me', Matlock."

"I know," he griffled. "At least, I know that *now*, after Soriah told me about the real purpose of the potion bottle you made me wear around my neck that very same night."

She narrowed her eyes. "And just what did she griffle to you about it?"

"Things," he griffled. "Things I wish I hadn't heard, frankly. Things that made me feel even more of a glopped-up clottabus than I already am." He untied the bottle, pid-padding back over. "I foolishly thought that these eyesplashers meant that I might have meant something to you."

"Well, then you are a splurk and nothing more."

Matlock ignored her. "When a true solitary hare-witch gives away her tears, it is always to a hare undertaking the three Most Majelicus tasks. The eyesplashers inside this bottle are simply there to absorb my feelings, Ursula. They're not about your feelings at all." He shrugged. "All this time I thought it meant something else, but really it's just a tzorkly trick so that you can re-live my feelings as I struggle to complete the tasks." He threw the bottle high in the air, catching it at the peffa-last blinksnap, watching closely as she flinched. "Look at you, so worried they might break and spill, and all the experiences and memories would be lost. And do you know what else she told me?"

Ursula stared blankly back, her white hare's face vilishly reforming into a mask of calm disinterest.

"She griffled to me that the *peffa-briftest* feelings – the most sought-after and saztaculous ones – are those where the majickal-hare stroffs. If those tears are drunk then the solitary white-hare witch gains the most ganticus amount of tzorkly wisdom and experience. They're highly prized. I suspect you could even sell some to your yechus friends. After all, they seemed quite keen on the luck thing, didn't they?"

Still, she griffled nothing.

"Right now," Matlock tried to smile, "things aren't exactly looking all that fuzzcheck for me. Chances are and peffa-high chances they are too – that Ayaani and I might very well be stroffed on this task. But I'm sure you'll find a way to collect your bottle from the Krettles once I've been made into hare soupy-soupy. In fact, I wouldn't be surprised if they didn't already have some sort of collection service for witches. I wouldn't put it past them, they seem peffa-well organised. And then you can simply ride away and mix it with your wine and drink them right down and discover exactly how it felt in those final few blinksnaps before I fell into their splutting cauldron."

"Why do you look at me in this way?" she quietly asked. "You're making me twizzly."

"And afterwards," Matlock continued, "you and this Ledel Gulbrandsen that I've heard so much about can ride off together into the sunset and..."

"Just be quiet!" she hissed at him. "No more of your griffles! You have nothing to be jealous of Ledel about."

"Jealous?" Matlock griffled, laughing. "I'm not *jealous* of him! I feel sorry for him! I barely know you, and yet you are one of the coldest hares, ever. To even imagine a lifetime with you would be completely glubbstooled!" He pid-padded over, holding the bottle out to her, trying to level his voice. "Here. Take it. Give it to another clottabussed hare just starting the three tasks. I'm sure you'll find plenty of eager volunteers."

She reached out, reluctantly taking the bottle and tying it round her neck, watching in silence as he pid-padded from the tent.

"So," an oidy voice griffled, "I'm guessing that it probably didn't go quite as well as expected? No hug between friends and the pair of you happily setting off to search the Icy Seas together?"

"No, Ayaani," Ursula quietly griffled, lifting the dripple into her lap and stroking her soft head. "It didn't."

"The thing about Matlock," Ayaani griffled, "and I've known him for quite a while, so please, trust me on this, is that although you couldn't ever really call him a saztaculous majickal-hare, he is quite caring in his own sort of glopped-up way."

"Then that makes him a splurk," Ursula griffled. "To be caring is to be trusting. Creatures take advantage."

"Just as you did, with your bottle of tears?"

"Of course. It is the way of a true solitary tzorkly white-hare witch. We trust no one, so we are never disappointed."

Ayaani let out a low whistle. "Sounds like fun, every pid-pad of the way."

Ursula frowned, then shrugged. "Too much is griffled about 'fun'. Fun is not tzorkly. It is for leverets and splurks."

Ayaani chickled. "You looked like you were having fun when you were selling all the luck."

"Nonsense! I was simply having too much wine, which was all Matlock's fault because he left me alone too long, whilst he was griffling to…" She suddenly stopped, frowning and shaking her head in disbelief. "It *can't* be right. It just can't."

But Ayaani nodded. "Oh, yes it is," she griffled. "However truly solitary you think you are, you still needed Matlock to get you your grimwagel wine. And then you even became russisculoffed when he took too long. All rather peffa-untzorkly and un-solitary, methinks."

"It didn't happen like that," Ursula whispgriffled.

"It did," Ayaani assured her, scrittling up to her neck and untying the oidy leather potion bottle. "Sometimes, methinks all this 'solitary' business is peffa-glopped." She gently placed the bottle into Ursula's paws. "And I also think it's about time you poured these tears away."

"But why?"

Ayaani studied her face for a snutch of blinksnaps. "Because I think that in just a snutch of blinksnaps, you might well get eyesplashy again. But this time they will be real tears, not ones to simply absorb the feelings of a clottabussed majickal-hare."

"And why would I be about to eyesplash?" Ursula griffled, trying to stay composed. "It would be... most splurked."

"Because," Ayaani told her, "perhaps you've realised the difference between being lonely and being solitary." She jumped back onto the glopped-grass. "Matlock might well be a splurk, but he's also a splurk I'd never be without. If you wish otherwise, then it's up to you. I suppose that would make you truly solitary. But from what I saw of your High Priestess, she didn't look too happy with the life she'd chosen. Having a wooden throne may be one thing – but methinks having a friend is quite another."

And with that, she left, scrittling back out of the tent, senses completely alert, looking for her master, finding him a short distance from the estuary bank, staring out to sea, the rising waters already beginning to soak his long purple shoes.

"I'd move back, if I were you," she called out to him.

"Well, you're not me," he griffled, back turned.

"And thank Oramus for that," she griffled. "As I'd have a peffa-hard job of making everything quite so glopped as you do."

He turned. "Is this why you've come? To make me feel even more of a gobflopper?"

"Partially," she admitted. "Although there is some method to it."

"Well, I'd really like to hear that."

"You will do," she griffled, "as soon as you pid-pad over here and get your clottabussed feet out of the water."

Matlock looked down, seemingly seeing the water lapping around his shoes for the first time. "I hadn't even noticed."

"Well, that doesn't surprise me. You're the last majickal-hare to ever really notice anything."

"Harsh," he griffled.

"But fair," she replied, watching him pid-pad up the gently sloping bank, before reaching down to put her in his hood as he always did. This time, however, she stopped him, vilishly brushing aside his outstretched paw. "Just sit down," she ordered, her oidy dripple's face set and serious. "This has to be griffled face to face, and you're going to listen to me without griffling another griffle."

He reluctantly sat on the damp grass.

"I have known you for so long," she began, "and in all that time you've never even stopped to wonder why it was that I chose you in the first place, why I determined that I would spend the rest of my sun-turns with you."

"Because I was born on the exact same sun-turn as you were," he griffled. "It wasn't as if you had a lot of choice, really. We were destined to be together from the very first sun-turn of our lives."

She tossed back her head, throwing her eyes to the lid and tutting. "Think!" she scolded him. "We dripples *choose* the majickal-hare we want as our master. Once, I had the choice of every majickal-hare in these dales, but still I went for a glopp-up like you. I'm clever, resourceful, cutting, and at times even quite fuzzcheck. What in Oramus' name would have ever persuaded me to choose *you*?"

"What do you mean?" he frowned. "It was just the way the sun-turns of our birth fell."

"No, Matlock," she griffled, her oidy black eyes boring into his "This was no accident or coincidence. You see, I *chose* to be born on the exact same sun-turn as you. 'Tis simply how it works. We dripples make our choices a long time before you hares are even a twinkle in your mahpa's eye."

His eyes widened. "You *knew* when I was going to be born?"

She nodded. "To the exact same sun-turn."

"But how?"

"They have a list," she simply griffled, pointing into the raining lid. "Up there."

"A list?" he griffled, astonished. "A list of hares yet to be born?"

"And your name," she told him, her voice deadly serious, "was the *last* one on it."

He frowned, trying to understand the full implications of what she'd just griffled.

"You, Matlock," she slowly explained for him, "are the last of the majickal-hares. They stop with you. Everything stops with you."

He let out a ganticus breath, pinching the end of his nose, frowning and trying to take it all in.

"It's the real reason I chose you," Ayaani griffled. "There were simply no other names left. All the others had gone. As the last dripple, I had no choice. I *had* to choose you."

He slowly turned to her, his voice shaking. "So it all ends with us?"

She looked out at the grey churning seas for a while, the light winds gently ruffling her fur. "What I'm saying," she griffled, "is that knowing what you now know – knowing that you are the last of the majickal-hares – perhaps you might not act like such a sulky clottabus for once, and go back into that guzzwort tent and ask Ursula peffa-nicely to be your friend again. After all, what do you possibly have to lose?"

Matlock rubbed his face, muttering and nodding to himself, before finally standing. "You're right, Ayaani," he griffled. "I have been a clottabus about this. A peffa-clottabus. She's my friend, and I've been a glopp-up to her."

Ayaani nodded.

"And I will go back in there and griffle to her how much I value her friendship." He began purposefully pid-padding through the rain.

"Wait!" Ayaani called. "You can't just go pid-padding straight back in there without knowing what you're going to griffle! You know what she's like. The wrong griffles, and she'll most probably vroosh you into some sort of gobflopped creature for ever!"

He thought for a moment, recalling Ursula's skill with the wand, flinching slightly.

"Give me just a snutch of blinksnaps with her, first," Ayaani griffled, trying to be reassuring. "I'm sure I can pave the way for you."

"You'd do that for me?" Matlock asked. "Even though I was the last majickal-hare on the list?"

"It hasn't *all* been glubbstooled," she smiled. "Once or twice, we've even had an oidy bit of fun on our adventures, haven't we?"

He nodded, smiling back.

"Just give me a snutch of blinksnaps, then you come in," she instructed. "Be confident, and be bold." She scrittled away, darting vislishly back inside the tent where Ursula still sat in the wooden throne, lost in thought, the potion bottle held tightly in her paw.

"Why are you here?" she asked, staring down at Ayaani. "Haven't you chickled at me enough?"

Ayaani scrittled up onto the wooden arm of the throne, grinning widely, and pointing to the opening of the tent, trying to control herself, her oidy paws jumping on her furry crimple with each chickle.

"Enough of this!" Ursula snapped. "Leave me now. Go back to your splurked master. I have no need for either of you, ever!"

Ayaani shook her head, reaching over and placing her oidy paw on Ursula's arm. "No wait, please," she managed to griffle. "This is going to be saztaculous! I've been telling Matlock a little spuddle."

Ursula narrowed her eyes. "A spuddle?"

Ayaani nodded. "He thinks he's the last ever majickal-hare. Honestly, he believed every griffle! He's going to pid-pad in here in a snutch of blinksnaps and ask you to be his friend again like a peffa-clottabussed glopper! It'll be saztaculous!"

"But," Ursula griffled, confused, "you've lied to your master?"

Ayaani nodded.

"This is not good, or tzorkly."

"Perhaps not, but it'll be funny," Ayaani insisted.

"I really don't think this is such a tzorkly thing to do for your master."

Ayaani blinked. "But you don't even like him," she griffled. "You think he is a splurk, remember?" She looked at the oidy leather potion bottle, noticing the stopper was slightly wet. "Have you been eyesplashing?"

"That is none of your business," Ursula snapped. "None at all!"

"Here we go," Ayaani griffled, watching as Matlock made his way nervously into the ganticus tent. "Let's enjoy it. This'll hopefully make us chickle."

"Why are you doing this?" Ursula hissed at her.

Ayaani looked at her with her oidy black eyes. "Perhaps your griffles about him finally made sense to me. He *is* just a glopp-up. And when he doesn't find the Tillian Wand, he'll stroff, meaning that I will also stroff. And all because of what a peffa-gobflopper he is. So methinks that in these last few hours, I'm entitled to one final chance to have a good chickle at his expense."

"Ayaani!" Ursula whispgiffled, shocked "You can't do that!"

"And why would *you* care about him?" Ayaani shot back as Matlock made his way closer. "Look at him, he's so clottabussed in those wet shoes. Do you know, I found him like that, just standing in the flood, looking out to sea, not even realising the tide was already at his ankles."

Ursula chewed on her bottom lip, watching Matlock every pid-pad of the way. "This is not good," she muttered.

Ayaani scrittled up onto Ursula's shoulder, whispgriffling into her long white ear. "Imagine that, Ursula Brifthaven Stoltz doesn't want to see a glopped majickal-hare humiliated in front of her? My, how the world can change peffa-vilishly. Now, let's have some fun."

They both watched, Ayaani trying her briftest not to smirk, as Matlock cleared his throat. "Ursula Brifthaven Stoltz," he began. "I know that I pid-padded out of here feeling russisculoffed with you, but I've just discovered something I never knew before, and it's made me feel even more of a clottabus than usual."

"Difficult, given his past," Ayaani whispgriffled.

"I haven't been much of a good friend to you, Ursula, and my griffles to you were glopped and unfair. However, as I now know that I am to be the last of all the majickal-hares…"

Ayaani let out a small snigger she vilishly tried to disguise as a sneeze.

"…I feel that the time is now right to griffle to you about how much I hold you dear to my heart as a loyal and trusted friend." He swallowed hard.

"Has he been practising this?" Ursula whispgriffled into Ayaani's ear.

"I told him to try and get some griffles together," Ayaani replied.

"Really? But these ones are so terrible."

"Hold on," Ayaani whispgriffled. "He's not finished yet."

"By my witch's hat," Ursula moaned, "I think you're right."

Matlock pressed on. "For much of my life, Ursula, I have lived humbly and simply, but also, perhaps, peffa-clottabussedly. And now, as I finally begin to discover many things about myself, things that make me twizzly or russisculoffed, happy or sad – I realise that perhaps it is all far too little, far too peffa-late. Things have happened, and will happen, that I have no control over. Destinies and times have been weighed out and measured – with so much, it seems to me, somehow fated to also end with me – the very last of the majickal-hares."

"Shall I clap?" Ursula whispgriffled.

"No, please," Ayaani spluttered. "It'll only make him worse."

Matlock suddenly dropped to one knee, paw outstretched, staring intently into Ursula's eyes. "I've been a fool," he griffled. "For there is one thing that I *can* change – one peffa-important thing. Ursula, accept my apologies, and be my friend again. Please be the friend of the last majickal-hare of all the dales."

"How long are you going to let him suffer?" Ayaani whispgriffled.

"About six more blinksnaps," Ursula replied, counting them in her head and studying Matlock's worried face intently. "Get up," she griffled at him. "All this begging is most untzorkly." She handed him the oidy potion bottle. "There are new eyeplashers in this bottle, Matlock. The old ones I poured away. I have no wish to experience your feelings from the past – but perhaps, one sun-turn, I just might wish to understand your feelings in the future." She narrowed her eyes. "And that, Matlock is *all* I will griffle about the matter until that sun-turn comes."

"*If* it ever does," Ayaani griffled. "The way everything's going glopped at the moment, it seems rather unlikely."

Matlock stood, re-tying the potion bottle round his neck. "What made you change your mind?" he griffled. "Was it because I am the peffa-last majickal-hare, ever?"

Ursula sighed. "That was just a spuddle Ayaani made up, you ganticus splurk."

He looked across at Ayaani, trying her briftest to look innocent. "This is true? You made it all up?"

She shrugged. "Well, someone had to do something," she griffled. "The pair of you were behaving like leverets. This way, we're all fuzzcheck again, and perhaps we can finally get back to finding this glopped Tillian Wand."

"But I really believed it," Matlock griffled, hurt.

"Well perhaps, Matlock," Ursula griffled, rising elegantly from the throne, "that was because you *wanted* to."

"I don't understand," he griffled.

"Once again, you have caused me no surprises whatsoever." She left them both, pid-padding purposefully outside, then standing with her hands on her hips, anxiously watching the rising flood.

"Your next eyesplash," came a voice from behind, "will be perhaps your most peffa-important one Ursula. But it must come from your heart, and you must be sure to use it peffa, peffa-wisely."

She turned, taking a breath as she saw the robed figure of Soriah Kherflahdle. "I thought you'd gone to Winchett Dale, Your Tzorkliness."

"I will, in time," the High Priestess griffled. "But first, I had to see something with my own eyes." She softly chickled. "I must griffle that the Matlock's dripple is one of the tzorkliest creatures I have ever known."

"Ayaani?"

Soriah nodded. "I saw the whole thing in there, Ursula, heard every griffle."

She coloured slightly. "Oh."

"The next eyesplasher that you weep will be for the life of true solitariness you now realise *isn't* the tzorkly way for you. Ursula, you need friends and companions – and perhaps one sun-turn, you might even begin to take their advice peffa-occasionally."

"That," Ursula muttered, "will never happen."

Soriah smiled. "Let the eyesplasher fall to the ground, then use it wisely."

"To do what, Your Tzorkliness?"

"You'll know when the time comes." Soriah clapped her paws twice and her vroffa-broom immediately roared over, the large sack of luck tied neatly beneath. "I've seen all I that needed to see, so now I must go. Help Matlock search the Icy Seas. Much depends on him finding the wand. He has found the half that floats in the lid, now he must find the half that lurks in the deepest black beneath the waves. And all the time, the spirit of Alvestra will be battling to get there first. It will be twizzly and peffa-dangerous, but it must be done for all our sakes; witches, wizards and dale-creatures alike."

Ursula looked back out to sea, a thick fog now slowly beginning to roll in. "But it's so ganticus," she griffled. "How do you even begin?"

"If you are getting close to the wand, then Alvestra will find you," Soriah griffled. "The moment she appears is the one you must be ready for."

"Me?"

"You and Matlock both." She mounted the broom, gunning the branches and loudly calling over. "Weep your eyesplasher, Ursula! Weep it for the solitary life you thought you wanted. Weep it for the splurk you think you've been. Use it to help all who live in the majickal-dales!"

A ganticus roar filled the skies as Soriah vilishly took off, the red-hot tips of her vroffa-branches soon lost in the low, hanging cloud.

Ursula watched the crimson dot disappear, feeling heavy sploinks of rain falling on the brim of her hat as the wind picked up, peffablasting her face. Close by, the flood had risen over the bank, the waters now freely running into the abandoned festival, already taking down distant tents and lines of black flags closest to the churning estuary.

She vilishly pid-padded back into the guzzwort tent. "We must leave," she griffled to Matlock, Ayaani scrittling back up into his hood. "The waters are coming. We must find higher ground."

They headed outside, vilishly pid-padding away from the flood between long rows of abandoned tents and stalls.

"What about your broom?" Matlock griffled. "Wouldn't that be quicker?"

Ursula stopped, then turned, pointing to a distant row of collapsing tents being swept away in the surge. "It would be if I hadn't left it over there," she griffled. "It will be gone. For now, we have no choice but to pid-pad."

They set off again, heading for the edge of the festival where the ground began to slope up and away into higher, surrounding woodland. A loud garrumbloom of thunder cracksploded above their heads, and the rain came down even harder, drumming and bouncing off the ground at their feet.

"Up there!" Ursula called, pointing to the line of trees. "We can shelter and be safe for a while."

They carried on up the wet slope, Ayaani peering over Matlock's shoulder, trying to wipe the heavy lidsplashers from her oidy eyes. Matlock helped Ursula up the last steep ridge until they stood in the shelter of the trees, looking back down over the devastated festival, watching tents, furniture and all sorts of tzorkly flotsam being washed away; cauldrons, guzzworts barrels, tables and chairs bobbing and turning in the thick, grey waters.

"Well, I guess that was lucky," Matlock griffled. "We only just made it."

"You're forgetting," Ursula snapped. "You only had *one* piece of luck, and you used that when I got you out of that sack." She paused for a snutch of blinksnaps, watching the ganticus guzzwort tent finally collapse, spreading itself like a huge octopus and slowly drifting away, a ganticus realisation occurring in her tzorkly hare's mind. "Which, of course, must mean that everything that happens from now on is somehow *meant* to be, because we no longer have luck on our side."

"So you're meant to be with me right now, stood here, watching all this?" he asked her.

"It is the only unfortunate and peffa-splurked conclusion I can come to," she reluctantly admitted. "Perhaps for me, all my ambitions are over; my dreams of being solitary, of one sun-turn being *Grand High Priestess of the Tzorkly Order of The League of Lid-Curving Witchery* – perhaps they simply end here, washed away, leaving me with just a splurked majickal-hare to griffle with under some wet trees."

Matlock tried to think of something more positive. "Well, I did think those thrones were really quite uncomfortable."

She turned to him, frowning. "I would have used a cushion, you splurk! You think I hadn't already thought of that?"

"Ursula," he asked, "can I griffle you a question?"

"You just have," she griffled, turning back to the flood. "And the answer is 'no' – because it will no doubt be a splurked question about Ledel Gulbrandsen."

"It is, yes," he admitted.

"Then my answer is peffa-definitely 'no'. Ledel is a good and noble wizard-hare and that's all I'll griffle about the matter."

Matlock didn't ask any more. Instead, the three of them silently watched the oncoming waters fill the field below and head slowly and inevitably towards the slope.

She turned to him. "You griffled to me you had seen a puzzle?"

He nodded. "Written in the creeping-green on the side of the Krettles' tower."

"What did it say?"

He recalled the griffles, griffling them slowly out loud:

Look to the lid, the sand and the sea,
And there, reflected in your sands of time,
Four dworps linked in all eternity,
A wand from a broom to make a Tillian shine,
There to be grasped, and taken by one paw,
According to Most Majelicus dalelore.

"That's all?" she griffled. "You're sure of it?"

He nodded. "My life depends on me remembering them."

"And mine," Ayaani added.

Ursula thought about the griffles, looking up at the thick bank of heavy cloud obscuring the full moon. "The 'four-dworps'?"

"Proftulous, Marellus, Flavius and Xavios – all named after the four stars that form The Great Broom," Matlock explained. "Only they've been moving, Ursula, realigning to form the shape of a wand, with the full-moon as its glowing tip. It's why I was so sure the Tillian Wand was a witch's broom. Everything just made so much peffa-perfect sense."

"Well, clearly not," Ursula griffled, unamused. "Once again, your clottabussed thinking was most splurked."

"At least I found half of it," he quietly griffled, slightly offended at Ursula's demolition of what he thought had been a most saztaculous piece of working out under what had been quite peffa-glopped circumstances. "I mean, it's not that easy trying to solve riddles when all you can see in your mind is a ganticus hour-glass full of your own heartbeats."

"Oh, for Oramus' sake, Matlock, nothing is *ever* easy!" she griffled. "Why do you always think it must be so?" She took a breath, pushing down any rising russisculoftulation, then tried another tack. "Other majickal-hares have found the Tillian Wand," she griffled, "so I see no reason why you can't do the same."

"But Chatsworth didn't," Matlock griffled. "He told me had, he even wore the red-robes though they weren't his. Baselott and Laffrohn took them from Trommel's stroffed body. So it turns out that my master was never Most Majelicus, yet he still made me do these tasks that I never, ever wanted to, and…"

She held up a paw. "So?" she griffled, staring into his eyes and frowning. "Why does any of that splurked stuff from the past even *matter?*"

Matlock swallowed, caught under her gaze. "Well…" he muttered, unnecessarily scratching at his paw, "…I don't suppose it really does, it's just that…"

"Because right now, Matlock, *all* you have to be worrying about is finding a wand." She grabbed his paw, squeezing it tightly. "Whatever has happened before, how it has happened, who has done what to whom and why – all of this is for another time, Matlock. Not now. Do you understand?"

He nodded. "You're really hurting my paw."

She squeezed even harder. "That's good, because you're finally concentrating on the pain of the now, instead of the glopp-ups of the past!"

"Yes," he squeaked, "I'm definitely concentrating on the pain of the now."

"Then let us turn our attention to what has to be done." She let go, watching Matlock blow on his paw. "We know the second half of the wand is somewhere out to sea. We also know that Alvestra will come for us."

"Alvestra?" Matlock griffled, getting twizzly. "The smoke witch?"

Ursula sighed. "When she appears, you will know you are close to the wand."

"Me?" he griffled. "I was hoping this would be a 'we' thing."

Her hare's eyes widened. "And why would *I* ever want to search the entire Icy Seas? It would be most dangerous, twizzly and peffasplurked."

"To help me?" Matlock weakly suggested. "After all, it is a peffaganticus sea."

"And for that reason alone, it is so obviously a completely hopeless task that I have no desire to be the oidiest part of it."

"But wouldn't four eyes be better than two?"

"You already have four eyes; yours and Ayaani's."

"Have you seen the size of her eyes? They're oidy, and peffa-black."

"Aha, but maybe this is making Ayaani all tzorkly for seeing underwater," Ursula griffled. "Not that I know how you are going to be getting under the sea in the first place."

Matlock looked out across the flooded estuary to the roaring waves now openly beginning to crash inland and roll to the bottom of the slope beneath them. "It just looks so cold and gubbstooled," he griffled.

"Exactly. Two more reasons why you won't catch me in it," Ursula griffled. "Can you even swim?"

"A little," Matlock admitted. "Sometimes Proftulous and I would go for a dip in Thinking Lake."

She frowned. "Methinks the Icy Seas will be an oidy bit more twizzly than your Thinking Lake. Besides, this isn't just swimming, this will be diving down, right to the bottom to find a sunken wand."

"I know," he griffled miserably. "You're right. The whole thing *is* just peffa-pointless and glopped. It's impossible."

Without warning, she suddenly bliffed him hard around the ears. "Ah! So now you are going to be Mr 'Giving-up' Matlock, are we? *Nothing* is impossible, Matlock, nothing!"

Ayaani, who had been listening quietly, scrittled onto Matlock's shoulder clearing her throat with a sudden sense of theatrical ceremony. "Ursula, you griffle that nothing is impossible. But how about Proftulous being named as the briftest-looking creature in all the majickal-dales? I'd say that was pretty impossible."

Ursula considered this. "Unlikely," she agreed, "but not *entirely* impossible. For if Proftulous was the *only* creature left, then he would have to also *have* be the briftest-looking."

"Ah," Ayaani griffled, raising an oidy paw, "but if he *was* the only creature left, who could name him as 'briftest-looking creature'?"

Ursula frowned, looking for an answer, her witchy-tzorkliness determined not to be beaten by a dripple. "By another creature!" she triumphantly cried. "The only other creature in the dales, who also just happens to be conveniently uglier than him."

"And can you *really* think of such a creature?"

Ursula tried for a snutch of blinksnaps, before finally shrugging. "You're right, I can't." She turned to Matlock. "I apologise. I make a ganticus mistake before. *Nearly* everything is possible – except Proftulous ever being named briftest-looking creature in all the dales." She angrily stamped her foot. "There. Are you happy now?"

Matlock flinched, an oidy bit confused. "I never griffled anything. It was Ayaani."

"Oh, so now you are going to blame your oidy-dripple?" She thrust her paws on her hips. "Well, doesn't that just make you the peffa-ganticus hare!"

Matlock tilted his head. "Ayaani – is she drunk again? Is the green-milky stuff wearing off?"

Ayaani watched Ursula carfully. "No," she quietly griffled. "Methinks she's like this all the time. You still glad that you made up being friends with her?"

"I seem to remember that was your doing, not mine."

"Hey! This could be the last sun-turn of my life!" Ayaani protested. "I'm allowed an oidy bit of fun."

Ursula, watching the pair of them squabble, suddenly began to chickle, starting with just the oidiest giggle, then slowly spreading to the rest of her body, holding her sides and growing in intensity, until she was hopelessly consumed, laughing out loud at not only Matlock and Ayaani, but also the sheer glopped and desperate situation they found themselves in.

Next, a single eyesplasher fell from her cheeks to the ground at her feet. She looked down in shock, remembering Soriah's griffles and the absolute peffa-importance of just this one tear. "Matlock!" she cried. "Come see!"

He pid-padded over, both he and Ayaani staring at the ground. "And I'm looking for?"

"An eyesplasher!" she griffled, keenly dropping to her knees to vilishly search amongst fallen leaves.

"An eyesplasher?" Matlock griffled, feeling that if anything, the sight of Ursula raking the ground with her paws was final proof that she was, in fact, quite completely clottabussed and beyond any kind of majickal help, whatsoever.

"It's here!" she cried, springing back up and showing him the peffa-perfect tear, now rolling along the spine of a fallen leaf. "The eyesplasher that could change everything!"

"Just look interested and be impressed," Ayaani whispgriffled in Matlock's ear.

"It's here!" she cried, springing back up and showing him
the peffa-perfect tear, now rolling along the spine of a fallen leaf.
"The eyesplasher that could change everything!"

He tried, closely inspecting the tear and making what he thought sounded like suitably appreciative noises. He looked at Ursula. "And what happens now, exactly?"

"I'm really not sure," she replied, studying it intently. "Something tzorkly, I suspect."

"Right," Matlock slowly griffled, totally at a loss, all three of them studying the lone eyesplasher for a long snutch of moments without anything remotely tzorkly happening at all.

"I think that the problem," Ursula slowly griffled, "is that perhaps we have to *believe* in it."

"Believe in an eyesplasher?" Matlock blinked, watching Ursula close her eyes, urging Matlock and Ayaani to do the same, muttering strange griffles under her breath.

"Now, let's try again," she announced. "This time, when you open your eyes – *believe*."

She slowly circled her paw over the tear, before letting it fall to the ground at Matlock's feet, the ground streaking with instant bright blue light, the tear beginning to grow right in front of his disbelieving eyes.

"It's happening!" she excitedly cried.

"What is?" he griffled, the tear now almost up to his waist.

"I have no idea!" she chickled. "But it's something peffa, peffa, *peffa-torkly*! I'd stand back if I were you."

He took a couple of pid-pads backwards as the ganticus tear continued to grow, hissing and frizzing, becoming a huge ball of streaking blue lightning. "It's…it's going to cracksplode!" he yelled, turning to run, only stopping when Ursula vilishly caught his arm.

"Get inside it," she griffled to him.

"Get inside?" he yelped in twizzled-panic. "Are you *completely* glubbstooled? I'll stroff if I take a single pid-pad closer!"

Without waiting to hear another protesting griffle, Ursula expertly spun him round and pushed with all her might, hurling him headlong into the ganticus lightning ball. A tremendous cracksplosion shook the forest, everything flashing the brightest blue, the ground trembling under Ursula's feet, before finally calm slowly returned, the only sound heavy raindrops sploinking the leaves above her head.

She looked at the ganticus tear and gasped. It was now a saztaculous bubble and trapped inside, frantically trying to rip its thick skin, was Matlock, his muffled cries barely reaching her ears.

"Be calm!" she shouted at him. "You are too splurked and peffa-twizzly! You'll break it!"

But just as she could hardly hear him, so her griffles were lost on Matlock, too. Inside, he tried not to get too twizzly, aware of his vilishly beating heart, doing his briftest to calm himself, pressing all over the bubble, looking for a way out.

"Methinks," Ayaani calmly observed on his shoulder, "that we're stuck. Bursting our way out will be impossible."

Matlock gritted his hare's teeth. "Weren't you the one griffling that nothing was impossible?"

"No, that was Ursula," she corrected him. "I was the one who simply destroyed her gobflopping argument with Protfulous-related logic."

He craned his neck to her. "That doesn't really help, does it?"

"And neither does that," Ayaani griffled, pointing outside, as Ursula began pushing the side of the ganticus bubble, the whole thing beginning to slowly roll along the ground. "Get pid-padding! Or we'll be spinning around and upside-down in no time!"

"What's she doing?" Matlock panicked, trying his best not to lose his footing, his paws outstretched as the bubble picked up speed, Ursula rolling it towards the edge of the trees and the grassy slope beyond. "She's…she's not going to push us down there, is she?" he griffled, turning, trying desperately to shout at the chickling witch still pushing with all her might. "What in Oramus' name are you even thinking of, Ursula!"

But Ursula kept on pushing and rolling the bubble to the edge of the slope, then finally sent it on its way with one last, ganticus push, watching as Matlock frantically pid-padded inside, picking up even more speed, before rolling straight into the rising flood with a ganticus splash and being slowly swept out to sea.

"Well," she griffled, dusting off her hands as the bubble finally sank below the waves. "You needed to search the Icy Seas, Matlock. And now you can. From now on, it's up to you."

She was about to turn away when a smoke-trail caught her

eye, high in the dark-grey lid, weaving between rainclouds before suddenly diving vilishly down into the sea with a small splash. She shuddered slightly. Innocent as it may have appreared, Ursula knew it could only be one thing...

Matlock was finally heading for the depths, and Alvestra wasn't far behind.

Far away, Laffrohn streaked across the rainy-lid on half of a broken vroffa-tree, high over the dales, following Garrick's directions to the top of a distant mountain with the largest castle she'd ever seen perched on its rocky summit.

She landed outside and crossed the drawbridge, holding Garrick's jangling bunch of keys firmly in her paw, fitting the largest into the ganticus oak creaker, slowly opening it and pid-padding through a vast entrance hall towards an enormous set of stairs at the far end. Flaming torches lit walls adorned with crumlush pictures of places and creatures she barely knew. Tapestries hung from the high roof, elaborately woven in exotic threads, depicting scenes from ancient myths and spuddles. She stopped under one, looking up, making out the embroidered figures of Alvestra and Tillian in a twizzly vrooshing battle far out to sea, watched by ferocious creatures, all eager to snatch and take the notorious wand for themselves.

She shuddered slightly, telling herself to go on, climbing the cold stone stairs, her soft pid-pads echoing off the flickering walls, all the time knowing that somehow every blinksnap of her long and majickal-life had led to this one point – this inevitable reckoning – the beginning of the end.

At the top she headed away from the stairs, through a series of long, dark corridors, each time finding the way blocked by another locked creaker, before unlocking it into more corridors beyond.

She was pid-padding purely on instinct alone, her whole being now completely consumed by her Sisteraculous, guiding her, drawing her to the inevitable conclusion that perhaps she'd realised for a long time, but never really had the courage to face or understand. She thought of her times at the The Vroffa-Tree Inn, the discovery Baselott had made about the ganticus flood, the plans they'd made to avoid it – and the many secrets she also knew he always kept from her...

It was time, she griffled to herself, for things to be revealed, players to be unmasked.

She pid-padded on, letting herself be drawn up a tall spiral staircase, the steep climb reminding her briefly of her sister and the once saztaculous tower that had been her home, but was now little more than a glopped-kitchen for boiling majickal-hares. She wondered how much of this had really started with her and Lily, remembering to her shame how she had run from Alvestra, knowing her sister was to be stroffed, fleeing for her own life, completely terrified and twizzly, unable to believe that such a precious, innocent life as Lily's could be taken away so cruelly.

A long, thin torch-lit corridor waited at the top of the staircase; at its end just one final oak creaker, heavy with iron hinges – Garrick's office. She pid-padded to it, heart beating heavily. Paws trembling, she found the last key on the ring, slowly turning it in the lock, taking a deep breath and pushing it open, knowing her journey was nearing its end; Baselott's thirteen pages of parchment, and all its secrets, would finally be revealed…

She pid-padded inside, making out a large desk, lit by a single candle, the rest of the room in almost complete darkness.

"You took longer than I thought," a voice calmly griffled from the darkness.

She looked to the ceiling, letting out an oidy sigh and smiling.

"How goes the vrooshfest?" it asked her. "I presume it's completely glopped-up, which is why it took you so long to get here?"

"No," she griffled, turning to the dark corner. "You'd be surprised, Chatsworth, you really would. It be going better than I could have ever hoped."

Chatsworth slowly stepped from the gloom, coughing slightly. He looked old and weary. His red robes seemed to merely hang from him, as if somehow, he'd already left them. He nodded. "That's because you could always be relied upon to pull things round," he griffled. "If anyone could make the Dale Vrooshfest a success in Winchett Dale, it would be you, Laffrohn. What did you do – the invisible-vrooshfest trick?"

She nodded.

He smiled, looking at her for a long time. "Dear Laffrohn, one of my briftest ever friends. And now, you have found me out to be the glopped majickal-hare that I am. A stealer of griffles. Not only that, but the last ever griffles of my master – the one hare who supposedly gave so much for me, who believed in me, and also gave me these very robes in order that I wouldn't have to complete the final two Most Majelicus tasks." He shook his head sadly. "And all he asked of me in return was to do just one oidy thing."

"To deliver the thirteen pages of revisions to Garrick after he had stroffed," Laffrohn nodded. "So they would remain safely locked away in this desk."

"Indeed," Chatsworth quietly agreed. "That was my one and only true purpose in all of Baselott's plans – to be loyal to him, even after he stroffed."

"But you weren't were you?" she griffled, holding the oidy key which unlocked the desk.

He slowly shook his head. "When did you know?"

"When Garrick griffled to me that the thirteen pages were still rolled up with an unbroken seal," she calmly replied. "Garrick may be a clottabus, but he's too greedy for drutts to ever bother opening some peffa-glopped griffles from a stroffed hare." She lightly drummed the desk with her paw. "But with you, Chatsworth, it would have been a peffa-different matter. I can see you now, taking the papers to Garrick, desperate to be knowing what's inside them, opening them, reading them – then keeping them for yourself."

She slid the key into the lock, turning and slowly opening the desk draw, pulling out the rolled, sealed parchment, breaking the wax and unfurling them to reveal just thirteen empty pages without a single griffle written on any of them.

She smiled, nodding, her suspicions confirmed. "So you gave Garrick these, instead, didn't you? Because you couldn't stand to not know what Baselott had finally written, what his peffa-big secret was that he'd never dared to griffled to either one of us about. You couldn't stand to simply have it locked away in a glubbstooled castle somewhere on a distant mountain." She let the blank parchment pages drop to the floor. "So you switched his griffles for these blank pages, didn't you? Then kept the original ones for yourself. It's why Baselott's revisions were never submitted for *Majickal Dalelore – Volume 68*, isn't it?"

Chatsworth nodded.

"Why, Chatsworth?" she pressed. "Why, after all your master did for you?"

He softly chickled. "After all he *did* for me, Laffrohn? Really? Taking me as a young leveret from my family out in The Great Beyond, bringing me back to this gubbstooled place of confusing majick, with its rotten rules and glopped-creatures?" He laughed, but it was as cold, hollow and empty as the castle itself. "And then," he went on, "Baselott, my so-called 'saztaculous' master, couldn't even be bothered to teach me the ways of real majick and dalelore. Oh, no – not for Chatsworth! Instead he schooled me in his own peffa-glopped science and logic, forcing me to study it, using me as some sort of private experiment, just as he did with his own griffling dripple!"

"Chatsworth," Laffrohn tried to griffle, "you be getting this all wrong…"

"Remember, Laffrohn?" he vilishly cut in, breathing heavily, "the very first dripple to ever griffle a griffle, and what did Baselott do to it? How did he repay its loyalty to him? He experimented, became obsessed, forcing it to try and make new noises, learn new griffles, sun-turn after sun-turn, until it finally weakened and stroffed."

Laffrohn nodded, careful her griffles didn't upset him further. Already, she could make out the beginnings of tears in Chatsworth's eyes. "But Baselott was a hare of science, Chatsworth," she gently griffled. "You couldn't have expected him to do anything else with a griffling dripple. And, sad as it was that it stroffed, it proved that the ways of dalelore were wrong, because for the peffa-first time a majickal-hare didn't stroff on the same sun-turn as his dripple." She reached out and took Chatsworth's paw, earnestly looking into his old eyes. "Don't you see? That was the turning-point for us all, Chatsworth. You, me and Baselott. His dripple's stroffing was what drove Baselott on with his experiments and researches that eventually led him to be finding about this ganticus flood, so we were able to make plans to get everyone safe up on Winchett Dale's High Plateau." She tried to smile at him. "Without that dripple, without me, without you – everyone would be in most peffa-twizzly danger right now. And whatever you may be thinking about him, however harsh or cruel you think he be to you, Baselott's really the one that everyone has to be thanking."

Chatsworth let go of her paw. "He made me wear these robes," he quietly griffled. "Most Majelicus robes that I'd never earned, simply stolen from his own master."

Laffrohn chewed her bottom lip for a snutch of moments. "Baselott didn't steal the robes, Chatsworth. I did."

Chatsworth's eyes widened. "You?"

She nodded. "Trommel stroffed as he nifferduggled at The Vroffa-Tree Inn. Baselott, he and I had all been griffling about how things had nearly gone peffa-glopped for you on your first Most Majelicus task. There was a terrible argument between us. Trommel went to bed and peacefully passed into Oramus' most eternal care. In the morn'up, I went to his room and fetched his robes, griffling to Baselott to give them to you, because neither of us wanted you to be stroffed on the remaining two tasks. Solving the riddle of Trefflepugga Path nearly cost you your life, Chatsworth."

"Because," he suddenly hissed at her, balling his elderly paw and bliffing the desk, "because Baselott hadn't taught me the ways of true majick! Don't you see? I had to complete that task using his peffa-glopped scientific vrooshers and logic! I wasn't given the same chance as normal majickal-hares! I wasn't even allowed to read the majickal-driftolubbs! I was forced to read whatever Baslelott put before me, then listen to all his glubbstooled thoughts and griffles about majickal-dalelore being wrong."

"Because he *cared* about you," Laffrohn griffled. "Can't you see that? He wanted you to be the first in a new dynasty of majickal-hares, ones that could use science and his invented vrooshers to bring new ways of majick to everyone, every living creature."

"No, Laffrohn," Chatsworth griffled, gritting his teeth, "he simply wanted me as just another of his experiments, like his dripple." He bliffed the desk a second time, russisculoftulation rising in his angry elderly voice. "And when it was proved that I could hardly even solve the riddle of Trefflepugga Path, he simply threw me his master's old robes, griffling to me that they were all I ever really needed to be Most Majelicus in the first place!" He looked at her, eyes pleading. "How do you think that made me *feel*, Laffrohn?

To know that I'm just a glopped experiment?"

"I don't know," she quietly admitted.

"I know you don't know!" he shouted at her. "Because all *you* could see was your peffa-glopped inn! And there you stayed, hidden underground, as Baselott secretly griffled to you about all he had discovered, and how saztaculous he was at being scientific. I sometimes had to pid-pad along, too, remember, but you barely noticed me! It was as if I didn't exist! You two made all the decisions and plans, didn't you? Nothing I ever griffled was important enough to be listened to! I was just peffa-glopped Chatsworth, who wouldn't have ever become Most Majelicus unless his robes were stolen from a dead hare!" He stopped griffling, breathing heavily through flared nostrils, trying to calm himself, watching Laffrohn closely. "But that all changed, didn't it, after I had done my duty and fetched Matlock to be my apprentice? After I had been told to go to The Great Beyond and bring back the most clottabussed looking, glubbstooled and peffa-glopped hare I could find, simply that he too would one day also fail the Most Majelicus tasks, in order that the Majickal Elders would no longer be suspicious of what you and Baselott were up to." He narrowed his eyes. "You used me, so that you could both use Matlock to save your own skins from being discovered going about your scientific treachery!"

"It wasn't like that," Laffrohn griffled, her voice beginning to shake. "We just had to be looking normal, that's all. If you hadn't gone and fetched Matlock, other creatures would have been wondering just why it was you weren't discharging your Most Majelicus duties." She anxiously cleared her throat. "It's…it's what creatures all expected of you, Chatsworth, to be fetching and training an apprentice."

He pointed an accusing paw at her. "And just to ensure that Matlock really had no chance whatsoever, you made sure his master wasn't even Most Majelicus, either! Even Trefflepugga Path knew Matlock was a total gobflopper on his first ever journey back from The Great Beyond – it took him right to Winchett Dale, for Oramus' sake!"

"Chatsworth," Laffrohn pleaded. "It wasn't like that…"

But he didn't listen, instead stooping down to pick the empty parchment papers from the floor, then waving them angrily in

He stopped, turned, gave her one final, long look. "To find Matlock," he simply griffled. "There's still much he needs to know. Goodbye, Laffrohn."

front of her face. "You're right. I *did* swap these papers! I deserved to be the only one that read Baselott's final revisions for *Majickal Dalelore – Volume 68*. Me – just me! Clottabussed old Chatsworth, the gobflopped hare, the one that always had to quietly sit and listen as you two griffled, the one that spent his time hidden away in a yechus burrow helping his master with glopped experiments. If anyone was entitled to know what Baselott had written on those pages, it was me, Laffrohn – and no one else. Because I had earned the right."

"And that's when you learned the truth about your dworp?"

His eyes widened. "Oh, yes! And *so* many other things besides, Laffrohn! The dworp that I had once been briftest friends with and had given me so much, simply for me to forget ever knowing anything about it, was just one oidy thing, just the *start* of what I discovered in those pages." He slowly reached into his robe pocket and pulled out thirteen pages of parchment, then slammed them angrily onto the desktop. "Read them!" he commanded. "Read the last griffles of Baselott, Most Majelicus hare of Nullitt Dale!"

Laffrohn gasped, jumping back at the sight of the papers. "These…" she whispgriffled, "…these are them? The *real* ones? You've had them all this time?"

He slowly nodded, breathing heavily. "They're yours to read now, should you wish. But be warned, Laffrohn, there are things in these griffles that you might not *want* to read, things that could very well haunt your nifferduggles for the rest of your days, as they have done mine."

Laffrohn put on her spectacles, taking a deep breath as the quilled griffles came sharply into focus.

"I am done here," Chatsworth quietly griffled. "Do with them what you wish." He pid-padded towards the door.

"Where are you going?" she asked.

He stopped, turned, gave her one final, long look. "To find Matlock," he simply griffled. "There's still much he needs to know. Goodbye, Laffrohn."

And then he left, pid-padding away down the long corridor, leaving Laffrohn quite alone at the desk.

10.

Vrooshers, Colley-Rocks and Vroffa'd Witches

For Lord Garrick, reluctantly in charge of the entire Dale Vrooshfest, the sun-turn couldn't have been more gobflopped. Or so he unwisely thought...

Laffron's sudden departure as main organiser and announcer had necessitated having to take the rather glubbstooled duty on himself, griffling to fellow committee members that 'the other announcer was such a gobflopp' and that he'd decided to step in and show them all how it should be done properly. One or two members, who had long suspected Garrick had always had a secret urge to hog the limelight at just such an occasion, raised their eyebrows, at which point Garrick had merely pointed them to the arrival of a completely non-existent and magnificent afternoon'up feast on the empty table, watching as they all eagerly tucked into whatever he told them was there.

Besides, their suspicions couldn't have been more wrong. The peffa-last thing Garrick wanted to do was to find himself stood in the middle of the grassy arena, announcing contestants through some glubbstooled creature's paw, as all the while, rumbles and garrumblooms from the distant thunderous lid were getting ever closer...

He looked across the sea of expectant creatures' faces waiting for his griffles, seeing in the far distance what looked like a ganticus burst of water suddenly shoot from the side of a mountain. "The tunnels," he muttered to himself. "It's going to be peffa-worse than I thought."

He vilishly beckoned Serraptomus over, the krate eagerly wheezing his way to his side. "The mirrit-tunnel entrance in Winchett Dale," he whispgriffled, ensuring Kringle's paw was nowhere near his mouth. "Are you sure it's safe and blocked?"

Serraptomus nodded officiously. "With grillions of colley-rocks, Your Lordship. Oversaw the whole operation personally."

"You?" Garrick frowned, trying not to feel too disheartened. "But you couldn't even organise a single tent."

Serraptomus thought about this, trying to find the right angle. "Ah, yes," he griffled. "And the reason for that is because at the time I was attending to the welfare, health and safety of all visitors to Winchett Dale by blocking the mirrit-tunnel entrance in the first place."

"Please don't griffle to me that it was just *you* doing it," Garrick sighed.

"Oh no," Serraptomus brightly replied. "I had a complete army of highly competent engineers under my total command."

"You're lying, aren't you?"

Serraptomus winced. "An oidy, oidy bit, yes. It was Laffrohn, Proftulous and a white wizard-hare called Ledel Gulbrandsen."

"But will it hold?"

Serraptomus shifted awkwardly from foot to foot. "It…should do, Your Lordship."

"Should do?" Garrick hissed, as the crowd began to get restless, eager for the next majickal-constestant. "Just what do you mean by 'should'?"

"Well," Serraptomus replied, glad to have been asked, and utterly convinced that his answer would be nothing but helpful, "the thing is, the colley-rocks can get a bit moody and…"

"And what?"

"Well…just sort of roll away if they want to. I mean, they're rather unpredictable like that." He tried to laugh. "And frankly, they didn't look best pleased to be all piled up on top of one another, either. Especially the ones at the bottom, proper russisculoffed they were. And Zhava, she's the Last Great Elm of Wand Woods who guards the entrance, can get quite a mood on her, too." He playfully elbowed Garrick in the ribs. "Between you and I, I don't really hold out much hope. After all, everything always goes glopped-up in Winchett Dale."

"Serraptomus?"

"Yes, Your Lordship?"

"Will you just pid-pad away now?"

"Very good," Serraptomus cheerfully griffled, happily pid-padding towards the edge of the arena, before suddenly stopping and turning. "We must have more of these little chats," he called out, a ganticus smile beaming on his proud, officious face. "It's so much nicer than when you get all russisculoffed with me!"

Garrick took a deep breath, tilted his head towards the lid, closed his eyes and exhaled loudly.

"I may have yechus feet," Kringle suddenly griffled, "but at least I'm not a total clottabus like him."

"He's *actually* in charge of Winchett Dale?" Garrick asked.

"Not really," Kringle admitted. "He's taken to carpentry recently. Spends a lot of time with the singing kraark, whittling things." He held his paw up to Garrick's mouth. "But, for now, I suggest you start griffling and get the next majickal-hare on before this crowd gets any uglier."

Garrick nodded, taking just the oidiest look at the distant mountain which now appeared to have two ganticus spouts of water geysering high into the air. He desperately hoped everyone was high enough on the plateau to avoid the coming flood, not really knowing where else there was to go. The limestone cliffs of Twinkling Lid Heights were far higher and possibly safer, but virtually impossible for most creatures to climb. The birds, he knew, would be safe. They, at least, could fly.

"Good gentlecreatures!" he announced into Kringle's paw, the young griffelot's ganticus beak obediently moving with every griffle. "Thank you so much for your extraordinary kindness and patience. And I'm sure you'll all want to give another ganticus round of pawplause to the peffa-talented and definitely-different, Felic, the majickal-hare of Ceedius Dale!"

"He was definitely clottabussed!" someone shouted back. "Worst thing I've ever seen at one of these vrooshfests, he was!"

"Oh, come, come," Garrick tried. "That's hardly the spirit of the Dale Vrooshfest, now, is it? It's the taking part that counts, rather than the winning, surely?"

"Well if you can't do the latter," the creature called back, "'then what's the point of doing the former? I mean, by your logic, we should *all* be taking part, not just majickal-hares, which, quite frankly, would lead to a never-ending vrooshfest full of performances of varying quality, thereby undermining the competitive element of what is, for us, very much a spectacle to see and enjoy, rather than be forced to take part in."

There was much nodding of heads and murmuring to this, Garrick having to eventually quell it by completely reversing his previous statement, and griffling to the crowd that, in fact, it's only winning that matters, and should contestants feel that they're not up to it, then they really shouldn't bother turning up in the first place – a sentiment that was more or less accepted by everyone except the unfortunate Felic, who still insisted that a saztaculous dancing, majickal-hare shouldn't be penalised by the judges simply because the crowd were too culturally backward and clottabussed to appreciate what a majickal-spectacular was – even if the competition vrooshers had turned out to be rather on the lame side during the actual performance itself.

"You just wait seven years!" he shouted at them all, trying to ignore the boos and jeers. "I'll be back, don't you worry!"

The unfortunate creatures of Ceedius Dale who had between them gone to great lengths and personal sacrifices in order to bribe Garrick with a ganticus pile of drutts to ensure that Felic won and left in triumph for a new career in Sveag Dale, simply sat tight lipped, trying their briftest not to imagine the mind-numbing horror of a further seven years of his clottabussed dancing. One of them mentioned something about it being 'one of life's bitter ironies', but the others all vilishly bliffed him on the head.

"So it gives me ganticus pleasure," Garrick continued, trying to restore order, "to introduce to you a peffa-special hare indeed. A white wizard-hare from across the Icy Seas. The very first one to ever have competed in a Dale Vrooshfest! Please put your paws, hands and wings together for the peffa-majickal Ledel Gulbrandsen!"

An excrimbly roar greeted the announcement, creatures all straining to get a look at the confident white hare pid-padding into the centre of the arena and casually letting fly with a series of elegant vrooshers that raced above their peffa-appreciative heads, looping and twisting in a saztaculous shower of brightly coloured sparks.

"Now this be more like it!" someone cried out.

"Just look at his robes!" another added, eagerly pointing. "They be all white and most crumlush, with saztaculous gems and riches woven in!"

"True," Felic sourly agreed, still smarting. "But if you look peffa-closely, I think you'll find one of his ears is longer than the other."

There then followed ten minutes of the most saztaculous vrooshers anyone had ever seen at any Dale Vrooshfest. Ledel commanded both the arena and the crowd with a peffa-extraordinary display that produced near-continual gasps of amazement, raucous pawplause, cheers and whistles. He majicked vrooshers of every colour and hue, expertly directing them from his wand, giving them impossible shapes, turning them into blazing trails of fire, smoke and ice, sending them high into the darkening lid, backlighting the clouds to form truly a saztaculous tableaux of moving majickal-pictures that re-created the many great myths and spuddles from The Land of the White Hares. All this, as his rousing musical-vrooshers also shot around the plateau adding a saztaculously dramatic symphony, leaving everyone wide-eyed and open-mouthed in peffa-amazement.

"I still say one of his ears is too big," Felic muttered as Garrick bliffed him, the tall chaircreature lost in the sheer spectacle, all thoughts of the imminent flood temporarily forgotten in the majickal, musical and vrooshing saztaculousness of it all.

The display finished with the entire lid ablaze with flashing colours, cracksplosions raining all round in a truly thunderous finale that merited every cheer, whoop and rousing round of pawplause that rang out over the whole of Winchett Dale. In the very centre of the arena, Ledel simply put away his wand and bowed, quietly signalling to Kringle to pid-pad over, raising his paw and waiting for silence to descend amongst the elated crowd.

"Creatures of the majickal-dales," he griffled. "I come to you this sun-turn as the first white wizard-hare to compete in your Dale Vrooshfest. For too long, the creatures of our lands have been distant, separated by our histories, beliefs, our ways of using majick, be they tzorkly, or otherwise. But truly, we are only really separated by just the one thing – the Icy Seas."

The crowd cheered.

"Despite what you might think," Ledel continued, "I didn't come here today to prove myself *Briftest Hare of All the Dales*…"

"Well, you just have done!" a lone bloated-vellup called out. "You're saztaculous! You can come for a bowl of niff-soup at my cottage anytime!"

Ledel smiled. "I came here for another reason entirely, to find and battle another majickal-hare – Matlock from Winchett Dale."

The crowd looked from one to another, not quite understanding.

"He has been described to me as 'the most clottabussed of all the majickal-hares' and 'a complete gobflopper from the most glopped-up of all the dales'."

"Steady on," someone from Ceedius Dale called out. "We've got Felic, remember?"

Ledel quietly chickled. "Indeed, you do. But here's the point, my friends, whatever we 'think' we may have, however things are griffled about, or changed, or half-remembered, all that we ever really know of one another is gained from actually being together – rather than assuming spuddles to be true, or listening to someone else's griffles. I came here to battle with Matlock. I now realise it would have been pointless and completely wrong."

"And over peffa-quick, too!" Slivert Jutt called out, still pouring invisible guzzworts for a long line of listening creatures. "Matlock is hopelessly gobflopped at doing any sort of battling things. He be more of a sort of herbs and potions kind of a hare, really."

"Which," Ledel called back, "is precisely the way perhaps he *should* be. For who is to griffle that any one of us is brifter or more tzorkly than any others, simply because of what we may or may not be able to do?" He took a breath. "We are all majickal, each and every one of us. And just as the Icy Seas are the one thing that separate us, so perhaps it is majick that really unites us."

"He's good," Garrick griffled to Felic, as another ganticus roar of approval shook the High Plateau. "Does a fine line in schmaltz-griffling."

"Still needs to work on his choreography," Felic sniffed, reluctantly joining in the pawplause. "I'll beat him in seven years, though, just you wait."

"Do you know," Garrick griffled, watching Ledel take a final bow and pid-pad from the cheering arena, "I'm not at all sure Mr Ledel Gulbrandsen *will* be here in seven years time."

"How so? He'll surely have a title to defend?"

"Because," Garrick griffled, "perhaps he has griffled all he really needed to griffle."

Felic frowned, clearly not understanding, pid-padding away to join a throng of other creatures all offering hearty congratulations to the saztaculous wizard who had travelled from The Land of the White Hares to share his tzorkly majick with them all.

However, one unfortunate consequence of such a saztaculous lid-vrooshing display was its sheer ganticus size and spectacle, making it clearly visible to any remaining creatures who hadn't already made their way up onto the High Plateau – including a pile of ever more disgruntled and russisculoffed colley-rocks stacked around the base of an elm-tree, deep in Wand Woods...

The pile had, up until this particular tipping point, remained remarkably stable and accepting of its collective duty to weigh down and keep the mirrit-tunnel entrance completely sealed, having spent most of the time since Protfulous, Laffrohn, Ledel and Serraptomus had left slowly rearranging themselves into a new pile which they all agreed was far better suited to such a dangerous and important task.

As a result, colley-rocks from the more glopped-up areas of Winchett Dale were made to take their places at the bottom; their grumbling, complaining faces pressed against the soft, forest floor. They did so, partly because the colley-rocks from more exclusive places griffled to them that this is what they *should* do – and partly because somewhere in their glopped colley-rock minds they already believed that to be bottom of the pile was somehow their rightful place. Here, they were free to griffle and grumble about being put-upon and squashed by those above as much as they wanted to, as they couldn't really be heard, anyway.

Next, those colley-rocks who considered themselves superior to those on the bottom eagerly made their way up the pile, positioning themselves around Zhava's trunk in the places they thought were most appropriate to their homes. If a rock happened to live in a more splendid part of the dale, then it reasoned that it shouldn't be sat upon by a rock who lived in a drearier place. Inevitably, squabbles broke out, for unlike the rocks beneath – who accepted being bottom of the pile – these colley-rocks were really quite particular about who should be above whom.

"I spend my sun-turns resting in a quiet glade," one griffled, turning to her neighbour. "Whereas you spend yours on the edge of Thinking Lake. Therefore, *you* should be *below* me."

"Nonsense," the other rock griffled. "I know for a fact you were bought up on Grifflopp Marshes, so don't come the old 'Thinking Lake' griffles with me! You only got to a quiet glade because you scrunched your strata at a slow-jarrock who took pity on you and carried you up there!"

"Complete rubbish!" the first offended colley-rock cried. "I rolled there all by myself! Now get down to where you belong!"

And so it went on for some considerable time, the second layer bickering, squabbling and re-arranging itself as the bottom layer simply got on with their principal duties of supporting them and moaning about how ignored and hard-pressed they were.

Eventually, however, the pile was two layers complete, now looking like a ganticus cone with Zhava's trunk poking through the middle. A casual observer (of which there are remarkably few in Winchett Dale, it has to be griffled) might have noticed the disparity between numbers in the first two layers; the colley-rocks on the wider, bottom part of the pile easily outnumbering those from the better areas above. The observer might also have reached a broader conclusion about this, but again, as this is Winchett Dale, its far more likely they would have simply wandered off to do something glopped instead.

Lastly, came the final layer of colley-rocks – the smallest layer, those few fortunates at the very top who were sat upon and squashed by nobody, affording themselves the briftest views of everything, as well as being as safe as possible from any imminent flooding. How did they justify their superior position? Well, in truth, they didn't. The peffa-strangest thing was that although they were just as rocky and colleyed as the other rocks, the rest of them just *let* them do it, as everyone was either too preoccupied with moaning or desperately trying to outsmart each other. Those few at the top, however, neither complained or argued and simply rolled right up to what they expected and accepted as rightfully theirs, settling comfortably in and pressing down without so much as a single thought for the two layers struggling beneath. They had always been top of any colley-rock pile, and always would be, it was as peffa-simple as that.

However, in this instance, the moment Ledel's saztaculous lid-garrumblooming vrooshers had filled the sky, those same colley-rocks at the top began to glimpse teasing parts of it through the dense woodland canopy above their heads.

"Oh, my griffles!" one gasped. "Just look at that! It's utterly saztaculous and just peffa-shindinculous!"

"Oramus with a hat on!" another griffled. "What on earth are we even doing here, guarding some sort of tree-tunnel, when quite clearly, there's a far more saztaculous time to be had up on the High Plateau?"

"True," the first rock griffled. "And if anyone should be rolling over to see the saztaculous vrooshers, it should be us. After all, we do anything we want. And there's so few of us that we probably won't be missed, anyway. Let the others do all the holding and pressing-down, it's all most uncomfortable and frankly rather undignified."

"Indeed," its neighbour agreed. "The whole business is making me feel quite ill. I think I'm currently sat on a rock from one of the more glopped places of the dale, and I'm just hoping I won't catch anything dreadful from it."

"Well, that's our minds made up," the first colley-rock griffled, turning to his fellow top-of-the-pile friends. "What say we all roll up to the High Plateau and catch the last of the fun?"

A suggestion that was met with immediate approval, the upper layer all vilishly rolling down onto the forest floor.

"We're off for a spot of fun now," they cheerfully griffled to the others. "You just stay here and do your 'saving-the-dale-from-imminent-catastrophe' thing, will you? Problem with us is we're really not the hero-types, never have been. Far brifter to leave all that sort of nonsense to you lot, really. You don't mind, do you?"

But instead of immediately objecting and calling them all cowards, the second layer of colley-rocks eagerly assured them that they would indeed stay by the tree, if only to ensure those unfortunate colley-rocks at the bottom stayed in their places – a task they all seemed to believe was far more important than rolling away and fleeing for their own safety.

For a long time, there was silence, as if the two remaining layers of colley-rocks were trying to work out just what had happened, how it was they'd been so easily deserted and left alone. If anything, those on the second layer began to get an oidy bit twizzly, as they were quite unused to not being sat on by anyone above them.

"What do we do now?" one whispgriffled. "We've reached the top of the pile, but it doesn't feel right."

"That's because we're not high enough," another chipped in. "They've gone, but we haven't really moved *up* at all. We're still just the same height as we always were."

"Excuse me," one griffled. "But why don't we do just what they did?"

"Leave the pile?" another gasped. "Now that we've *finally* got to the top?"

"Yes," she nodded. "We just all leave and roll away up onto the High Plateau."

"But what about those below us?"

"What about them?" she griffled. "We'll be up on the High Pleateau, safe and having fun. Why should we bother about them?"

The rest of the colley rocks in the second layer didn't need to think too hard about this and soon began rolling down the pile and away into Wand Wood, leaving just the final, bottom layer.

Gradually, peffa-slowly, they rolled their heads around, looking to the lid, scrunching and grinding against one another, unable to believe what they were seeing.

"We're off for a spot of fun now," they cheerfully griffled to the others. *"You just stay here and do your 'saving-the-dale-from -imminent-catastrophe' thing, will you?"*

"They've all gone and rolled off!" one gasped. "That's it, me brothers! Look at us now – we've finally gone and made it to the top of the pile!"

"Because," another one griffled, starting to chickle, "We *are* the pile! It's just us, now! No more being sat on by others! Those sun-turns are peffa-definitely over!"

"Over!" the remaining rocks all cried out in unison.

"Things have finally changed," the first colley-rock griffled to them all. "This pile now starts and ends with us! We are its top, its middle and its bottom. How long have we longed for this moment, me brothers, this defining blinksnap in our history?"

"Not sure," one griffled, shrugging. "Say maybe twenty moon-turns? Thirty?"

"I don't mean literally!" the first colley-rock griffled. "I meant it as a sort of figurative statement that was more to do with a collective yearning by us with which to express the negativity of our overall years of suppression by an uncaring and unjust colley-rock society that seems to have finally fled the self-made wreckage of its own…"

It was unfortunate, because as fascinating as the colley-rock's hopes and plans for a newly emerging single-strata'd colley-rock society might have been, the rising floodwaters chose that very blinksnap to finally cracksplode through the thin earth under Zhava's roots, throwing the shocked, protesting tree backwards and shooting a ganticussly powerful geyser of underground flood-water high into the forest canopy.

"Roll for it!" the colley-rock cried. "To higher ground, me brothers, vilish!"

Up on the High Plateau, the unexpected cracksplosion caused heads to turn, the startled crowd anxiously looking down into Wand Wood to see the powerful jet spurting high above the trees.

"What be going on?" one demanded.

Garrick, knowing the importance of keeping everyone as calm as possible, put Kringle's paw to his mouth. "Everyone! Your attention please! There is nothing to be alarmed about. The good folk of Winchett Dale have simply put on a majickal-fountain display for you all to enjoy as part of this memorable vrooshfest!"

"Have we?" Slivert Jutt called over, looking confused and scratching his head. "Not sure we be organising anything at all, really."

The other creatures began to get an oidy bit restless and twizzly, now beginning to point at similar jetting geysers peppering the distant landscape.

"They be everywhere!" someone cried. "All over the dales!"

Again Garrick appealed for calm. "Creatures!" he griffled. "This is simply all part of the display! Why not take a snutch of blinksnaps to enjoy it? After all, Winchett Dale has gone to quite saztaculous lengths to prepare it all for you."

He urgently summoned Serraptomus over. "Who's next in the arena?"

"That'll be Matlock the Hare," the wheezing-tweeded krate officiously confirmed. "Our very own majickal-hare from Winchett Dale."

"Good," Garrick griffled. "Hopefully he'll put on a suitably saztaculous display that'll take everyone's minds off all these cracksploding mirrit-tunnels."

Serraptomus unwisely chickled. "You see, I did warn you that the colley-rocks wouldn't hold, didn't I? You can always trust old Serraptomus to griffle to you when there's a ganticus glopp-up coming."

Garrick frowned icily. "Just send the majickal-hare into the arena."

Serraptomus took a less than officious breath, scratching awkwardly at the side of his face.

"What is it?" Garrick asked, russisculoffed.

"Well, the thing is..."

"Yes?"

Serraptomus lowered his voice to a whispgriffle. "It's...it's not really Matlock, you see. He couldn't make it, Your Lordship. So he's sent Proftulous, his dworp, instead."

"Couldn't make it?" Garrick griffled, pulling an astonished face. "To his own vrooshfest?"

Serraptomus tapped the side of his nose twice, trying to be confidential. "He's been called away on sudden, urgent Most Majelicus business, Your Lordship. His dworp's all ready to step in, though. Or should I say, lump-thump."

Garrick looked towards the edge of the arena where Proftulous, dressed in a shabby, ripped green robe, stood nervously waiting with just an oidy twig in his ganticus paw. "Please don't tell me this is actually happening," he quietly moaned.

"We think he looks quite like a majickal-hare," Serraptomus tried. "Especially with those robes on. Quite caught me out, they did."

Garrick shook his head, staring at the ground for a snutch of moments, hoping against all hope that it might just somehow swallow him up, thereby neatly relieving him of the total and utter glopp-up of this most peffa-glubbstooled sun-turn. "Can the dworp do any vrooshers?" he heard himself asking.

"Oh, I doubt it," Serraptomus brightly griffled. "After all, he's only got an oidy twig for a wand. It's hardly going to work, is it? Useless, if you ask me."

Garrick was lost for griffles. In all his time as a peffa-important chaircreature, he hadn't ever encountered anything quite so saztaculously glubbstooled as this. Griffles defied him, refused to even begin to form themselves. He remembered Laffrohn, how she had left him in charge, telling him he might even be remembered as a true hero one sun-turn – Lord Garrick, the selfless creature who'd saved all the creatures of the majickal-dales in the face of a ganticus flood. They might even erect a statue in his honour, but then again, he reasoned, if his present situation was anything to go by, it'd most likely be of him, holding the paw of a big-beaked grifflelot with yechus feet, and Serraptomus chickling like a clottabus at his side.

"Shall we do the announcing?" Kringle asked him.

"Do you know," Garrick smiled, looking to the ever darkening skies and trying to smile, "I'd be ever so peffa-pleased if you could do it for me."

"Me?" Kringle griffled, brightening. "Really? I mean, I've never had the chance to put my own paw to my mouth before."

"Well, now you have."

"But," the anxious grifflelot griffled, "what if it makes my voice sound all glopped?"

Garrick rolled his eyes. "How *can* it? It's *your* voice, the same one you always use, from that very same ganticus beak of yours! It'll just be louder, that's all."

Kringle thought about this. "You're right!" he griffled, beaming as broadly as his beak would allow, raising his paw and loudly clearing his throat. "Creatures of all the majickal-dales! 'Tis the moment you've all been waiting for; the highlight, the finale, the ganticussly saztaculous end of our peffa-shindinculous contest!" He removed his paw, looked up at Garrick. "Am I doing all right?"

Garrick nodded, as the first heavy drops of rain began to fall. "Fine. Just keep going."

The paw went back. "So it gives me the peffa-greatest pleasure to be able to introduce the last majickal-hare of the competition – our very own Matlock the Hare from W*iiiiiiiiiiii*nchett D*aaaaaaaa*le!"

The crowd all roared, turning their heads to where Proftulous waited, Ledel by his side, encouraging him to lump-thump into the arena.

"Go on," the white wizard-hare griffled to him. "It'll all be fine. Just go out there and give it your briftest shot."

Proftulous took a deep dworp's breath. "But I don't be knowing any saztaculous vrooshers," he griffled, trying to be heard above the noise of the crowd. "I'll really gobflopp."

Ledel looked up into his doubting eyes. "This isn't about vrooshers, Proftulous. This is about you being tzorkly."

"Like you?"

"No. Like *you*. Like Proftulous." He pushed Proftulous lightly on his reluctant back, turning to the eager crowd and getting them to clap in unison, grillions of paws encouraging Proftulous to the centre of the arena with every hesitant lump-thump.

Serraptomus, sensing Proftulous' twizzliness, swiftly pid-padded to his side. "Saztaculous stuff, Proftulous!" he cried over the excrimbly crowd. "Hope you have a truly amazing vroosher ready?"

"That be the problem," Proftulous shouted back, brandishing the oidy twig. "I've never done one before."

"Crivens!" Serraptomus frowned. "Then why in Oramus' name have you gone and dressed up as Matlock? Seems a bit clottabussed, if you ask me."

"Because," Proftulous griffled, grinding his teeth and trying not to bliff the confused krate, "you told me to in the first place, remember?"

An oidy flash of recognition briefly flickered in Serraptomus' eyes. "Oh yes, I did, didn't I? Well, briftest of luck!" He vilishly pid-padded away leaving Proftulous alone at the centre of the arena. The crowd gradually quietened and the rain began to steadily fall, a situation Fragus the disidula from Winchett Dale quickly seized upon by 'selling' dozens of invisible umbrellas amongst the crowd.

Kringle pid-padded over, the wet grass slopping under his yechus feet, offering up his paw as high as it would go, Proftulous having to almost bend double to speak into it, rain steadily dripping from the end of his yechus nose. "Good and noble creatures of all the dales," he began, his voice faltering as a heavy garrumbloom of thunder rolled over nearby hills, "I have something to be griffling to you that be peffa-difficult to griffle."

"Well don't griffle it then!" someone shouted, his paw held aloft, sheltering his family under a non-existent umbrella. "Just get on with the vrooshing, as I think these umbrellas are an oidy bit glopped!"

"Nonsense," Fragus called over, still handing them out to eager paws desperate to shelter from the rain. "You just has to take it down and put it up again. Any clottabus knows that!"

The creature did so, miming the action, seemingly content that this had corrected the problem.

At the edge of the arena, the first of the colley-rocks arrived, rolling over to Garrick through the rain, looking utterly confused. "Are you in charge of this here Dale Vrooshfest, good creature?"

"Unfortunately," he griffled, his robes heavy with rain.

"So where are all the saztaculous tents, stalls, rides, guzzworts, food and essential vrooshfest facilities?"

"It's a long story," Garrick griffled. "Too peffa long, frankly." He pid-paded away through the restless crowd and looked over the edge of the plateau, seeing the waters rapidly rising in Wand Wood, vilishly becoming a ganticus lake, with just the tops of the last few trees poking above it. "Oh, my juppers," he quietly griffled, pid-padding back to find Serraptomus.

"I don't care how you do it," he whispgriffled in the wheezing krate's ear, "just make sure all eyes are on the dworp. I want all eyes in the arena, you hear me?"

Serraptomus nodded, swallowing hard and wincing. "And if I do, will I be excused washing-up duties until the last of my sun-turns?"

"Put it this way," Garrick hissed at him. "If you don't, *this* will be the last of your sun-turns!"

Serraptomus vilishly pid-padded through the increasingly wet and restless crowd, joining Proftulous and Kringle in the centre of the arena, grabbing the paw and swiftly putting it to his own mouth. "Good creatures!" he wheezed, trying to smile. "Although it isn't common practise to interrupt a majickal-hare's vrooshers..."

"He hadn't even started, yet!" a complaining wilting-jutter called out. "He's just been stood there, not griffling a griffle."

"This true?" Serraptomus asked, looking up at Proftulous.

The wet dworp nodded. "I had meself some griffles to be griffling," Proftulous tried to explained. "I been working them all out in my head while I be waiting. It's just that when I gets meself out here, it all be going." He looked at Serraptomus. "This just be too peffa-difficult for me."

A slow paw-clap began breaking out. Creatures began to boo and hurl invisible fruit, jeering loudly, Serraptomus ducking to dodge them.

"Proftulous," he urged. "Please, just try. You *must* at least try!"

Proftulous simply frowned at the russisculoffed crowd, quietly growling at them.

"I mean," Serraptomus tried, "look at me. I'm just a hopeless, clottabussed krate. I can't remember the last time I ever did *anything* officious. I just wheeze and whittle wood. That's all I ever really do. Most of my sun-turns are right peffa-gobfloppers, but it doesn't stop me trying."

Proftulous slowly turned to him as the jeers grew louder, looking down at the hopeful krate, rain bouncing from his officious head. He slowly knelt down. "Look into my eyes, Serraptomus," he griffled. "What do you see?"

Confused, Serraptomus peered into the yechus eyes. "I...I just see me," he griffled. "Just me, reflected there."

"Exactly," Proftulous griffled, his voice suddenly completely calm. "And who is to griffle that it *isn't* you? For right now, I see something of me in your eyes. But it isn't simply a reflection,

Serraptomus, it's something that perhaps I've been hiding from for too long."

Serraptomus blinked back, totally confused, not understanding a single griffle, yet sensing in his officious Sisteraculous that somehow this one moment in a mud-glopped, rain-sodden field was peffa-important. Something had happened to Proftulous that would change everything.

"You wanted a vroosher for a todel-bear?" Proftulous griffled to him, standing and brandishing the oidy twig. "Very well, Serraptomus. For services to being a peffa-glopped-up krate who really prefers whittling, here comes your very own todel-bear!"

Proftulous screwed up his yechus eyes, lifted them to the lid, rain pounding off his face, spreading both his arms out wide and smiling the most peffa-crumlushed and contented smile as a mighty garrumbloom of thunder cracksploded immediately overhead, blinding lightning thumping into the arena, causing everyone to cry out in sudden, excrimbly shock.

"Be staying where you all are!" Proftulous roared at them all. "The todel-bear will not be harming any of you! He just be here for some todelling is all!"

The watching creatures rubbed at their eyes, their vision gradually returning. "Where is it?" one called through the rain.

"Wait," Proftulous griffled. "He be coming right now."

Through the mist and the heavy cloud came the beginnings of truly ganticus lump-thumps, shaking the sodden ground, as an enormous grey bear's head rose over the edge of the plateau and roared louder than any thunder heard in any of the dales.

"It be here!" Proftulous cried.

The bear roared again, hauling itself over the edge of the plateau until it stood some hundred feet high, dressed in a long grey robe, easily striding over the crowd and lump-thumping its way into the centre of the arena, turning and roaring again.

"Nobody is to be getting twizzly, now," Proftulous cried, standing under the ganticus creature, his own yechus head barely reaching above its grey, furry ankle. "This be a fuzzcheck bear, a peffa-good bear. It not be here to be doing us any harm." He looked up into the rain. "Are you?"

The todel-bear looked down, snorted through its nose and shook its ganticus head.

"See? He just be wanting to be our friend."

To Proftulous' surprise, however, the crowd began to jeer. Russisculoffed cries of 'There's nothing there!' and 'Where is it then?' began to fill the arena.

The todel-bear roared once more, taking a ganticus lump-thump backwards, the earth shaking under its feet.

Proftulous held up his hands. "You can't be seeing it?" he griffled, pointing up at the bear. "It be here, right here! I be majicking it for you!"

"But you don't even *look* like a majickal-hare!" someone shouted back. "You look like some great glopped clottabus in glubbstooled robes! There's no way you could be majicking *anything*! You just be trying to get clever and smart with us! There's nothing there!"

Proftulous' jaw hung open. "You...really can't be seeing it? Or hearing it? Or feeling its ganticus lump-thumps shaking through your softulousses?"

"You're a fake!" a twisted-grittler cried. "You've made it all up! There be no such thing as a todel-bear!" It turned to the others. "Anyone else ever be hearing about a todel-bear?"

They all shook their heads, as once again boos and hisses started all around the arena.

But from the side, Garrick looked on, completely unable to believe just what he was seeing, urgently calling Serraptomus over, and pointing to the ganticus bear roaring back at the hostile crowd. "Is it safe?" he asked.

"Is what safe?" Serraptomus griffled.

"The bear, you great clottabus! The todel-bear! Is it safe? Is it going to stroff us all?"

Serraptomus looked back into the arena, wheezing slightly. "What bear?" he griffled. "There's no bear, Your Lordship. Just Proftulous getting all russisculoffed."

"You...you *really* can't see it?" Garrick griffled.

Serraptomus shook his head.

Garrick pushed him aside, vilishly making his way into the centre of the arena, ignoring the russisculoffed boos and chanting, the rain driving against his face. "Tell me," he urgently griffled to Proftulous, pointing up at the ganticus bear who was now staring curiously down at him. "Is this *thing* safe?"

"Of course he be safe," Proftulous griffled. "He simply be here to be doing some todelling."

Garrick swallowed hard, trying to keep what might have remained of his sanity. "Are you even aware, dworp, that Serraptomus *invented* the todel-bear purely to try and persuade me to award the Dale Vrooshfest to Winchett Dale? It doesn't even exist. Even *he* doesn't know what one is! The whole thing was just a desperate figment of his clottabussed imagination!"

Proftulous looked up at the huge bear, whose grey robes alone would have made two guzzwort tents. "Doesn't exist?" he griffled, smiling slightly. "Now this be most peffa-confusing." He leant down and whispgriffled in Garrick's ear. "Methinks you know all too peffa-well that it exists. Methinks you can be seeing it as well as I can."

Garrick furiously wiped the rain from his eyes, pointing at the russisculoffed, jeering crowd. "It's just made up, for Oramus' sake! Even *they* can't see it!"

Proftulous softly chickled. "And they be the same creatures that be 'seeing' an entire vrooshfest that doesn't exist, aren't they? Methinks p'raps they don't be making the briftest judges about such things, don't you?"

Garrick's face was a peffa-perfect picture of defeated, glopped misery. "I don't know," he moaned. "I...I just don't know any more." He appealed to Proftulous. "I don't think I really know *anything* anymore. What's real, or unreal, what exists, or what doesn't – it's all just...beyond me."

Proftulous put a reassuring paw over the humbled chaircreature's rain-sodden shoulders. "Bet you'd like to see it todel, though, eh?"

Without waiting for an answer, Proftulous nodded up at the ganticus bear, causing another ear-splitting roar as it bent down and offered a truly ganticus open-paw at Garrick's feet.

"Step on," Proftulous griffled, "and let him show you exactly what todelling be."

"Step on?" Garrick yelped, crying out as Proftulous pushed him onto the outstretched paw and he was vilishly lifted high into the air, right in front of the ganticus and formidable bear's face, each of its teeth twice as large than him. A rough tongue the size of a pink blanket suddenly shot from its mouth and licked him, Garrick squirming and yelling throughout.

Next, the todel-bear delicately sat Garrick on the bridge of his nose, the peffa-twizzly chairperson trying not to look down, simply staring into the huge eyes, each as large as one of the oaken-creakers in his distant castle.

"Well, what do we have here?" it griffled. "It be Lord Garrick, if I not be mistaken."

"Please don't eat me!" Garrick blurted out.

The todel bear chickled, Garrick nearly slipping and falling. "Eat you? Why would I eat you? Your softulous is so wretched with cowardly corruption, my crimple would be peffa-glopped for a moon-turn."

Garrick vilishly nodded. "Indeed," he nervously agreed. "I'd taste yechus, really glopped. Much better you just put me down, perhaps?"

"Time for todelling, methinks," the bear griffled, picking him up with his ganticus claws and vilishly raising him up above his head. "Up you be going!"

Garrick desperately hung onto a long claw, scrabbling to haul himself back into the safety of the open paw, wondering just how much higher he was going to go, looking down and seeing the snarling bear's head far below. It felt as if he'd been lifted almost to the lid itself, whisps of dark rain clouds soon disappearing as he continued ever upwards, becoming whiter as the todel-bear's arm reached even higher. Garrick simply shut both eyes, clinging on, wondering just when it was he would be dropped, and how long it would take to fall to the ground and stroff.

He didn't have to wait long…

The paw began to slow, Garrick now feeling warm sun on his face, opening his eyes to the clearest blue sky, his rain-sodden robes gently steaming in the quiet serenity of the moment. He sucked in his breath, looking all round, seeing nothing but beautiful clear blue calm and realising in that one blinksnap that somehow everything had *always* been like this. Regardless of all his glopped ambitions, his greedy deals and lazy drutt-fuelled life, they were as nothing to the saztaculous quiet above the clouds. Far below, he could make out just the oidiest, distant echoes of the jeering, booing crowd drifting up in warm winds that seemed to almost caress his face. Nothing seemed to matter any more, except this. Nothing had any meaning or reason, as if everything had stood completely still. Whatever was happening far, far below had no impact on this endless, everlasting peace...

Then, as he was still lost in the crumlush moment, the todel-bear's paw began to tilt, throwing him to one side. He frantically tried to reach out for a ganticus claw, but was effortlessly flicked away and sent plummeting, falling straight back down into the bank of cloud, unable to breathe, completely and utterly twizzled, eyes tightly shut, feeling the cold and darkness return, winds whistling all round, rain pounding at his face as the noise from the vilishly approaching vrooshfest grew and grew in his terrified ears...

But without warning, he suddenly stopped, jerked to a standstill just inches from the onrushing ground, his wet robes pinched between the todel-bear's claws, righting him onto his shaking feet to stand before Proftulous.

"You be enjoying your todel?" the smiling dworp asked. "Methinks some creatures just likes it for the ride." Proftulous winked at the breathless chairperson. "But p'rhaps they be the ones that can *always* see a todel-bear in the first place."

Garrick struggled for griffles, wide-eyed. "It's...saztaculous up there," he eventually managed. "Completely crumlush."

Proftulous looked towards the ridge of the plateau and the flooding dale beyond the baying crowds. "Methinks the way these waters are rising so vilishly we might not be safe." He pointed towards the village of Winchett Dale, now totally submerged. "It won't be much longer and all the floody will be easily reaching us."

Garrick, still trying to get over his todelling and not quite sure if his feet really were firmly on the ground, looked towards the distant skyline of Twinkling Lid Heights. "Up there," he griffled. "It's far higher. We'll all be safer."

Proftulous nodded. "It be higher, alright. But it's too far away.

The dale be flood-glopped. We'd never get up there." He watched Garrick carefully, seeing if the chairperson would finally work it out.

"I know!" Garrick griffled, pointing up at the todel-bear with an excrimbly finger. "We use the bear! It can take us across!"

Proftulous nodded, slowly smiling. "It be a most fuzzcheck plan," he agreed. "Save for one oidy thing."

"What's that?"

Proftulous pointed to the russisculoffed crowd. "I believe these folk would firstly have to be *seeing* the todel-bear for it to be able to help them."

Garrick looked at Proftulous. "You mean...you mean, I have to...convince them that this ganticus bear actually exists?"

Proftulous nodded, the rain bouncing from his yechus head. "It be seeming like the briftest place to start."

"But they clearly *can't* see it!" Garrick protested. "How can I griffle them that it exists?"

"Well," Proftulous griffled, beckoning Kringle over through the driving rain, and putting his paw to Garricks lips, "methinks you'd best use this."

"Where are you going?" Garrick cried, watching as Proftulous lump-thumped from the arena. "You can't just leave me!"

"I can, and I am," Proftulous griffled. "Me needs to be finding Ledel. You just be sorting everything out all fuzzcheck and proper for everyone."

"But..." Garrick moaned, watching Proftulous disappear into the booing crowd, then feeling the eyes of thousands of creatures settling on him, all soaked through to the skin, fur and scales, huddling under invisible umbrellas in torrential rain, waiting for his announcement.

He cleared his throat, all too aware of the ganticus foot right next to him, reminded of the briefest moments of contented bliss he'd felt above the clouds, bathed in the warm blue, a seeming grillion miles away from the muddy, rain-soaked, glopped-up misery he now found himself in.

"Griffle something!" a voice called out. "We're all waiting!"

He nodded, squeezing Kringle's paw, part of him almost relieved when the peffa-strange creature gently squeezed back. It was the moment, he knew; the time for truth, however much they'd despise him for it. He took a deep breath, knowing it was the only way to try and save them all.

The rain began to ease as he started to griffle, creatures looking to the thinning skies, some even putting away their non-existent umbrellas.

"Majickal-creatures of all these dales," he began. "It has been a peffa-long and saztaculous sun-turn, I think you'll all agree. And even if it did start out like a typical Winchett Dale gobflopper with the singing kraark's glubbstooled showstopper about his milky-white eye, I think each and every one of us would like to thank the good creatures of this most clottabussed dale for nonetheless rising to the occasion and putting on a most peffa-shindinculous Dale Vrooshfest for us all."

"Get on with it!" an irate-jortle called out. "Just griffle us who the winner is!"

Cries of 'Ledel, Ledel, Ledel' began to ring around the plateau, creatures stamping their feet in the glopped-mud.

Garrick appealed for calm. "Before I announce the winner… there's something I have to griffle to you all, and it's peffa, peffa-important."

"Has the guzzwort run out?" a confused twolp shouted, licking his three lips. "Only it were right nice, it really were. Briftest I've had at one of these fests."

"No, it's not the guzzwort," Garrick griffled, taking a long, deep breath. "Although, perhaps, in a way, it is."

The creatures looked back, confused, the rain finally fading to just the finest drizzle as the beginnings of the oidiest glimpses of sunshine broke through overhead.

"You see, good creatures," Garrick continued. "The guzzwort you've all been enjoying so peffa-much, the fine food, pies, soups and cakes – the tents, stalls, banners, flags and all the saztaculous things that make a vrooshfest…" He took another deep breath. "… none of it exists. Not a single mug, bowl, plate, umbrella or anything else. It's all false, made up. Everything."

Above him, the todel-bear gently mumbled, its approving toes slightly clutching at the bright-green sunlit grass.

"Hang on," a committee member called across, "are you seriously griffling that we've been eating nothing but air all sun-turn?"

Garrick nodded.

The committee creature thought about this, muttering to himself, before griffling, "That'd explain everything. I must have had at least twenty-pies, and don't feel a thing. Normally, I'm lying on the floor looking peffa-glopped at this point."

Gradually, the realisation began to spread amongst the stunned crowd as thousands of shocked creatures looked round and saw the empty pleateau as it truly was for the first time, unable to believe just quite how easily they'd been fooled. Next, they began to get restless, and Garrick, sensing it would soon turn into russisculoftulation, quickly put Kringle's paw to his mouth, griffling urgently into it "Good creatures, if there is one single creature who is most responsible for this glopp-up, then it's me. I alone have led a glubbstooled committee of gobfloppers that have done nothing but take bribes and lazily feast every sun-turn, while you have believed in the integrity of ourselves and the Dale Vrooshfests. Good creatures, I can now griffle to you that what we did was wrong."

A swollen-premble raised a webbed paw. "Begging your pardon, Your Lordship, but I don't think there be a single one of us stood here that didn't already know you lot were all corrupt gobfloppers. 'Tis simply the way of all committees in these dales, right the way through. You see, for us, the Dale Vrooshfest is more about the day out, really. It's what we all look forward to – and of course, discovering who be named *Briftest Majickal-Hare of All the Dales.*"

One of the other committee members stood, outraged at what he'd heard. "What, *all* of you realised we were useless?"

The crowd nodded as one.

The committee member humbly sat back down, muttering and shaking his head to fellow members around the empty table.

The swollen-premble, sensing that he had become spokescreature for the crowd, pressed on. "We look around ourselves now, and probably feel an oidy bit clottabussed that we saw things that weren't real, feasted on food and drank guzzworts that never existed – but as far as I can be telling, we've all had a saztaculous sun-turn here in Winchett Dale, and most probably one we'll all be remembering for the rest of our moon-turns." He frowned slightly. "All except for the singing-flapper and his white-eye business. And the hare from Ceedius Dale, the dancing one. They were both truly glubstooled. Dreadful."

"So you *really* don't mind?" Garrick asked them, relief coursing though him. "You're not really, really peffa-russisculoffed?"

"Just be griffling to us who the winner be," the swollen-premble griffled, "then we can all be making our peffa-long journeys home before any more of that lid-splashy comes down." He threw away the imaginary umbrella he was still holding. "Because these things are heavier than you think."

Garrick awkwardly scratched the back of his neck. "Well, creatures, here's the problem. The peffa-ganticus problem. For while it was greed that made me choose Winchett Dale to host this extraordinary Dale Vrooshfest, it…er…appears there might have been another reason I was completely unaware of. A much more important reason." Far above him, the todel-bear muttered its approval. "For while we've all been here up on the High Plateau, we've been safe."

"Safe?" someone cried out, alarmed. "Safe from what?"

Garrick took a deep breath. "Turn around, and you'll see."

The crowd slowly turned seeing the edge of the plateau dropping away to the rising floodwaters. A ganticus gasp began to vilishly change to rising, twizzly panic. Creatures began pid-padding and lump-thumping to the edges, trying to find any way of escaping that wasn't straight down into the dark-brown, churning waters.

"We be surrounded!"

"We're all going to be drowney-stroffed!"

"The waters still be rising! What of our homes? How do we get back to our own dales?"

The peffa-twizzly crowd began to close in on Garrick and Kringle, urgently demanding answers. He held up his hands. "Please, there's no reason to get so twizzled! I have a plan to get us out of here."

"Like what?" someone angrily sneered. "Some sort of ganticus invisible bird that you've bribed to fly us all out of here?"

"Sort of," Garrick hurriedly griffled. "Sort of very like that, indeed. You see, I'm reliably informed, and can griffle from my own recent experience, that some creatures can't see a good thing when it's standing right in front of them." He took a vilish breath. "So now, I want you to do just that. Really open your eyes and see the ganticus todel-bear that's stood next to me."

"What in Oramus' name are you griffling about?" a female shuttock cried. "This be no time for any more of your glubbstooled todel-bear trickery!"

The rest of the crowd agreed, pressing forwards.

"Please!" Garrick pleaded, scrambling up onto the todel-bear's ganticus foot. "Just see it! Please! Look at me – I'm not floating in air. I'm on its foot! It's so ganticus that it'll be able to get you up to Twinkling Lid Heights! You'll all be safe! Just see the bear! *Please* just see the todel-bear!"

The crowd stopped surging, following Garrick's arm as it pointed towards the distant limestone-cliffs across the rising waters, realising just how high they were, knowing how much safer they'd all be if they could somehow get up there.

One cautiously pid-padded forward, holding out an arm for Garrick to haul it up onto the ganticus grey foot. It let out a peffa-astonished gasp. "I see it!" it cried to the others. "It's true! I can see it now! I'm on its foot!"

Far above, the todel-bear let out a roar, creatures suddenly ducking and as he bent down and dropped his open paws to the ground with a ganticus garrumbloom, causing a desperate surge to climb on, creatures pushing and kicking others out of the way, completely twizzled, frantic to be taken to the safety of the heights.

Garrick reached down through the crowd and managed to pull Kringle up onto the ganticus foot, vilishly putting his paw to his mouth. "No one must get twizzly!" he cried. "It'll take more than one trip! Everyone will get there if we all remain calm!"

The crowd dropped back as the todel-bear gently raised its paws laden with twizzled creatures then slowly lump-thumped to the edge of the plateau and cautiously entered the flood, the water rising almost up to his shoulders, the remaining creatures all watching, barely able to take a breath as he began forcefully wading over what had once been Grifflop marshes.

Around him, the dark waters rushed and churned. He nearly slipped right over, fighting the current, turning his back to the surge and sidestepping towards the sheer cliffs of Twinkling Lid Heights, before finally reaching out and majickally extending his ganticus arms to the very top, allowing the peffa-twizzled creatures to scramble to safety.

"Well, I'll be a disidula's-uncle!" a short-legged teppit on the High Plateau called out as the todel-bear made his way slowly back through the deep flood. "They're safe! The todel-whatsit has saved 'em!"

"But the water's still rising!" a twizzly gompfer cried, pointing. "There's not enough time for it to make more trips across! We'll all drown and be stroffed!"

The creatures, now caught in a most panicked peffa-twizzle, vilishly stampeded towards the edge of the plateau, barely waiting for the ganticus, juzzpapped creature to haul itself over before jumping straight onto it, clinging onto anything they could; wet robes, paws, arms, ears, even its eyebrows. In just a snutch of blinksnaps the todel-bear was covered in a sea of scrambling, shouting creatures, frantically trying to stay on as he tried to right himself for the return journey.

"There's too many of you!" Garrick screamed through Kringle's paw. "He can't take you all at once! Wait for him to come back! There's too many of you!"

But the creatures were having none of it, still desperately piling themselves up onto his head, reaching down to help others, hauling on the wet, grey robes, more creatures leaping from the edge of the plateau as the huge bear set slowly back off into the deep, churning water, looking like a single, ganticus ball of peffa-twizzly creatures, moving deeper and deeper into the rising flood.

And then, it happened…

The todel-bear lost his footing, stumbling in the surge, creatures falling into the churning froth and being swept away, their screams soon lost in the rising waters.

"Oramus, have mercy on us all," Garrick griffled, unable to take his eyes from the terrible spectacle, watching the todel-bear suddenly lurch dreadfully sideways, crashing into the swell and being dragged under with one final, desperate roar, taking last of the clinging creatures with him.

Garrick sprinted to the edge of the plateau, looking for signs of life breaking the waters, seeing none, knowing that at that precise moment the creatures were all tumbling, drowning and stroffing in the yechussly glopped flood.

"Oramus! Help us!" he cried, pushing shocked and stunned creatures out of the way, stumbling back into the middle of the plateau, lifting his arm to the lid and pointing angrily. "How can you let this happen? Where *are* you! Your creatures are stroffing! Your dales are flooding! Everything's going glopped, and you're nowhere!"

A paw clumped onto Garrick's shoulder. He span round, wild-eyed with twizzly-rage to see Proftulous pointing to the skies as a ganticus, distant roar slowly filled the lid.

"P'raps Oramus has been sending us these," he griffled as the first wave of airborne witches roared thankfully into view, circling the plateau and diving straight into the waters, rising out a blinksnap later each with a splutting, gasping creature on the back of their brooms and flying straight to the safety of Twinkling Lid Heights, before returning to dive again.

"By my griffles!"Garrick gasped, yelping for joy. "It's *The League of Lid-Curving Witchery!*"

A snutch of moments later and the lid was thick and black with thousands of roaring witches, diving into the flood and rescuing drowning creatures then flying them to the distant limestone cliffs, as those that remained on the High Pleateau cheered in excrimbly relief, unable to believe what they were seeing.

"What about the bear?" Garrick asked, pacing along the edge of the plateau, urgently staring into the churning waters. "Why aren't they rescuing the bear?"

"The bear be gone," Proftulous griffled to him. "And now I think it be time for you to join the others on Twinkling Lid Heights. So be getting on one of those vroffa-brooms while you still can."

"And you?" Garrick griffled as a cackling witch landed nearby and beckoned him over. "What about you?"

Me?" Proftulous griffled, watching as another witch in green

"P'raps Oramus has been sending us these," he griffled as
the first wave of airborne witches roared thankfully into view...

and golden robes landed right by Ledel Gulbrandsen. "I'll be along in just a snutch of blinksnaps, don't you be worrying about that." He waved as Garrick vilishly took to the sky, then pid-padded over to join Ledel and the witch, now the last remaining creatures on the plateau, the floodwaters already spilling onto the wet grass, trickling and puddling over the boggy ground.

Ledel was already bowing to her as Proftulous arrived.

"And you," she warmly smiled, turning, "must be Proftulous, famed dworp of Matlock the Hare, the same dworp who is rumoured to have once eaten the entire collection of majickal-driftolubbs at one sitting."

Proftulous flushed slightly. "It not be that difficult. I was mostly eating a ganticus tweazle-pie at the time."

"Really?" she griffled, raising an eyebrow. "That's not the way I've been hearing it, good dworp. Griffles reached my ears that those driftolubbs made you Most Majelicus and it was far from any splurked accident."

Proftulous shifted awkwardly. "Sometimes, griffles has a way of getting glopped when they be passed from many mouths to even more ears, methinks." He looked at her. "And you must be being Soriah Kherflahdle, *Grand High Priestess of the Tzorkly Order of The League of Lid-Curving Witchery.*"

She raised another eyebrow. "You know much about me for such a clottabussed dworp?"

He paused, an oidy bit stuck. "It be the green and golden robe and hat. Makes you be looking all peffa-important, so I be thinking you had to be the most peffa-important of all the witches, and everyone knows that be you." He took a breath. "So...all your witches be getting here in just the peffa-right blinksnap."

Soriah just chickled at him. "How many others know?"

"Know?" he griffled.

She nodded, then turned to Ledel, who was looking more bemused than ever. "Did *you* know, wizard? Surely you would know, the peffa-tzorkly and saztaculous Ledel Gulbrandsen, living hare-legend from across the Icy Seas – surely you can see it?"

Ledel blinked a snutch of times. "See it?" He turned to Proftulous. "Would anyone mind griffling to me what's going on?"

"Well," Proftulous griffled as the pair of them watched Soriah skipping and chickling in the flood. "As far as I can be making out, it appears that we be standing up to our ankles in rising waters, while she be jumping and splashing about like a clottabussed leveret."

"Correction," Ledel pointed out. "The flood might very well be up to your ankles, but it's almost up to my knees."

Proftulous looked down, seeing Ledel's gown floating around his waist like a suddenly blooming white rose. "You be right about that," he griffled, effortlessly lifting the wizard-hare up onto his shoulders.

"I generally am about most things," Ledel griffled, looking at Soriah splashing through the rising waters, oblivious to the obvious danger. "Begging your pardon, Your Tzorkliness," he called out to her, "but I think it's time we took flight."

Proftulous waded across, grabbing Soriah's vroffa-broom before it floated away, then lifting her out of the water and awkwardly perching her on his other shoulder. "So," he griffled, "methinks now be the peffa-perfect blinksnap for us all to be flying away."

Soriah was still chickling, her face bright and resonant with so many different thoughts and possibilites. "It's just all so good!" she griffled. "And yet it's also all so bad! It's neither one thing, nor the other. It's saztaculous, but also splurked! And yet, it also makes sense – of everything! The past, and the future!"

"We really have to be leaving now," Proftulous insisted.

She turned to him. "Oh, Proftulous, *what* a future! I can see it all. Will he do it? Will Matlock actually do it? But he *has* to, doesn't he? He has to for *all* of us!" She laughed out loud. "For everything! Everything that is, has been and will be – and it will all come down to one peffa-splurked majickal-hare!"

"Then can I humbly suggest," Ledel griffled, trying not to get too russisculoffed, "that you spend a little less time thinking about it, Your Tzorkliness, and more time starting your broom? We really don't have much time left."

She suddenly looked across, as if seeing Ledel for the first time, bursting out into loud laughter again, pointing right at his annoyed face. "And you!" she griffled. "You're a part of this, too, Ledel! Only you can't see it yet, can you? You can't see an oidy bit of what's *really* going on, can you? Not the oidiest, oideist bit!"

"What I can see," Ledel griffled, gritting his teeth, "is that right now the waters are dangerously close to stroffing us all. Frankly, I'd rather griffle about what I may or may not 'see' when we're up on those cliffs. Until then, I suggest it's vroffa-time, rather than griffle-time."

She raised both eyebrows, her eyes widening as something else suddenly made peffa-perfect sense. "Oh, yes," she griffled, "I can see why *you* were chosen, Ledel. Calm under pressure with a sharp, tzorkly mind. And believe me, when it all *really* starts, when this finally begins, you're going to need a ganticus lot of that, Ledel, a peffa-ganticus lot of it."

"P'raps the only thing we should be starting," Proftulous pleaded, the water now over his chest, "is this broom of yours."

Soriah, nodded, smiling, seemingly content to finally grasp the broom, closing her eyes and whispgriffling to it, the vroffa-branches bursting into roaring-life as she and Ledel climbed on, reaching down to help Proftulous struggle onto the back, the three of them finally setting off into the lid over the vast lake that now covered the whole of Winchett Dale, save for the small ridge of Twinkling Lid Heights, crowded with creatures and witches, all pointing to the skies and cheering as they landed.

"P'rhaps next time," Proftulous griffled, climbing off, relieved to finally have his dworp's feet on solid, stony, ground, "we won't leave it to the peffa-last blinksnap." He lump-thumped away through the excrimbly crowds towards a quiet spot at the edge of the cliffs, looking down at what had once been his home just a few short hours earlier.

Soriah followed him, pid-padding to his side. "I just wanted to griffle that I won't griffle a griffle to anyone."

He looked at her. "I be liking your hat."

She smiled, putting a paw to her lips. "Your secret's safe with me."

"What, that I be liking hats?"

She chickled. "No. The other one." She looked out over the flood, the waters still rising and gradually creeping up the cliff-face. "Is it all going to be crumlush in the end, Proftulous?"

Proftulous took a long time, his yechus brow creasing. "I not be knowing anymore, " he quietly griffled.

"But it *had* to happen, didn't it?" she griffled. "Wasn't this all somehow meant to be?"

"P'raps," he griffled, feeling an oidy bit choked, not wanting to cry, not now, not when he had to be at his strongest.

"Can I ask one last question? Then I won't griffle another griffle about any of it."

He nodded.

"Why does it have to be Matlock? Why him? He's done nothing wrong, or glopped or splurked."

Proftulous frowned, his yechus lips moving, trying to find an answer, a cold, wet paw reaching up and rubbing the side of his face, hoping she wouldn't notice the single eyesplasher that fell to the ground at his feet.

The Tillian Wand

11.

The Icy Seas, Legends and Statues

"Well," Matlock announced as the ganticus bubble slowly sank and bumped against the bottom of the seabed, "I'm supposing that somehow you have a plan for all this, Ayaani?"

"Not as such," she replied, peering into the gloom, making out occasional gawping eyes of startled fish outside.

"Then please tell me you're working on one," he griffled, pushing against the bubble and feeling the full weight of the cold sea pressing back against his paw. "Please tell me that somehow you always knew this was going to happen, and that somewhere inside that dripple's brain of yours, you'd already come up with a tremendously saztaculous plan."

"You're still angry about the Ursula thing, aren't you?"

"Frankly, yes," Matlock admitted. "You lied to me, Ayaani. You told a ganticus spuddle about me being the last ever majickal-hare which made me look like a peffa-clottabus and…"

"I can't believe you're still russisculoffed over that!" she griffled. "Honestly, how much time do you waste thinking about, oidy, clottabussed things that no-one else would even bother about? For Oramus' sake – just look where we are, stuck in a bubble at the bottom of the Icy Seas! Yet all you can do is griffle on about some spuddle." She scrittled down his robes. "Don't you think that really, you have far more peffa-serious things to worry about?"

She scrittled down his robes. "Don't you think that really, you have far more peffa-serious things to worry about?"

"Plenty," Matlock agreed. "Far too many. So many, in fact, that I can't even begin to sort them out in my head in the first place. So as such, I'm simply worrying about whichever one happens to pop into my mind at the time – which right now is your disgracefully glopped disloyalty to me."

She slowly folded her arms and looked up with black, glaring eyes. "Light your wand. Now!"

Knowing it was always unwise to refuse Ayaani when her face was set, Matlock reached into his robe for his wand, the bright red frizzing tip illuminating the inside of the bubble, turning everything a deep shade of pink and startling a group of fish to vilishly swim away into the darkness.

"Make it brighter," she ordered.

"Brighter?"

"Oh, Matlock, just do some majick for once! Make it brighter. We need to know where we are and precisely what's out there."

Matlock frowned, his brow creased. "That's just the point, though. That griffle 'precisely'."

"What in Oramus' name are you on about?"

"Well," he griffled, trying to explain. "Have you ever felt so twizzly, that really, you don't actually *want* to know what's out there? Like, if you're nifferduggling at night, and you suddenly wake up and hear a strange noise deep in Wand Wood, and it's getting closer and closer and..."

She stared blankly back. "Not really. Chances are, it'd most likely be that clottabus Proftulous, lump-thumping around, looking for tweazles."

"But that's just it, Ayaani. I wouldn't think like that." He reluctantly peered out into the darkness. "And what happens if it *wasn't* Proftulous? What happens if it was really something far more yechus and twizzly, with ganticus claws and teeth and..."

"Matlock," Ayaani griffled, "just light the wand properly. We're going to see what's out there, and that's the end of it. Because really, however cosy this is, I've no desire to end up stroffed in a witch's tear on the bottom of the Icy Seas with just a twizzly majickal-hare for company."

He gripped the wand tighter, the pinking glow flashing yellow for a blinksnap, briefly illuminating more of the gloomy seabed. "But what if the smoke-witch is out there?"

She sighed. "Sometimes, Matlock, I despair, I really do. If Alvestra *is* out there, then it means that we're closer to finding the other half of the wand. Don't you understand? She's as keen to find it as we are. She stroffed trying to get her yechus hands on it, so she's not likely to give up now."

"I'm just getting rather twizzly right now, that's all," he griffled. "Everything's so dark out there."

"Lift me up," she instructed. "I need to griffle to you, eye to eye."

Matlock did so, stooping and lifting the earnest dripple to his face.

"For far too long," she griffled, "in fact, ever since I've known you – you haven't even *begun* to notice the peffa-important and obvious things that have been going on all around you. You've never once stopped to look up and see, use your ears to listen, or even begin to griffle the obvious questions, let alone look for any answers. You've simply been Matlock the Hare, in and about your business of being rather less than majickal in Winchett Dale."

"This is going to turn into one of your serious griffversations, isn't it?"

"Just listen. For all of my life with you, I've been silent, as all dripples are with their masters. But, as you know, solving the riddle of Trefflepugga Path changed all that. I can griffle now. I can finally begin to tell you things that might sound glopped, but really, I think you ought to know."

"Trefflepugga Path," he mused. "Now that *does* seem a peffa-long time ago."

She silenced him with a look. "Last even'up at the inn, you griffled that life wasn't about answers, but questions. The snoffibs knew grillions of answers, but not to the right questions. Answers aren't the thing, Matlock, and neither are questions."

"So what is 'the thing', then?"

"Choices."

"Choices?"

She nodded, firmly holding his eyeline. "It's only if we *choose* to ask the right questions, Matlock. And then, afterwards, if we ever choose to also try and find the right answers."

A shoal of blue ziller-fish swam by, rocking the bubble.

"Go on," he griffled.

"I had a choice," she griffled. "I had a choice to bind my sun-turns in these dales to a single majickal-hare master – to faithfully serve him according to dripple-lore, like generations of my kind before me."

"And I'm peffa-grateful you chose me," Matlock assured her. "You've always kept the cottage and potionary tidy, made quite the most crumlush niff-soup and brottle leaf brews, and…"

"I didn't."

"Oh, but you did," he insisted. "Quite the most slurpilicious brews, soup and…"

"No," Ayaani griffled, her face deadly serious. "I meant, I didn't choose *you*."

A ganticus shock coursed through his softulous. "You didn't… you didn't choose *me*?" He could barely get the griffles out.

Ayaani shook her head.

"This is a joke," he griffled, his tongue suddenly far too dry. "Another one of your peffa-glopped spuddles." He looked at her for a long snutch of moments, the only sound his quickening breath. "Isn't it?"

Again, she shook her head.

"But…I don't understand," he griffled, looking all round, yet seeing nothing, unable to believe even the oidiest griffle of what he'd just heard. "It's not true. It *can't* be. You chose me. You peffa-definitely chose me!"

"No," Ayaani calmly replied. "I chose another majickal-hare. But it became impossible. My life was in danger, and he knew that, so he gave me to you, knowing in his Sisteraculous that it was the briftest way for all of us to live."

"Who was it?" Matlock urgently griffled. "Who did you chose, Ayaani? Who's your real master?"

"And the answer to that question comes from one you've never even thought to ask," she griffled. "An easy question, a peffa-obvious question, one that despite everything you now know, has never occurred to you for even the oidiest, oidiest blinksnap." She scrittled up onto his shoulder. "Think, Matlock! Find the one question you *really* have to ask yourself to understand the choice my master had to make. Think."

"I can't," he griffled. "I'm so…confused and so…peffa-vexed by all this." He turned to her. "You *really* didn't choose me?"

"Not at first," she confirmed, as his heart sank even further. "You weren't the one, Matlock. You *became* my master, but you weren't ever my *true* master. I chose to be with you when it all went peffa-twizzly and glopped."

"What went peffa-twizzly and glopped?"

"Again, that isn't the question you should be asking," she griffled. "You're sounding like a snoffib now, all panicked because a thinking-machine isn't giving you right answers."

He nodded, becoming twizzly. "Because I need *you* to give me them, Ayaani! You know – just tell me!"

"The answer isn't mine to give, but yours to find and realise for yourself."

"Stop griffling riddles!" Matlock griffled, russisculoffed. "You *are* mine! You've always been mine! You chose *me*, for Oramus' sake, not some other majickal-hare!"

"Just think," she calmly griffled. "Think about what has been under that clottabussed nose of yours all the time."

He tried to calm his twizzled russisculoftulation, taking a snutch of deep hare's breaths to make sense of it all. For no matter how glopped he felt in the knowing, the look on Ayaani's face told him that this time, she wasn't telling spuddles. It was no joke, no tall story to make him look clottabussed. Every single griffle was true – she belonged to another master. But who?

Then – curiously – almost unnoticed to him, the more he tried to clear his mind and find the peffa-glopped, elusive question, the more his wand began to glow more brightly. Gradually at first, then emitting a pulsing yellow light that seemed to swirl and dance inside the bubble, becoming brighter by the blinksnap, as if sensing that somehow Matlock was about to finally stumble upon a revelation so obvious, so important, that in itself, it would be majickal enough to begin shedding light on so much that finally needed to be revealed…

He thought of many things; of all he knew to be his every truth; his quiet and crumlush life in Winchett Dale with its clottabussed creatures and villagers, his sun-turns and even'ups of making potions, tending his cottage garden, griffles with friends at the inn, sitting around the blazing piff-tosh, a mug of guzzwort in his paw, smiling his familiar curling smile.

"The question is," he quietly griffled, as Ayaani listened to each and every griffle, "the question is…"

"Yes?"

"Why didn't I 'see' anything earlier?" The wand pulsed a whiter, more intense light, illuminating the beginning of rocks and underwater caverns nearby. "The question is – *how* could I have missed so much?" He turned to her, his orange hare's eyes intent. "Why didn't I ever see things for what they really were?" He bliffed his forehead in frustration. "For Oramus' sake! I had a dripple that wasn't even mine, a Most Majelicus master who simply wore stolen red robes! I just thought everything was fine. I never began to even question why it was that…"

Ayaani watched as he suddenly stopped griffling, the obvious question finally occurring. "You never even questioned 'what', Matlock?"

He let out a breath, trying his briftest to manage the oidiest smile. "Why it was that Chatsworth never had his own dripple?"

She nodded, gently putting her soft head against his.

"It was Baselott, wasn't it?" Matlock griffled, his mind finally clearing and beginning to see the truth. "His own dripple had stroffed, and as a scientist he would have wanted to repeat the griffling experiment – but this time with you, with Chatsworth's dripple."

She tried to smile. "Chatsworth couldn't stand the thought of it, couldn't have it on his conscience. He was racked with guilt for his lost dworp, shamed and twizzly for wearing the Most Majelicus robes of another hare. He wouldn't let me be used in another of his own master's experiments. And regardless of whatever you might think of him, Matlock, no matter how cold or cruel you think he is – to me, my master is still the noblest of all majickal-hares."

Matlock tried not to feel utterly glopped by the admission. "So he gave you to me?"

Ayaani nodded. "It was the only way. Even though I couldn't ever griffle to him, I understood why. We both knew the danger was peffa-real. We'd been in the underground burrow for too long, hiding away, watching Baselott obsessing about his theories and experiments. It would only have been a matter of time before he started on me."

Matlock frowned. "It's why you found his diary so easily when we were down there, wasn't it? You knew exactly where it was, because you'd already lived there."

She nodded. "Yes, I knew where he kept it, and that you probably needed to read those griffles, Matlock, more than anyone else. You needed to open your eyes and begin to see just exactly what's been going on."

But instead of opening them, he shut them, needing to think. "Ayaani," he slowly griffled, "please forgive me. It's just that all of this is so…peffa-difficult to take in. It's quite completely glopped. You've been Chatsworth's dripple all along?"

Again, she tried to smile.

"So why tell me now?" he asked her. "After all these many moon-turns we've been together, after all our adventures and glopp-ups, why tell me something as truly glubbstooled as this? Why not just keep it quiet and let me carry on believing you'd chosen me, and that Chatsworth was truly Most Majelicus, and that everything in my life was always as crumlush as it ever was? Why, Ayaani?"

"Because," she slowly griffled, "it wouldn't have been the truth."

He let out a long slow breath, the bubble now shindiculously bright with light. "But perhaps," he griffled, "sometimes it's brifter if the truth *isn't* always griffled, Ayaani. Sometimes the truth can make someone feel completely glopped."

"True," she tried to explain, "but the moment I recognised the entrance to the burrow under the thinking-machine, I realised what I had to do. I knew in my own oidy Sisteraculous that we hadn't been bought there by some sort of glubbstooled accident. It was all too much of a coincidence." She looked him in the eye. "Don't you see, Matlock? *None* of this is chance. Everything is happening for a reason. Something, or someone is making sure that everything we're doing has a purpose to it." She put her oidy paws around his neck. "What I'm trying to griffle is that despite everything being glopped and twizzly at the moment – I still think that somehow we're being looked after."

He tried to smile.

"It's why I had to show you Baselott's diary," she griffled. "Because I think that whatever it is that's helping us – I think it *wants* the truth to be known. It's why it keeps taking us to all these places. Remember Trefflepugga Path? Everything seemed pure chance, yet everywhere we went had a purpose that bought us both here, right now, to this glopped witch's bubble-tear at the bottom of the Icy Seas.

"Matlock, I don't know where we're going, or how we'll get there, or if we'll ever find the Tillian Wand. All I know is that you deserve to know the truth about yourself. Chatsworth may be my true master, but I also know deep in my Sisteraculous that whoever would have been your dripple would also have been the peffa-luckiest dripple in the history of all the dales. For while Chatsworth might be the noblest, truly you are the peffa-kindest majickal-hare, even if you are annoyingly clottabussed at times." She hugged his neck a little tighter. "You're right, we've had some saztaculous adventures together, you and I. Sometimes, even with that yechus great clottabus Proftulous, too. And I will be forever grateful for those. After all, it was because of you that I was finally able to griffle."

"Yes," Matlock admitted, "although I'm rather beginning to regret that now."

She smiled. "And do you know the reason why you never saw what was going on around you? The *real* answer to your question?"

"Because I'm a glopp-up?"

"Trust," she griffled. "It's because you trusted. It's because you still do. That's what makes you who you are, Matlock. You trust. And not only in your Sisteraculous. You trust creatures, the trees and animals of the forest, each blade of grass in the meadows, every drop of lid-splashy that falls. That's what makes you so peffa-special, Matlock. That's why you've been chosen to do what you'll have to do. Because no other creature could ever, *ever* be called upon do it. But you *will* do it, Matlock, when the time comes – because you will always trust. And in doing so, you will change everything. Everything."

"What?" he griffled to her. "What's this thing that I'll have to do? Do you know?"

"One thing at a time," she griffled, peering outside into the heavy, icy waters. "Right now, we have to be concerning ourselves with finding a wand from an ancient spuddle." She turned to him, nodding to herself. "It's strange, but I think I finally recognise my own part in all this; to help you find the Tillian Wand, so you can go on and do what you really have to do. I don't know how long this bubble will last, or even how safe we are inside it, but right now the one thing I do know is that the peffa-last thing I can see is a wand of any kind."

"And you'll tell me what this is all about after we've found it?"

"I don't think I'll have to," she griffled to him. "I think you'll simply know."

Matlock looked out, scanning rocks and corals, seeing creatures scrittling across and swimming by, getting closer, lured by the light inside. "Well, from all that's happened so far," he griffled, "this Tillian Wand is unlikely to be an actual wand. After all, the first half was a moving star constellation, which means the second half could be almost anything."

"True," Ayaani admitted. "So where do we start to look for something that could be anything at the bottom of the sea?"

"Do you miss him?" he suddenly asked her.

"Who?"

"Chatsworth."

"I did – to start with. Peffa-much so. But not any more. As soon as he gave me to you, I was safe. Baselott couldn't get his paws on me for his griffling experiments. Everyone knows a majickal-hare apprentice always has a dripple. If I'd suddenly gone missing when I was with you, creatures in Winchett Dale would have wondered what had happened to me. So I was safe when I was with you." She thought for a snutch of blinksnaps. "And, I also have a feeling in my Sisteraculous that somehow Chatsworth didn't need me any more, anyway. He had other things to do, other journeys to pid-pad along. As did I. As did you. As do all of us." She began pushing at the side of the bubble, rocking on the sandy bottom. "Well, don't just stand there like a clottabus, push!"

Matlock set himself against the clear bubble wall and together they began rocking it back and forth, trying to free it from the seabed, a thick sandy cloud rising all round, startling curious creatures outside.

"It's no use," he moaned. "We're hopelessly stuck."

"Push harder!" Ayaani puffed.

They set to again, straining and pushing, but only succeeded in grinding themselves frustratingly further into the seabed.

"It's useless!" Matlock griffled, panting heavily. "We're just gobflopping. We're stuck here, and that's the end of it."

"It *can't* be," Ayaani insisted. "We haven't come all this way for it to end here. We just need to push harder, that's all."

"No," Matlock griffled, suddenly struck with a powerful extrapluff as he looked around the bubble and the clouding sand outside. "It's not about pushing, Ayaani. Not at all."

She stared at him, confused.

"This bubble we're in," he explained, becoming excrimbly, "and the sand outside. Don't you see? It's like a mirror of the ganticus hour-glass in the Krettle's tower!"

"Really not with you on this one," she griffled.

"The ganticus glass bowl in the bottom of the hourglass," he griffled. "It's like we're already in it. And in the hourglass everything works downside-upsie. The sands falls *up* into the top bowl, Ayaani. Don't you understand?"

"Not really."

He turned to her, smiling. "We need to think like the Krettles do, Ayaani, live like the Krettles do – we need to be all downside-upsie about this."

"Methinks your mind's gone downside-upsie," she muttered.

"We don't push this bubble, Ayaani – we pull it!" He passed her the frizzing wand and grabbed the skin of the bubble with both paws, heaving it towards him, his whole face contorting with the effort.

"You'll break it!" she squealed. "We'll drown!"

"Not today!" he cried, suddenly letting go, the whole bubble jerking forwards out of the sand and surging upwards, drifting in the currents before settling on a rocky outcrop festooned with scrittling staffel-crabs. "Not *ever* today, Ayaani – for this is the sun-turn we find the Tillian Wand!"

"This is so glopped," she quietly griffled.

He took a breath, chickling with relief, reaching out for the bubble wall again and plinging them even further this time, right over a shoal of startled blue-shlurpfins.

"Stop!" Ayaani cried. "You don't even know where you're going!"

"You're right," he griffled, plinging the ganticus bubble once more, hurtling them over a dense coral bed set with drifting tentacle weeds dancing in the bright light of the frizzing wand. "So why change the habit of a lifetime? Just use those oidy black eyes of yours to spot anything that might be a wand."

Together, they plinged their way forward, picking up speed, bouncing and bumping over rocks and reefs, trails of vilishly swimming fish parting before them as they went deeper and deeper, a pure white, bouncing ball of light in the peffa-glopped darkness.

"You're going too vilishly!" Ayaani griffled. "I can't see anything properly!"

"You'll know it when you see it," Matlock griffled, pulling and plinging the bubble again. "Others have found the Tillian Wand, Ayaani, and so can we."

"Slow down!" she griffled. "Your heart will be beating too fast! Our sands will be running out!"

But Matlock kept plinging, using just his Sisteraculous to guide him, sensing deep inside that although the Icy Seas were truly ganticus, they were somehow getting closer.

Up ahead, he made out the beginnings of an entrance to an underwater cave, deep in a sheer blackened cliff-face crawling with gropps, gill-spiders and razor-legged pluckel-crabs.

"Careful," Ayaani warned him. "They don't took too friendly to me."

"I say we get closer," he griffled, plinging the bubble again.

They bounced to the entrance, the yechus creatures on the rock face sensing their opportunity, scrittling over the outside of the bubble, poking and testing it with their long sharp legs and pincers; vilishly becoming a frenzied mass of black, crawling bodies, all desperate to cut, bite, stab and tear their way inside.

"Probably not your briftest idea," Ayaani icily observed, her eyes following the twizzly hoard of russisculoffed creatures. "What are they, anyway?"

"Not the oidiest idea," Matlock griffled, the outside of the bubble now completely covered. "But methinks we're about to find out just how strong Ursula's eyesplasher really is."

He looked up as a horribly familiar, muffled chattering noise filled his long hare's ears, the creatures' eyes now glowing bright red, oidy sharp teeth spinning like hundreds of needles in their blackened mouths.

"They're going to bite right through!" Ayaani cried.

Matlock grabbed the wand, waving it inside the bubble. "Take us where we need to be!" he griffled to it. "Take us away from here! Take us to our fate and destiny!"

"Couldn't you just have griffled, 'take us to the Tillian Wand?'" Ayaani sourly griffled, scrambling back inside his hood.

"It doesn't work like that, remember? It takes us to where we need to be."

"Well, why are we still here?" she cried out, the first hard jet of icy water raining down on them from the pierced bubble above. "It's not working! Do something else!"

"Like what?" he cried, as a long, thin, thrashing leg worked its way inside.

Ayaani took a breath, then vilishly scrittled back down, grabbing the frizzing wand and plunging it with all her might through the side of the bubble wall, releasing a ganticus jet of trapped air, propelling them at speed right down into the underwater cavern, the shocked creatures falling away and stroffing against the side of the jagged rocks.

"It's collapsing!" Matlock cried. "We won't be able to breathe!"

"Then I suggest you take a ganticus breath," she griffled. "And get ready to swim."

"Where?"

"Anywhere but here!"

Holding the wand in one paw, Ayaani in the other, Matlock took his deepest breath and swam out into the icy waters, feeling the frizzing wand leading his arm, pulling them both deeper into the pitch black tunnel, his lungs feeling like they would burst from the effort, before finally surging upwards and breaking the black waters, leaving him gasping for breath, his coughs and splutters echoing around a huge and most unexpected cavern.

He held the wand aloft, slowly turning in the still water, gradually making out what looked like a small beach in the distant corner, complete with a small wooden hut. He vilishly began kicking out towards it as Ayaani scrittled onto his back, her oidy teeth chattering from the stinging cold.

"What is it?" she griffled, shivering.

"No idea," Matlock gasped, struggling to keep the wand aloft to light their way. "But it looks like there's a fire inside. There's smoke coming from the chimney."

Splashing, they headed for the shore, stepping out and pid-padding to the small tumbledown hut, drawn by the welcoming glow inside. At the old wooden creaker, Matlock reached for the handle with a shaking paw, slowly pushing it open.

"Hello?" he griffled, cautiously stepping inside and finding what appeared to be a surprisingly crumlush and tidy room, a blazing pifftosh in the corner, and over it a gently bubbling cauldron. Everything was saztaculously welcoming and cosy. There were armchairs, thick woollen rugs and candles lit in the windows.

"Well, this is unexpected," Ayaani whispgriffled.

"Why are you whispgriffling?" Matlock whispgriffled back, aware he was dripping water over the floorboards.

A noise caught him, and he turned to see an old, beaming witch making her way slowly down a small wooden staircase, lightly pid-padding over to shake his paw with a warm smile.

"Oh, my peffa-goodness," she griffled, "now just who's washed up to Alvestra's cottage this time?"

Matlock flinched. "You're…Alvestra?"

The oidy old witch nodded brightly, gently taking the wand from his paw. "I don't think we'll be needing this for now, do you?"

Instinctively, heart pounding with twizzles, he turned back to the wooden creaker, jumping as it slammed shut in front of his face. He tried the handle, desperately twisting and turning.

"Oh, dear. Now just what are you getting all twizzly about?" the witch griffled. "Are you being much displeased with me?"

"Open the creaker," Matlock managed to griffle, trying to stay calm. "Release your spell and open this creaker right now!"

"I sense you're being all displeased with me," she griffled, shuffling over to an old armchair and slumping into it with a satisfied groan. "Just like all the others. They all be being most displeased with Alvestra. Every one of them. It be quite juzzpapping after a while, all this displeasing."

Desperate to escape, Matlock raced towards an open window, the shutters also slamming with a loud crash. "Let me out." he griffled. "Now!"

"But you not be having any soupy-soupy yet," she griffled. "And you be all peffa-cold and wet. Come sit by the fire, hare. Dry yourself and griffle with Alvestra about exactly what be displeasing you. For you do seem most peffa-displeased, indeed."

"Just give me back my wand and let me go," he griffled, trying to steady his vilishly beating heart.

She pointed at him with a long, thin finger. "Sit."

"I'd rather not."

"But I'd *like* you to. And your not sitting is beginning to be displeasing me, hare."

To his horror, two oidy puffs of smoke rose from her eyes, each a perfect ring, then forming eyes of their own before drifting across the room and studying him intently.

"You really are right twizzly, aren't you, hare? And all because of Alvestra."

He waved a paw through the smoke, watching as she sucked the two trails back into her eyes. "I need my wand back," he tried to griffle, swallowing hard. "For without it, I'll never find the Tillian Wand you also seek. Without me, Alvestra, you'll never get it."

She softly chickled. "And do you know, hare, just how many of your kind have griffled to me those exact, same griffles? Here be just a snutch of them." She snapped her bony fingers and a cupboard flew open to reveal rows of hare skulls, their empty sockets ghoulishly peering out. "And these be just my favourites. The most slurpilicious ones. I always keep them if they be peffa-slurpilicious. What be your name?"

"Matlock," he griffled.

"But you not be having any soupy-soupy yet," she griffled. *"And you be all peffa-cold and wet. Come sit by the fire, hare. Dry yourself and griffle with Alvestra about exactly what be displeasing you…"*

She frowned for a moment, looking at him carefully for a peffa-long time, the silence heavy between them. Next, she began nodding and mumbling to herself, staring at her hands in her lap, then finally looking back at him. "Very well. And so it begins."

"What does? What begins?"

"The end," she simply griffled. "The end begins with Matlock the Hare. Everybody be knowing that."

"What do you mean?"

"Everything is already foretold, Matlock." She gestured to the empty chair by the piff-tosh and the splutting cauldron. "Come sit with me. Warm and dry yourself. It's time for my supper, and I mean you no harm."

He nodded, knowing deep in his Sisteraculous that somehow he didn't have any other choice *but* to sit. Every exit was blocked, and without his wand, to even think of escaping would be truly peffa-glopped.

He tried to close his nostrils to the awfully yechus smell rising from the bubbling cauldron, watching as Alvestra ladled herself a bowl of the peffa-glopped soup, greedily slurping the first mouthful from a steaming wooden spoon, thick slimy trails running down her chin.

Throughout, her eyes were as bright and welcoming as ever. "Now, I'm supposing that you have many questions to be asking me," she griffled. "But before you be doing that, I just want to griffle that you be in no danger here, Matlock. None at all. I may look old and glopped, but really, I not be all that displeasing, am I?"

"Can I have my wand back?" he asked.

She thought about it for a snutch of moments, blowing on her soup then spooning in another mouthful, chewing and swallowing. "No."

"But I need it to find the Tillian Wand."

"And you don't have much time left, do you, Matlock? Which must be most displeasing to you, methinks."

"But not to you, presumably."

She turned to him, smiling slightly. "Whether you find the wand is of no real consequence to me, Matlock. I shall be displeased, but others will come after you. 'Tis the way, you see?" She suddenly held out the bowl under his recoiling nose. "See these stringy chunks in here? 'Tis all that remains of the same hare you saw stroffed and boiled last even'up. Meat's too bruisy, and there be too many carrots in it. Though Lily be griffling to me that you be most helpful with the chopping and throwing in."

Matlock pushed the bowl away, trying his briftest not to look at it. "If you're really Alvestra," he griffled, "the great and ganticus Alvestra, cunning witch who did battle with Tillian himself for possession of the Icy Seas – then what are you doing here, all alone, eating yechus soup in a glopped-hut?"

"You don't be liking my home?" she asked, an oidy bit shocked. "I try to be keeping it as crumlush as I can, but it be getting too much for me these sun-turns."

"Just how old are you?"

She brightened at this, the glint back in her eye. "Older than you could ever be thinking in that clottabussed hare's brain of yours, Matlock. Twice as old as you could ever be imagining, three times."

He looked around. "And you live here? This is all you do?"

"Not all the time. Sometimes I be doing the smoke-trick, like I be doing with you outside the burrow." She started to chickle. "That be pleasing, seeing the peffa-twizzly look on your face."

"But the rest of the time, you're here?"

She nodded. "Because I have become something that I can't ever be. I've changed too much over the years."

Ayaani crept cautiously onto Matlock's shoulder. "How?"

"Griffles," Alvestra went on. "Griffles, legends and spuddles about me – have all *changed* me, Matlock. So many myths, so many pictures, so many tales written in books and majickal-driftolubbs. So many tapestries, statues and stories passed down from eager mouths to listening ears, all changing the truth of what really happened." She leant towards him, her old face set. "When you become legend, Matlock, it changes *everything* about you. You're no longer who you are, or who you ever really were. You simply be whatever folk and creatures needs you to be. What you did, and why you did it, are all changed and twisted by others."

She smiled slightly, remembering. "And there were times, Matlock, a grillion moon-turns ago, when it was sometimes most pleasing for me to make myself all smokey and drift down chimneys to listen to creatures griffling about me. Oh, I'd hear such spuddles about the many peffa-glopped and terrible things I was supposed to have done, and I'd be thinking 'Alvestra, truly you have become so much more twizzly and peffa-fearful than you could ever imagine'."

"But then it changed?"

She nodded, slightly closing her eyes. "I began to see that I was being used all over these dales. Creatures would griffle about me to their youngsters, 'Get upstairs for nifferduggles, or Alvestra will come for you!' Others with ganticus power would use me to threaten an entire dale, griffling that unless they obeyed, I would stroff them all. It was all nonsense, of course, just spuddles from a splurked legend. I just be a witch that stroffed. All I really be doing now is scaring and eating majickal-hares."

Matlock frowned, recalling Soriah's Kherflahdle's griffles at the Estuary Festival, "But if you're…stroffed…then don't you become a part of the dales like all other witches?"

"What do you know of this?"

"I have friends who are witches," he explained. "They griffled to me about it. One of them wants to be a far and distant mountain when she stroffs."

Alvestra smiled at this. "A most tzorkly and crumlush idea, methinks. Most pleasing."

"And you?" he asked. "What did you want to be?"

She snapped her fingers and the shuttered windows slowly opened. "That," she simply griffled, pointing outside. "I wanted to be that most ganticus and tzorkly cavern out there, Matlock."

"The cavern?"

She looked at him. "You think this is a splurked idea? Only that will be making me most displeased."

"No, no," he quickly griffled, anxious not to displease her in any way at all. Instead, he pid-padded to the window, wondering just how far he would get if he tried to leap through. "It's just so cold and dark out there."

"And lonely?"

"Yes," he griffled. "I'm just supposing that it wouldn't be everyone's choice, that's all."

Instantly, she flew at him from the chair; suddenly snarling, hundreds of needlesharp teeth spinning in her yechus mouth, smoke pouring from her eyes. Ayaani yelped and scrittled back into Matlock's hood as the enraged witch grabbed him by his robe and flew them all straight out of the window and high into the dripping cavern roof, the dark waters far below his dangling feet.

She spun him to face her. "Choice?" she hissed, red eyes blazing. "What do you know of *choice*, Matlock? Is it your choice that you're here with me now, just a precious few blinksnaps from being stroffed? Did you ever really *choose* to become a majickal-hare, to undertake the three splurked Most Majelicus tasks? Did you? Answer me!"

"No!" he cried, completely twizzled. "I chose none of it!"

"Now we're finally getting somewhere!" she screamed, the cavern walls echoing with her yechus chickling. "Matlock, *The Hare Who Changed Everything*, finally sees the light! And that be most pleasing old Alvestra, indeed!"

Matlock's whole softulous shook. "I don't know what you're griffling about. I'm just a clottabussed majickal-hare from Winchett Dale. I can't change anything – I never do."

Again she cackled out loud. "Oh, but you *will*," she griffled. "It has been foretold, Matlock. You are *The Hare Who Changed Everything*. And after you have stroffed – spuddles will be told of you, great and saztaculous legends will be written in your name. Your face will be on every picture, every tapestry, every book, every driftolubb. All creatures in these dales will know of Matlock the Hare. And then you will become like me, Matlock, a legend – an oidy shadow of what you really are, but one that everyone will believe is *real*. And just like me, you'll be trapped by it. Your legend will become your prison guard. You will no longer be able to live, or pass into Oramus' most eternal care. You will be a nothing, a ghost listening to glopped spuddles portraying your life as it never happened."

"Please let me go," he griffled. "Just give me my wand, and I'll be on my way."

The teeth span even more vilishly. "And what spuddles will be told, what pictures will be drawn, what tapestries woven of *this* particular moment, I wonder? How will the grifflers and spuddlers tell our story, eh? I expect they'll have you in golden-armour, with a mighty wand, vrooshing me all over this cavern, chickling loudly as you battle the peffa-yechus Alvestra! Matlock the hare-hero, in another saztaculous tale everyone will know and love!"

She took a breath, her teeth slowing, retracting, her face gradually returning. "There will be music, songs, statues – perhaps even festivals in your name. At first, like me, there will be an oidy part of you that will feel honoured and most pleased. But then you will no longer see yourself in any of it. You will have stroffed in the memories of the creatures you now know, and those yet to pid-pad through these dales. You will try to close your ears to the spuddles, your eyes to the books and pictures. But they will be bigger than you. The last of you will be gone, stroffed by the very thing you became in the minds of others." She closed her eyes. "You will have given everything – but got nothing."

Matlock didn't griffle a griffle, shivering with shock and cold, high in the freezing cavern.

She opened her eyes, smiling brightly. "But right now, Matlock, you *do* have a choice. And it be a most pleasing one. A peffa-pleasing one."

"What choice?" he managed to ask.

"Stay here with me," she griffled. "Spend your last few hours cosy by my crumlush piff-tosh. We can griffle and chickle. I can tell you the real spuddle of the Tillian Wand, not the one so many have heard and changed. And when your sands finally run out, you will be taken to the hourglass, boiled-up and made into soupy-soupy. It won't take long. The waters are peffa-hot, and the Krettles are most expertly pleasing at the boiling of majickal-hares. Next, you'll find yourself safe in Oramus' most eternal care, as just another hare who failed the second Most Majelicus task. History will soon forget you. Make the choice, Matlock – for your sake and no one else's. Be *The Hare Who Changed Everything*. But choose to change everything about *yourself*. Deny the destiny that has been shaped for you. Stay with me, and I promise that your skull will have the most pleasing pride of place in my collection."

He took a deep hare's breath. "But I choose *not* to do that," he griffled, watching her face begin to turn yechus once more.

"Because, for whatever you or any other creature might think about me, I'm not going to spend my last few hours sitting in a hut, waiting to be boiled into soup."

"Then you are even more of a peffa-splurked wandlewheimer than I thought!" she cried. "A truly clottabussed majickal-hare!"

"Then I'd rather you stroff me right here and now," he griffled to her. "And if not, then I'd peffa-much appreciate you putting me down so I can get on with trying to find the Tillian Wand."

She cackled full in his face, teeth angrily spinning.

"And truthfully," he went on, " I don't know anything about *The Hare Who Changed Everything* – or what that even *begins* to mean. Everyone's always griffling to me that I'm 'special', or that one sun-turn I'm going to do something truly saztaculous. But for me, whether my destiny has been decided or not – I choose to go on, rather than become a bowl of soup that simply gave up."

"You be most displeasing me," Alvestra growled, smoke beginning to pour from her blood-red eyes. "Most displeasing me indeed! I shall have the Krettles boil you so slowly that it will take a whole even'up for your fur to be falling off!"

"That's assuming I don't find the wand,' he reminded her, spluttering in the thick smoke.

"Even if you *do* succeed, Matlock," she hissed, "you'll wish you hadn't. It will simply be the beginning of the most ganticus of all ends. There will be no pid-padding back for you, ever."

"Just put me down and let me be on my way."

Ayaani whispgriffled from his hood. "And what way would that be, exactly?"

"Not totally sure at this precise blinksnap," he quietly griffled. "Just trying to work out how to get us down, first."

But before he could griffle another griffle, the smoke thickened, forming arms that wrapped themselves around and began pulling him vilishly though the cold, cavern air.

"One more thing you need to see!" Alvestra's voice screamed from somewhere above. "One more place you need to visit!"

He struggled to breathe in the choking cloud, dimly aware he was lurching and turning, hurtling so vilishly he felt as if his hare's smile would be torn from his face. He tried to take a breath, twisting and desperately fighting for air, arms and legs blindly thrashing as they flew through the darkness.

"Not far now!" Alvestra's voice called from somewhere in the chaos, as gradually the smoke thinned, and he felt the ground rushing up beneath him, glimpsing flashing, brilliant blue skies far above his head.

"See?" she griffled as they landed, Matlock taking a huge breath, peffa-grateful for firm ground under his feet, warm sun drying his robes and a feeling of calm flooding his entire softulous. "That didn't be taking so long, did it?" She pointed to a ganticus white stone building a little way off. "What do you be thinking of it? You think it be most pleasing?"

In all truth, he wasn't the oidiest bit certain where he was, let alone in any state to make critical judgements. He looked around, rubbing the smoke from his eyes, seeing immaculate lawns, well tended footpaths and the most saztaculous fountains sending cascading water into ornate ponds abundant with ganticus lillies and saztaculous flowers. All manner of oidy creatures foraged and scrittled nearby, some pushing wooden wheelbarrows laden with spades and forks, busy about their business of happily tending everything.

Then he noticed something else. Everywhere was completely silent. Although fountains shot high into the air, waterfalls ran over lavish rockeries, meadow-bees and iridescent hammer-flies hummed and buzzed all around – nothing made even the oideist sound. He shook his head, wondering if his ears were blocked, but clearly heard them loudly flapping around the sides of his face.

"Where are we?" he whispgriffled to Alvestra.

"The Saztaculous Garden of All Spuddles," she griffled. "And there's really no need to whispgriffle. No one can hear us, Matlock. We don't exist." An oidy creature scrittled by, pushing a wheelbarrow. "Go on," she urged. "Try and griffle to it."

"Hello?" he griffled to the creature, now earnestly forking and turning soil in a nearby flower bed.

"Try and touch it."

He gingerly reached down, gasping as his paw passed right through.

"They're tenders," Alvestra explained. "They tend to these

gardens. Theirs, Matlock, is a most crumlush world, full of chickling, griffling and much singing. Look." She pointed to a group of oidy creatures nearby, all busy griffling with one another. "We see them, but can't hear them. They can neither see or be hearing us. We only exist as legends to them. Who we *really* are means nothing to them. Nothing at all."

Matlock sensed an oidy flicker of sadness in her eyes. "And I'm guessing that be displeasing you?"

She half-smiled, then turned to the ganticus stone building in the centre of the silent garden. "Come. Follow me. What I really want to show you is in there – The Saztaculous Hall of All Legends."

Matlock pid-padded by her side, trying to get used to the strange sensation of crunching on gravel without making even the oidiest noise. "So, are we…?"

"Alive?" she griffled. "Oh, peffa-much so. And perhaps, Matlock, that be the most displeasing thing about it all."

Matlock only began to realise just how truly ganticus and impressive the hall was the closer he actually got to it. A huge set of white marble steps led up to a saztaculously ornate creaker, set into a wall decorated with dozens of carved legends – some he remembered from being told as a wide-eyed leveret himself, others he couldn't even begin to possibly recognise. Ganticus heroes did battle with peffa-yechus monsters on land, sea, and in the air.

"Watch," Alvestra instructed.

Matlock's eyes widened as each carved figure slowly turned to face him before dropping to their knees, offering their flaming swords and weapons, bowing reverently as the ganticus doors slowly opened. "What are they doing?" he whispgriffled, as something stirred deep in his Sisteraculous, coursing through him like iced water.

"Welcoming the greatest of all the legends," Alvestra simply replied. "*The Hare Who Changed Everything.* You, Matlock."

He shook his head. "No," he griffled. "Not me. It's a mistake."

"'Tis already written. Follow me."

But Matlock stayed put, frozen to the spot, unable to take his eyes from the stone tableaux, barely noticing Ayaani scrittling up onto his shoulder. "Methinks it's time for one of those things of yours," she griffled.

He turned to her. "A deep hare's breath?"

She nodded.

"Am I dreaming? Am I alive, stroffed? What *is* this place?"

She looked around. "Methinks it's just a ganticus hall in a silent garden."

"I know that, but…" He tailed off.

"What?"

"I just have this peffa-strange feeling in my Sisteraculous."

"Sort of twizzly and scared?"

He swallowed. "No, not twizzly – just…strange. I can't describe it."

She shrugged. "Then don't bother. Just do the deep-hare's-breath thing and let's go inside."

"I really don't know that I want to."

"What? Do the breath, or follow the witch?"

"The breath thing. Honestly, sometimes it's quite painful. It sort of twists my smile. Have you seen the size of my mouth?"

"Matlock," Ayaani sighed, "it's your signature. Just do it, and let's go."

Still feeling strangely twizzled, he tried his briftcst to take a deep-hare's breath.

"Well, that was pretty glopped," Ayaani muttered, unimpressed, as they pid-padded through the doorway and into the ganticus hall. "I mean, if ever there *was* a time for a saztaculously ganticus deep hare's-breath, that was surely it. Honestly, how many more chances like that do you think you'll get?"

"Please be quiet," Matlock griffled, looking all round, stunned by the overwhelming size and spectacle of the huge hall. Truly, it was vast, more ganticus than anything he'd ever expected or encountered. Bright light flooded the enormous space from windows set high in the walls, illuminating dozens of statues on enormous plinths, each taller than any tree in Wand Wood he'd ever seen.

Alvestra suddenly appeared at his shoulder. "Impressive and quite pleasing, don't you think?"

He nodded, completely transfixed.

She pid-padded to the nearest statue, pointing up at the carved figure standing on top of a yechus monster lying across the plinth. "Behold the legend that is Corvola of Miltdown Dale. Armed with his mighty club and sword, he slew the evil and peffa-glopped Telecanth in a battle that lasted for nearly seven moon-turns."

"I know this spuddle," Matlock nodded, pid-padding closer and slowly reading the carved griffles on the plinth. "I remember it from a driftolubb I had as an apprentice." He looked up at the fearsome statue. "Truly, he's just like I remember him, a mighty warrior. And Telecanth, the yechus monster, is every oidy bit as twizzly."

"You would like to meet them?"

He turned, confused. "Meet them?"

She nodded. "However saztaculous and wondrous this place may appear to be, Matlock, it's really just one ganticus stone prison. Yes, the walls are pleasingly clean, the white marble floor be all polished, the statues be most impressive – yet for those that live here, those that are imprisoned, it is nothing more than a ganticus white dungeon where they remain trapped, unable to pass into Oramus' most eternal care, held against their will by becoming legends they were never wanting to be in the first place.

"Only two of us are allowed to be free from this place; Tillian and myself, as our legend was chosen to be the finding puzzle on the Most Majelicus task you now undertake. It allows us to roam the dales and be free from this dread place. But for every other creature who became legendary, Matlock, their place is here, these pure white walls their eternal home. As they will be yours, too, when the time comes."

Matlock watched as she clapped her hands and two small, wretched figures appeared from behind the enormous statue, each chained by the neck to a heavy iron ring on the side of the plinth.

"Here they be," Alvestra griffled. "Here be Corvola and Telecanth – as they *really* are – as they really *were*, and as they always have been."

If Matlock's jaw could have done, it would have dropped to the floor.

Ayaani, watching in confusion from his shoulder, managed to get the griffles out first. "Those two gobfloppers be Corvola and Telecanth?" she gasped. "*The* Corvolla and Telecanth?"

Alvestra nodded.

"But how?" Matlock griffled, frowning heavily. "They just look like a sort of squidged disidula and a bricklepine holding a branch."

"Branch?" Alvestra griffled. "Surely, you mean 'a most ganticus and mighty club in order to stroff the peffa-twizzly and most yechus Telecanth'?"

"No," Matlock insisted, pointing at the forlorn bricklepine. "I meant, 'branch' – and frankly, quite a glopped one, at that. I doubt it could even stir a cauldron, let alone stroff a ganticus monster."

"Well, it *didn't*, that's why," the bricklepine politely griffled. "Not always good to believe in legends and spuddles, dear hare."

"Most peffa-definitely not," the disidula agreed. "Sure, my name's Telecanth, and he's Corvola, but really all that happened is that one sun-turn he's out climbing a tree for some larking when I goes pid-padding by, underneath. He falls out, right onto me, and – boom! – that's me and him both stroffed by the same broken branch. Next, we finds ourselves in here, chained up for all eternity – and all because I went for a pid-pad, and he went larking."

Matlock rubbed a paw through his ears. "Wait – are you really griffling that you're the *real* Telecanth and Corvola?"

"Well," Corvola griffled, adjusting the heavy chains around his neck and clearing his throat, "I suppose that depends on just what you mean by the griffle 'real', dear hare. Have you never heard tales from strangers about a saztaculous place you simply *must* visit, only to find that when you get there, it's really quite glopped and a complete waste of time? It's just the same with us. The same with *all* of us. You can look at us as simply the end of a journey you've heard so much about that ends up disappointingly glubbstooled."

Matlock turned, a great chorus of clinking and jangling now filling the hall, as all around, similar figures in chains slowly emerged from behind their legendary and saztaculous statues to stand in front of the plinths.

Alvestra pointed to them. "Everyone you see here, Matlock, is a legend you have either read or heard griffled about. All the great spuddles from all the dales are held here, right in this hall, chained by the griffles of others, for the rest of time itself."

He looked around, unable to believe his hare's eyes. He knew enough spuddles and legends to know that at least he should have recognised Borth the Ungloppable, Sharombleez the Flurp and Sivertson the Most Mighty. Instead, they turned out to be a juzzpapped pondblarper, a leaning jutter with a sore nose, and a short-necked grapple who clearly looked extremely embarrassed about the whole thing.

"And up there," Alvestra griffled, pointing towards the vast roof as a stone witch on a broom began roaring around the hall above their heads, "that one be me!"

Matlock looked from the stone witch to the old and oidy one by his side. Its hat was much bigger, flapping eagle's wings poked from its back and it had six arms; two holding the broom, the other four each waving a vrooshing wand.

"The wings are a nice touch," Ayaani observed. "Where did they come from?"

"The same place as the arms," Alvestra replied, pointing to Ayaani's mouth. "From here. From mouths that make griffles – griffles that became lies and exaggeration; griffles that changed the way we were into what we've become in creature's minds. Creatures tell our stories for their own reasons. But they always need us to be much more legendary than we really are." She pointed to a small green and white sazpent who could barely slither because the heavy chain around its neck was so tight. "That's Kruffanor, most mighty and peffa-yechus beast ever to roam and lay waste to the dales. Grillions, we are told, fear him."

Matlock nodded, pid-padding towards the sazpent. "I used to sometimes lie awake, unable to nifferduggle because you made me so twizzly."

"Sorry about that," Kruffanor griffled. "But, really, you have to blame Oramus for all this."

"Oramus?"

"Of course," the sazpent went on. "*He* needed us. *He* needed legends of ganticus monsters being defeated by saztaculous heroes that at some point, just when they thought they'd be stroffed, call on *His* most ganticus and eternal powers to slay their foe. It sort of makes Oramus look brifter than *He* really is, you see."

The less than heroic Corvola eagerly agreed. "Our legends only exist to make creatures believe that no matter what happens in their lives, if they call on Oramus, they'll overcome everything."

"So," Matlock frowned, looking at them all, struggling to make sense of things, "it's Oramus that keeps you all here?"

They nodded.

"And *He* made all this?" Matlock asked, arms spread to the building.

At this point, perhaps the oldest creature Matlock had ever seen shuffled forward on bare feet, dressed in rags, its ears torn and whole face sagging under a weight of peffa-wrinkled fur. It's griffles were low and angry, brimming with russisculoftulation. "Oramus didn't make these statues," it growled, pointing an accusing paw. "Clottabussed creatures like *you* made them, hare!"

"Me?" Matlock griffled. "I've never been here in my life."

"Approach!" the elderly creature commanded. "My chains are too tight. Come closer so that I can see you!"

Ayaani urgently pulled on one of Matlock's ears, whispgriffling into it. "Not really sure that going anywhere near it would be such a fuzzcheck idea, Matlock."

"Why's that?"

"Oh, for goodness sake, Matlock! Look at the statue he's under! Don't you know who that is?"

Matlock squinted, trying to read the distant plinth. "Schlott?"

"Exactly," Ayaani whispgriffled. "Schlott. Now do you understand?"

"Not really. Never heard of him."

She vilishly bliffed her oidy forehead. "Matlock! Schlott! *The* Schlott!" She pointed at the statue. "Look at him, for goodness sake! He slew the Afligator!"

Matlock stared blankly back.

"*Please* tell me you've heard of him," she griffled, her voice almost begging. "Even *you* can't have kept your clottabussed hare's head in the ground for that long."

"Of course I've heard of him."

Ayaani breathed a ganticus sigh of relief. "Thank Oramus for that. I thought you were joking."

"I heard of him just now when you told me about him. He blew down an abbrolatt, or something?"

"He slew the Afligator!" she cried in pure frustration. "*The* most ferocious beast that ever lump-thumped across the dales!"

"But isn't the whole point," Matlock griffled, calmly pid-padding up to Schlott and looking him square in his angry eyes, "that you most probably did nothing of the sort? You most likely choked after swallowing a neffle-fly, or something."

There was a long and very awkward pause. "Two, actually," Schlott eventually griffled. "And one of them really was quite ganticus. For a neffle-fly, that is. Lots of lesser creatures wouldn't have been able to take it like I did."

"Well, you clearly *didn't* take it, did you?" Matlock pointed out. "Because presumably you choked, stroffed and ended up here."

"S'pose," Schlott griffled, humbled but still keen to impress. "But it really was ganticus. Far from your average neffle-fly, was that one. Doubt there's been one that big, since." He frowned slightly. "Anyway, hare, the point is this. I was the first one here. The very first of all the dale-legends. One moment I was choking on the fly, the next I found myself in here, chained to a ganticus block of stone. Then flying hammers and chisels appeared out of nowhere, vilishly chipping away at the block, sculpting it. Griffles began writing themselves on the plinth, a story of my life, but not my actual life, a life retold and written by Oramus *Himself* – the Legend of Schlott and the Afligator." He pointed to the plinth, eyes ablaze. "And what a legend it is, hare, griffled by creatures in these dales for grillions of years – how bravely I battled with the ganticussly yechus Afligator, how it almost stroffed me, save for me crying out to Oramus at the last possible blinksnap, whence *He* gave me the power to finally raise myself and thrust my spiked, majickal lance into its glopped heart!"

"When all you really did was swallow a neffle-fly?"

"Two," Schlott vilishly corrected him. "Anyway, not long after I'd been here, other ganticus stone blocks started appearing. Then more creatures came, all chained like me, and the hammers and chisels got to work on their legends, too, creating all that you see before you now. You don't believe me? Look at my chains and see for yourself the griffles of others that keep us all here."

Matlock peered at the chains, studying the links closely, realising to his open mouthed amazement that each one was indeed a swirling, dense mass of spinning griffles.

"We did nothing wrong," Schlott griffled to him. "None of us did anything heroic, or legendary. Yet we're all here, chosen by Oramus for reasons we'll never know, to further *His* power. Only Tillian and Alvestra are free. The rest of us remain here, forever."

Matlock frowned, turning to look at their faces, watching them in their chains, a forlorn parade of confused creatures imprisoned by legends they knew nothing about. "I honestly don't know what to griffle," he told them. "All I can griffle is that this isn't the Oramus I recognise. None of it."

They all turned to the rear of the hall, silently pointing to a truly ganticus set of doors which seemed to run from the bottom of the polished marble floor to the heights of the immaculate white roof.

"You want me to go in there?" he asked them.

"Probably not such a good idea," Ayaani advised from his shoulder. "All things considered."

"All things considered?" he griffled back to her, "I can't help but remember that it was you getting peffa-twizzly about someone who had merely swallowed a couple of neffle-flies." He looked back into the expectant faces, all silently urging him to go through the huge doors.

"Listen," Alvestra suddenly griffled to him, her face alert. "What do you hear in there?"

Matlock listened, gradually making out a small but insistent chipping and tapping.

She smiled. "The hammers and chisels have been at work, Matlock. Oramus has been shaping your destiny. Go through those creakers, for you're the only one who can. See your future. See what you become. See how history will remember the great and most saztaculous Matlock – *The Hare Who Changed Everything.*"

"But I need to find the Tillian Wand," he griffled.

"All that you seek, lies through that doorway. Though what you'll find, how it will shape you, will no longer be of your will or making. Go – see for yourself. And if you ever do find the wand – then it *really* begins, Matlock, the final part of your true destiny."

"You griffled that my destiny was already written. Where?"

She softly chickled. "On thirteen pages of parchment, Matlock.

Hidden, but read. Everything was already quilled by another of your kind, many moon-turns ago."

"Baselott?" Matlock griffled. "The revisions he wanted to make to *Majickal Dalelore – Volume 68*. The ones he wrote before he stroffed?"

"Strange to be thinking," Alvestra griffled, tickling Ayaani under her chin, "that all this really started when just one dripple griffled. To think how that changed so much, just one griffle from a mouth so innocent and oidy." She sighed. "Sometimes, life can be so peffa-displeasing, and in quite the most unexpected and splurked ways."

The ganticus white doors slowly began to swing open.

"It's time, Matlock," she griffled. "Methinks the chisels have finished their work." She reached into her robes and threw him his wand.

He caught it. "Why are you helping me?"

She looked to the ceiling and the floor. "As above, so below, Matlock. 'Tis the way of all tzorkly witches. Go now. Hesitate, and the doors will close, your time will run out, and I will be feasting on you. Lily and Jericho Krettle will soon be lighting their cauldron. Go, while you still have a beating heart in your softulous."

Matlock turned to Ayaani, perched on his shoulder. "You know when you griffled to me that I wouldn't get another chance to take a deep hare's breath?"

"I know," she conceded. "I griffled too soon."

"How many this time, do you think?"

She looked up at the huge doors, trying not to get too twizzly. "At least three, methinks. Really deep and ganticus ones."

He tried to smile, took three deep breaths, then pid-padded into another vast hall, but this time empty save for just one truly ganticus statue in the very centre, twice the size of the others. "Oh…my…drifflejubs," he slowly whispgriffled, staring up at it in shock. "It's me!"

Together, he and Ayaani stood at the bottom of the massive plinth, looking up at an enormous stone statue of a truly ganticus majickal-hare resplendent in full armour, a huge round shield over one arm, the other holding a frizzing wand high into the air. It wore iron pointed shoes, its cloak was exotic chainmail, and two long ears poked from a saztaculously ornate helmet. On its shoulder, replete in her own fearsome armour and a vicious spear in her paw, was a dripple, its mouth open in a silent, blood-curdling roar.

"I must say," Ayaani griffled, carefully considering it. "They've done my teeth rather well. Not sure about your smile though, it's not nearly as curly and clottabussed as your real one."

Behind them, the massive doors suddenly closed with a thunderous, echoing garrumbloom.

"I'd also griffle," she calmly observed, "that we're pretty much trapped."

Matlock began to read the carved griffles on the huge plinth, running a paw over them.

"What does it say?" she asked him.

"You really want to know?"

"It'd help," she griffled. "Seeing as I can't read. Is it about us – me and you?"

Matlock nodded, slowly reading aloud the carved griffles:

THE LEGEND OF MATLOCK THE HARE

MOST MAJELICUS OF ALL HEROES
WHO CHANGED EVERYTHING

Many moon-turns ago, a most clottabussed and splurked hare was brought from The Great Beyond to train as apprentice in Winchett Dale. To many, he wasn't the oidiest bit heroic at all. Most of Winchett Dale simply thought of him as a long-eared gobflopper who always glopped up his vrooshers, and spent far too much time in his cottage garden. And really, because they were from Winchett Dale (the most peffa-glopped, gubbstooled and splurked of all the majickal dales), it wouldn't take even the most spuzzed-wuzscrittler to realise just how dull, tedious and ordinary Matlock really was.

"Well, it all seems pretty accurate so far," Ayaani griffled, satisfied.

"I don't even know what a 'wuzscrittler' is," Matlock griffled, frowning. "let alone what a spuzzed one's supposed to do."

"Well, they obviously seem to know a lot about you."

"I think it's just being used as an example," Matlock griffled, nodding to himself. "Perhaps they simply ran out of comparisons."

Ayaani frowned at him. "Read on. Don't stop there. Get to the bit about how I got all my armour. That's got to be a saztaculous part."

He cleared his throat:

> However, despite not really concentrating on his studies, or reading his majickal-driftolubbs, to the peffa-amazement of everyone, Matlock did manage to finally become a majickal-hare…

"Oh, wait!" Ayaani called out, getting excrimbly. "I know what this is, Matlock! This is one of those spuddles that you griffle to clottabussed, gobflopping youngsters. You know the sort of thing – 'If Matlock the Hare could do it, then so can you'." She playfully bliffed him on the head. "Wow – your utter dullness is going to help glubbstooled creatures everywhere. It's as if the peffa-boring life you've led actually has some purpose! After all, who's going to want to be more peffa-boring than you? Oh, that's *so* peffa-good to know, it really is."

He frowned at her. "You want me to keep reading?"

"Of course. Get to me. Get to me."

"You're enjoying this far more than I am, aren't you?"

"Immeasurably. Just get on with it."

Matlock sighed and began reading aloud once more:

> …and when he did, for many moon-turns he led a most peffa-dreary and unexceptional life. However, Oramus – as He always does – had other plans for this most gobflopped of all hares…

Matlock stopped, "I'm really not liking the tone of this, frankly. It's all quite insulting."

Ayaani eagerly pointed up at the impressively ferocious, armoured statue. "But the point is, Matlock, that somehow you become *that*. A peffa-hero! Now keep reading, we haven't even got to me, yet."

"But that's all there is," he griffled. "I've reached the end. There's no more griffles. The rest is just blank."

"Blank?" Ayaani frowned, angrily looking at the plinth. "But there must be more. We've had lots of saztaculous adventures, you and I. Just think of Trefflepugga Path. Is there no mention of that?"

Matlock shook his head. "Not a single griffle."

"It's like," a ganticus voice suddenly boomed from high above their heads, "your life never really happened, isn't it?"

Matlock jumped, looking up, then crying out in shock as the ganticus statue suddenly bent right down and inspected him closely, its huge stone nostrils twitching as it sniffed him.

"You smell…musty," it boomed.

Matlock tried to control his twizzliness, a peffa-difficult task as the statue's head was almost the size of his entire cottage. "It's…it's from the underground lake at Alvestra's," he managed to griffle. "It made my robes all wet and glopped."

The ganticus eyes narrowed. "But you smell *peffa*-musty."

"And we were trapped under the sea," Matlock vilishly griffled, his voice shaking. "We were plinging our way round in a bubble, and then it got attacked by schillercrabs and burst, and it's been a really, *really* peffa-long sun-turn and…"

The statue began to chickle, the heavy stone armour crunching and grinding. "Plinging your way around the sea in a bubble? Attacked by mere schilercrabs? Smelling all musty and garbling like a startled leveret?" It pointed a huge claw to the uncompleted griffles on the plinth. "Are you honestly surprised none of your story is here, Matlock? It's just all so glubbstooled and…un-heroic."

"That's not true!" Ayaani shouted, startling the ganticus stone dripple, who yelped and vilishly scrittled for cover inside its master's huge stone hood. "We've had all sorts of twizzly adventures!"

The statue inspected her closely. "And you must be Ayaani – the legendary griffling dripple?"

"Not yet," she challenged. "I'm not legendary yet. I'm just plain Ayaani from Winchett Dale, thank you."

The statue smiled, amused. "Such spirit for one so oidy. Impressive. More than the long-eared gobflopper you choose to ride around with. Griffle me this, though, Ayaani – just how would *you* be prefer to be remembered? As an oidy dripple, glopping around with a musty, long eared clottabus; or as the saztaculously brave and defiant Ayaani, ready to do battle at a blinksnap and inspire all future dripples with legends of her twizzly and most shindinculous adventures?"

"To be honest," she griffled, "when you put it like that, it does sound quite appealing."

"Because," the statue went on, "what does history ever *really* griffle to us anyway? Truth? I don't think so. History is given to us by others; from spuddles, legends, tapestries and pictures. No creature ever really knows the 'truth' about history. It's used for compliance, to patch over glopped events, twist and turn them into another reality. And of that, and your part in any future history, you'll have no choice." It reached around the plinth, effortlessly lifting two heavy collared chains. "These will be yours when the time comes. You will both live here, with me. This will be your home, forever."

Ayaani looked around the empty hall. "Perhaps we need to work an oidy bit on the furniture side of things?"

"Fools!" the statue roared. "You *dare* to mock me, *The Hare Who Changed Everything*?"

"Just thought that a couple of chairs might help," she griffled. "Looks like there's an awful lot of standing around to do."

"Chairs?" it bellowed, standing upright on the plinth, angrily thrashing the ganticus shield with its huge stone wand.

"Perhaps even a piff-tosh?" she added. "And a kettle to make a brottle-leaf brew?"

"Ayaani," Matlock quietly griffled. "I really don't think this is the time to be…"

"Just have your wand ready," she hissed at him.

"For what?"

She threw her eyes to the ornate ceiling in despair. "To vroosh the chains, you ganticus clottabus!"

"Chains?"

"For Oramus' sake, Matlock! Yes, the chains! They're made of griffles, don't you understand? History is shaped by griffles. *Our* history will be told and changed by griffles. They're the most peffa-dangerous things of all. Vroosh the chains, and break the griffles locking us into this peffa-glopped place."

He nodded. "Fuzzcheck idea. I was just about to griffle the exact same thing."

"No, you weren't."

"I was. I was simply a bit musty, that's all."

Ayaani shook her oidy head, loudly shouting to the statue way above their heads. "I mean, you can hardly be calling yourself *The Hare Who Changed Everything*, if you can't even change this place into something a bit more friendly and comfortable, can you? What happens if we have visitors round? It's all going to be an oidy bit embarrassing, isn't it?"

"*Visitors?*" the statue roared.

She nodded, scrittling from Matlock's shoulder up the entire length of the statue to perch on its ganticus nose. Beneath, Matlock silently made his way to the back of the plinth, looking at the heavy iron rings that held the griffle chains in place, his Most Majelicus wand already frizzing bright red at its tip.

"The thing is," Ayaani informed the frowning statue, "Matlock and I are used to certain home-comforts, which frankly, I don't see anywhere here. Like beds to nifferduggle in, for instance."

"What will you need beds for?" it griffled. "You'll already be stroffed when you get here. No one sleeps when they're stroffed!"

"Well, that doesn't seem very well worked out," Ayaani griffled, trying to glance down, hoping Matlock was busy vrooshing the griffle chains. "How can you enjoy a crumlush brew in bed, if you haven't had a right good nifferduggle first?"

The statue sneered at her, nostrils flaring. "You're wasting my time with your clottabussed griffles."

She nodded. "So imagine just how russisculoffed you're going to get when you have to listen to them for all eternity? Because, really, I can griffle on and on about quite the most oidy things for a peffa, peffa-long time. Matlock has learned to close his ears by now, but what with yours being quite so ganticus and heroic, they'll be listening to me griffling on and on about kettles and chairs and brews and beds and cupboards and..."

A loud cracksplosion suddenly shook the hall, the statue crying out in rage as it looked down and saw a large plume of red smoke rising from the plinth below, an angry swarm of oidy griffles billowing up in a dark cloud behind it.

"The other one!" Ayaani cried out, vilishly scrittling down onto the plinth. "Vroosh the other chain, Matlock!"

*A loud cracksplosion suddenly shook the hall,
the statue crying out in rage as it looked down and saw
a large plume of red smoke rising from the plinth below...*

Floored by the force of the cracksplosion, Matlock vilishly got back onto his hare's feet and aimed his wand at the remaining chain, eyes closed as he shot out a second bright red vroosher. Another ganticus garrumbloom cracksploded around the hall, thousands more griffles swarming up and away, joining the others, smashing and bursting through a high window and soaring away into the clear blue lid outside.

"You clottabussed fools!" the statue roared, watching the fleeing griffles. "What have you just done?"

"Griffles are the only reason you're here," Ayaani shouted back. She pointed to the plinth with an oidy paw as one by one, the carved griffles now also beginning to disappear. "Soon there will be none left – and no reason for you to be trapped here, either."

The ganticus statue slowly dropped from the plinth to the floor, bending low to watch the last of the griffles fade to pure white stone. "But where will I go?" it griffled, becoming twizzly, a low and ominous clacking slowly filling the hall.

"Nowhere," Matlock griffled, dusting himself down and watching as the first chisel and hammer flew across and began vilishly chipping away at the statue's armour. "Because you weren't ever 'here' in the first place. You were just a history of me waiting to be written. You never existed – you weren't ever 'me' – because I'll never be *The Hare Who Changed Everything*."

The statue whirled on him, crying out as more hammers and chisels flew in, now vilishly chipping away at its face. "You ganticus clottabus!" it cried, sharp stone raining down all around. "Don't you see? It's already begun! You're changing a history that was already determined, Matlock! I may stroff, but what you have so foolishly done *will* change everything! You'll *never* escape your destiny – or any of ours!"

Hoards more chisels joined the others, hammering great cracks and chunks out of the roaring statue, sending them crashing to the floor, the stone dripple crying out in peffa-twizzled fear; the last terrifying sound it made before finally the entire statue fell to the floor with a thunderous garrumbloom, a huge white dust cloud racing across the marble floor and slowly climbing the echoing walls.

And then, there was simply quiet...

"Well," Ayaani managed to griffle through the choking cloud, scrittling back up onto Matlock's shoulder, "I guess that's another story tell to the gand-leverets about. Thank goodness that's over."

"Erm," Matlock griffled, making out dozens and dozens of chisels now lined up and pointing directly at them both through the clearing dust. "I'm not really sure if it is, to be honest."

"Duck!' Ayaani screamed, as the lethal tools sailed over, just missing the tips of Matlock's ears, and hurtling towards the ganticus doors at the far end of the hall, crashing into them and attacking the heavy wood – slicing, splintering chopping.

Matlock immediately set off after them, wand frizzing in anticipation.

"What are you doing?" Ayaani griffled.

"Right now, my friend, we're going to change a little more history!" he cried, sending a bright red streaking vroosh cracksploding into the last of the disintegrating doors and following the chisel hoard into the other hall, shouting to all the startled legends to come out from behind their plinths, vrooshing each of their heavy chains, ganticus dark griffle clouds swirling and breaking away, the grateful band of released legends each gradually fading from sight as the hammers and chisels furiously hacked and chipped their statues to just peffa-glopped piles of harmless stone.

At its end, Matlock and Ayaani were left stunned in the dusty chaos, panting heavily, watching the last of the chisels chasing Alvestra's ganticus flying statue high above their heads, attacking the vroffa-broom, until it too finally dropped to the ground, smashing and cracksploding into a grillion pieces with a deafening crash.

They both looked around the demolished hall, chisels dropping onto piles of stone like stroffed meadowflies, their majick spent. Just the plinths remained, cleaned of all griffles, each and every legend just piles of rubble and dust.

"Well," Matlock griffled, putting away his smoking wand, "there's fun, and then there's ganticus fun like vrooshing an entire hall of peffa-twizzled statues."

Ayaani griffled nothing, instead pointing to a familiar, elderly figure in a dust-laden witch's hat, coughing as she emerged from behind a nearby pile.

"Alvestra?" he griffled to her, confused. "You're still here? But I've released you from your legend. You should have become your underwater cavern by now."

She shook her head. "'Tisn't as easy as that for Alvestra. The others have all passed on to Oramus' most eternal care. But I am a witch, Matlock, and more than that – a witch that's bound to this life by the second Most Majelicus task. Just as Tillian, Jericho and Lily Krettle are, too. We all 'live' in this state purely to serve the task, Matlock. It's what we've been chosen to do. And as long as the task exists, we shall be remaining trapped within it. I shall be turning to smoke, frightening young dale-creatures and eating hare soupy-soupy for as long as majickal-hares undertake it. For the task is far stronger than any legends, Matlock. It is *real*, it is now, not history or twisted griffles. True, you have finally freed the others, and for that they will be most peffa-grateful. But in doing so, you have also changed so much more. Come."

He followed her out of the hall and back out into the harsh sunlight, hardly able to believe his hare's eyes. Gone were the saztaculously ornate gardens and oidy creatures carefully tending them. Instead – simply a barren field leading to a sheer cliff-face, and beyond just a dark raging sea stretching to a distant horizon. "Where's it all gone?" he asked. "Where are the fountains and flowers, the paths and crumlush lawns?"

"If there are no legends to tend, Matlock, then why tend them? The gardens are no more. They never existed. You changed *everything*."

"But," Matlock griffled, looking over the empty field, "I just wanted to free those poor creatures in there."

"Indeed," Alvestra griffled. "But in doing so, you have done so much more, Matlock. Remember what Schlott griffled to you – we legends existed as important examples of Oramus' great powers. We fuelled creatures' belief in *Him*. But now, thanks to your vrooshing, there are no legends left. Soon, not even the oidiest memory of them will remain in creatures' minds. Grillions of pictures will simply be blank, tapestries will be unravelling, their threads falling to countless floors, books will be empty. It will be as though they never existed."

She looked at Matlock for a long time, the wind from the sea picking up and peffa-blasting round them both. "Many creatures believed in

Oramus simply *because* of those legends, Matlock. They were proof of *His* eternal prescence. Now that belief will be gone, too."

Matlock's hare's eyes widened. "You mean...?"

She nodded, lowering her voice to a whispgriffle. "It will be like *He* never existed, either."

He struggled to take it in, turning to the sea, paws over his mouth. "What have I done?"

"Changed everything," Alvestra quietly griffled, the edges of her hat and robe beginning to swirl with dark, rising smoke. "Just as the legend foretold, Matlock. *It* has won, not you."

"But I can change it all back!" he insisted, getting twizzly and reaching for his wand. "I can vroosh it all just how it was."

She shook her head. "The chains are broken, the griffles have fled and flown away into the winds. Everything is different now, Matlock, and all because of you."

"But only because I wanted to do the right thing!" he insisted, voice cracking. "Those poor creatures were trapped in there. I wanted to release them"

"And in so doing, you made completely the *wrong* choice," Alvestra griffled, gradually becoming a dark cloud of thick smoke. "And yet...perhaps you never *had* that choice to even make, Matlock. After all, you merely did what others had already decided. And for that, perhaps one distant sun-turn, they might even thank-you – the clottabussed hare from The Great Beyond they all used to change everything. Most pleasing for them."

"This isn't pleasing at all!" he shouted at her. "This is truly most peffa-glopped and dreadful!"

She chickled. "I think, Matlock, that all along, you'll find that you've served others peffa-well in ways you never even thought possible. It's probably why they picked such a gobflopper like you to start with; blind to the obvious, deaf to what you really needed to hear, unaware of anything except your dreary, gubbstooled life in Winchett Dale."

"Where are you going?" he griffled, the smoke swirling higher into the lid as a flash of lightning ripped across the darkening lid, a powerful storm beginning to roll in from the churning sea. "You can't just leave me here!"

"I must return home," she griffled, as the first heavy lidsplashers began to fall. "To my cottage under the sea. I'm hungry. A great tide is coming, Matlock. The moon is ganticus. Many of the dales will already be flooded. Your time is nearly at an end. You have done all that was asked of you. You changed everything, just as the legend foretold. Now it is time for you to stroff. Your sands will be reaching just the last, oidy trickle. Soon, you will be soup, Matlock, your destiny fully achieved. But I will be keeping my promise to you. That skull of yours will have pride of place in my collection, no matter how stringy and yechus you are."

He brandished his wand, angrily aiming a bright red vroosh into the centre of the swirling smoke. "I will not stroff!" he cried at the top of his voice. "I am Matlock the Hare, from Winchett Dale, and I have done *nothing* wrong, ever, in all my years in these dales!"

"Indeed," Alvestra griffled. "Nothing at all. Except, of course, destroy all creatures' faith in Oramus. We witches have the power now, Matlock. With Oramus vanished from so many minds, creatures will turn to our way – the Tzorkly Way."

"A friend once griffled to me that 'tzorkly' means 'to rise above'!" he shouted up at her, heavy lidsplashers pounding his face. "It's not about power! It never has been!"

"Perhaps it wasn't *then*," she griffled, drifting through the heavy rain towards the cliff edge, "but it is, now. You made it that way, Matlock. You – and you alone. I bid you goodbye, and good-stroffing. Show heart, not twizzly fear at the end – that way the boiling won't seem to last as long."

And then she was gone, vilishly streaking far out to sea, lightning forking and flashing as she finally plummeted into the churning surf below.

Ayaani crept up onto Matlock's shoulder, pulling the hood over both their heads. "I'm thinking this'll probably take at least eight. Maybe even ten. Be a first, wouldn't it – double-figure deep breaths?"

"Ayaani," he quietly griffled, turning to her under the hood. "I think I've gone and done something really, *really*, peffa-glopped and completely clottabussedly glubstooled. I think I've destroyed Oramus."

The oidy dripple thought about this for a snutch of moments as the rain pounded down. "Well," she eventually griffled, "perhaps all you've *really* done is destroy creature's faith in *Him*, Matlock. I mean, you have difficulty in making a cloff-beetle salad to go with your niff-soup, so quite how a gobflopper like you could ever destroy Oramus is really quite beyond me."

"But what if I have?" he asked her. "What if it's all true, and I've actually become the clottabussed *Hare Who Changed Everything*? Think, Ayaani – think of those legends back in that hall. Try and remember some of their names. I can't remember a single one. Not a picture of them, not a single griffle of their spuddles. They've all just gone, vanished from my mind. And Oramus, too, Ayaani – I feel *Him* fading, as well." He suddenly threw back his hood, vilishly pid-padding to the edge of the cliffs, just stopping short, sending a trickle of oidy rocks plummeting below.

"Probably not such a fuzzcheck idea," Ayaani observed, looking down from his shoulder at the raging sea, the clouds parting to reveal a truly ganticus full-moon powering the tide. "I say we find some shelter, rather than standing up here like clottabussed-splurks."

But Matlock was too juzzpapped, twizzly and, above all, just too peffa-russisculoffed to even hear her griffles. Instead, he got out his wand and sent a bright red vroosher screaming into the thundery-lid. "Oramus!" he roared at the moon. " I've asked you for help many times, as all your creatures do. Why? Because I believed in you! And I suppose I still do – I still believe that somewhere you look over us. But I don't see you caring anymore! And the more I come to know about myself and my life, the more I realise that perhaps you *never* cared! You used me, Oramus, every peffa-glopped pid-pad of the way! Why would I be still be stood here, right now, after destroying so much, if it hadn't all somehow been part of your plan – your will?

"Are you fed up, is that it? Juzzpapped with us all? Did you just want to fade from our memories, lay waste to these dales, then wash us all away, like we never even existed?" He shot another bright red vroosher screaming out to sea. "Well, I won't let that happen! As long as my last few heartbeats remain, and my name is still Matlock the Hare, I shall use them to try and *really* change everything!"

"Matlock!" Ayaani griffled, vilishly bliffing his ears, and pointing to a small beach at the bottom of the cliffs. "Just shut up and look down there!"

Matlock looked, following her oidy paw and making out an small orb of bright yellow light floating along the beach, and under it, a most curious creature in what looked like a red and white striped suit, bathed in the orb's warming sunlight, waving up at him and pointing to a set of stone steps cut into the cliffs leading the way down.

"Who's that?" Matlock quietly griffled.

"No idea," Ayaani replied. "But frankly I'd prefer to be down there under his sunlight, rather than up here in all this lidsplashy."

"How many?" Matlock asked her.

"I think just two this time," she griffled, trying her briftest to smile through the driving rain.

"Then two it is," he griffled, taking two deep breaths and pid-padding to the steps before carefully making his way down to the beach below, paws held against the side of the sheer cliff-face, trying his briftest not to slip and fall on the wet stone.

At the bottom he stepped onto firm, wet sand; roaring, breaking waves filling his long hare's ears. He looked across at the suited figure still beckoning him into the welcoming burst of light. Cautiously, he pid-padded towards it, seeing two large, translucent eyes on either side of a thin, grey face, and realising that the brilliant yellow orb was in fact attached to the creature itself, held above its head by what looked like a long, thin fishbone jutting from the centre of its flat, grey forehead.

"I'm really not sure of this at all," Matlock muttered, the creature beaming a friendly smile from a thick-lipped mouth full of razor-sharp teeth.

"Hey," Ayaani reminded him. "We've already stroffed Oramus. This fishy-fellow isn't going to be too much of a challenge."

They stopped at the edge of the sunshine.

"Do come on in, Matlock," the creature politely griffled in a pleasantly bubbling voice. "My name's Tillian, and I've been waiting for you for quite some time."

12.

Heights, Krellits and Sea-Wizards

It was late afternoon, the lid was darkening and the vast crowd of dale-creatures trapped up on the blustery cliffs of Twinkling Lid Heights were beginning to get increasingly restless. The flood was still rising and many were tired now, juzzpapped and wet through from the afternoon's heavy rain, huddling in groups, asking passing witches and majickal-hares to light small fires with their wands from whatever wood and kindling they'd been able to scramble and find nearby.

Inevitably, perhaps, creatures began to split, fracturing into their own dales in smaller groups, each seemingly determined to turn their backs and isolate others. Old arguments and russisculoffed squabbles began to break out, creatures suspecting those from other dales had somehow bought secret hoards of hidden food and guzzworts that they were now refusing to share.

At the very far end of the cliffs was a smaller group – the creatures of Winchett Dale, mostly in good humour, but occasionally looking out over the vast lake below at what had once been their village and crumlushed homes.

"Well," a portly-nunkel griffled, putting his arm round his wife. "At least we'll not be having to be fixing that hole in the roof, now, will we?"

"You'll not be getting out of it that easily," she griffled. "When this flood be gone, I be wanting that hole fixed, you mark my griffles!"

Goole, the one-legged, one-eyed kraark always keen to further his singing career, had decided that the flood presented a most ganticus opportunity to be remembered for lifting everyone's spirits in their hour of need – and hopefully get himself a season in Sveag Dale into the bargain – deciding that a truly saztaculous singing showstopper was called for, and he was just the kraark to deliver it.

Unfortunately, the majority of the other creatures didn't seem to share his enthusiasm, and he soon found himself being bliffed and harried away, mostly before he had managed to get a single griffle out. Undeterred and still keen to impress, he resolved to scrittle straight to the heart of the matter, setting off through the disgruntled crowds to find the residents of Svaeg Dale themselves. For surely, he reasoned, if any creatures would be the ones to finally recognise his ganticus talents, then it had to be them.

"Afternoon'up, good Sveagsfolk," he introduced himself, flourishing his damp tricorn hat and bowing generously. "I come to regale you with a saztaculous showstopper to enliven this peffa-glopped situation."

"Are you the flapping-fool that was squawking about his yechus milky-white eye this morn'up?" one asked.

"The very same," Goole beamed. "Though I'd griffle it was more like 'singing' than 'squawking'."

"That be a matter of opinion," the creature grumbled.

"Listen," Goole continued, undaunted, "I don't suppose you be knowing who I should griffle to in order to be getting myself a right crumlush singing opportunity in your dale, do you?"

"You see those cliffs over there?" the creature griffled, pointing through the crowds. "Go throw yourself over them."

It took at least another dozen rejections before Goole finally returned to a small rock where the remnants of the ploffshroom band sheltered against the steadily rising wind. "Any luck?" one of them griffled.

Goole shook his head.

"What happened to your hat?"

"A muted-plindle stepped on it," Goole griffled, adjusting his badly crushed tricorn, sighing. "Sometimes it strikes me, good band of musical-shrooms, that I must've simply been born before my time."

"Well that's all right then," the trinkulah player brightly offered. "You can blame your mahpa and pahpa for that."

"That's right!" Goole beamed, clearly pleased. "I can, can't I? It all be their fault that I'm not saztaculously successful with ganticus plies of drutts. I thank you most humbly for your observation, good rhythmical-ploff."

"Anything to help," it yawned. "So, that's it, is it, then? No more showstoppers? Finally hanging up the beak for good?"

"Not necessarily," Goole griffled, tapping the side of his head with a ring-jangling wing. "I've been thinking of changing the act."

"Saztaculous! Does that mean we're not needed any more? What a relief."

"Nothing of the kind," Goole griffled, wrapping his wings around the three disappointed ploffshrooms. "We're a team, you and I. An unstoppable singing and rhythm combo."

"Just when I thought the sun-turn couldn't get any worse," one of them muttered.

Goole pressed on. "What I've been thinking, me brothers, is that times are changing – and we must change, too. We've got to be able to do something more involving, more elaborate, crumlush and exotic. Mere hundred-verse showstoppers aren't enough for today's more sophisticated audiences. Creatures want a fresh experience, something new, something…"

"Can I just get one thing straight?" the ploffshroom asked. "Are you griffling that we won't ever have to play *Milky White Eye* again? Because it's completely glubbstool and peffa-embarrassing."

Goole held up his wings in shock. "Whoa! Slow down there! I'm not griffling about dismantling the spine of the act! No – I'm just griffling about adding a new and saztaculous dimension to it."

"Which is what?" the nuttar-player asked.

"Stories."

"Stories?"

Goole enthusiastically nodded, his one good eye impossibly

bright. "We tell a story, then do a showstopper about it. Tell another story, do another showstopper. Then another story, another showstopper. Then another…"
"We get the picture."
Goole frowned. "You think it's a gobflopper of an idea, don't you?" All three nodded.
"Well, this is where I'll prove you wrong!" he boldly announced, awkwardly standing on his wooden leg and calling a crowd round. "Creatures of these dales!" he cried. "Come gather for a saztaculous distraction from your woes! Prepare yourselves for a brand new entertainment experience, the like of which has never been seen or heard before!"
"You're not going to sing again, are you?" a thin-pullit asked, already shielding her twizzled youngster's ears. "Only last time it made us all feel quite ill."
"Madam," he smiled at her, his voice steadily rising to a triumphant crescendo, "this time I can honestly griffle to you that you'll be stunned, shocked, amazed and saztaculously enthralled; as I bring to you all, for the peffa-first time, live, right here on this very glopped and flooded afternoon'up – the highlight of the saztaculous Dale Vrooshfest – the official premier of 'The Legends of Time!'"
"What's that, then?" someone asked.
Goole flushed slightly. "The name of me new show."
"No, I meant, what's a legend?"
Goole narrowed his one good eye. "What's a legend?"
The rest of the crowd nodded, staring right back at him. "It just sounds like something you made up," a greebuck griffled.
Goole, his oidy kraark's brain working furiously, began to get flustered. "Well," he griffled. "A legend is…a legend is…is a…"
"Is a what?" the greebuck griffled.
"Is a story!" Goole finally griffled, relieved to have remembered. "A story about some sort of creature that does something saztaculous, then it all goes a bit glopped, then it has to fight something yechus that nearly defeats it, before doing an oidy bit of praying to Oramus who comes and makes everything crumlush for everyone again."
"Never head of such a thing!" a wilting-stuffel shouted from the crowd. "Never heard of this Oramus, neither!"

Others began to agree, becoming bored and wandering back to their fires.

"Wait!" Goole griffled after them. "Don't go! I haven't started the show yet!"

One of the ploffshrooms lightly tapped his wooden leg. "Goole," it griffled up at him. "Maybe this is another one of your ideas that's simply too far ahead of its time. Let them go. No one knows what a legend is, who this Oramus is, or anything." He tried smiling at the confused kraark. "But at the end of the sun-turn, think of it this way – you can still blame it all on your mahpa and pahpa."

"But," Goole griffled, watching the last of the crowd drift away, "*everyone* knows who Oramus is. And all the great and saztaculous legends of the dales." He stared down at the confused ploffshroom. "Don't they?"

It simply stared silently back.

"Oh, come on," Goole tried, trying to chickle. "For a start there's…there's…"

"Who?"

He frowned. "You know, there's that…legend thing…that did that thing…and then…probably did something else…and…"

The ploffshroom shook its wide, creamy head. "And Oramus? What's that supposed to be; a place, a creature, a tree, a chair, what?"

"I had it a moment ago," Goole slowly griffled, scratching at the side of his head with a flaxen wing. "It's just that now I can't seem to remember anymore." He thought for a snutch of blinksnaps, frowning heavily under his damp, crumpled hat. "Though, on reflection, I'd probably say Oramus is…a chair. Yes, I think that's it. Definitely a chair."

The ploffshroom pulled a face. "A chair that saves things?"

"Why not?" Goole shrugged. "We can still make a saztaculous entertainment experience out of it. After all, just because it's a chair, why *couldn't* it save anything?"

"Like what?"

The confused kraark thought long and hard. "How about," he eventually griffled, "a table?"

"It saves *a* table? This is it, is it, your ganticus idea for a new show? A chair called Oramus that saves a table?"

"Well," Goole sheepishly admitted, "it's a start, isn't it? I mean, it's still very much a work in progress. You see, the chair probably wouldn't actually save the table until right at the very end, just when everyone's getting really peffa-worried about it. And, of course, there'd be a host of saztaculous other furniture-related adventures, too."

The ploffshroom sighed. "Goole," it tried to griffle in its most reasonable tone, "just how many saztaculous adventures do you think a chair could have?"

"Like I griffled," he muttered, tutting and scrittling away, "it's just a work in progress."

Some distance from the confused ploffshrooms, Proftulous stood silently at the edge of the cliffs, a grillion thoughts crossing his clottabussed mind. To others, he would merely have looked quite lost in his own oidy world, unaware of anything around him.

Soriah Kherflahdle pid-padded back over, flanked by witches pushing crowds out of the way. "Makes you wonder, doesn't it," she griffled to him, looking out over the water, "if it's ever going to stop."

Proftulous simply stared straight ahead.

She took out her wand and sent a harmless vroosher streaking and fizzing into the water. "Splurked, isn't it, to know that for all this majick, all our vrooshers and spells, something as simple as a most ganticus full-moon can cause all this."

"No majick can be controlling the tides," Proftulous quietly griffled.

Her voice was suddenly cold, her griffles little more than a sneer. "But you used to have something you could call on for help, didn't you, something dale creatures would pray for?"

"Oramus," he muttered.

"That's right!" she replied, opening her eyes in mock surprise. "The saztaculous and ever-present Oramus. The ganticus hare in the moon that looked after all *His* creatures. Do you know, I'd almost forgotten." The smile faded. "But your Oramus didn't look after *all* of us, did he, Proftulous? Certainly not us witches and wizards. We just had ourselves and our tzorkly majick. Oramus never came to us when we needed help. I wonder why that was, Proftulous, I really do."

"I not's be knowing," he griffled. "I just be a clottabussed dworp who be missing his briftest friend."

She beckoned him down, whispgriffling into his ear. "A new age is coming, Proftulous. A new beginning. For too long witches and wizards have been denied what is rightfully ours – a belief in something or anything beyond ourselves. And how wonderful it is that finally, all you dale-creatures know exactly what that feels like in your final few hours before we take to the sky on our vroffa-brooms and leave you here to drown, denied of hope and prayers, victims of a forgotten god who turned his back on you when you needed *Him* most."

"Matlock will do something," Proftulous insisted. "He'll save us and make everything saztaculous and crumlush again, you'll see."

"Matlock?" she cried, startling creatures nearby. "You really believe that that splurked gobflopper of a so-called majickal-hare could save *anything*? The last I saw of him, he couldn't even fetch a glass of grimwagel wine for his witch-friend without getting it all wrong!" She pointed to the rising waters below. "That's where your 'Matlock' will be, Proftulous – somewhere out there, trying to search the entire Icy Seas for a wand that doesn't exist, simply to fulfil his own splurked ambition to be a Most Majelicus hare." She angrily thrust a pointed paw towards a huddled group of miserable looking hares dressed in red robes. "Look at them. Most Majelicus hares. Yet, really, what is so majickal and saztaculous about any of them? Have they saved us from the flood? No – it was witches that saved you all from drowning – witches! Most Majelicus hares are nothing more than glubbstooled creatures in red-robes. Where is their majick now? They can do nothing. Yet your 'Matlock' – your briftest friend – spends his last few hours trying to be exactly like them."

Proftulous shook his yechus head. "You be all wrong," he griffled. "He'll be finding a way to be saving us."

"You ganticus, tweazle-eating fool!" she hissed. "You, more than anyone, know that everything Matlock has done is a destiny he can't change, no matter how hard he tries to pid-pad away from it!"

Proftulous simply turned away, looking back out over the vast floodwater, just one or two distant peaks still visible in the darkening distance. "Matlock will be back," he griffled, jaw set.

"How can you be so sure?"

"The birds," he quietly replied, pointing to a nearby group of assorted fluff-thropps, short-wings, drep-flappers and coated miffle-terns. "They haven't flown away. They be waiting for him."

She shook her head in bewilderment. "Your faith in Matlock betrays you as perhaps the most clottabussed splurk of all, Proftulous. Just how do you think he'll save you? In a peffa-ganticus, majickal boat?"

"P'raps," Proftulous griffled, frowning and slowly pointing back out over the flood. "P'raps just like that peffa-ganticus boat what be approaching right now."

Soriah squinted out to sea, making out a large shape moving closer, immediately summoning a line of witches to the cliff, ordering them to draw their wands at the peculiar looking vessel. "What is it?" she cried out to the furthest witch.

"It be some sort of ganticus raft, Your Tzorkliness," the witch replied, squinting and holding a bony hand under the brim of her hat. "There be creatures on it. It looks like they're sort of rowing it. And they look like…"

"They look like what?" Soriah demanded.

"Krellits!" the witch suddenly cried out in twizzly-fear. "Long, long-nosed krellits from Trefflepugga Path! They've survived, and they be coming straight for us!"

Immediately, creatures began backing away from the cliff as her griffles spread amongst the anxious crowd. One witch, so peffa-twizzled by just the thought of encountering the dreaded long, long-nosed krellits, wasted no time and immediately took to the lid on her broom, desperate to escape.

Soriah spotted her, narrowed her eyes and calmly took aim with her wand, sending out a bright green vroosher that instantly downed the fleeing witch in a thunderous cracksplosion. "Everyone stays where they are!" she shouted at the rest of them. "Witches, hold your line! Get ready to vroosh when I griffle you to!"

Serraptomus, sensing a quite splendid chance to be peffa-officious, began ushering crying dale-creatures away from the snarling line of cliff-top witches. "Just everyone stay calm," he appealed. "Make sure all youngsters are accounted for." Next, he ordered a line of krates to guard the throng, before jauntily making his way over to Soriah.

"Creatures of the dales are secured and their twizzles quelled," he officiously informed her.

She looked distastefully into his puffing, eager face. "Quelled?"

He nodded. "All expertly, officiously organised by my peffa-good self."

She raised her eyebrows. "Listen, you perfectly ghastly lump of glopp, I'm quite capable of being officious by myself, you know. I've had more than enough practice."

Serraptomus began to colour slightly under her intent, tzorkly gaze. His collar suddenly felt too tight. "Just…doing my briftest to help," he stammered, aware her frizzing wand was now pointing directly at his midriff. "I didn't mean to deny you any officiousness, really I didn't."

"So you want to help me, do you?" she slowly griffled, sensing an opportunity of her own in the pitiful wheezing creature.

Serraptomous puffed out his chest proudly, a button from his tweed jacket unfortunately plinging straight into her eye. "Born to help and serve, I am," he griffled, scrabbling on the ground for the button. "Chief Officious Krate of Winchett Dale, ready and reporting for help duty."

"Good," she nodded, directing the wand at his feet and lifting him effortlessly off the ground under a frizzing green vroosher. "Then I suggest you take a little trip down to that boat and find out exactly what those long, long-nosed krellits want."

Before he could even squeak the oidiest griffle of objection, Serraptomus was hurled over the edge of the cliff, the vroosher powering him straight into the large boat of waiting krellits below. A blinksnap later, he landed in a peffa-painful and wholly undignified crash.

Instantly, he shot to his feet, ready to defend himself, both fists clenched in front of his face, desperately scrittling about and trying to look as menacing as possible. "Any of you krellit glopp-ups come any closer," he warned, "and I'll bliff you clean off your pid-pads!"

"Perhaps," a smoothly cultured voice assured him, "we might take your threats an oidy bit more seriously, if it wasn't for the fact that you have both eyes closed, and the vast majority of us are actually sitting down."

Serraptomus stopped scrittling and peffa-cautiously opened just one eye, realising he was standing right in the middle of the boat, with pairs of confused looking long, long-nosed krellits sitting in rows on either side on what appeared to be piles of books. Each pair also held a long branch with another soaking book tied to its end to form a kind of feeble, makeshift oar.

Indeed, the more Serraptomous looked around as the boat bobbed in the rising surf, the more he realised that the whole structure appeared to be made entirely out of books that had been hastily lashed together – and clearly, not very effectively. Water poured through the gaps, forcing the juzzpapped, miserable krellits to use their long trunk-like noses to try and suck as much in as possible, before blowing it back in arcing jets over the soaking sides.

Taking a deep breath, he turned to the politely cultured voice, seeing a smiling long, long-nosed krellitt obviously trying his briftest to keep up some sort of appearances under what were – understandably – quite glubbstooled circumstances. Its skin was quite the most yechus Serraptomus had ever seen, riddled with deep cracks and erupting boils, and yet a golden monocle perfectly framed its left eye. It also wore a tattered scarf and dirty white leather gloves, making for a look that Serraptomus suspected might have made the krellitt appear almost dashing on any other occasion.

"I'm Tiftoluft," the krellit griffled, beaming widely, snaking out its long nose and sliding it into Serraptomus' paw to offer a friendly shake. "And welcome aboard my saztaculous drifting-tub of driftolubbs!"

"Your…what?" Serraptomus griffled, heart-pounding, trying not to look too twizzly as he kept a sharp, officious eye on the others. As lizard-guardians of Trefflepugga Path, every dale creature knew all too well that if the path took offence to your journey, then long, long-nosed krellits would soon be crunching on your bones. Beyond that, peffa-little was known of the fearsome creatures, yet the very mention still struck terror into even the most hardened dale hearts.

However – most peffa curiously – the more Serraptomus looked around, the less he began to fear them. For regardless of their reputation, they looked simply rather sad and clottabussed, drifting around in a glopped boat of books, dismally trying to jet the water away with their long, long noses.

"My saztaculous drifting-tub of driftolubbs," Tiftoluft repeated, still beaming. "It's what we call the books. We took as many as we could from our place in Trefflepugga Path before the waters came, then we few survivors built this." He bliffed the side of it, unfortunately sending a pile of loosely tied books straight into the sea. "What do you think of it, eh? Not bad for a bit of krellit construction, I'd say – not bad at all."

"But it's sinking," Serraptomus pointed out.

Tiftoluft nodded and adjusted his monocle. "Good point, peffa-good point. Problem with driftolubbs is once the parchment gets wet, the whole thing gets soaked through. Becomes little more than a sponge. Bit of an oversight in the planning process. Probably would have been more helpful to make the whole thing out of pastry." He looked up at the curious crowd of witches and creatures anxiously peering down from the top of the cliffs. "Still, at least it got us this far. Thought we were going down a fair few times, frankly, but then spotted you lot from a distance and decided we might as well make a row for it." He lowered his voice to a more confidential tone, his long nose wrapping itself around Serraptomus' flinching shoulders. "The thing is, good krate fellow, is that we could rather do with leaving the old drifting-tub pretty soon. Just wondering what the chances are that your witch friends up there could vroosh us up onto those cliffs before she finally heads for bottom of the drink?"

Serraptomus swallowed hard. "You want…you want to go up there?"

Tiftoluft nodded, trying to offer his friendliest smile. "Now, I'm all too peffa-aware that we long, long-nosed krellits come with… a somewhat unfortunate reputation. And I can well understand a partial reluctance to save us, but I'd just like to offer you my complete and total assurance – on behalf of all of us – that we'll do our utmost not to stroff and eat anyone once we're safely up there."

It was too much for a krellit seated nearby. "No we won't!" he griffled in outrage, struggling with his makeshift oar. "We're long, long-nosed krellits, and the peffa-first chance we get, we'll all be crunching on their bones!"

Tiftoluft adjusted his monocle and tutted loudly, looking

scathingly at the russisculoffed creature. "And what exactly, was the last creature *you* ever stroffed?"

The krellit shifted awkwardly on its soaking book pile, mumbling something inaudible.

"Didn't quite hear that," Tiftoluft griffled.

"A berry-scrittler," it quietly replied.

"A berry-scrittler," Tiftoluft agreed, nodding. "And from what I remember it was absolutely oidy, and afterwards you complained of a glopped crimple for a whole moon-turn."

"Right!" the embarrassed krellitt shouted, throwing away his oar and standing precariously on the wet, wobbling book pile, his shocked partner having to wrap its trunk around his lizard's legs to stop him falling, "I want everyone on this so-called boat to listen to me!"

The entire crew turned, the only sounds the bobbing of the raft and water pouring through the sides.

"I don't know about the rest of you," he griffled, "But what's the point to having a peffa-fearful and twizzly reputation if we can't get to use it once in a while, eh? And right now – well this is the peffa-perfect chance! If anyone's entitled to a bit of stroffing, eating, crunching and terrifying – then it's us! After all, how long do we all spend stuck behind desks, endlessly handwriting all these majickal-driftolubbs for hares that never even bother reading them in the first place? It's just glopped up and pointless!"

"That's all you do?" Serraptomus asked, surprised.

The krellit turned, shrugged with its trunk. "More or less. Sometimes we clean the bones from a few unfortunates that've stroffed on Trefflepugga Path, but most of the time it's just sitting and scribing." He waved a trunk over the damp books. "I mean, who do you think actually writes all these, anyway? They may be majickal, but I can assure you, they don't write themselves, you know."

The other seated krellits nodded, mumbling amongst themselves.

"Each and every sun-turn," the krellit explained, "you'll find us slaving away, making eternal copies of these clottabussed, pointless things." He picked one up and opened it, showing Serraptomus the sodden, ink-smeared pages. "Hours of work, sweat and toil there is, in every page, and for what? The only oidy glimmer of hope we had – the *only* thing that kept us at our desks all that time was the thought that every other creature thought we were terrible and yechus; truly the most twizzly, feared and frightening creatures in all the dales."

"Well, I certainly always thought you were terrifying," Serraptomus griffled, trying to make the creature feel brifter, but also heartily relieved to discover the truth. "So you don't actually stroff anything at all?"

"Peffa-rarely," another seated krellit towards the back of the sinking boat chipped in. "And only then if we're really, really hungry." He reached around and bought out the wet book he was sitting on. "It's all in here, *Majickal Dalelore – Volume 68* – if anyone could be bothered to read it. We've got three whole pages just to ourselves; all about long, long-nosed krellits, everything you'd ever need to know." He tossed the slim volume at Serraptomus, who made rather a stumbling hash of catching it. "Careful, krate – that's the very first one that was ever written. I've spent years and years of my life copying it, over and over again. But you can have it now. I really can't stand the sight of the clottabussed thing any longer."

Serraptomus made a show of trying to flick through the wet pages, the book awkward in his paws. "Thank you," he politely griffled, about to hand it back. "Only, it's not much use to me as I can't read."

"Ah, but it'd be worth the most ganticus pile of drutts, though," another krellit added, the water now up to its shivering knees. "That's the original *Majickal Dalelore – Volume 68* you've got there– the very first one, and without a single revision." He lowered his griffles. "There be wisdom in there, krate, that harks right back to when Oramus *Himself* was said to pid-pad over these flooded dales."

"No idea what you're griffling about," Serraptomus replied, nonetheless tucking the oidy book into his tweed jacket pocket. "Not a clue who Oramus is – or any of the rest of it, frankly. But if you say it's worth a ganticus amount of drutts, then I would very much like to humbly accept it and…"

"I say we all mutiny!" the standing krellit suddenly cried at the top of his voice. "Come on, all of you! Put down your oars, and let's

*Serraptomus turned to Tiftoluft, quite confused. "Are they always as glopped as this?"
"Pretty much," Tiftoluft griffled, using the chaos to expertly slip his long,
long-nose inside Serraptomus' tweed jacket and remove the priceless driftolubb.*

scale these cliffs! Let us twizzle and terrify those creatures up there! Let us be fearful and frightening! Let's stroff and eat them all!"

An excrimbly roar greeted the announcement, the whole krellit crew abandoning their oars into the sea to stand and shake their fists at the watching crowds above.

Serraptomus turned to Tiftoluft, quite confused. "Are they always as glopped as this?"

"Pretty much," Tiftoluft griffled, using the chaos to expertly slip his long, long-nose inside Serraptomus' tweed jacket and remove the priceless driftolubb. "I tend to let them get a bit carried away at times. Lets off a bit of steam, really. They normally just run round their desks for a bit, make a right peffa-racket, maybe stroff something then eat it. They soon settle back down to work again." He winked at Serraptomous. "It's the secret to managing krellits. They're peffa-skilled, but alas, not that bright. Just give them something harmless to get angry about every so often, let them have their rant, then quietly sit them back down again. It's really peffa-simple. Managed ranting and working, I call it."

"They're not…" Serraptomus griffled, nervously looking at the howling krellits, "…they're not going to eat me, are they?"

"Would have thought so," Tiftoluft griffled, bliffing a hard finger straight into Serraptomus well-padded ribs. "Lots of officious fat and meat to be stripped and crunched from those bones, I'd wager."

"Then please stop them!" Serraptomus begged, getting twizzly again. "Get them back into their seats, or something." He began to wheeze and whine. "I don't want to be stroffed and eaten. I'm yechus, completely peffa-inedible – one bite would glopp their crimples for many moon-turns! Please, just griffle them to stop!"

"Oh, I wouldn't worry too much," Tiftoluft smiled, pointing to the rising water inside the boat. "By the look of this drifting tub, we're all going to drown long before you're stroffed and eaten." He looked to the cliff-tops, rubbing his chin thoughtfully. "I wonder if that lot'll simply watch, or if that witch friend of yours will vroosh you back up from the sea at the last possible blinksnap?"

Seraptomus began madly waving his arms at the cliff-tops. "Vroosh me back up!" he yelled. "Or I'll drown, or get eaten! Or both!"

Tiftoluft lightly tapped him on the shoulder with his nose. "You see, what you have here, krate, is your very own chance to be a hero. You simply have to calm down and see it, that's all."

"What do you mean?"

"Simply convince your friends that really, we're all harmless."

Serraptomus vilishly blew out both cheeks, pointing at the baying krellits. "But just look at them! Who's going to ever think that lot are harmless?"

"If you don't, then we all drown," Tiftoluft simply replied, grinning broadly. "And frankly, I suspect you're the only one of us that those witches up there will listen to."

"But how? They all think I'm the most peffa-clottabussed krate in all the dales. The peffa-last thing they'll do is ever listen to me!"

"Then perhaps," Tiftoluft calmly replied, "now's the time to change all that." He stood on a wobbling book pile to avoid the water. "But please be vilish about it, there's a good chap, the last thing I want is my scarf getting wet." He clapped his gloved hands loudly, addressing the unruly krellit mob. "Enough of this glubbstooled mutiny! The krate needs quiet to griffle to the witches!"

The krellits slowly calmed down, one or two of them realising they were now waist-deep in water.

Serraptomus looked up at the cliffs. "Er…," he began, cupping his paws and calling up. "You sent me down here to see what these charmingly good creatures wanted…"

A bright blue vroosher streaked straight down, cracksploding into the sea, rocking what was left of the sinking boat and showering them all in spray.

"All they want to do is stroff and eat us!" A witch called back from the cliffs. "We all heard them!"

Serraptomus frantically waved his paws as a chant of '*Let them all stroff and drown!*' quickly broke out from above. "No, no, no!" he shouted. "You've got it all wrong! They were only doing that to try and make you twizzly. All they really do is sit behind desks on Trefflepugga Path copying out books! They're not frightening at all!" He pointed at Tiftoluft. "Just look at this one! He wears gloves, scarves and a monocle!"

The chant began to fade as more creatures peered over the cliffs at the bizarre spectacle of a short, fat krate trying to defend the most dreaded creatures the dales had ever known.

"And their noses," Serraptomus went on, suddenly holding Tiftoluft's in the air, "just look at them! They're really glopped!" Caught in the hysteria of the moment, he began painfully twirling Tiftoluft's long, long-nose above his head so that it made a high-pitched whistling noise through its shocked nostrils. "Do you think they'd let me do this, if they were really as peffa-terrifying and twizzly as you all think?"

One or two chickles broke out from the watching crowd. Others began pointing and clapping as Serraptomus quickly went from nose to nose, swirling and twirling, sending a variety of different notes whistling high into the air. "All they do is copy books!" he cried, managing to twirl a nose in each paw as the two unfortunate krellit owners winced in pain. "They're not going to stroff and eat anyone!"

By now, the whole of the cliff-top was pressing to the edge, keen to see the peffa-strange scene, krates and witches having to try and hold them back for fear of being pushed over themselves.

Soriah, sensing the danger, sighed heavily and sent down the first vroosher, lifting a snutch of sore-nosed, but peffa-grateful krellits up onto the cliffs, the crowd vislishy parting to give them room, before immediately diving in with hands, wings and paws to try and whirl the tempting long, long noses for themselves.

Other witches followed suit, sending out their rescuing vrooshers, hauling wet krellits from the sinking boat of books up onto the safety of Twinkling Lid Heights, until finally just Serraptomus and Tiftoluft remained.

"You think I'll be a hero, now?" Serraptomus asked, as a blue streaking vroosher shot down and lifted them both into the air.

"Wouldn't have thought so," Tiftoluft griffled. "Creatures have short memories. Heroes and legends are forgotten far too peffa soon. Any clottabus knows that."

Up on the cliffs, the creatures watched the last of the boat sink beneath the flood, some beginning to remark just how much higher the waters had recently risen. It was choppier, too, swelling from a gusting wind that peffablasted their faces.

As the rest of the creatures busied themselves going back to their fires or chasing long, long-nosed krellits, Soriah Kherflahdle once again joined Proftulous at the edge, looking down where the boat had been just a snutch of moments earlier. One or two pages of parchment bobbed in the swell. "All that majickal-hare wisdom," she griffled. "Finally gone."

He turned. It was getting darker now, and alongside him, groups of witches had set about constructing much larger fires, lashing their vroffa-brooms together, bringing as much wood as they could find and piling it on top to make a series of beacons on the edge of the sheer limestone cliffs. "Wisdom never be gone," he quietly griffled. "The griffles be gone, but the wisdom still be all around us, just as it always is."

She softly chickled. "But a new age requires new wisdom, Proftulous. New tzorkly wisdom, perhaps?"

"They be one and the same," he griffled. "Only you can't be seeing that."

She frowned, turning and viciously aiming a green vroosher at a distant huddle of Most Majelicus harcs, expertly setting their robes on fire and watching as they rolled on the ground. One drew out his own wand and foolishly tried to retaliate. Instantly, over twenty witches broke from the beacons and vrooshed him where he stood.

"You think," she asked Proftulous, "that *he* had wisdom? Just because he wore a red-robe and thought his Most-Majelicus wand a match for ours?" She paused, looking into his eyes. "Do you really think *any* of them have any wisdom?"

"Majick not be wisdom," Proftulous griffled, watching the Most Majelicus hares tend their badly scorched friend. "Vrooshers not be wisdom."

"But the tzorkly way *is*, Proftulous," Soriah griffled. "We are the ground and all things upon, above and below it."

"No," he griffled. "You're just witches. And your new-age will end up just as clottabussed and glopped-up as any other age. Just because it be new, doesn't be changing anything."

She smiled. "Except, we're not *just* witches." She nodded to a nearby witch who lit the closest beacon with a frizzing wand. In a snutch of blinksnaps others were also set ablaze, forming a line of roaring vroffa-broom fires burning savage orange in the darkening lid. "Or have you forgotten about the wizards too, Proftulous?"

The ganticus crowd of creatures began to surge forward, drawn by the beacons, hundreds of witches quickly forming a line between them, wands drawn.

Soriah pid-padded to the front, standing alone in the heavy, twizzly silence. "The time," she loudly announced, elaborately brandishing her own wand, "is nearly upon us. For too long, these dales have been…"

"Speak up!" someone griffled from the crowd. "Can't hear a thing back here!"

She frowned, cleared her throat, then tried to griffle at the peffa-top of her voice. "I am Soriah Kherflahdle, Most Tzorkly High Priestess of the League of Lid-Curving Witchery and…"

"Still no good," someone else called out. "None of us can hear a griffle!"

Creatures at the front tried to turn and hush the objectors behind, causing a few choice griffles of their own to begin racing round the increasingly restless crowd. Thwarted from her speech, Soriah was also becoming increasingly rusisculoffed with what should have been – on parchment, at least – the relatively simple business of informing everyone that they were shortly to be stroffed in order for the New Tzorkly Age of Witches and Wizards to begin. How something so simple could suddenly go quite so splurked, was beyond her.

It was the tall, clottabussed figure of Slivert Jutt, landlord of the Winchett Dale Inn, who finally broke from the unruly crowd, pid-padding over with a ganticus beaked creature, the likes of which she'd never seen before, at his side.

"Sorry to be a'bothering of you," he griffled. "Only I sees you be having trouble griffling, so's I bought Kringle for you."

Soriah looked down at the bizarre creature, completely bemused.

"You just be sticking his paw next to your grifflehole like this," Slivert demonstrated, lifting Kringle's long arm to his mouth. "Then when you be doing the griffling, it be Kringle's ganticus beak what be moving and making it all peffa-heary and fuzzcheck for everyone."

"I'm sorry," she griffled, lost. "I've not the oidiest idea what you're griffling about."

"Then be allowing me to be a'demonstrating," Slivert replied, lightly bliffing Kringle twice on the beak, before his voice boomed out over the whole of Twinkling Lid Heights. "Now look here all you good dalesfolk, let there be no more pushing, shoving, bliffing, twirling krellits' noses or bad griffles from one to another. We all be in this together, so I suggest we all be getting on with one another as briftest as we can."

The ganticus crowd turned to face him.

"Now," he went on, "from what I can be seeing here, I has a long line of witches with wands at my back, then behind them there be the beacons, and lastly there's just a long drop into the sea – which, as I griffle, is probably getting shorter and shorter, as it be rising so fast."

"Any chance I could have the paw, now?" Soriah asked him, frowning. "Only I do have peffa-important things to griffle. In fact, I've actually been planning this speech for quite some time, and I really don't want it to go splurked."

"In a couple of blinksnaps," Slivert assured her. "Just settling these good folk down for you. If this be your peffa-ganticus moment, then you'll be wanting an appreciative crowd." He unwisely dug her in the ribs. "P'raps you be wanting me to be warming 'em up with a snutch of me amusing guzzwort-based anecdotes?"

Soriah's eyes widened. She seized the paw, bliffing Slivert with such force he was sent hurtling into a startled group of witches behind. Next, she cleared her throat, took a deep breath and bought Kringle's paw gradually to her lips. "As I was griffling before..."

She got no further, the crowd instantly demanding that once again they couldn't hear her. Confused, she looked at the paw, tapped it a snutch of times, blew into it and tried again.

"Get the other fella back on!" a stunted-moople demanded. "At least we could hear him!"

"S'right!" a crumpled-disidula cried out. "And he was going to give us some funny stories, too!"

Soriah angrily bliffed Kringle's beak. "Why isn't this thing working? Answer me, you splurk!"

Kringle looked up at her. "Me wants a hat."

"A hat?"

He nodded. "A hat that be like yours. One of the witchy hats. All pointy and crumlush."

"You want a witch's hat?" she gasped.

"And a robe. And one of those flying brooms, too."

She slowly shook her head. "Just griffle me this isn't happening, please."

"I want to be all witchy," Kringle earnestly went on, "with a big robe to be covering my yechus feet, and a wand, and…"

"*A wand?*"

"Then I'll be making my paw work for you, and you can be doing all your griffling."

"Are you *actually* trying to blackmail me?" Soriah griffled.

"Yes," Kringle simply replied, tapping the side of his beak with his paw. "You be needing this, and I want to be all witchy."

The increasingly restless crowd left Soriah no option but to quickly order her witches to provide a hat, wand, broom and robe – a process that in itself took far too long, squabbles braking out over who it was that should loose their tzorkly dignity and prized possessions; all of which seemed to please the chickling crowd no end.

Eventually, order was restored, and Kringle stood proudly next to Soriah dressed in a black pointy hat, a long robe and a vroffa-broom in his paw. Apparently content at last, he offered up his other paw to a peffa-frustrated Soriah.

Taking a deep breath, she tried to calm herself, finally ready to deliver the speech she had waited to griffle for so long. This time, when she spoke, her griffles boomed out clearly over the watching crowd.

"The time," she griffled, smiling, "is nearly upon us. For far too long…"

A loud garrumblooming rumble suddenly shook the whole cliff, hundreds of creatures crying out in twizzled panic as the ground shook beneath their feet.

Kringle looked up at Soriah. "What be that?"

She sighed, threw away his paw. "That," she griffled to him, peffa, peffa-russisculoffed, "is the end of my speech. Or was *meant* to be!"

The ground shook again, flaming beacons sending out showers of hot sparks spraying over the cliffs.

Kringle let out a twizzled yelp. "What be happening?"

"It's the arrival of the Sea Wizards," Soriah angrily griffled. "They're always exactly on time!" She stamped her feet in rage. "All I wanted to do was finish my speech before they came. Just that one oidy thing! I had it all planned, all rehearsed! Griffle-perfect, I've been – for years! But, oh, no – *you* had to go and splurk everything, didn't you? You wanted to be a witch! You went and wasted all that time when I was supposed to be griffling!" She bent over, peering intently into Kringle's terrified eyes. "Do you have any idea just how peffa-splurked it is to be really looking forward to telling everyone they're about to be stroffed by Sea Wizards, then miss the chance because of some big-beaked fool?"

Another ganticus garrumbloom shook the cliffs, this time sending an entire flaming beacon hissing into the churning swell below.

"Does this mean I can't be witch anymore?" Kringle griffled, nervously looking towards the remaining beacons.

She bliffed him away in rage, storming through the terrified crowds to the cliff edge and screaming into the darkened sea. "Please, not now! I haven't done the speech yet!"

The whole of the cliff shook as another ganticus wave hurled itself into the flaking limestone, huge chunks breaking away and sliding into the russisculoffed waters below. Proftulous fought his way through the crowds to the edge, wheeling Soriah round to face him. "What have you done?" he griffled. "Stop this! Now!"

She screwed up her face, sneering, practically spitting the griffles out. "I only did what you always needed me to do, Proftulous."

"No-one must stroff!" he cried, the cliffs shaking again, a ganticus wall of heavy pounding spray raining down like jagged ice.

She smiled, relishing the panic in his eyes. "You thought all this could be achieved without anyone stroffing, Proftulous? Then you are a fool!" She turned as a truly ganticus wave, twice the height of the cliffs made its way through the darkness towards them with a terrifying roar. "How much longer can you lump-thump away, Proftulous? How much longer can you hide? Behold your legacy, Proftulous! The Sea Wizards are here to sweep away the last of the dales and herald the new tzorkly way!"

The ganticus wave gathered pace, bearing down, the terrified crowd screaming out in twizzled fright, knowing they were just a snutch of blinksnaps from being swept away and stroffed…

…however, at the very last, to everyone's peffa-relief and complete amazement, it stopped, holding itself over the cliff, reshaping, rising further into the lid to form the shape of an enormously ganticus robed wizard, rippling and flowing, its two black whirlpools eyes looking down on the scene below.

Others joined it, as ganticus wave after wave each reformed into huge water-wizards until finally they all stood in line, surrounding the cliffs, their wands vast columns of seawater with waves breaking on both ends.

The voice, when it came was the loudest anyone had ever heard. "Which of you is Soriah Kherfladle?" it asked, as another great sheet of limestone fell into the sea.

"I am!" she shouted from the edge of the crumbling cliff.

The Sea Wizard nodded. "Then take your witches and leave," it boomed. "Your purpose is done, and you shall be spared. Take to the lid and fly away while we stroff what's left."

It was only at this moment that some of the witches began to mutter amongst themselves, pointing to the last few flaming beacons. One of them bravely approached Soriah, awkwardly tugging at her green and golden robes. "Please, Your Tzorkliness," she quietly inquired, "but did he just griffle that we're all free to fly away?"

Soriah nodded.

"The thing is…" the witch nervously coughed, "You see…the thing is…"

"The thing is *what*?" Soriah snapped.

"Well…we've gone and burnt all our brooms making the beacons."

It took a snutch of moments before Soriah could take this latest blow in. Her mouth opened, then closed, then opened again, as she slowly turned to the last remaining heaps of burning vroffa-brooms.

"Is there some sort of problem?" the Sea Wizard boomed out from above. "I told you to leave!"

Soriah took what was most likely her deepest witch's breath, ever. "The thing is…" she began, "We seem to have an oidy bit of a problem with the whole flying away thing, really." She tried to chickle. "Only we've...sort of...gone and burnt all our brooms."

"Sort of?"

"Well, definitely, really," she griffled, trying to make light of it. "Yes, we've definitely burnt them. Each and every one. Ashes, the lot of them."

The Sea Wizard considered this, slowly swishing towards his equally bemused water colleagues to decide what to do. The twizzled crowd waited expectantly. Eventually they all nodded and slowly swished back into position.

"It's fine," the Sea Wizard boomed out. "Not a problem."

"It isn't?" Soriah griffled, relieved.

"Not at all. We'll just stroff you alongside everyone else."

"What?" she cried. "But you can't do that!"

"Why not? The New Age of Wizards is certainly a lot less of a mouthful. Easier to remember, we think. Catchier. Probably drop the whole 'tzorkly' thing, too. More your bag than ours, really."

"But the new age is about wizards *and* witches!" she pleaded. "It would be like..."

"Like what?"

Her twizzled mind vilishly fought to find an example. "Like grimwagel wine without the glass."

The Sea Wizard shrugged, sending a great wall of water cascading below. "Fine. Just drink it from the bottle." He turned to the other wizards, who all swished and nodded.

"Please," Soriah begged, "please don't stroff us." She pointed to the dale-creatures. "Just stroff them. They're the old way!"

"Look," the Sea Wizard sighed, "we're wizards, not mathematicians. How can you even begin to calculate the chances of us descending into ganticus crashing waves to stroff all the dale-creatures, but somehow not stroff you witches in the process? It's going to be a peffa-lot easier if we stroff the lot of you, frankly."

"Couldn't you just try and land all on the ones without the pointy-hats on?" a witch suggested, her friends immediately agreeing with this idea.

Another witch had a different approach. "How about if we all linked arms and stood together in a really solid bunch, then sort of jumped and held our breath when you all splashed down on us? Maybe we'd all float up together?"

The Sea Wizard shook its huge watery head. "Look at us, we're absolutely peffa-ganticus. The weight of all this water crashing down on you would flatten you thinner than a cauldron handle in a blinksnap. Worth a go, though," he congratulated her, looking around. "Any other suggestions, or shall we just get on with it?"

"I have a suggestion," a bold voice called from the crowd, creatures parting as the white robed figure of Ledel Gulbrandsen marched purposefully to the front.

Seeing him, Proftulous immediately pushed through, grabbing him by his shoulder. "What you be doing?"

Ledel looked him in the eye. "They can't stroff their own kind, Proftulous," he griffled. "It's part of the Wizard's Code." He took out his wand, the bright blue tip already frizzing, pid-padding forwards and looking up at the ganticus watery figures. "Great and most tzorkly Sea Wizards!" he cried. "I am Ledel Gulbrandsen – Arctic wizard-hare from across the Icy Seas! If you decide to crash down and stroff us all, then you will stroff me, too! A wizarding law will be broken! I command you to leave these creatures in peace!"

The vast crowd waited, holding their breath as once more the Sea Wizards swished together to consider this new dilemma.

"Very well," the leader griffled, swishing back. "We've had an oidy bit of a think about it and decided it's probably best if you just jump in, swim around for a bit while we get all the crashing and stroffing done, then we'll take you back to your homeland afterwards. That suit you?"

"No," Ledel griffled, flexing his paw around his frizzing wand. "It doesn't."

Another Sea Wizard moved its ganticus bulk closer, towering over to inspect Ledel as cold, heavy water poured down onto the hushed crowd. "What are you even *doing* here?"

"I came for the Dale Vrooshfest," Ledel griffled. "To prove that wizard-hares are more tzorkly and more majickal than ordinary majickal-hares. I came to prove myself *Most Briftest of All Majickal-Hares*."

The dark whirlpool eyes opened in admiration. "Oh, I see.

Jolly good. And did you win?"

"It really doesn't matter," Ledel griffled. "None of it does; not winning, not losing, not majick – it's all about other things."

"Really?" the Sea Wizard griffled, sitting carefully on the edge of the cliff between the last of the flaming beacons. "So griffle to me, Mr Gulbrandsen of *so* much high principle – what is it that you think *really* matters? Or wait, no – don't. Please spare me from a predictably splurked speech about the majickal-nature of all living beings, how really we're all the same, regardless of who we are, how we dress, what we look like – and that true majick really beats inside the softulous' of us all, should we only take the time to find it. Honestly, I can't tell you how much I get bored of those."

"Choices," Ledel fired back.

"Choices?"

"Choices matter. Making them at the right time." He lifted his wand, breathing heavily, aiming it at the ganticus figure. "And perhaps knowing which choices to make matters even more. After all, who tells us such things? What guides us? Are they tzorkly, or majickal, or something we don't even have the oidiest idea about?"

The Sea Wizard slowly stood, anxiously looking at the frizzing wand.

Ledel pointed at the crowd. "These dale creatures, they're not my kind. They'll griffle to you that it's something called their Sisteraculous that guides them, griffles them what to do. Majickal-hares trust things called 'extrapluffs'. We witches and wizards have 'the tzorkly way' – but in the end, it's not about sensing or knowing which choice you should make – it's what you *do* with it. Whether you choose to follow it through."

Proftulous vilishly lump-thumped over as Ledel drew back his vrooshing arm. "What are you doing?"

"Choosing to defy the code," Ledel griffled, turning to Proftulous and smiling. "I liked your Todel Bear, though. Quite made my life."

And then, before Proftulous could stop him, Ledel flung his arm forwards, sending out a saztaculously tzorkly screaming blue vroosher straight into the startled Sea Wizard who roared in twizzly pain. Another vroosher followed, then another, Ledel laughing all the time, twirling and dancing, vilishly sending streaking blue vrooshers from behind his back, over his head, throwing the wand from paw to paw, twisting and turning, the ground shaking and garrumblooming as vroosher after vroosher hit home.

"You're breaking Wizard Law!" the Sea Wizard boomed, as yet another of his companions fell stroffed back into the sea with a ganticus, roaring crash. "Stop!"

But Ledel carried on, heartened at the site of so many Sea Wizards slicing back into the churning waters, vrooshing and vrooshing under the ganticus full moon, his bright blue streaks like lightning against the ever darkening lid.

Next, he bounded to the very edge of the cliffs, eager to vroosh those trying to fall back into retreating waves, their roars filling the lid, spray fountaining into the air. Some tried to raise their ganticus wands to strike back, but Ledel was too vilish, they were too slow – until the final Sea Wizard suddenly reached down a ganticus, watery hand and thrust him high into the night-sky, Ledel still vrooshing as it roared out in twizzled pain.

Protulous lump-thumped to the edge, panting heavily, as far above, the Sea Wizard let out one final, agonised roar and crashed into a solid wall of plunging water. Ledel, with one last effort, managed to leap away, falling to the ground, tumbling to the edge and then right over the cliff, just managing to grip onto a piece of crumbling rock with one straining paw at the very last blinksnap.

"Help me," he called to Proftulous, wide-eyed with twizzly-fear. "Pull me back up!"

Proftulous lump-thumped over and crouched down, looking back at the cheering crowds running towards them. "I…can't," he griffled.

"You can!" Ledel cried. "Just pull me up! Proftulous, please! You can do it! Take my paw and pull!"

Proftulous took a deep breath, rubbed at his yechus face with his paws, then reached down and gently prized Ledel's paw away from the edge, turning away so as not to see the complete confusion in the wizard-hare's eyes as he finally let him fall away into the unforgiving darkness below.

He stood just as the excrimbly crowd reached him, held out his shaking paws. "I couldn't be saving him," he griffled. "He just be slipping right through my paws."

The crowd hushed, one or two pid-padding to the edge, peering down into the black.

The tall blue-robed figure of Lord Garrick stepped forward, frowning. "He's stroffed?"

Proftulous nodded. "He be too wet to be holding onto."

Garrick reached up and put an arm around him. "You tried your briftest, Proftulous. Only you and Ledel even dared to get that close. Truly, you are the bravest of all dworps." He turned to the sullen crowd of witches and dale-creatures. "Good folk, something happened here this even'up of most extraordinary and saztaculous courage. Between them…"

Kringle pushed through them, dutifully supplying his amplifying paw.

"Thank you," Garrick griffled, putting it to his mouth. "Good folk, something happened here this even'up of most extraordinary and saztaculous courage. Between them, Proftulous and Ledel Gulbrandsen, two creatures from entirely different sides of the sea, came together to beat those ganticus monstrosities and save us from all being stroffed. It is only because of their bravery that we are still all here. The waters are calmer now – as so must we be, too." He pointed to the huge full moon that watched over them all. "By tomorrow morn'up, the tide will have gone, these lands – our dales – will emerge, allowing us to pid-pad back to our homes and begin again. And perhaps this will be our new age – an age to rebuild and pull together and…"

A ploffshroom with a trinkulah vilishly scrittled over in the moonlight and looked up at him. "Excuse me, but do you want a bit of backing to this? Only it's quite an emotional moment, and I do a neat line in rousing melodies in a minor key."

Garrick looked down, frowning. "I've sort of lost the flow of the griffles now."

"Only asking," the ploffshroom griffled, tutting.

The rest of the creatures; shocked, stunned, relieved and saddened by all they'd seen, began melting away back to their fires, griffling amongst themselves of the saztaculous and most tzorkly bravery of Ledel Gulbrandsen. Witches joined dales-creatures, Most Majelicus hares warmed their paws beside long, long-nosed krellits, residents of rival dales collected wood together, then sat griffling about the most spectacular Dale Vrooshfest there had ever been – the sun-turn they'd all come to Winchett Dale.

Soriah Kherflahdle found Lord Garrick on the edge of the cliffs, staring out over the flood, the moon a peffa-perfect reflection in the still, dark waters below.

"Dreadful isn't it?" she griffled.

"Oh, I don't know," he griffled, "it all seems quite strangely crumlush to me."

"I didn't mean the splurked view, I meant not being able to make the ganticus speech when your moment finally comes."

He turned and looked at her. "I don't really think I ever had that much to say."

She walked further on, finding Proftulous sitting by the last flaming beacon. Frowning, she sat next to him, dangling her legs over the cliff. "So, are you going to push me over too, then?"

"He be slipping."

She faced him. "Sad thing was, he never really *had* any choices, did he? For all Ledel may have griffled about making the right choice, it all finally came down to your choice, didn't it?"

Proftulous griffled nothing, staring at the moon, frowning heavily, his yechus brow twisted and creased. "You don't be knowing anything about me."

She stood, smiled, leant over and whispgriffled into his ear. "I know you dropped him, Proftulous, and I know why. You sit here thinking about choices you made, when really, you don't have any left, do you? I'd have thought you'd have joined the other creatures by now – I'm sure they'd give you quite the hero's welcome by their fires."

"I think you should be leaving me," Proftulous quietly griffled. "I not wish to be griffling any more."

She nodded, looked at him for a long while then slowly shook her head and pid-padded away, unaware that far, far away in a ganticus white hall, the chisels were already at work, shaping a ganticus block of stone that would soon become the first of the new Dale Legends – Ledel Gulbrandsen – the Hero of Twinkling Lid Heights.

13.

Betrayals, Treachery and Sisters

As the sea flowed slowly out of the dales, more land rose from the receding flood. Tips of distant mountains became whole again, occasional rooftops could be glimpsed emerging from moonlit waters. Above, the cloudless lid played host to the brightest full-moon, quite ganticus and saztaculous, the four stars of the constellation of Tillian clearly visible in a straight line next to its yellow surface, so close it looked as if the moon would merely need to take the oidiest breath to suck them all in.

It would be morn'up before creatures could return to their homes and discover just how flood-glopped their dales had become. But for now, they were safe up on Twinkling Lid Heights, occasionally leaving their fires to wander to the cliff-top and look over the stilled serenity, quietly watching tops of trees gradually reappearing far below.

For Laffrohn, the last few hours had been peffa-long ones. With no option but to take to the lid on her broken vroffa-tree after leaving Garrick's Castle, she'd spent the time aimlessly circling, far above the flood, occasionally stopping to hover in mid-air, taking out the thirteen pages of parchment from her smock and re-reading them, questions fighting for space in her mind.

She wondered if she should return to Winchett Dale, but realised the folly of such an idea. The flood was now too high and doubtless would have already reached the helpless creatures there. Whatever her and Baselott's plans had been to ensure the Dale Vrooshfest take place up on the High Plateau, she now knew how much they'd underestimated the ganticus tide. It was far stronger, far higher than they'd ever expected. Looking down, she realised the whole of Winchett Dale would now be underwater, the plateau completely flooded. She hoped that perhaps some birds had escaped, flown to the safety of Twinkling Lid Heights – but as for the others, they would surely have stroffed and drowned. For all their careful plans, she realised full well that in the end, she and Baselott hadn't managed to save the dales at all. The moon was simply too ganticus, its hold on the tides too strong. His science, his logic, and her majick – had finally meant nothing in the unstoppable face of it; all was surely lost.

She thought too, of Chatsworth, and how he had secretly carried Baselott's revisions with him for so long. She wondered how many times he had paused to take them out to read them, perhaps furtively looking to see if anyone else was watching. She tried to understand just why it was that he'd never thought to tell her, show her the parchment. Didn't he trust her? There'd been so many opportunities after Baselott had finally stroffed. How many times had Chatsworth come to The Vroffa-Tree Inn, alone? Why not simply share them with her?

How close, she wondered had they ever really been? How close had *anyone* been – Baselott, Chatsworth, or her? Friends, on the surface, yes. But with too much hidden away. Too many stories untold. Too many secrets kept.

High in the twinkling-lid, she read from the pages once more, slowly shaking her head, imagining Chatsworth reading them, finally realising just why it was he never confided in her.

They weren't revisions at all. They were a letter to Chatsworth.

Dear Chatsworth,
Firstly let me say that I use the griffle 'dear' in no other context but politeness. It's not meant to infer any affection, and I would be peffa-disappointed to think you took it thus. It is merely a formality and not meant to disguise my complete disappointment in you one oidy bit.

By now, of course, you will have realised that you are no closer to finding my revisions than you have ever been. Doubtless this might enrage you – or then again, you might be peffa-relieved. As I sit here writing, I am imagining you, Chatsworth, reading these pages, desperate for their knowledge – my knowledge – which frankly I never had the oidiest intention of ever giving to one so spineless, clottabussed and cowardly as you.

Why did I entrust you with the task of taking these pages to that greedy fool Garrick? Because I knew you would fail. The moment I am stroffed, you will read them – I am sure of it. Next, of course, you will have to deliver them to Garrick, who is, in some senses, just as untrustworthy as you. You won't trust him not to open them and read them for himself. Doubtless you'll find some solution – it wouldn't be difficult, not even for a clottabus such as yourself. There's plenty of spare parchment, you'll most likely just give him thirteen blank sheets of it.

You won't be able to griffle to Laffrohn about your deception, either, will you? The shame would be too much. How would you ever admit to her that the 'revisions' you read were simply a letter outlining just what a glopp-up you are?

So you will be left with these. I suspect you will most probably burn them or some such – perhaps throw them far out to sea, or bury them under a rock in the darkest forest. But these griffles, Chatsworth, the ones I'm writing – and you'll all too soon be reading – will live inside your mind for the rest of your miserable life.

Perhaps you think me cruel – or unjust in some glubbstooled manner. But you have been caught out, Chatsworth. If you'd simply delivered these pages to Garrick as I asked – then none of this would have happened, would it?

I advise you not to read on – but I'm certain you'll ignore this, also.

I had no intention of ever having an apprentice, let me make that peffa-clear. The thought of having some clottabussed leveret to teach in the ways of majick that I already knew to be quite glopped, was utterly pointless and a waste of my valuable scientific time. However 'rules' laid down by others demanded that once I had passed the three Most Majelicus tasks, I must spend the rest of my life dressed as a red-robed fool, searching for hares like yourself in The Great Beyond to train as apprentices, according to Majickal Dalelore.

Of course, such a prospect offered me nothing. *You* offered me nothing, Chatsworth – save the chance to perhaps be the next subject of my experiments.

Why was I so loathe to have you around? Because I had already completed the three tasks without ever using a single vroosher. Mostly, they were merely enfeebled puzzles, simply requiring a minimum of logic, and no majick, whatsoever. As such, they were an insult to a hare of my advanced knowledge and understanding. All those hours of study that Trommel, my master, had forced upon me, making me read the majickal-driftolubbs proved useless. Potions he had me making, spells he had me memorising, vrooshers he had me practising – all were without even the oidiest purpose in completing those clottabussed tasks.

Afterwards, dressed in the red-robes of the Most Majelicus hares that I now despised, I set my mind to thinking about the folly of all this. How was it possible that we hares alone were the only majickal-creatures in all the dales? After all, it seemed to me that it was only us that made potions, performed spells and vrooshers with our hawthorn wands. Why were we so different? What was to stop a disidula doing the same? Or an abbrolatt, or a leaning jutter, or even an officious krate? Was it simply because hares were the only creatures to be called from The Great Beyond? Was this the place where true majick lay?

I spent time travelling the mirrit-tunnels, determined to find answers. I pid-padded to other dales, resplendent in my red-robes, griffling to whoever I could, hoping to find even the oidiest clues. The answer was always the same – Oramus, in His wisdom, took the form of a hare, and in His time upon these dales, created all living things, and all we see around us. From here he passed to the moon, and lives there still, watching over us all.

The world as I perceived it had gone quite glopped.

I visited many dales in my quest for answers before realising there weren't any to be found. Why? As a logician, I needed to know. The greatest of all libraries – the one in Alfisc Dale, would surely provide answers. But instead of forbidden wisdom, I simply found empty books full of blank pages, lurking behind elaborately ornate covers. Residents pid-padded around with them, dressed in their saztaculous finery, using them as little more than useless items of jewellery, pretending to griffle of stories they'd read inside, adventures they'd discovered. I searched the entire library, yet didn't find a single book that had even the oidiest griffle written upon its pages. Slowly, I began to realise that our knowledge is only passed to us by those peffa-few in these dales who can actually read – mostly majickal-hares, whose only 'real' knowledge is gained from the ancient griffles they are forced to read from the majickal-driftolubbs in the first place.

All, it seemed to me, had been prepared a peffa-long time ago.

I realised too, *why* there were no answers to be found. It was peffa-simple, and perhaps had been staring me in my hare's face for far too long – there were no answers because there were no questions. Everything was just accepted. We dale creatures simply did what was asked of us, without ever once stopping to question why we were doing it.

But back to you, Chatsworth, and here things might get an oidy bit glopped. Forced as I was to fetch an apprentice hare, I took the mirrit-tunnels, this time stumbling upon The Vroffa-Tree Inn at the very centre. It was the first time I had met Laffrohn, landlady to all Most Majelicus creatures. I also met witches on my travels and learned from them. They have a saying – 'as above, so below' – it isn't the same for dale-creatures, Chatsworth.

You may be shocked to learn of my association with witches. Why was I, a hare of science and logic, griffling with flying-hags in rags? The point was this – they had no 'rules', Chatsworth. They had no 'Oramus" – just a belief in the nature that surrounds them. Their 'majick' is 'tzorkly' – inherited, not learnt or taught. A witch's wand makes our mere hawthorn efforts look like little more than an oidy twig.

After griffling with Laffrohn, I took the mirrit-tunnel, pid-padding along its long, twisting length, until finally emerging in a field in what I knew to be The Great Beyond, where I took cover, aware my strange appearance would mark me out as easy prey to lurking predators. You were the first leveret that I saw, Chatsworth – all alone. Gradually, I noticed others, pressed down in the long grass, as if they'd already sensed my presence. It was all too easy. You actually began to come towards me and didn't seem worried at all. It was then that I knew you were perfect. How could anyone be that clottabussed, that trusting? And better still, the others kept themselves hidden, as if they wanted me to take you, not them.

You came so close that I just reached out, swept you up and pid-padded vilishly back to the tunnel entrance. It was only then that you got twizzly and cried out for your mahpa. I should have dropped you there and then, returned for a braver specimen. But I carried on, down into the tunnel, soon realising to my horror that we were being followed. Your mahpa was behind, bounding on all fours, gaining on us. You struggled, bucked and kicked, crying out for her. Then the most saztaculous thing happened – the tunnel took her. She stroffed, unable to take another bound into its forbidden Most Majelicus darkness, sucked into the mud, all trace of her gone. I was safe.

I carried on, realising just how lucky I was to have you, Chatsworth – a leveret born from a truly clottabussed mahpa who so easily gave her own life in a glopped act of bravery that achieved nothing. As her offspring, you would surely be just as clottabussed as her! If I could use my methods to turn you into a Most Majelicus hare, then it would prove my life's work wasn't in vain. The rules of the Majickal Elders would finally be shown to be wrong. Extrapluffs and majick weren't necessary – just science and cold logic. I was eager to begin.

However, much to my dismay, you soon proved to be perhaps the most glubbstooled choice I could ever have made. Each and every sun-turn, you sat around glopped, pining for your mahpa and didn't apply yourself to my studies even the oidiest bit. Merely teaching you to pid-pad properly on hind legs almost exhausted my patience with you. You were worse than peffa-useless, the most gobflopped subject of a scientific experiment I could ever have acquired.

Trommel would sometimes visit to check on your pathetic

progress, griffling to me that these things take time, always with an amused smirk on his face. I had no patience for his feeble observations – it was hard enough for me to convince him I was training you the 'proper' majickal way, instead of secretly using my own methods. However, one sun-turn, he discovered the truth and tried to forbid me from my researches, insisting I was wrong and placing everyone in great danger. I pretended to stop, but kept on, nonetheless. Trommel's 'wisdom' was simply his own twizzly-fear of change, a desperate hare clinging onto all he believed, refusing to see it for the shallow, empty promise it really was.

I continued teaching you my ways, but also schooled you in old-majick, too, in order you might realise just how irrelevant it really was. I made you read – forced you through page after page of the majickal-driftolubbs, comparing them with my own notes made from experiments which disputed every so called 'fact' on the faded parchment. No doubt you might remember these times as harsh, or cruel, but for the experiment to be 'proper' you had to know of *both* ways – then choose the direction you wanted to pid-pad along. But once again, you disappointed me – preferring to spend your sun-turns playing with your dripple and your dworp. I would set you tasks, but then notice you outside, all three of you playing, as if everything should be simply endless fun. You were turning out to be no brifter than any of the other dale-creatures. It was all most peffa-glopped.

The rest, you know. The Most Majelicus robes you wear belong to another – Trommel, my master – as this was the only way to complete my experiment – to make you some sort of success. Chatsworth, when I think of you – which fortunately isn't too often – it is simply of a red-robed fool who in the end had to be saved from the final two Most Majelicus tasks as he would have surely stroffed trying to complete them. You had every chance to learn from me, to become more than me, to inherit my researches and methods, but you chose not to. Everything about you is a disappointment. Even in my last snutch of hours, it pains me to think that somewhere in that coward's heart of yours still lies a belief in the old ways of majickal-dalelore – despite all I tried so peffa-hard to teach you. It makes me despise you even more.

Soon, I will stroff, and make my way to join the Majickal Elders. No doubt Trommel will be waiting for me, furious about my so-called 'treachery' to dalelore. And here, time will be on my side. I will have the chance to griffle to them first, long before you arrive. And, of course, I shall be dutifully contrite, peffa-apologetic, shaking my head all the while and pretending to be most ashamed of my actions.

Next, I shall ensure they see your pathetic attempts to train your own majickal-hare as just as treacherous as anything I ever did – if not more so. Because, remember, you and your peffa-glopped apprentice, Matlock, have broken more rules than I ever did. You took him without ever being truly Most Majelicus. You taught him dressed in the stolen robes of a stroffed hare. When I have finished griffling to the Majickal Elders, your crimes will be seen as *far* worse than mine. You may think this unfair – but the truth is that my griffles will be listened to long before yours are even uttered, and I'll happily use them to blame you for as much as possible. In doing so, and begging 'forgiveness' I'm certain to be be accepted amongst them, allowing me to pursue my investigations without the oidiest suspicions, dressed in the blue-robes of a Majickal Elder myself.

I suggest you destroy this letter. Although, knowing you to be the clottabus you are, you'll most probably keep it, thinking that perhaps it has some value, some future worth. It doesn't and it won't.

You have your own hare now – this Matlock creature. Perhaps, in some way, you feel that he's the answer to your problems, the justification for your dull and glubbstooled life. He won't be. There is already too much at stake that you know nothing about. I noticed you gave your own dripple to him – doubtless to thwart any further griffling experiments I may have wished to conduct on it. You most likely thought it an heroic act of kindness, an unselfish gesture – but really, it simply showed me how little you've grown since the confused leveret who would wake from his nifferduggles, all eyesplashy and crying for his mahpa. You gave away your own dripple simply because you were afraid for its safety. How cowardly of you – how weak. Who knows what progress I could have made with it – the benefits my experiments would have uncovered? And even if your dripple was to stroff, then it couldn't have been for a finer cause – scientific investigation.

I taught you forbidden vrooshers that I myself invented, vrooshers that could change so much, make things far brifter for so many dale-creatures. But will you ever use them? I very much doubt it. The 'Mutato-Corpore' – the greatest of all my discoveries – the changing spell. Will you ever have the courage to finally use that spell, Chatsworth? And what would you choose to change, if you could? I suspect your answer would be 'nothing' – as you have never realised the most fundamental principles of science, logic and the eternal links between choice and change.

One sun-turn many years from now, a ganticus flood will cover the dales. Nothing can stop the power of the moon and tide. The devastation will be almost total. Lives, homes, dales and faiths will all be destroyed. And yet, in the aftermath – perhaps you will seize the opportunity to rebuild things using my proven scientific methods, rather than a glopped belief in a majickal way that will have failed everyone so cruelly.

I sincerely hope that you do.

High in the twinkling lid, under the light of the ganticus moon, Laffrohn slowly blew out her cheeks. She'd lost count of the number of times she'd read the letter, wondering all the while how Chatsworth had managed to keep it from her. He'd never once griffled about his mahpa stroffing in the mirrit-tunnel, or any of his other worries and woes. His life was to her mostly a mystery. She knew him simply as her good friend Baselott's apprentice – a hare that could be trusted, a hare that always seemed faithful to his master, despite everything.

She thought of Trommel's robe – how he and Baselott had argued deep into the night before the elderly hare had finally gone to bed, Baselott still insistent that Chatsworth shouldn't be forced to undertake the second Most Majelicus task. She remembered finding Trommel's body the next morn'up – the older hare having passed peacefully into Oramus' most eternal care during the night. A brief image of herself taking the robe and giving it to Baselott crossed her troubled mind, together with the look of pure relief on his face. At the time she thought it was because he was relieved Chatsworth wouldn't stroff trying to solve the puzzle of the Tillian Wand. But now, she knew differently. Baselott's joy in watching Chatsworth awkwardly dress in Trommel's robes was simply the look of the scientist whose experiment is a complete success. Chatsworth had indeed finally become a Most Majelicus hare. But it all mattered so much more to Baselott – and for the most peffa-glopped and glubbstooled reasons. The moment she'd reached for Trommel's robes was the blinksnap she became trapped by her own glopped deed. The die was cast.

And yet, if she really thought about it, perhaps it had been cast many years before, as she'd vilishly sprinted away from a falling tower, far, far away…

She looked down, seeing parts of the dales gradually emerging from the flood. Tips of forests rose from the water, mountains stood taller. Beginnings of sloping dales were just visible in the bright yellow moonlight. It was peffa-quiet, as if the entire landscape was still in shock. Occasional gusts of wind lightly rocked the broken vroffa-tree she sat on.

"So where to, then?" it asked her. "Looks like there's some places down there we could try to land on."

She closed her eyes, thinking.

"Only," the tree went on, "we've been up here a peffa-long time, and it's all very well for you to be just sat there doing nothing – but you try to glide motionless with half your trunk missing. It's not easy."

Laffrohn smiled, lightly patting the side of its bark. "I think there's really only one place that I can be going to."

"The Vroffa-Tree Inn?" it hopefully griffled. "Back through the tunnels to the cavern – see if we can find it?"

"No," she quietly griffled. "Somewhere else. Somewhere else entirely."

"Suit yourself," the tree griffled. "You always do, anyway. I'm just the branches in this operation."

They headed away, flying through the lid to the peffa-last place Laffrohn ever wanted to go to, yet knowing that really, she had no other choice. The pull inside her was too strong, pressing into her mind, refusing to be ignored.

There were candles burning inside, some at the arched windows, looking as if they'd only just been lit. Creatures scurried and scrittled across the round walls, searching for cracks to hide in.

She steered with her knees, speeding over floodwaters, scanning the darkened landscape, looking for the one place she knew she had to go. She dropped down, streaking across the flood, the moon a peffa-perfect reflection on its stilled surface. Up ahead, she saw the tops of a distant mountain range, sensing she was close, rising to fly over them and sweeping down again, seeing an island of land, and on its surface, breaking through and rising up to meet her – the downside-upsey tower of Jericho and Lily Krettle.

It was time to settle things with her sister once and for all.

She dismounted, her feet squelching in the sodden earth. The tower, too, looked quite glopped – the ivy hanging off in wet trails, soaking stonework glistening in the moonlight. There were candles burning inside, some at the arched windows, looking as if they'd only just been lit. Creatures scurried and scrittled across the round walls, searching for cracks to hide in.

All was perfectly quiet. Waiting.

A sudden voice at her side. "We be wondering when you'd finally be stopping by, Laffrohn."

She span round, seeing the face of Jericho Krettle. "I need to be griffling with Lily."

"Oh, you *needs* to, do you?" he griffled. "After all this time, and suddenly you *needs* to be griffling with your sister?" He lifted a short, stubby finger, pointing it accusingly. "But p'raps she no longer wants to be griffling with you, Laffrohn. P'raps it be too late for displeasing griffles that should have been griffled a peffa-long time ago."

A window opened above and Lily Krettle leaned out. "Be sending her up, Jericho, my lovely."

He looked up, frowning. "It not be right, Lily. She can't be just turning up and having a griffversation whenever she be wanting it. She left us to stroff, remember? Just pid-padded away as vilishly as possible when things got too twizzly."

"She still be my sister," Lily warned him. "Bring her up, or it be most displeasing me."

"Very well," he griffled. "Though I not be thinking this be a good thing at all, my lovely. Not one oidy bit of it." He turned to Laffrohn, spun his needle sharp teeth just inches from her face. "Although p'raps it be time for some cowardly-sister soupy-soupy."

Laffrohn griffled nothing, holding her ground until he finally chickled then led her inside the tower and up the long, winding spiral staircase to the round room at the top. She paused to take it all in, her heart beating vilishly, eyes drawn to the splutting bubbling cauldron and the ganticus hour-glass in the centre, just a small trail of sand left rising into the upper bowl.

"It be the final heartbeats running out," Lily announced from the cauldron, a large knife in her paws. "He'll be along all too soon. His sands almost be gone. Come, join me. There be the chopping up and throwing in of vegetables to be done." She smiled. "It'll be like old times, methinks, like when we be helping mahpa with all the preparation."

Laffrohn slowly pid-padded over, ducking between low-hanging chains. "I not be here to be helping you," she griffled.

Jericho chickled coldly. "Just like when you be running away and letting Alvestra be stroffing us both – your very own flesh and blood?"

Lily waved the knife at him. "Now Jericho, my lovely, how does that be helping anything? Here be my younger-sister and I haven't been seeing her for so peffa-long – and you be getting all russisculoffed and not be making everything pleasing."

He shook his head then set back to tending the chains, readying the heavy mechanism above the hourglass.

Laffrohn took a deep breath. "I always thought I'd know what to griffle when this time finally came," she told Lily. "Sometimes, I be imagining it in my head, and it all be so easy. I'd be looking at you, you'd be looking at me, and then we'd both be smiling and hugging. But now I don't think it'll be like that."

Lily snorted, chopping vegetables, the knife blows echoing round the stone walls. "Nothing's ever like you imagine it to be in your head," she griffled. "I never imagined I'd be having a sister who would run away all twizzly and leave me to Alvestra. But you did."

"I was young."

"We *both* were," Lily shot back. "*All* of us were. But between us – you, me and Jericho – we could have used our majick to defeat her. Jericho and I never stood the oidiest chance."

"I be sorry, Lily," Laffrohn tried. "I be thinking about you most every sun-turn."

Lily chickled, throwing chopped vegetables into the bubbling cauldron. "From where, Laffrohn? From your crumlush inn, all hidden and safe, deep under Trefflepugga Path? With all your cosy fires and Most Majelicus friends, your guzzworty even-ups and saztaculous griffversations? Is that where you be thinking about your sister, stuck in this peffa-glopped downside-upsey tower, with nothing to do but be making more curtains and eating hare soupy-soupy?" She pointed a blackened ladle, her sharp, pointed teeth beginning to slowly spin in her mouth "You not be thinking about me at all, Laffrohn. I can be seeing right into your mind. I be half-witch now, and so be Jericho. We both have the spirit of Alvestra inside us – and she shows us just how glopped your twisted griffles are. You not be my sister anymore– no more than this cauldron or this ladle be. You just be Laffrohn, landlady of The Vroffa-Tree Inn, and as such you being here is most displeasing."

"What happened?" Laffrohn quietly asked, beginning to slowly back away. "What happened after you stroffed?"

Jericho Krettle chickled from across the other side of the room. "Well, I can be griffling to you what *didn't* happen, Laffrohn. We were forbidden from passing into Oramus' most eternal care. There was witch in us, all glopped and mixed up. We'd become like a soupy-soupy ourselves – a stew of dale-creatures and witch. Things had gone downside-upsey for us, so we be sent here, guardians of the task to keep safe the same wand that had caused us to be stroffed in the first place."

Lily nodded, still stirring the splutting cauldron. "But while we've been here, Laffrohn, we've been doing much thinking. We always wondered why it was that Alvestra came looking for the Tillian Wand in our tower in the first place. Why would she even *think* it would be here? The legend tells of Tillian throwing one half high into the lid, the other deep into the Icy Seas. So why would Alvestra come to our home?"

Laffrohn took a short, shallow breath. "Because she'd already looked everywhere else?" she griffled. "Your castle be simply another place for her."

Again, Jericho chickled, pid-padding across to the hour-glass, watching the last grains of sand making their way increasingly vilishly into the upper bowl. "So, it all be just one peffa-big coincidence, be it?" he griffled. "She just happened to be flying around and thought she'd come and see if the wand be here?"

"Most probably," Laffrohn griffled.

"And you *really* be believing in such ganticus coincidences, do you?" he griffled, staring her in the eye. "Because Lily and I don't be doing any such thing."

"I don't know what you be griffling about."

Her sister chickled. "Oh, Laffrohn, why be coming here after all this time and try to confuse us with your griffles? It be most glopped. Alvestra obviously came because someone had griffled to her that the Tillian Wand was here. Someone had been managing to persuade her. She be desperate and old, weary of all her searching. She would go anywhere to finally find it."

"And then," Jericho coldly griffled, "she be meeting *you*, didn't she?"

"No," Laffrohn griffled, frowning heavily and backing away. "That not be true!"

Lily slowly pid-padded towards her, the chopping knife tight in her paw. "You couldn't be standing the thought of what Jericho and I be having, could you? You be jealous and all twisted up with it. You be wanting me back as your sister. It's why you be coming and taking me out for pid-pads. You told Alvestra when Jericho would be on his own. You griffled to her that the Tillian Wand was somewhere in our castle."

"No!" Laffrohn indignantly insisted, frowning. "None of that be true! Not an oidy griffle of it! You be getting this all wrong! I not be jealous of anything!"

Lily shook her head. "So when you and I be out pid-padding, Alvestra arrived and began vrooshing the place to dust and rubble. It's how we saw it, Laffrohn, remember – when we pid-padded back? And you tried so hard to stop me from running in to protect my dear Jericho, didn't you? Screaming at me, you were, holding me back and griffling that he'd already stroffed, that Alvestra's majick be too strong for us. But I rushed inside, while you pid-padded away as vilishly as you could."

Jericho began hauling on some chains; wheels and cogs now

turning loudly in the yechus room.

Lily closed in. "You probably be thinking that that be the end of it when you see the tower all falling down. You probably be thinking no one would ever know just what you'd done. But we became part-witch, Laffrohn. Alvestra's mind met with ours. We soon discovered the truth of why she was there, and exactly who had led her to us."

"But she be a witch!" Laffrohn tried, getting twizzly. "No one can be trusting the griffles of a witch!"

Lily slowly shook her head. "The only griffles I can't trust are those of the peffa-glopped creature that once be my sister. The sister that left me to stroff, then hid away, deep underground, growing vroffa-trees for witches brooms in order she never be suspected of ever having done the most displeasing thing she did. T'was the promise you made to Alvestra, wasn't it? That you'd always grow vroffa-trees for witches."

Laffrohn flinched, looking over her shoulder, suddenly crying out as Jericho expertly wrapped a large chain around her and roughly dragged her to the wall, securing her to an iron ring. "What you be doing with me?" she cried, struggling.

Lily chickled. "You never wanted to be separated from me, Laffrohn, did you? Well, now you never will. You can be joining Jericho and I for the rest of your sun-turns, right here, eating the slurplicious hare soupy-soupy. There'll be another one along all too soon. His name be Matlock. In a snutch of blinksnaps we'll be making him all boily. 'Tis a most excrimbly thing to see."

Laffrohn watched in horror as thick, black smoke began pouring from her sister's eyes.

"Ah!" Lily cried out, grinning widely. "I see Alvestra has decided to join us this time. He must be a most special hare, this Matlock." She lightly tapped the end of the knife against Laffrohn's cheek. "Methinks we're all going to be having a most pleasing and excrimbly party. And we be most pleased that you finally be joining us, Laffrohn. Most pleased, indeed."

14.

Tillian, the Tower and the Puzzle

Stepping under the bright yellow orb attached to the top of Tillian's head was quite simply saztaculous. Even Matlock, who had seen and done many majickal things in his lifetime, couldn't ever have begun to imagine something quite so unexpectedly shindinculous.

The moment he took his first hesitant pid-pad under the light, everything changed as he suddenly found himself on a most surprisingly crumlush, warm and sunny beach; frittle-gulls cawing in a bright blue lid above, waves gently lapping at flat, golden sands, the cliffs alive with hanging plants, trees and nesting creatures, all enjoying the warming sun, faces upturned, chickling and griffling to one another.

Confused, he stepped back out from the light, vilishly returning to the wretched, windswept, rain-sodden beach in a blinksnap.

"You can stay out there if you really want to," Tillian's bubbling voice griffled. "But most prefer it here in the warm with me."

"But," Matlock managed to griffle above the roaring of the angry sea, the rain driving into his face, "I just don't understand."

"What is there to understand?" Tillian griffled. "Out there, it's glopped. Under here, it's crumlush. It all seems peffa-simple to me."

Matlock took a cautious pid-pad back under the glowing orb, finding himself once again on the saztaculous beach, squinting to adjust to the warming sunlight, looking all round, still unable to believe his hare's eyes.

"Just stay close to me at all times," Tillian griffled. "As long as you're under my light, everything's crumlush. Follow me, and we'll have a little griffle."

Matlock pid-padded by Tillian's side, safe under the warming orb, occasionally daring to poke an arm out from under it, immediately feeling the rain pounding down, before vilishly pulling it back under.

"You'd be surprised how many do that," Tillian griffled, opening his arms as widely as possible, tentacles dancing from the end of his red and white striped sleeves. "Thing, is, because the orb-thing is pretty much a permanent fixture on my head, I can't ever pid-pad outside it. Leaves me sort of trapped. Can't even stretch a tentacle out into the real world." He wrapped an arm round Matlock's shoulder, the pale tentacles exploring his wet face. "Still raining out there, I see. Is it bad, this flood?"

Matlock frowned, looking at the calm blue waters stretching right to a flawless horizon, all without the oidiest hint of the raging storm outside. "How," he griffled, "is any of this possible?"

Tillan's translucent eyes widened on either side of his large, grey head. "Possible?" he griffled. "How is *anything* possible? Being possible is surely what makes anything probable, depending on the probable possibilities."

"Think you've probably lost me there."

"Probably, or possibly?"

"Definitely," Matlock griffled. "You've definitely lost me, now."

Tillian sighed. "I just wish that one sun-turn, they'd send me a hare with a little more grey-matter. Just adds to the frustrations, really, when a chap like you finally turns up, then turns out to be just another clottabus." He lazily kicked at the sand. "But if you want the real answer as to how this permanent sun is 'possible' – look no further than Oramus. And perhaps just the oidiest bit of my own foolish greed, too."

"I've really no idea what you're griffling about," Matlock confessed. "But you knew my name just now?"

Tillian nodded, looking out across the calm, clear blue sea. "Really, on this sun-turn, *the* sun-turn everything changes, it could only have been you, Matlock, couldn't it?" He adjusted his pin-

"Just stay close to me at all times," Tillian griffled. "As long as you're under my light, everything's crumlush. Follow me, and we'll have a little griffle."

striped jacket, tentacles playing with the buttons, leading him over to two red and white striped deckchairs and a small table with two steaming mugs. "Sit," he instructed. "I think you'll find your brew's still warm."

"My brew?" Matlock griffled, looking at the mug as Tillian settled into one of the deckchairs.

Tillian ignored the question, Matlock awkwardly settling into the other chair, both of them looking out over the idyllic scene, Ayaani contentedly warming herself, her soft and most crumlush face upturned to the bright yellow sun.

"Long, long ago," Tillian began, "I stroffed on this very beach, an unfortunate loser in a rather pointless battle for control over the seas with a peffa-persistent witch. All most embarrassing, frankly. Forgot to factor in the moon and tides, found myself washed up here. Alvestra thought she'd got the better of me, but fortunately, just at the last, I managed to break the wand she sought, then throw half into the lid, half into the sea."

"I've met her," Matlock griffled. "Just now, at the top of the cliffs, she was with me."

"And how's she doing?" Tillian asked. "Always felt an oidy bit sorry for Alvestra. Poor old dear never got my wand, and also drew rather the short-straw in this whole task business. I've heard she has to live in some sort of underwater hovel, eating hare soupy-soupy and occasionally turning herself into smoke. Sounds dreadful."

"It's certainly not as crumlush as being here," Matlock admitted, beginning to slightly relax for the first time in a peffa-long while.

"Well," Tillian griffled, "Let's just griffle it was one of the *only* benefits of stroffing first. As a wizard, I quite expected to *become* this beach, as we witches and wizards don't really go in for all that 'dale-creatures ascending into Oramus' most eternal care' nonsense. Quite prefer to spend our time down here, thank you, just being things; lakes, mountains, trees, whatever we feel drawn to. Means we can spend our eternity without all those splurked committees of Majickal Elders trying to griffle us what to do all the time. Much more peaceful, our way. More natural, perhaps."

He shifted slightly, took a sip from his brew, dozens of small tentacles wrapping themselves around the mug. "Thing was, though, I was in a bit of a fix. Didn't find myself here after I stroffed – found myself 'up-there' instead." He pointed up into the clear blue lid. "Just couldn't understand it. Thought there had to be some peffa-ganticus mistake. I waited around for a while, then was eventually called before *The Elder Committee for the Instigation of Most Majelicus Tasks*. And let me griffle you this, Matlock, if ever there was a more clottabussed bunch of blue-robed fools in one room, I defy you to find it."

Matlock griffled nothing, just listening.

"Well, naturally," Tillian went on, "I griffled to them that there'd been a splurked mistake, and demanded to know why I wasn't already a beach. There was a lot of important sounding mumbling and whispgriffling, which frankly I knew to be a glopped attempt to try and make themselves look important. Next, one of them griffles to me that they have been asked by Oramus to find a new Most Majelicus task. Apparently, the old one was much too easy – something to do with majickal-hares having to try and eat an oak tree. Most simply figured out all they had to do was crunch on an acorn and that'd be it, they'd pass."

"Not Matlock," Ayaani yawned, gently falling into nifferduggles under the crumlush sun. "Believe me, he'd have tried to eat the whole tree."

Tillian smiled. "Anyway, Oramus had charged this bunch of clottabussed fools to come up with a new, far harder task, and they wondered if it might be a good thing if it involved witches and wizards in some way." He chickled out loud. "Well, of course, the blinksnap I heard these griffles, I knew they had to be desperate. Witches and wizards, combining with dale-creatures? Majickal-Dalelore finally needing the help of The Tzorkly Way? It was a most splurked idea, yet one I foolishly thought I could play my own way.

"They explained that the oak-tree task was so easy there were now far too many Most Majelicus hares pid-padding around the dales, all eagerly waiting to become blue-robed Majickal Elders when they stroffed. As a result, it was getting crammed up there – with new committees having to be established most every sun-turn simply to give the fresh arrivals a job to do. I myself had to go through seven sub-committees before they would agree to any of my proposals. Whole thing was a peffa-splurked mess, Matlock. No one knew what they were doing. No direction or guidance from Oramus, and just committee after committee of blue-robed Majickal Elder hares doing precisely nothing of any importance, whatsoever."

Matlock looked up into the lid, trying to imagine it all. "But you ended up back down here?"

"Indeed, but not before Oramus *Himself* had to step in to sort things out properly. All rather twizzly, really, as *He's* quite a russisculoffed force to be reckoned with – even for an unbeliever like myself. Got on with *Him* alright in the end, though."

Matlock turned to him. "You've met…Oramus?"

Tillian nodded, chickling. "Oh, yes. Almost felt quite sorry for the chap, really. Surrounded by clottabussed hares, *He* was, more arriving every sun-turn, all eager for their blue-robes and places on committees."

Matlock held his breath, scarcely able to believe what he was hearing. But then again, he couldn't really believe the place he was listening to them in was real, either, although every hare's sense told him that it was. He saw things, smelt them, felt the warmth as his rain-soaked robe dried, tasted the brew he sipped at, heard the relaxing swish of gently breaking waves almost hypnotic in its calming rhythm just a short distance away. He *was* on a crumlush beach. He *was* griffling to a creature called Tillian. It *had* to be real.

"Anyway," Tillian griffled. "Oramus, finally asks me if we couldn't just make the new task be the finding of my wand. Turns out that was why *He* had me sent up there in the first place."

"Just like that?" Matlock asked, shocked. "It all got decided?"

Tillian nodded. "A way needed to be found to stroff majickal-hares before they could become Most Majelicus. By cutting down numbers, it cut down committees. As simple as that, really."

Matlock frowned. "So…so the task was purely created to stroff majickal-hares?"

"More or less," Tillian shrugged. "*His* reasoning was – the harder the task, the less that live – the less *He* has to deal with. All made perfectly peffa-good sense to me. It was almost tzorkly, in a curious way."

But," Matlock griffled, still frowning, "I've always been taught that becoming Most Majelicus was the most saztaculous thing a majickal-hare could ever do. Only the briftest ever wear the red-robes and will eventually become Majickal Elders."

Tillian chickled out loud, enjoying the moment, lightly bliffing Matlock's lap with his tentacled arm. "The briftest? Oh, my dear Matlock! Do you know there was a committee up there called *The Elder Council to Investigate the Real Need for Cavern Owl's Beaks*. It met twice every moon-turn and had four of its own sub-committees deciding on beak-length, height, overall-width and tuning. It was a mess up there, an absolute splurked mess."

Ayaani stretched out on Matlock's shoulder. "I think I'm getting this, now," she griffled. "We're not meant to succeed, are we? Ever?"

"Probably not," Tillian admitted. "One or two lucky ones do, but to be honest, it's mostly soupy-soupy for you lot. Shame, but that's how it is. If you'd been born earlier, chances are you'd have eaten the acorn, become Most Majelicus for a while, worn the red-robes, stroffed, made your way to Oramus, then found yourself on a committee to find out what noise a pie makes when it's thrown at a tree."

"There's a committee for that?" Ayaani asked.

"It's only a research sub-committee at the moment," Tillian admitted. "Carrying out a lot of tests across the dales. Different pies, trees, distances, speeds, that sort of thing."

Ayaani sighed. "So what happens now? Sorry to press you, only I presume the last of our sands will be running out rather vilishly, and we're nowhere nearer to finding your wand."

Tillian looked surprised. "You don't like it here? Most who get this far find it quite a pleasant place to spend their last snutch of heartbeats. Sit there, they do, in that very chair, just griffling away with me, enjoying the sun, then suddenly – vroosh! – they're gone, and it's another one for the Krettle's cauldron." He lightly nudged Matlock in the ribs. "Of course, you're welcome to pid-pad back outside into the pouring lid-splashy, if you want. Wouldn't ever want to keep a chap in here against his will."

"Where's the wand?" Matlock griffled.

Tillian smiled. "Well, it wouldn't be much of a puzzle if I simply griffled you where it was, now, would it? Whole point was to make it difficult to stroff as many of your kind as possible."

Matlock turned to him, suddenly struck with something. "None of this is real," he accusingly griffled. "You're part of an old legend, and I've just destroyed them all. So you shouldn't even be here – you're not real. I released all the legends."

Tillian softly chickled. "Well, you see, that whole 'legend' business was one of the first things I had to sort out with Oramus. Not for me to be chained to a peffa-glopped statue of myself, no thank you. If *He* wanted my help in this task, then *He* had to provide me with certain things to get it." He gestured to the saztaculous beach. "This being just one of them. And the suit and chairs, of course. I have a new one sent down each year. Decided on the red-stripe this time. You like?"

Matlock stood. "I can't sit around listening to this. I need to find that wand."

"And what makes you think you'll succeed where so many others have failed?"

"I've already found half of it – the four stars in the twinkling-lid."

"And I'm supposed to be impressed? You've found *half* a wand? Do sit down, there's a good fellow. There's more to griffle, yet."

"I don't have time."

Tillian pointed to the brew-mug. "Is it still warm? If it is, then you still have time. Not much, but perhaps enough. But, by all means, leave on a perfectly peffa-pointless search if you want to – or you could stay here and perhaps learn something you might need to know."

Realising he had no other real choices, Matlock reluctantly sat back down, holding the brew in his paws, nervously checking its warmth. "So griffle what it is that I need to know."

Tillian settled back into his own deckchair, eyes fixed on the horizon, crossing his tentacled arms over his chest. "Oramus and I had an oidy problem with the task."

"Which was?"

"Alvestra. She was still very much alive and looking for my wand, scouring the seas, desperate to find some, or any trace of it. Without it, she wouldn't ever have control over the seas she craved.

And if she found it – then clearly there'd be nothing for majickal-hares to try and find in the first place. We needed her stroffed before she found it. Majickal-Elders set to work on the splurked business of stroffing her, sworn to secrecy, answerable to only Oramus. It took many years, but eventually a place was found, a tower – and a way of leading Alvestra to it, convincing her the wand lay inside."

"The Krettle's tower?" Matlock griffled.

Tillian nodded, sighing slightly. "I sometimes wonder if those two creatures didn't get the most peffa-glopped deal of all. Young sweethearts with a crumlush life ahead of them, lovely creatures, both."

"Really?" Matlock griffled, remembering the spinning teeth, the chopping knives and clanking chains. "They're truly yechus."

Tillian smiled. "Now, maybe. But not *then*, Matlock. Back then they were that most saztaculous of all things – completely innocent. It's what made them so ideal. All that young innocence and hope would blend with Alvestra's tzorkly greed when they all stroffed together."

"What happened?" Matlock griffled.

Tillian shifted, his voice slightly shameful. "After the deed was done, they came to Oramus, but with Alvestra now a living part of them. As such, none of them could ever move on. We had trapped all three. Part witch – Jericho and Lily wouldn't ever be allowed to pid-pad in Oramus' most eternal care. Alvestra – now part dale-creature, wouldn't ever become the saztaculous underwater cavern she so desperately wanted to be. Together, they had no other option but to agree with becoming guardians of the new second Most Majelicus task. They've done it, ever since, trapped within it, but also faithfully serving Oramus in *His* duties. And if you want to know why, Matlock, then the sad truth is this – it's the only way they can really exist as anything at all."

Matlock rubbed at his brow, still remembering the horror of the Krettle's tower, the hourglass and the yechus, splutting cauldron. Next, he thought of Alvestra, sitting in her wooden hut on the cold, dark shores of the underground cavern – wondering just how it was that the creature he'd always known as the saztaculous, forgiving Oramus could have ever been so cruel. If it wasn't glopped enough that *He'd* found an impossible task simply to stroff majickal-hares, Matlock now discovered the very creatures in charge were completely trapped by it, too. He frowned, trying to re-imagine Jericho and Lily Krettle as a young, married couple, full of hope for a future they'd never enjoy for a single sun-turn.

"But," Tillian brightly griffled. "I suppose it's not all splurked news."

"Why?"

"Well, at least I got this beach out of it. And the suit. Not forgetting the chairs, either." He sighed. "Not that it's much of a reward. More of a prison, really. I'm just as trapped as they are, only the view's marginally brifter. To start with, anyway. After a while, all this perfection just gets on your nerves." He pointed a mass of white squirming tentacles at Matlock. "It's what makes me long to be someone like you, Matlock."

"Like me?" Matlock griffled. "But I don't have anything. Everything's going glopped, and there's a ganticus chance I'm about to be stroffed and eaten."

"Exactly!" Tillian enthused. "Which means change, don't you see? Things will change for you. You'll be vilishly boiled up into soupy-soupy – but afterwards, you'll find yourself happily pid-padding around one of Oramus' many eternal-dales *He* keeps for stroffed hares like you. Pretty soon, you'll forget about tasks, Winchett Dale, wands, beaches and chairs – everything you ever thought 'mattered' down here. You'll have new friends, new experiences, a new life. It'll be that most crumlush of things, Matlock – change."

"Not if I find your wand first," Matlock reminded him.

Tillian frowned. "How many years do you think you could sit here without getting utterly peffa-bored with it all?" He lightly flicked the glowing orb above his head. "This glubbstooled sun is the deal I made with Oramus. At the time it was all I wanted. I was fed up of the sea, its dark, frozen depths. I wanted to be on land. If I couldn't become a beach, then I wanted to live out the rest of my sun-turns enjoying the most crumlush one in all the dales. So *He* gave me this majickal-sun, secured it to my head with *His* very paws. Only now, I'll never escape it. Asking for it was the most glopped and splurked thing I ever did. Perhaps it was why Oramus agreed in the first place. *He* knew full well how easily I would soon tire of everything."

Matlock screwed up his face. "Are you *actually* asking me to feel sorry for you – after all you've done?"

"Not one oidy bit of it," Tillian griffled, standing. "What you have to remember is that it was a ganticus tide that first stroffed me here. I knew full well that in time, there'd be another, just like the one that's flooding these dales now. I also realised just why it was that Oramus gave me my own sun – it was so I'd never see the real sky again, the moon again, the stars, or the alignment of their constellations. I would be forever blind to the true tzorkly majick of the tides, powerless to act."

"Why are tides so important?" Matlock griffled.

"Because they are *time*," Tillian explained. "Here, there is no time. Every blinksnap is like the last. Look around you. My 'sun' never moves. Under here, there is no morn'up, no even'up, no night. Just this sun. And when you're trapped, the one thing you miss most can be the very same thing that traps you. You, Matlock, are trapped by time that's running out – I am trapped by time that doesn't exist. Because, really, in the end, it all comes down to grains of sand; either in a ganticus hourglass, or on a saztaculous beach."

Matlock watched as he reached down and picked up a large handful of sand, letting it slowly run through his tentacles.

"The sands of time," Tillian griffled, "wait for no creature – not even Oramus. Once set in motion, they are unstoppable – just like tides, Matlock, and the ganticus flood that the moon has bought over these dales. It was simply its *time*, that's all. History repeats itself. Chaos rules, and I fear Oramus *Himself* has finally turned his back on us all. The age of dale-creatures is at an end. Sea Wizards will rise from the depths to stroff any survivors. Together, they will band with witches to form a new age of tzorkly-majick, the old ways drowned and forgotten." He looked into the clear blue lid. "It's been coming for a long time, Matlock. Right now, you and your dripple are probably the last dale-creatures left alive. On your journey, you have destroyed legends, faith, history – and now, I'm peffa-much afraid, the time has come for you to be stroffed as well."

"Matlock!" Ayaani whispgriffled into Matlock's ear. "Don't listen to him. It's *not* going to happen, you hear me? We are not going to stroff! We must never give up, ever!"

Tillian chickled, removing his jacket, his skin dry and scaly beneath. "Hate this bit," he griffled. "Spent so long on the beach, it get's harder and harder to go for a dip. Strange, when you think how many grillions of years I spent in the sea." He turned to Matlock, hanging his striped jacket neatly over the back of the deckchair. "Do you mind if I keep the trousers on? – only it saves a bit of time that frankly, you really don't have any more."

Matlock nodded, not knowing what to griffle.

"So," Tillian announced, "here's what's going to happen. Basically, as you've got this far, there's two choices. Either you can forget about this wand business and we can simply griffle a bit more until you find yourself back inside the hourglass at the Krettle's tower – or we can actually go through with you trying to complete the task."

Matlock frowned. "I'd almost definitely prefer to go with the latter one."

Tillian sighed, looked quite disappointed. "You sure? Either way, it'll make no difference. Your finding task is one of the peffa-hardest that's ever been set. It's almost as if you're meant to stroff more than any other majickal-hare who undertook it. And frankly, it'd save me a lot of unnecessary bother having to go through with it all."

"I just think getting this far probably earns me the right," Matlock griffled.

"You sure?" Tillian griffled. "Even if you succeed, you'll still be last dale-creature alive. The others are already drowned by now. Why not just finish your brew and wait for the cauldron with an oidy bit of dignity?"

"Dignity's never been his strong point," Ayaani griffled, setting her face. "Can we just get on with it?"

Shaking his head and mumbling, Tillian slowly began setting off into the churning sea, the pouring rain and wind immediately returning the blinksnap he left.

"Do you know?" Ayaani sourly observed, lidsplashy stinging

her face. "I'm beginning to think sitting in the sun wasn't such a peffa-glopped idea."

"What happens now?" Matlock griffled, following Tillian to the water's edge, foaming waves streaming over his long purple shoes, soaking the end of his robes. "Where's he gone?"

They waited for a snutch of blinksnaps, Matlock looking into the ever darkening lid, the ganticus moon and the four stars of Proftulous, Marellus, Flavius and Xavios still in a perfect line on its edge.

"Well, half the wand's up there," Ayaani griffled, pointing. "And presumably, the other half's still somewhere in the sea."

Matlock kicked at the water as a wave sucked itself back, leaving a perfectly smooth bank of dark, wet sand. "Then we're no further forwards than when we were hopelessly plinging ourselves around in a bubble, are we?"

"But surely reason suggests that it *has* to appear to us at some stage?" Ayaani griffled to him. "We just have to be in the right place, that's all."

"*Reason?*" Matlock griffled, becoming russisculoffed as another wave surged around his knees. "Since when has reason played even the *oidiest* part in any of this?"

"Well, I don't want to be worrying you," she griffled, looking out to sea as a ganticus ball of yellow light began to make its way vilishly towards them under the surface. "But perhaps it's about to, now."

"Oh, my drifflejubs!" Matlock cried, as the huge orb broke from the surface, rising high into the lid, and underneath, attached by a long spike into its head, the largest sea-creature he had ever seen roaring up in a gantucis cracksplosion of foaming spray and thrashing tentacles. Glowing lights flashed in exotic rainbow patterns all over its white, scaly softulous. "Whatever it is, it certainly doesn't look reasonable to me!"

"Pid-pad!" Ayaani cried. "Vilish!"

A ganticus tentacle flashed out, easily wrapping itself around them both, its giant suckers opening and closing like mouths, tiny sets of spinning teeth buzzing inside, effortlessly lifting them above the sea, higher and higher, towards a yechussly snapping black mouth, opening and closing like an angry set of ganticus cupboard doors.

"Your wand!" Ayaani screamed. "Vroosh it with your wand!"

"Can't reach it!" Matlock griffled, struggling in the tentacle's tightening grip. "It's too tight!"

"Then bite it! Use those hare's teeth and really, *really* bite it!"

Matlock twisted, puffing heavily, straining to lean closer to the pulsing tentacle, trying to avoid the gripping suckers desperate to bite him first.

"Now!" Ayaani yelled at him. "Do it now – or we're eaten!"

Twisting one final time, Matlock felt the tentacle under his chin, vilishly opening his mouth, closing his eyes and sinking his teeth deep into the thrashing mass.

Above, the creature roared, Matlock biting again, over and over, its huge black mouth peffablasting them in yechus sea-glopp, the tentacle suddenly uncurling, whipping away in outraged pain and plunging Matlock and Ayaani straight back into the churning sea.

He took a ganticus breath and dived under, trying to kick for the shore, russisculoffed tentacles pounding down into the water all around; cutting, swathing and searching.

He surfaced, lungs bursting, but feeling the relief of firm sand under his feet. Crying out in pure-twizzled terror, he began wading waist-deep for the shore, the huge sea creature letting out a ganticus roar that ripped through the entire twinkling-lid as it spotted him far below.

Ayaani, clinging to Matlock's neck, vilishly scrittled down his robes, searching his pockets, bringing out his Most Majelicus wand, its bright red tip already frizzing. "Vroosh it!" she screamed. "Vroosh it now!"

Matlock stopped, turned in the water, gasping at the sheer size of the creature, its mouth opening again, black translucent eyes fixed, bearing down, crashing through the dark waters, its whole yechus softulous lit from the huge orb on top of its head.

He took aim…held the wand steady…and let the vroosher fly…

It streaked away, powering towards the oncoming creature, Matlock falling back into the sea with the ganticus force of it. A blinksnap later, another terrifying garrumbloom tore through the lid as the vroosher thundered into the vast orb, the creature crying out as the huge yellow light cracksploded into a grillion flaming pieces; falling, hissing and splutting as they hit the sea below.

"Move!" Ayaani cried. "Peffa-vilishy! Move!"

Matlock turned back to the shore, wading as vilishly as he could, stumbling in the dark waters, waves breaking over his back, pointing the wand behind him, paws shaking, blindly letting fly with another red vroosher.

"Hurry!" Ayaani squealed. "It's gaining!"

He hauled at his heavy robes, lifting them from the sea. "Why did I ever learn to pid-pad?" he moaned, surging forwards. "If I was back on all fours, we'd be out of this!"

He pressed on, the water now thankfully just to his knees, finally able to pid-pad onto the firm wet sand and higher up onto the beach, heading for the cliffs, heart pounding.

"Stop!" Ayaani called from his shoulder, pulling on his hood to spin him round. "Look!"

He stopped, breathing heavily, looking back towards the shore and seeing the ganticus creature now lying on the cold wet sand at the edge, its tentacles slowly reaching back into the sea, trying to drag itself back in.

Instinctively, Matlock pid-padded back towards it.

"What are you doing?" Ayaani gasped.

"We've got to help it," he managed to griffle, panting heavily.

"But it just tried to stroff us!"

Matlock nodded, then pointed to the oidy pieces of red and white striped material hanging in tatters high up on its long, scaly softulous still gently pulsing with fading light. "It's Tillian," he griffled. "How he really is."

"Fine," Ayaani snapped. "We've seen that. Now let's go find his wand."

"But don't you see?" Matlock griffled almost overcome with excrimblyness, pointing at the long flat shape in the sand. "He *is* the wand, Ayaani! Look at the light. See how majickal it is." He pid-padded closer, cautiously stepping over stroffing tentacles, looking up into the ganticus translucent eyes, not really knowing what to griffle – whether to feel elated he'd finally found the wand, or peffa-glopped it had taken stroffing Tillian to do it.

"I'm sorry," was really all he could offer to the ganticus creature; although in his heart, he meant every griffle.

The eyes glowed brighter for a moment. "About the trousers? Are they terribly ripped and glopped-up?"

Matlock nodded.

"Why…is it so dark? And cold?"

"Because I vrooshed your sun," Matlock griffled.

It tried to look to the top of its head. "Oh," was all it could griffle.

"I'm really peffa-sorry."

"I feel like this has happened to me before," it slowly griffled. "A long, long time ago."

"I think it did," Matlock griffled. "Then you became trapped on this beach, and you've been here ever since."

It frowned slightly. "And is 'ever since' a long time?"

Matlock nodded.

"Then it's all most puzzling. Most puzzling, indeed, little fellow. Who are you?"

"Matlock. Matlock the Hare from Winchett Dale."

The creature moaned softly, its tentacles hardly moving now, occasionally reaching out for the sea and slapping the cold, wet sand. "And is it nice in Winchett Dale?"

"Yes," Matlock quietly griffled. "Most crumlush."

The creature smiled. "Then you are peffa-lucky, Matlock the Hare from Winchett Dale." It let out a deep gurgling rumble, slowly closing its eyes in pain.

"Can I help?" Matlock asked, reaching for his wand, hoping there was something – anything – he could do. "What can I do to help?"

"Nothing. The sea will take me, now." Tillian looked around one final time, seeing cliffs bathed in saztaculous moonlight, flat sands shimmering with reflected stars in watery pools. "It's really rather nice, here, isn't it? Sort of place a chap might actually want to become once it's all over." He half-smiled, then closed his eyes as the glowing lights under his skin gradually faded to nothing.

Matlock simply stood, not knowing what to do, but becoming aware that the sea was moving, not in a ganticus wave, but gently, swelling forwards to surround the ganticus creature, pulsing and illuminous in the darkness. He pid-padded backwards, watching in astonished amazement as the glowing waters gathered up the stroffed creature and floated it back out, finally pulling it down into the depths, leaving just a long wet scar on the shore.

For a long time, neither Matlock or Ayaani griffled a single griffle, staring out to sea, lost in what had just happened, both of them knowing it was something quite saztaculous, yet also peffa-glopped. Tillian had been finally released from the beach that had kept him trapped for so long – but in so doing, they'd lost their only chance at finding the wand. It had been there, right in front of them, as large, majickal and twizzly as Tillian himself – but in the end, they'd simply let the sea come for him, watching as it took him slowly back to the depths.

It was Ayaani who broke the silence. "I quite liked the first bit," she griffled, "when we were on the crumlush beach with him. The second bit, in the sea, well, that was far too twizzly and glopped – and the last bit…well, that has to have been the strangest thing I've ever seen."

Matlock nodded.

She looked around. "I wonder if it's happened yet?"

"What?"

"If he's finally become this beach. It'd feel strange wouldn't it – to be standing on him?" She looked back out to sea for a moment. "You know why I'm griffling all this glubbstooled nonsense, don't you?"

Matlock nodded, sighing slightly. "Because neither of us wants to admit that by freeing Tillian, by finally having the second half of the wand right in front of us, all flashing and peffa-majickal – we've missed the only chance we ever had to solve the puzzle."

"Couldn't have griffled it brifter myself," Ayaani quietly admitted. "We came close – peffa, peffa-close – but in the end, we couldn't do a thing about it. We just…we just sort of let him go."

Matlock took a deep hare's breath, lightly stroking her head with a wet paw. "Perhaps, it's because somehow we knew it was the briftest thing to do," he quietly griffled. "And maybe that's all we were ever truly meant to do."

They were both considering this, when an elderly voice rudely interrupted their thoughts, vilishly pid-padding down the stone steps behind them. "Matlock!" it urgently cried. "Come to me at once! There's not a blinksnap to lose!"

They both turned, Matlock taking a sudden breath as he saw the red-robed figure of his master step onto the sand at the bottom. "Chatsworth?" he frowned, vilishly pid-padding over. "How in Balfastulous' name did you get here?"

The old hare looked at his former apprentice, panting heavily. "Not for you to know the precise details. Let's just griffle that sometimes Baselott's invented spells and vrooshsers aren't quite as glopped as they seem. But not a griffle to anyone that I've been using them – I'm in more than enough trouble as it is." He looked towards the long scar on the shoreline. "Tillian?"

Matlock nodded. "It was. He stroffed. The sea took him. I failed the task, missed my chance."

"Not yet, Matlock," Chatsworth griffled, looking him in the eye. "You're still alive, still here, so you must still have time. And that means time enough to give me your robes."

"My robes?"

Chatsworth nodded, griffling urgently. "The promise we made at the Krettle's tower, you remember? That when the time came, you'd wear my robes? That time is now, Matlock. Give me yours, and take mine."

Matlock frowned as a distant garrumbloom of thunder rolled far out to sea. He looked into the face of his old master, suddenly having to choke back an overwhelming sense of anger. "*Your* robes?" he griffled, accusingly. "But they're not your robes, are they? I've seen where you and Baselott hid away. I read his diary, Chatsworth. They're Trommel's robes, stolen from his stroffed body." He took a deep breath, unable to stop the griffles. "All this time, and you've never been Most Majelicus at all! Everything's been a lie, from the very first time you took me from The Great Beyond."

"Matlock," Chatsworth insisted, trying to stay calm, "we really don't have time for this. Just give me your robes."

"*Time?*" Matlock griffled, chickling out loud. "What would you ever know about time? You had all the time in the world to tell me the truth, but you chose not to. You never even undertook this task, Chatsworth! Baselott thought you were too glopped, that you'd stroff too easily."

"Please," Ayaani urgently griffled on his shoulder. "Do as he says. Keep the promise and wear the robes. Even if that's *all* you do, even if you hate him for the rest of your sun-turns – just keep your promise. I've never asked you to do anything for me – ever. But do this one thing, Matlock, please."

He searched both their imploring faces, looking up at the moon and the four stars next to it, shaking his head, trying his briftest to decide what to do, remembering a crumlush cottage on the edge of Wand Wood that now seemed so peffa-far away, the times he'd shared there as an excrimbly young leveret, being taught the ways of majick by his Most Majelicus master, Ayaani always on his shoulder, both she and Chatsworth doing their briftest to teach and guide him in the ways of dalelore.

He closed his eyes, feeling the extrapluff coursing through his entire softulous, griffling to him exactly what to say. "Your dworp was called Marellus," he quietly told Chatsworth. "It's the star right next to Proftulous."

Chatsworth took a sudden breath, looking up into the twinkling-lid and slowly smiling, the one great mystery of his life finally solved. "Of course," he griffled. "How could I ever have been such a clottabus?"

"Perhaps," Matlock griffled, unbuttoning his green velvet robe, "it's because you spent so much time with me."

"And never for one moment regretted even the oidiest blinksnap of it," Chatsworth griffled, passing his own red robe to Matlock. "Please, just wear it for me. I want to see you as the most saztaculous Most Majelicus hare that ever pid-padded in all these dales. Just this once."

Matlock reluctantly took the robe, passing his to Chatsworth, pushing his arms through and feeling the heavy red material on his shoulders, taking the red cap and sliding it over his long ears, before finally awkwardly standing before his master as a fully-robed Most Majelicus hare.

Chatsworth beamed, elderly pride writ ganticus on his face. "Never thought I'd live to see the sun-turn," he griffled, vilishly dressing in Matlock's robe and pulling the green cap down over his old ears. He reached into a pocket, pulled out Matlock's wand and passed it to him. "And, of course, no Most Majelicus hare should ever be without one of these."

Matlock simply stood, the wand idle in his paw. "Why would I need it?" he griffled. "I've done what you asked, I've worn your stolen robes. And any blinksnap now, I'm about to be made into hare soupy-soupy. It's over, Chatsworth, it's finished."

"Has it?" Chatsworth smiled.

"I must be seen to fail the task and be stroffed," Matlock insisted. "It's always been that way. I tried, I really did – but really, I never stood even the oidiest chance of ever finding the Tillian Wand, did I?"

"Indeed, Matlock," Chatsworth griffled. "It's true – you must be seen to be stroffed." He turned away and whsipgriffled something in deep concentration, then turned back, his elderly face now a peffa-perfect mirror of Matlock's own. "And so you shall."

Matlock's mouth hung open in peffa-disbelief. He was looking at himself.

"Another of Baselott's forbidden experiments," Chatsworth griffled. "The *Mutato Corpore* – or changing spell. He thought I'd never use it. But, once again, he was wrong."

"What…" Matlock barely managed to griffle, his mind glopped with a grillion twizzly possibilities, "…are you going to do?"

Chatsworth chickled. "What am I going to do? Something I should have done a peffa, peffa-long time ago, Matlock. Stop this whole mess, once and for all. I am going to be 'seen' to be you. For what could be more fitting, and give me more pride than that?" He stepped forwards, gave Matlock a long hug, patting him on the back and whispgriffling in his hare's ear. "This is far from over, Matlock, believe me. In some ways, it's only really just beginning. You will need to be strong, as I won't be able to help you anymore. Always trust yourself – be that hare I found out in The Great Beyond, and stay true to it at all times, whatever happens."

"But, Chatsworth, I…"

"Stand back," Chatsworth suddenly griffled, looking towards the sky, the sand at his feet beginning to dance and swirl. "It's coming. The sands have been sent. Your time is over – and now mine is done, too."

"Chatsworth!" Matlock cried, sand rising and stinging his face, forcing him backwards. "No!"

"Why would the sands ever take a Most Majelicus hare?" Chatsworth called out to him. "It's me they want – clottabussed Matlock, the majickal-hare from Winchett Dale!"

Matlock raised a paw over his eyes, trying to see as Chatsworth fast disappeared in a vilishly swirling tornado of sand.

A green-robed paw suddenly shot out. "Ayaani!" her true master called across. "Would you care to join me for our greatest ever adventure?"

"No!" Matlock griffled, as Ayaani scrittled down his robes. He vilishly scooped her up with his paw. "You *can't* go! Not you, Ayaani – you can't leave me!"

She looked at him, tried to smile. "I always knew it would be this sun-turn," she griffled. "We dripples always do. I must leave to be with my master, now."

"Please," he desperately griffled. "Don't go. Stay here with me!"

She effortlessly wriggled away, scritting towards the swirling sand, before stopping and turning to him one final time, looking him up and down. "My Matlock, a Most Majelicus hare at last." She smiled the warmest and most crumlush smile. "And I meant every griffle of what I once told you. Your dripple would have been the luckiest dripple in all the history of these dales; the peffa, peffa-luckiest. Good-bye, Matlock."

The sand blew harder, roaring across the beach, forcing Matlock back to the cold, wet cliffs, pinning him to the rock, unable to move, his anguished cries lost in the roaring winds…

"Well," Lily Krettle griffled, wiping her paws on her apron as the green-robed hare dropped into the bottom of the ganticus hourglass. "Here be the next one for the soupy-soupy, right on time, as usual." She turned to her sister, chained to the wall. "It be most pleasing, don't you think, Laffrohn, when it all be going good and crumlushly?"

Laffrohn's eyes widened at the twizzly sight. She'd never seen anything so dreadfully glopped, watching Jericho hauling on the heavy chains, slowly lifting the ganticus hourglass into the air. It was Matlock inside, she knew it, trapped and about to be boiled alive.

He'd failed the task as he was always meant to – Matlock, the hare she had shared so much with, now about to stroff before her very eyes. She struggled against the chains, but they were too heavy, too tight.

"Just stop!" she screamed out to her sister. "Please, just stop!"

"Now, why would I be wanting to do that?" Lily griffled, looking up into the glass. "It just be a hare that not be finding the Tillian Wand, like so many others. So it be boiling time, Laffrohn. You remember how we used to make soupy-soupy at our mahpa's? She always griffled that you and I be making the briftest, most slurpilicious soupy-soupy."

"Please," Laffrohn begged, her eyes following the hourglass as it made its way slowly towards the splutting cauldron. "Don't!"

Laffrohn chickled. "Oh, you just be getting twizzly with all the dropping in, aren't you? I be like that in the beginning. My advice is to be closing your eyes so you not be seeing it. P'raps try and be singing a song so you don't be hearing all the boily-screaming. You be surprised how vilishly it all be over."

The hauling suddenly stopped, clanging chains echoing round the yechus room, Laffrohn watching as Jericho Krettle peered up at the trapped hare, closely inspecting it. "He not be looking all twizzled and afraid," he slowly griffled, frowning. "In fact, he not be looking the oidiest bit twizzly at all."

Lily pid-padded to his side, and together they studied the majickal-hare smiling down at them. They looked at each other, quite confused, then jumped as it suddenly banged on the glass.

"Is this going to take much longer?" its muffled griffles asked. "Only, I've got a slight fear of confined spaces."

Lily and Jericho looked at each other, stunned. "You…you want to be boiled up…more vilishly?" Jericho asked.

"If you wouldn't mind. It all seems to take far too long, if you ask me. Why the hourglass thing? If you'd dropped me straight into the cauldron I'd be done by now, wouldn't I?"

A swirl of thick black smoke surrounded the glass, becoming a yechus face topped with a black witch's hat, turning to the confused Krettles. "Why has all the hauling stopped? I be hungry!"

"Avestra, please," Lily griffled, "Jericho stopped because this hare be most suddenly strange."

"Strange?"

"He not be one oidy bit twizzled. Not one bit at all."

Alvestra looked closely into the ganticus glass bowl, smiling. "Well, that's because it be Matlock from Winchett Dale in there! He be the most clottabussed hare of them all. He be *The Hare Who Changed Everything* – only now, he'll be changing into soupy-soupy!" She barked at Jericho. "Haul away, you spinning-toothed splurk! Let's get him dropped in. I be hungry and wanting his skull!"

Laffrohn watched in horror as Jericho set to the chains again, his face straining, the ganticus hourglass swinging ever closer to the vilishly splutting cauldron, unable to keep her eyes from the calm figure inside, who even turned and smiled as he passed by.

"Oh, Matlock," she whispgriffled. "I be so sorry. So peffa sorry."

Then, quite the strangest thing happened – Ayaani appeared on his shoulder and gave Laffrohn the oidiest wave. She sucked in a breath, everything suddenly making a new kind of sense as she remembered the parchment letter she'd read – how Chatsworth had given his own dripple to Matlock to save it from more of Baselott's griffling experiments – how Ayaani had only ever really been Chatsworth's dripple, not Matlock's...

An eyesplasher fell as she struggled to wave back – knowing that in those final moments, somehow Chatsworth had won – using spells Baselott had always told him he'd be too clottabussed and cowardly to ever use. He'd become Matlock with the *Mutato Corpore* – and was now about to take his place in the vilishly splutting cauldron.

"I think," she suddenly cried out to Chatsworth, as Jericho hauled the hourglass right over the splutting cauldron, "I think you've done it!"

Inside the hourglass, Chatsworth, the only hare forced to wear stolen red Most Majelicus robes, the hare who'd watched his own mahpa stroffed in the mirrit-tunnel, the hare who'd never known the name of the loved dworp he missed so much – turned to her one last time, his smiling face disappearing behind steam-covered glass.

"Marellus," he silently mouthed to her. "My dworp was called Marellus. Matlock finally found it for me."

Laffrohn screamed as a ganticus clang shook the room and the bottom of the hourglass opened, plunging Chatsworth and Ayaani into the boiling cauldron below.

"You be looking away, now, sister!" Lily Krettle cried, Jericho vilishly reaching in and throwing out the steaming wet robes onto the cold stone floor.

"More curtains, my lovely!" he griffled, teeth spinning as he began hauling the empty hourglass away. "'Tis a good job we be liking green."

Next to the cauldron, Lily chickled, puffing as she stirred it with a ganticus blackened ladle. Alvestra drifted over, her thick black smoke peering in and sniffing the rising steam. "Be there dripple in there? Oh, this be most good, dripple-seasoning!"

"Be fetching some bowls and chairs!" Lily called across to Jericho. "It's be ready soon, and we'll all be having a most pleasing bowl of slurpilicious hare soupy-soupy by the fireside." She angrily turned to Laffrohn. "Oh, do be stopping all your commotion and eyeplashers, sister! You'll be getting your bowl after we be finishing ours."

Alvestra swirled over to the wall as Jericho busied himself setting up chairs by the cauldron. "You do seeming to be most upset, Laffrohn," she griffled, studying her peffa-curiously.

Laffrohn lifted her head, looking the black face straight in its fiery red eyes, trying not to choke on its thick smoke. "This will all end," she defiantly griffled. "It has to. This peffa-glopped yechussness can't win. It just can't."

The smoke chickled, folding in on itself, becoming smaller, being sucked in by Alvestra herself until nothing remained but the small figure of the elderly witch. She smiled at Laffrohn, reaching out to take an eyesplasher from her cheek, examining it carefully on the end of her long finger. "This not be about 'winning', Laffrohn. It wasn't about 'winning' – ever." She flicked out her tongue, tasted the tear, reading its significance, then nodding approvingly. "Your eyesplasher be for the stroffing of a peffa-good friend."

"He was a good hare," Laffrohn quietly griffled, her eyes on the wet green robes. "The briftest of all hares."

"Who couldn't even find one oidy wand," Alvestra chickled.

Lafffrohn struggled against the chains. "And neither could you!" she shouted. "You spent most of your glopped-life looking for it, obsessed with it, but you didn't even get close! You lost, and Tillian won."

Alvestra smiled, shook her head. "It was never about 'winning', you splurk. It was about change – and choices." She chickled, pointing back at the empty hourglass. "Just change, and choices. That's all it ever really was. Nothing else. Just that."

"No," Laffrohn angrily griffled. "There is something else. Hope."

"Hope?" Alvestra griffled, pulling a face. "So what would you have 'hoped' for, Laffrohn? That somehow, your splurked friend Matlock had found the Tillian Wand? That we weren't all about to eat him? What 'hope' did he really ever offer?" She spun around, chickling out loud. "And you dare to griffle to me about 'hope', chained to a wall? You dare to griffle about 'winning' and 'losing'? What 'hope' is there now for the majickal-dales? What creatures will still be left alive to win or loose *anything*?"

"It be ready," Lily called from the cauldron, ladling three bowls of steaming hot soup.

Alvestra smiled at Laffrohn. "I do hope he be tasting better than he be doing his vrooshers."

"You never knew him," Laffrohn coldly griffled, watching as Alvestra sat with the Krettles, reaching out for her bowl. "And I hope you be choking on him!"

Alvestra slowly raised the steaming spoon, tutting. "'Tis like I just griffled, Laffrohn – all hope be gone."

The three of them blew on their spoons, Jericho and Lily's teeth starting to spin, drool dropping from their slowly opening mouths as they took the first mouthful…and the second…but on the third, it happened…

Jericho simply dropped his bowl to the floor, soup running from his mouth, jolting in his chair, eyes rolling into the back of his head.

"What be happening?" Lily cried. "What be happening to my lovely?"

From the wall, Laffrohn triumphantly called over. "You've all just eaten the wrong hare! It was Chastworth, Matlock's master – not Matlock! You've stroffed a hare that never undertook the second task – and now you all be paying for it!"

Lily turned to Alvestra, dropping her own bowl onto the stone floor. "This be…true?" she managed to griffle, her confused eyes also rolling to white, her teeth barely spinning. "We…be stroffing?" She fell to the floor beside her husband.

Alvestra stood, enraged. "This is the soupy-soupy of another hare?" she hissed, trying to pid-pad to Laffrohn, stumbling, the bowl outstretched. "It was Matlock! I saw him there, all clottabussed inside! He be stroffed and boiled, I tell you – him and his griffling-dripple – they both be in this soupy-soupy!"

"Matlock is alive," Laffrohn calmly griffled, watching Alvestra stumbling against the side of the ganticus hourglass, falling down and trying to pull herself painfully across the floor with just her long, bony fingers. "It *is* the end. But not for him – for you, and this yechus, glopped-up task."

Alvestra crawled to the chains at the bottom of Laffrohn's feet, slowly holding up the half-eaten bowl. "Eat," she griffled, smoke starting to pour from her body. "You…look…hungry."

Laffrohn struggled, trying to kick out, crying out in peffa-twizzled fright as Alvestra rose up one final time before suddenly screaming and dropping away, her thick cloud of yechus smoke rushing through an upturned window as the bowl fell to the floor, tumbling over the wooden boards, as the whole tower now began to move, spinning slowly, preparing to make its final journey…

The beach was cold, empty and quiet – the only sound the distant sobbing of a red-robed hare, slumped at the very bottom of the sheer cliffs. The rain had stopped, the seas calmed a little, the ganticus moon still hanging saztaculously in the twinkling lid, peeking from behind passing clouds returning to a pitch-black horizon.

Head bowed in his arms, ears flat against his damp back, Matlock used the red sleeve to wipe away his eyesplashers, never having felt so juzzpapped, confused, glopped and peffa-broken in all his majickal-life. Everything was gone – everything he'd ever known and loved; Winchett Dale and all the creatures who lived there, Wand Woods, his crumlush cottage, Chatsworth, Ayaani and Proftulous. Without ever wishing to, he'd somehow managed to destroy legends, history, even Oramus – and was now most probably the last ever dale-creature to pid-pad across the once saztaculous and majickal lands. It was all simply too much for him, nothing really mattered any more.

A pair of bright red shoes suddenly appeared on the sand beside him.

"Well," a stern voice griffled, "I can't say the red really suits you, but I suppose it's less splurked than the green."

"They're all gone, Ursula," he quietly griffled without bothering to raise his head. "Everyone. It's over. It all ends here."

She sat by his side, listening and staring out to sea as Matlock explained all that had happened since he and Ayaani had left in the eyesplasher bubble and headed into the depths of the Icy Seas.

After, neither griffled a griffle for some time.

"Well, this is peffa-dull," Ursula eventually griffled. "Sometimes, Matlock, I really don't know why I bother."

He slowly lifted his head, turned to her, frowning, quite unable to believe what he'd just heard. "Why *you* bother? What have you *ever* bothered about, except yourself?" He tore the potion bottle from around his neck, thrusting it into her paw. "This was all you ever bothered about, wasn't it? Collecting my experiences, so you could drink them down." He stood, began pid-padding towards the steps. "Well, enjoy yourself, Ursula. I think you'll find there's some truly 'tzorkly' ones in there – like how it felt to watch Ayaani and Chatsworth taken from me. I bet that'll taste really sweet for you, washed down with your grimwagel wine!"

"Aren't you going to even ask me?" she calmly griffled.

He stopped. "Ask you what?"

"How I found you?"

He threw his head to the twinkling-lid, chickling bitterly. "Ursula, why would I even be the oidiest bit *bothered*? Haven't you been listening? Don't you even begin to realise what I've been through, what's happened to me? Look at me, I'm wearing the robes of a stroffed hare and..."

"I used these," she griffled, reaching into her robe and pulling out three glowing pieces of green light dancing in her paw.

He narrowed his eyes. "Luck? But how?"

"I stole them, you ganticus splurk, at the Estuary Festival. Honestly, what sort of friend do you think I am that I'd let Soriah

Kherflahdle fly away with all the luck in the world without helping myself to a few oidy pieces, first?"

Matlock pid-padded back. "But we don't have any luck left," he griffled, transfixed by the bright lights. "I only ever had one piece and…"

She waved her other paw at him, tutting. "Only ever had *one* piece? Think about it, Matlock. You met me, was that not lucky? You lived in Winchett Dale – wasn't that lucky? You had a dripple that griffled, a Most Majelicus dworp and wand – weren't they all lucky?"

"But I don't have them anymore," he insisted. "None of them. Don't you see? What point is luck, if all it becomes is glopped memories?"

She stood, suddenly throwing the green lights as far as she could, Matlock watching as they hissed and disappeared on the wet sand. "You clottabussed splurk! Luck is always around if we bother to look for it it. You stand there, all glopped and sad, griffling on about how you've only ever had one piece of luck, when all your life you've been lucky! But it's only now, when it's all gone splurked that you *finally* begin to realise it."

He turned, began marching up the stone stairs, paws over his long ears. "Don't want to hear any more of your glubbstooled griffles, Ursula! You don't understand anything, about me, or anything else. Just drink your precious bottle of tears – see how many of them are really mine!"

She vilishly followed him up the steps. "Stop being such a clottabus! Look around you. Others may be stroffed, but you are alive. Chatsworth sacrificed himself so that you could complete this task. Whatever you may have thought of him, whatever you may have discovered, is pointless. Nothing will ever change what happened. But you have the choice to change what *will* happen, Matlock. And only you." She took a breath, pulling on his robe, staring into his confused eyes. "And that, my splurked friend, is luck – *real* luck – not oidy bits of green majick."

He looked away, chewing on his bottom lip, having difficulty swallowing, missing the comforting weight of Ayaani snuggled in his hood. "But I just don't know what to do anymore."

"Find the wand," she griffled. "Chatsworth has given you more time. Find it."

He pointed far out to sea, shaking his head. "I did find it," he griffled. "It was there, right on the beach. It was Tillian. I had my one chance and missed it."

Ursula looked at the ganticus moon, the four stars lined next to it. "But half is still up there, isn't it?"

He sighed, shrugging. "Truthfully, Ursula, I just don't know any more. I'm not even sure that I care, either."

She frowned, pushing past and vilishing pid-padding up the steps. "Well, I do, Matlock! You may have given up and gone all glopped, but I care! Ursula Brifthaven Stoltz doesn't give up on her friends, no matter how splurked they are!"

He pid-padded after her, puffing and panting, amazed at her energy. "You never told me!" he shouted.

"Told you what?" she called back.

"How you found me?"

"Luck!" she griffled. "And I didn't find it in some splurked sack, either!"

"Where are we going?"

"To get lucky again – and find this splurked wand of yours!"

Matlock breathlessly followed as she seemed to sprint up the rest of the steep steps, his feet stumbling and slipping on the wet stone, catching himself with his paws, trying not to look down at the sheer drop below. A cliff-bat suddenly flew from a crack beside him, his shoes sending a snutch of small stones tumbling far below as he yelped in twizzly fright.

"Hurry up!" Ursula called from the top. "We don't have long."

"But there's nothing there!" he griffled, managing to scramble up the final few steps before stepping onto the grassy ledge, his sides aching from the effort.

"Too many niff-soups and guzzworts for you, methinks," Ursula frowned as he gasped for breath. "More pid-padding around Winchett Dale for you in future."

He ignored her, gathering himself and looking round the empty cliff-top, waves from the retreating tide rolling and crashing on the distant shore.

"Griffle me the puzzle," Ursula ordered, pid-padding away, looking at the moon and line of four stars. "The one you found on the side of the tower."

He closed his eyes, thinking back to the ivy griffles he'd first seen glistening in the moonlight in Wand Wood, scarcely believing with all that had happened, that it had been just one sun-turn ago. He cleared his throat, saw them in his mind, began griffling them out loud:

Look to the lid, the sand and the sea,
And there, reflected in your sands of time,
Four dworps linked in all eternity,
A wand from a broom to make a Tillian shine,
There to be grasped, and taken by one paw,
According to Most Majelicus dalelore.

She nodded, made him repeat them, thinking all the while, closing her eyes in peffa-deepest concentration, then suddenly opening them, her face bright and excrimbly. "It's in the first line!" she called across. "It tells you what to do! Look to the lid, the sand and the sea!"

"I don't understand," Matlock griffled, pid-padding over. "I just don't know what you're..."

He got no further, as suddenly the ground began to shake beneath him, the whole cliff-top garrumblooming and rumbling as the Krettle's tower slowly drilled itself up through the grass, ganticus chunks of earth being thrown in all directions as it emerged from the ground, before finally stopping and standing still and tall against the twinkling-lid.

"It's the tower!" Matlock breathlessly cried, running around the base to find Ursula, who had already ducked between the upturned crenulations, a frizzing wand in her paw, vrooshing the wooden trapdoor above her head. "What are you doing? You can't go in there! The Krettle's will stroff you!"

"*I'm* not going anywhere," she replied, the trapdoor swinging open. "You are. The task is yours, not mine." She looked at him intently. "Matlock, I may be a peffa-splurked witch at times, but I'm still tzorkly, and I think that somehow this tower is the key to solving the puzzle. Use it to find the wand – use it to find the lid, the sand and the sea." She pushed him up through the trapdoor. "Be careful – but be vilish. You won't have long!"

"You don't fancy pid-padding along with me?" Matlock weakly griffled, using the light of his frizzing wand to find the spiral staircase.

"Matlock," she calmly explained. "You may well be a friend. But you're also a most ganticus splurk, and frankly I'd rather not stroff with you." She vrooshed the door shut and he was left in darkness with just a glowing wand for company, slowly reaching out and putting his first foot on the bottom stair, hearing distant chains ominously clanking far above his head.

"How many now, Ayaani?" he whispgriffled, wishing she was there to answer. "I think four. Yes, I'll go with four." He took four deep hare's breaths and began slowly climbing, his heart beating heavily in his peffa-twizzled softulous.

It was darker than before, no candles burnt from twinkleabras rising from the floors. It was quieter, too – the only sound coming from heavy iron chains slowly swinging against each other in the breeze drifting though the open, upturned windows.

Stopping halfway and gripping the frizzing wand tighter, he summoned all of his courage. "Hello?" he managed to griffle. "Is anybody there?"

He thought he heard a noise somewhere above his head. Every oidy part of him screamed to turn and run, the peffa-glopped memories of his previous visit still far too strong in his twizzled mind.

"What do you think, Ayaani?" he nervously whispgriffled. "We go further?" He put a foot on the next step. "It's what you would have griffled us to do, isn't it? Go right to the top?"

He let out a breath, then yelped as the whole tower suddenly lurched, stones on either side slipping and grinding in the walls. He looked up, watching a crack streak down and open like lightning, oidy pieces of rock falling away, followed by a cloud of settling dust slowly giving way to just the heavy silence once more.

"Hello?" he called out again, his wand out in front of him. "Answer me, if there's anyone there. It's not safe in here. Chatsworth? Ayaani? Can you hear me? We've got to go."

455

Another noise from above, but more distinct this time, a voice calling out. Heart thumping, he bounded vilishly up the rest of the staircase, the tower walls now openly slipping and crumbling all around, the iron staircase shaking under his unsteady feet. Reaching the last hatch, he aimed his wand and vrooshed his way inside, hauling himself into the yechus, round boiling room at the very top.

"Laffrohn!" he gasped, seeing her chained to the wall, rushing over. "What happened?"

"There be no time for that, Matlock," she vilishly griffled. "It all be over. The task be finished. Alvestra, Jericho and Lily be stroffed. The tower be returning to Tillian one final time. Go find his wand, and save yourself!"

He looked around, breath coming in short gasps as he saw the bodies of Jericho and Lily Krettle by the splutting cauldron. "Chatsworth?" he griffled. "Ayaani? Where are they?"

Laffrohn simply looked at him, shaking her head. "They ended this glopped task, Matlock – and that be the briftest thing to remember. No more majickal-hares will ever be boiled and eaten in this yechus place again."

A large stone loosened itself from the ceiling, crashing down and narrowly missing them both. He cried out in rage, stumbling as he aimed the wand at the iron loops on the wall, letting fly a vroosher that missed completely, thundering into the shuddering wall by Laffrohn's head.

"No time for that!" she yelled at him. "Just be finding that wand!"

"Where?" he griffed, turning blindly, the whole tower slowly beginning to tip. "Where is it?"

A second heavy stone fell from the ceiling. Matlock looked up, glimpsing stars twinkling through the gap, a fierce extrapluff griffling him to go up onto the roof. He turned to Laffrohn. "I'll be back."

"Stop griffling and just go!" she urged. "Or I swear I'll never serve you another guzzwort in The Vroffa-Tree Inn again. Ever!"

He climbed onto a dangling chain, heaving himself up to the gap, his whole softulous straining as he painfully pushed himself through, the tower shaking beneath his feet as he stood – breathlessly – at the very top…and *finally* saw the Tillian Wand…

"Here to be grasped and taken by one paw!" he cried out to the twinkling-lid.
"According to majickal-dalelore! Tillian Wand – I have found you! You're mine!"

...glistening in the moonlight, the peffa-perfect alignment of moon and stars, reflected in all it's majickal glory in the long puddled scar by the shore.

"By the hare's ears of Oramus!" he gasped, "There it is, reflected in my sands of time!"

The tower rumbled again, lurching even further as he reached out a trembling paw to the distant reflection, grasping the night air, hoping he could somehow pluck the wand from the wet sand…

"Here to be grasped and taken by one paw!" he cried out to the twinkling-lid. "According to majickal-dalelore! Tillian Wand – I have found you! You're mine!"

He shut his eyes, closing his paw around the distant shape, immediately feeling the most saztaculous pulsing of something long and heavy; a ganticus, majickal feeling coursing right through him as he opened his eyes and saw the prized wand for the first time, solid in his own paw, taken from the reflection; sea-shells, coral-jewels and crab-diamonds shindinculously clustered around it – its bright blue end already frizzing in anticipation.

"It's here!" he shouted down to Laffrohn. "I've found it! I've found the Tillian Wand! I'm coming down to get you!"

She looked up through the shuddering gap. "No time!" she griffled. "It's collapsing! Leave, Matlock – and use the wand carefully!"

"No!" he griffled. "I'm coming down!"

"The wand controls the sea, Matlock!" she urgently griffled, as another ganticus stone crashed down through the tower. "Use it peffa-wisely!"

Matlock cried out as more stones began tumbling away, sending him pid-padding vilishly to the very edge of the collapsing tower, teetering over, trying to hold himself back as he felt a ganticus jolt beneath him, then heard a sudden roar peffa-blasting his face as he was vilishly pulled up and away into the twinkling-lid, finding himself on the back of what appeared to be an entire vroffa-tree, Ursula in front, flying them both high over the beach.

"Stop!" he called out. "We've got to go back for Laffrohn! She's trapped inside!"

Ursula turned the half vroffa-tree around, streaking back to the cliffs, both of them watching as the tower collapsed into a ganticus pile of rocks and twisted metal, spinning and burying themselves into the shaking ground. Chains disappeared like thrashing, sazpents. The yechus, black cauldron grew spinning teeth and ate its way into the churned mud, before finally, the hourglass itself burst into a grillion pieces of glass, the trapped sand swirling up and over the cliffs, drifting on the breeze to finally settle like harmless dust back on the beach far below.

A snutch of blinksnaps later, nothing remained.

Ursula circled, Matlock searching for the oidiest trace of anything. "She's gone," he quietly griffled. "Laffrohn's gone. We couldn't save her."

"Laffrohn is tzorkly," Ursula griffled. "She will always be somewhere."

"But where?" he griffled, looking everywhere.

"Wherever she truly wants to be," Ursula calmly answered. "Wherever she really needs to be. It's the tzorkly way." She briefly looked over her shoulder. "You have the wand?"

Matlock held out his paw, showing her.

"Fine," she griffled.

"No!" he objected. "It's *not* fine, Ursula. Not fine at all. None of this 'fine', or tzorkly, or saztaculous, or fuzzcheck, or Most Majelicus, or peffa-shindinculous!" He held out the wand. "All this effort, all this loss – for this? How many have stroffed looking for this, Ursula? It's just a wand, that's all – just another wand!"

She turned the vroffa-tree, gunning the branches, streaking inland so vilishly Matlock was nearly pulled right off the back.

"Where are we going?"

"To use it, you splurk!" she cried out. "Where's the nearest mirrit-tunnel? We're going for a ride!"

"We can't enter the tunnels!" Matlock shouted back, desperately trying to cling on. "One of us needs to be Most Majelicus or we'll be stroffed the blinksnap we fly inside!"

Ursula chickled. "Well, that must be *you*, you clottabus! You wear the same robes Chatsworth wore. You *are* Most Majelicus now, you ganticus splurk! Just like Chatsworth was. He never completed the three tasks, did he? Yet those robes let him use the tunnels, just like they'll do for us."

They flew on over the ganticus flood, Matlock seeing for the first time just how many of the dales had been glopped by the ganticus tide, knowing in his hare's heart Winchett Dale's High Plateau would have been deep underwater, too. Tillian had been right – everyone at the Dale Vrooshfest would surely have drowned and stroffed. He closed his eyes, not wanting to see any more. Whilst he'd been pointlessly chasing a wand, so many others had needed his help. Were he and Ursula really the last ones left alive – flying above it all, with just a wand to show for everything?

How could everything have gone so glubbstooled in just a single sun-turn?

"There!" Ursula suddenly shouted, pointing to a distant mountain up ahead, a large geyser of water spurting from its slopes. "Is that a mirrit-tunnel?"

Matlock opened his eyes, looking. "I think so," he griffled. "It could be – I'm not sure. I don't recognise anything."

"Well, that's good enough for me!" Ursula cried, steering the broom straight at the spouting entrance. "Use the wand, Matlock! Vroosh the water back through the tunnel!"

Matlock held the Tillian Wand steady in his paw, taking a deep hare's breath and aiming right at the tunnel entrance, letting fly with a bright blue vroosher that tore through the night into the spurting floodwater, driving it back down into the tunnel, hoping and praying Chatsworth's red Most Majelicus robes would keep them safe.

They screamed in, Matlock vrooshing the solid wall of water and driving it back, the saztaculous, roaring power of the Tillian Wand shaking his whole softulous as they flew deeper and deeper into the pitch-black.

"It's working!" he cried.

"Shut up and keep vrooshing, you splurk!" Ursula griffled, using all her tzorkliness to expertly steer the tree through tunnel after tunnel; around corners, along adjoining tunnels, up and down, emptying each one, gradually driving the entire, roaring floodwaters back into the Icy Seas.

At the end, all the mirrit tunnels were empty, Matlock and Ursula effortlessly flying inside, and he was finally able to stop the powerful vroosh, his arm aching and from the effort. They finally arrived at the ganticus cavern at the very centre, once the saztaculous home to The Vroffa-Tree Inn, now just a broken wooden bridge over the still, dark lake.

Ursula landed the tree, patting it gently and thanking it, its ends still glowing from the flight.

"Where's the inn?" Matlock griffled, watching as Ursula vrooshed the torches on the sides of the cavern walls, their familiar orange glow flickering around the many tunnel entrances. "Where's The Vroffa-Tree Inn?"

Ursula pointed to a tunnel on the far side of the cavern, steadily glowing a pulsing bright blue. "I'm no expert," she griffled. "But methinks it's probably moved to a new home."

Matlock looked into the tunnel and closed his eyes. Somewhere, in the peffa, peffa-distance, he could almost hear the familiar sound of rolling waves. He smiled for the first time in a peffa-long time, content and sensing – perhaps for the first time in his life – that despite what he thought about everything, it all made a most curious kind of majickal sense – if not for him, then for others that he'd somehow managed to help on their way...

A thought occurred – not an extrapluff – but something far stronger, a glimpse almost, of a distant even'up, far into the future, in another place entirely. It was of Laffrohn, a smile on her crumlush face, serving him a guzzwort and lightly bliffing him on the ears as a piff-tosh crackled and warmed them nearby.

He opened his eyes, looking across at Ursula, who also opened hers then looked at him and smiled. "I'll be having a grimwagel-wine," she griffled. "Never could stand guzzworts."

Together, they flew out from the tunnels, back out over the dales, now looking saztaculously glorious and shindinculous in the moonlight, all traces of the flood gone, heading for Winchett Dale's High Plateau, seeing cottages, villages, forests, woods and trees far below.

"Look!" Matlock cried, pointing down to a majickally moving twisting landscape of mountains, valleys and rivers. "Trefflepugga Path is still here!"

Ursula griffled nothing, flying on to what she knew to be the distant beginnings of Winchett Dale – seeing a ganticus glowing beacon way up high on the sheer limestone cliffs of Twinkling Lid Heights, then gradually making out a surging line of grillions of creatures, waving and cheering at them both as they circled above.

Matlock looked down, barely able to believe his hare's eyes. "They're alive!" he griffled, breaking into the most ganticus curving smile, bliffing Ursula's back in pure, saztaculous exhilaration. "They're safe!"

"You do that again," she warned, "and you'll be far from safe, you splurk."

The huge crowds parted, allowing Ursula to finally land the juzzpapped vroffa-tree, excrimbly creatures of all descriptions eagerly surging forward; witches, disdulas, krates, leaning-jutters, fluff-thropps, mottled-regglers, foffles, flute-beaks and many more – all lifting Matlock and Ursula high into the air as pawplause rang out over the whole of Winchett Dale.

A short distance away, a rather nervous looking krate lightly tugged on Lord Garrick's long blue robes.

"Erm," Serraptomus griffled, awkwardly clearing his throat. "Does this mean I'll still have to be washing-up for the rest of my sun-turns? Only, I think you'll find that surely, in the end, Winchett Dale really *did* deliver quite the most saztaculous of all the Dale Vrooshfests."

"Well, it was certainly unforgettable, I'll griffle you that," Garrick agreed. "And as for washing-up – well, it really depends if there's going to be any committees to wash up for, doesn't it?" He smiled at Serraptomus. "And frankly, I'm not so convinced they're such a peffa-good idea anymore."

Proftulous barged past, vilishly lump-thumping through the crowd, desperate to see his peffa-briftest friend, bursting through and giving Matlock the most ganticus hug, effortlessly lifting him and turning excrimbly circles. "You be coming back!" he griffled. "You be vrooshing everything all crumlush again and be coming back to us! I knew you would, Matlock, just knew it! No one believes me, but I just be knowing it!"

"That's probably enough hugging for the moment," Matlock managed, face pressed against Proftulous' chest. "And spinning around, too. I never want to see anything else spin for a peffa-long time."

Proftulous set him down, the crowd quietening as Soriah Kherflahdle made her way over, turning to Ursula. "So," she griffled, "you found a way, didn't you? You found a way to help the hare."

Ursula bowed. "I think, Your Tzorkliness, perhaps we found a way together."

Soriah considered this, raising her eyebrows. "And maybe that is a good thing. Not a tzorkly thing – but perhaps a good thing." She turned to the crowd, snapping her fingers as Kringle dutifully pid-padded over and offered up his paw.

He winked at Matlock. "It's been a peffa-long sun-turn, I can tell you. Still working, I am. Believe me, you've missed out on one ganticussly, peffa-glopped adventure up here."

"Oh, I wouldn't be so sure about that," Matlock quietly griffled, watching as creatures hushed themselves to hear Soriah's griffles.

"Creatures and witches of all the majickal-dales," she began, Kringle's beak sending her griffles right across Twinkling Lid Heights. "We stand here, safe and alive, thanks to many things. This sun-turn could have been the most spurked for all of us. Some have stroffed along the way, and we must never forget them, and ensure their stories are told across the generations to honour the sun-turn we all gathered in Winchett Dale. It is both our majickal and tzorkly duty to them – to remember those whom this sun-turn *truly* belongs to – for now, and evermore."

The crowd slowly broke into pawplause – as far away, in a vast white hall, majickal-chisels began working on two new ganitcus blocks of stone, alongside the saztaculous statue of Ledel Gulbrandsen. One was to take the shape of a much-loved landlady of an inn hidden deep under the mirrit-tunnels that run throughout the majickal-dales. She held a guzzwort in one paw, a bowl of niff-soup in the other, and had quite the most knowing, crumlush smile.

The second was simply of a majickal-hare, merely standing, wand at his side, dripple on his shoulder, seemingly without the oidiest heroic trace about him. Underneath, the chisels were already carving his griffles onto the ganticus plinth:

*The lake settled and the creaker opened.
Three figures pid-padded outside, looking round.
"Well," Laffrohn griffled. "Methinks it's not
such a bad place to be starting over."*

CHATSWORTH
THE HARE WHO CHANGED EVERYTHING

Even further away, at the end of a peffa-long and gently glowing blue mirrit tunnel, lay quite the most majickal and tzorkly cavern, its roof adorned with saztaculous sea-emeralds, diamonds and shindinculous gemstones of every colour and size. To one side was a small beach, and on it a hut, with just the oidiest warming glow coming from inside. It was empty, and yet somehow, alive.

All was still, until there came a ganticus bubbling from the middle of the lake, vividly glowing the same majickal blue. A long chimney rose from the centre. Then a roof and windows, water pouring down the steadily rising walls. A thick wooden creaker followed, and lastly an entire garden of broken vroffa-trees, all majickally growing and restoring themselves in their saztaculous new home.

The lake settled and the creaker opened. Three figures pid-padded outside, looking round.

"Well," Laffrohn griffled. "Methinks it's not such a bad place to be starting over."

"It needs a peffa-lot of cleaning-up in there, though," Lily Krettle griffled. "We don't want it to be looking all peffa-glopped when the first Most Majelicus customers arrive."

Jericho Krettle looked towards the small hut, seeing an oidy trail of black smoke drift slowly from its chimney and float past them into The Vroffa-Tree Inn. "Do you know," he smiled, putting a paw around them both, "methinks we might just be getting some extra help with the cleaning up. And that be most pleasing."

"Most pleasing indeed," Lily griffled, as together the three of them made their way happily back inside.

Gifts, Even'ups, and Trials

The next few sun-turns passed in a frenzy of activity, as witches and dale-creatures set about returning to their homes, determined to put right the glopped-up mess and restore life to how it used to be before the ganticus flood.

Some didn't want to leave Winchett Dale, instead staying around to help the clottabussed villagers clean and repair their cottages, then enjoying even'ups at the inn, griffling and chickling over guzzworts by the roaring piff-tosh as Slivert Jutt presided over everything with his knowing smile.

With all their vroffa-brooms burnt in the beacons, Soriah Kherflahdle ordered *The League of Lid Curving Witchery* to go with the other creatures to their dale-homelands and use their tzorklyness to help rebuild all that had been flood-glopped. She herself stayed in Winchett Dale, planting the half vroffa-tree deep in Wand Wood next to an elderly elm, where it vilishly grew a saztaculous set of vroffa-branches, allowing her and Serraptomus to begin making and whittling new brooms. Once the pile was complete, Soriah re-summoned her witches, watching alongside him with quiet satisfaction as one by one they flew away into the lid.

"It's been quite the strangest few sun-turns," she griffled.

"Indeed," Serraptomus nodded. "And also highly officious, too.

Lot of brooms to be whittled and made, there. Job peffa-well done, methinks."

She turned to him, smiling slightly into his earnestly puffing face, lightly tucking a dangling thread back into his jacket. "Can I ask you something?"

"Most certainly," he griffled. "We dale-creatures and witches are most fuzzcheck friends, now. Ask away, Your Tzorkliness."

"What does 'officious' actually mean?"

He coloured slightly, furiously thinking, frowning and puffing out his cheeks. "Well, I think it means...I mean, it probably means...I'm fairly certain that..." He stopped, looked at her, lowered his voice to a whispgriffle. "Can I be peffa-confidential with you, Your Tzorkliness?"

"Of course."

"Thing is," he awkwardly explained, "back at krate-school, when they were doing the 'Being Officious' lesson, I had a bad case of the snunks and...sort of missed it."

"And you never thought to ask your teachers?" she griffled.

He shrugged, shaking his head. "I just didn't think it mattered that much, really." His eyes suddenly brightened and his voice filled with pride. "But I got top-marks in the 'Puffing Out and Wheezing' classes, I really did. They griffled they'd never had such a saztaculous wheezer in the school, ever."

She smiled. "How do you see me, Serraptomus?"

"See you?"

"Sometimes, creatures see me differently to how I really am. How do you see me?"

He frowned, not quite knowing what to griffle. "I see..." he began, swallowing hard, "...someone I never thought I'd enjoy whittling broomsticks and griffling with."

"And who knows?" she griffled, climbing onto her own broom and firing up its branches, "perhaps one sun-turn, we'll do it again." She lightly tipped the edge of her green and golden hat, then streaked into the lid, Serraptomus watching until she became just the oidiest dot, then wondering why his jacket felt suddenly heavier than normal, a mystery solved when he reached into the inside pocket and pulled out quite the most exquisite and saztaculous whittling knife he'd ever seen.

Similar things happened right across the dales when the witches left. Creatures began to find tzorkly gifts hidden in their homes; oidy witch's hats, cauldron ladles, saztaculous candles that seemed to burn every colour, bottles of grimwagel wine and even small vroffa-brooms, perfect for youngsters to play on, and sometimes – when they were safely nifferduggling in their beds – for their mahpas and pahpas to have a secret ride on, excitedly griffling and chickling as they flew low over the trees, feeling like excrimbly youngsters themselves.

Soon, most every creature agreed that despite what they thought and had been told, *The League of Lid-Curving Witchery* were really rather fun, and should they ever return, a warm welcome would be kept in the dales – together with a peffa-generous supply of guzzwort.

Goole, ever eager to spot a one-eyed singing opportunity, found a whole new appreciative audience in the tzorkly-cacklers, and was regularly invited to perform his clottabussed showstoppers for them, the ploffshroom band doing their briftest to keep up the tempo and avoid being eaten by the chickling witches as they did so. Within a single moon-turn, '*My, My, My…Milky White Eye!*' was the most popular song to stir a splutting cauldron to, and had vilishly become the favourite curtain-raiser for raucous, tzorkly even'ups out. Some witches even wore eye-patches and coloured their eyes especially for the occasion.

Lord Garrick returned to his castle to consider his future, determined his lazy life of committee-based luxury would come to an end. It was a most honourable intention. After his time in Winchett Dale, he'd come to realise that perhaps there was more to life than drutts and endless gluttony. There were other things he wanted to do, places to explore, saztaculous things he still yearned to see. However, when his russisculoffed family members informed him that all the tents at the Estuary Festival had been washed away in the flood, resulting in a ganticus overall drutt-loss, he was faced with no other option but to set up a brand-new committee to investigate just how such an occurrence could be prevented in future. Although, to his credit, he never once attended himself, having left the task to a group of colley-rocks that he felt fully confident wouldn't ever arrive at any conclusion, whatsoever.

At his small crumlush cottage on the edge of Wand Wood, Matlock tried to pass his sun-turns without ever thinking about the saztaculous events of the Dale Vrooshfest, mostly keeping himself to himself, quietly tending to his potions and his cottage garden. He hung Trommel's red-robes at the back of his small wardrobe, unable to part with them, but never wanting to wear them again, keeping them merely in memory of Chatsworth, who he'd finally come to realise really was the most saztaculous master any majickal-hare could ever have had.

At night, he would often light a piff-tosh, then make himself a small bowl of niff-soup, staring into the flames and griffling to Ayaani, telling her of all he'd done during the day, occasionally reaching out to stroke the empty place where she should have been, his hare's eyes closing, trying to remember the crumlush puff of her breath on his paw, the way she would take his empty bowl and return with a steaming mug of brottle-leaf brew, as together they'd griffle long into the night about quite the most clottabussed things, simply glad to be with one another, making their plans for the next sun-turn which would inevitably go glopped-up.

Proftulous came regularly to visit, concerned for his briftest friend, trying his briftest to cheer Matlock up, but never really knowing quite what to griffle. Everything he thought of was inevitably connected to either Chatsworth or Ayaani in some way. Sometimes, he and Matlock simply sat in silence the whole even'up, before Proftulous would lump-thump away with a heavy heart, not even bothering to look for tweazles as he sadly set back off home through Wand Wood.

One even'up, just as he was leaving, Matlock stopped him at the creaker. "Proftulous," he griffled. "I want you to take this. Destroy it, before it glopps anything else."

Proftulous looked at the Tillian Wand. "But it be yours, Matlock," he griffled, confused. "You be finding it. The task be all ended, so it can't be going back. It be yours now, Matlock, forever."

"I don't want it," Matlock quietly griffled. "I never wanted it. It cost too much. I never wanted to lose Ayaani or Chatsworth,

Laffrohn – or any of them. Take it, please. Destroy it."

"But it be most majickal," Proftulous griffled, getting twizzly. "I don't know that I should be destroying it."

"Please," Matlock griffled. "Just take it. I never want to see it again."

Knowing Matlock wouldn't change his mind, Proftulous took a deep breath and slowly took the wand, then gave him a long hug. "I'll be destroying it for you, Matlock."

"Thanks," Matlock griffled, looking Proftulous straight in his dworp's eyes. "You really are my briftest friend. You do know that, don't you?"

Proftulous nodded, trying to smile, struggling to say something, but no griffles coming as he slowly shut the creaker.

Inside, Matlock sighed heavily and vrooshed out the fire, making his way up the small wooden staircase, hoping he would be able to get some nifferduggles.

Which was when he heard it… A most saztaculous sound that made his whole softulous soar with majickal elation – Ayaani's voice, calling out to him from the other side of his bedroom door!

"Ayaani!" he cried, shaking with pure excrimbly emotion, vilishly opening the creaker and rushing inside…to find himself in a corridor with a long line of seated creatures on either side, all turning to look at him.

"Ayaani?" he griffled, utterly confused. "Where are you?"

Behind, the creaker slammed shut. He rushed to it, ganticus extrapluffs telling him to get out as vilishly as possible, but it simply melted away, becoming solid wall. He took a pid-pad backwards in shock, bliffing the wall with his paw, then reaching for his wand and trying to vroosh it back open.

"None of that vrooshing and getting twizzly works here, Matlock," a kindly voice he half-remembered, griffled. "Briftest thing is simply to wait like the rest of us."

He turned, still unable to take any of it in, looking at his once Most Majelicus wand, not even beginning to frizz, now just a useless piece of hawthorn in his paw.

Again, the voice griffled. "Why not come and sit down? I suspect these things take longer than we're led to believe."

He looked along the two rows of creatures, spotting the raised paw waving at him. "Estrella?" he griffled, remembering his time in the lidservatory. "Is that you?"

The nullitt astrologer smiled quite crumlushly.

He pid-padded over, stopping, then turning, pointing to the blank wall. "What's going on? My cottage is through there," he griffled, mind racing. "I have to get back. I heard Ayaani, then raced upstairs and..."

Beside his mother, Spig leaned over. "And then you most probably fell, I expect," he helpfully griffled. "Easy way to stroff, that. Just one oidy slip, and that's your lot."

Nearby, other nullitts nodded, Matlock recognising Forticus Grik politely raising his lizardy hand. "Or perhaps the chimney fell through the roof and landed on top of your head?"

"Wait," Matlock griffled, "are you griffling to me that I'm...?"

Estrella smiled. "Stroffed? We all are, Matlock. Every one of us here. T'was the ganticus flood that did for us. Us nullits never went to the Dale Vrooshfest. The waters came, and that was that. We ended up here."

"But," Matlock griffled, frowning heavily as he tried his briftest to understand, "I'm *not* stroffed. I'm still alive in Winchett Dale. I just came through my bedroom door and ended up here." He looked at the wall again, breathing heavily, the dreadful truth sinking in. "There's been a mistake," he griffled, beginning to panic. "I can't be stroffed! I'm not stroffed, you hear me?"

At the far end of the corridor a ganticus door opened, bright light flooding in behind a hare dressed in quite the most saztaculous silvered robes. "Matlock the hare!" it called out to him. "Approach!"

The other creatures all bowed, Matlock shielding his eyes against the sudden light, trying to make out who it was. "Something's gone wrong," he griffled to it. "I'm not meant to be here."

"Just get on with it," the hare griffled. "The last thing we want to do is keep the Majickal Elders waiting."

"Majickal Elders?" Matlock griffled pid-padding towards the shindinculously dressed hare, realising he was carrying a series of rolled-up scrolls under his arm. "But that's *good* news, isn't it? Peffa-good news. They'll know this is all a ganticus mistake. They'll send me back to Winchett Dale peffa-vilishly."

"Not completely sure it's going to be that sort of a trial, really," the hare griffled as Matlock drew level. "More you explaining why it is that you've broken so many of Oramus' rules. You'll probably end up in some sort of truly splurked punishment that lasts an eternal lifetime. Not that I'm any kind of an expert, I'm quite new around here myself." He held out a white paw. "I'm Ledel Gulbrandsen, by the way. We haven't met, but I've heard quite splurked things about you. What do you think about the ears?"

"Your ears?" Matlock griffled, completely ambushed.

"Peffa-perfect length, each and every one of them." Ledel griffled, slowly and luxuriously running a paw up to their tips. "Quite impressive, what they can do up here."

"What trial?" Matlock asked, still utterly confused. "I'm dreaming, aren't I? Yes, that's it. This is just a glopped-dream, and really, I'm safely nifferduggling in bed, and…"

"Listen to me," Ledel griffled, cutting across, his voice suddenly deadly serious. "This is the peffa-last place I want to be as well, you splurk. I stroffed, fully convinced I'd forever be the spirit of a tzorkly-forest, back in my homelands. But, like you, I ended up here. And worse, it's all *because* of you. You're not dreaming, you're here, whether you like it or not. So get used to it." He paused. "You're going on trial, Matlock, and unfortunately I'm the only oidy hope you've got. I've been made your counsel – the poor fool tasked with defending you. Now, follow me, or we'll be late."

"I don't understand a single griffle of what you're griffling about," Matlock tried to explain, pid-padding after Ledel into another long corridor also bathed in the brightest white. "There can't be a trial – I've done nothing wrong!"

Ledel stopped, turned to him. "Thing is, I haven't really bothered looking into your case, as I've spent most of the time getting my ears done and choosing the robes – which, I really do think set them off in a truly tzorkly combination. But from what I've been allowed to see, there's a pile of charges against you. Not that it bothers me in the slightest. I never liked you that much in the first place."

"I'm Ledel Gulbrandsen, by the way. We haven't met, but I've heard quite splurked things about you. What do you think about the ears?"

"Because of Ursula?" Matlock griffled, reaching around his neck for the bottle of her tears but not finding it. He cleared his throat, trying not to admit how alone he suddenly felt without them. "She told me about you, what a saztaculous wizard-hare you were – the absolute peffa-briftest."

Ledel waved away the griffles with his paw. "Let's just get this over as vilishly as possible so I can get out of this splurked place. Just try and look truly sorry and gobflopped – if nothing else it'll make me look even more saztaculous standing next to you."

"I just want to go home," Matlock griffled, trying not to get too twizzly, as he and Ledel made their way towards a ganticus set of doors opening into a vast room full of blue-robed majickal-hares, all turning to stare at him.

"Don't griffle anything until you're asked," Ledel whispgriffled, pulling out a short length of chain. "Would you mind just wrapping this around your wrists?"

"What for?"

"It's not obligatory, just thought it'd add a bit more drama. I mean, we're stuck here, might as well try and enjoy it. How are my ears, still looking good?"

"Ledel," Matlock whispgriffled, trying to stay as calm as possible, "please answer this next question, peffa, peffa-honestly. Have you *ever* done anything like this before?"

"Never," Ledel replied. "Whole thing came as a complete shock. Something about fate and destiny. Seems it was always going to be this way. You and I, thrown together, facing this lot. Me, in totally the wrong place; and you, not even stroffed yet."

They both looked into the room, the sea of waiting Majickal Elder's studying them both peffa-carefully, noses and long ears twitching, some already pointing and shaking their heads.

"Still, look at it this way," Ledel griffled, trying to smile. "How much worse can things really get?"

Matlock took his deepest ever hare's breath. "I think," he slowly griffled, "we're about to find out."

Griffle Glossary

Welcome to the 'griffle-glossary'; a peffa-handy 'start-griffling' guide to the language of the dales. Whilst far from comprehensive, it intends to give the interested observer a beginner's guide to 'griffling', and perhaps a further oidy glimpse into the world of Winchett Dale…

Good luck, and good 'griffling'!

Abbrolatt – (n) Slow moving, yet largely harmless giant *moffashlobb* – eats tops of trees, so *shortwings* have to be careful. Won't really mean to squash you with its feet, and will *eye-splash* for many *sun-turns* if it does. Useful for scaring long, long nosed *krellits* away. Not as effective at scaring short, long nosed *krellits*, though…
Bliff – (v) To lightly strike something, as opposed to using a *peffa-bliff* (n) to cause some really glopped-up damage.
Blinksnap – (n) The *oidiest* moment; from the time it takes the average creature to blink an eye. (All except grated-joolps, who for peffa-long and complicated reasons that can sometimes cause embarrassment, are the only creatures in Winchett Dale to take more than a minute with each blink.)
Briftest – (adj) What you know as 'the best'.
Chickle – (v) To laugh. From the guttural noise created by much mirth-making.
Cloff(s) – (n) Chores. From the *cloffing* noise made at the back of the throat by creatures doing chores, who'd much rather be doing *fuzzcheck* things instead!
Clottabus – (n, colloquial) A bit of a fool. Distinct to Winchett Dale, after Clottabus the owl once tried to actually prove he could turn his head a full circle, and found himself back to front for nearly a whole *moon-turn*.
Creaker – (n) Door; from the noise most often associated with opening one.

Crimple – (n) Stomach. Traditional repository for *tweazle-pies* and *niff-soup*. Can tend to grumble if too full.

Crumlush – (adj) The feeling you get inside when all's *saztaculoulsy* well. Cosy, warm, lovely.

Ebberback – (n) A type of beetle, tastes *yechus*, so don't bother. From the same family of *Coleodaletera*, frequently seen skrittling all around the dale and sometimes on some of the more *glopped-up* creatures themselves. Examples include – *murp-worms, slidgers, dilva-beetles, cloff-beetles* and water-dwelling *slipdgers, jellops* and *blurfs*. Not to be confused with *mirrits*, which are quite another *saztaculous* thing, entirely.

Eye-splashy(ers) – (v/n) To cry; tears.

Excrimbly – (n) Exciting, or excited – as in '*becoming all peffa-excrimbly*' at the thought of something *saztaculous* about to happen.

Foffle – (n) Small cheese-eating creature, much like an *oidy* kitten, with a hard belly and long pointed nose, who will guard your *piff-tosh* all night from *frizzing* embers, softly *greeping* as he does so.

Freggle – (coll n/slang) Much the same as a *snutch* (meaning 'few') *freggle* is most often used in association with *guzzworts*.

Fritch – (n) Most popular board game in Winchett Dale. Involves putting up tiny fences to wall your opponent in. *Ganticus* opportunities for cheating, and Matlock is most definitely not allowed to use any *vrooshers* during the game!

Fuzzcheck – (sl) When everything's completely *graggly* and fine! Used by Winchett Dale to approve of a really good *vliff*.

Ganticus – (adj) Somewhere between 'large' and 'huge'. Although *peffa-ganticus* is most definitely vast.

Garrumblooms – (n) Deep rumblings, of the kind sometimes made by *Foffle Mountain*; or more likely from Proftulous if he's eaten too much *tweazle-pie* for his supper. At this point, most creatures tend to make their excuses and go outside…

Gobflop – (n) To fail at something.

Glopped-up – (n phrase) When something has gone wrong.

Glubbstool – (n) When something has gone *peffa*-wrong! Not the sort of *sun-turn* you'd ever want to remember – could well be time for a *crumlush brottle-leaf* brew in front of the *piff-tosh*…

Greep – (v) Contented noise made by *foffles*, as they slide their hard undershells on any cinders that might pop from your *piff-tosh* during the

night. Helps to keep them warm during the winter months.
Griffle(s) – (n) Word(s). (Also used in verb-form – *'to griffle'*)
Grimwagel Wine – (n) Splurked tipple of witches, largely taken in a *ganticus* glass or tankard. Comes in varying colours and strengths. Pleas ensure never to drink a glass of 'home-made' Grimwagel Wine – as it will most likely be the last thing you'll ever do.
Guzzwort – (n) The favourite *even'up* drink of Winchett Dale. Brewed on the premises of the *saztaculous* Winchett Dale Inn, landlord Slivert Jutt's *crumlushly* famous ale is a rich, nutty bown slurpilicious treat. However, it can sometimes lead to a slightly *glopped* and *glubbstooled* head in the *morn'up*... (Visitors to Winchett Dale Inn: please be warned NOT to drink from Jericho Krettle's tankard, as even though he is a peffa-infrequent visitor, he's peffa-particular, and will bliff you quite severely if he finds out.)
Juzzpapped – (n) To feel really tired, especially at the end of a *peffa*-long and *glopped-up sun-turn*.
Lid – (n) The *crumlush* and *saztaculous* sky above all our heads.
Long, long-nosed Krellits – (n) Avoid these at ALL COSTS!
Majelicus – (adj) *Peffa*-majickal, the most majickal majick, that can't be *vrooshe*d from books, tinctures or potions, the very heartbeat of our majickal world.
Moondaisy – (n) Small, singing yellow and blue flower found in Wand Wood. We even have our own *Moondaisy* choir – auditions are *peffa*-hard, though, and most *moondaisies* will merely hum a bit, and never really have the chance to showcase their true floral singing talents to a wider audience beyond just a few *skrittling druff-beetles*.
Moon-turn – (n) The time taken for the moon to turn full-cycle – 28 *sun-turns*, or 'month'.
Niff – (n) *(niffcapiscum dalus)* Orange vegetable, similar in appearance to peppers, grown all over the dale, mostly in creatures' back-gardens, picked anytime from June onwards, and used in a variety of *slurpilicious* dishes, the favourite being sliced, roasted *niffs* lightly tossed in a *cloff-beetle* salad.
Oidy – (adj) Tiny, really *peffa*-small...
Nifferduggle(s) – (n) Sleeping. To go to *nifferduggles* is sometimes the most *crumlush* part of our *sun-turn*...
Parlawitch – (n) Official language of all witches, both in the dales, and

also solitary white hare-witches living across *the Icy Seas*. Developed over countless generations, *Parlawitch* is a combination of traditional witch-*griffles* blended with distant Scandinavian dialect. However, you don't have to be fluent in *Parlawitch* to griffle with a witch, as by and large, they have learnt to *griffle* many languages in their *vroffa*-broomed travels, but having a few *Parlawitch griffles* on hand is always polite, and perhaps the *briftest* way to ensure they don't get *russisculoffed* and try and turn you into some *yechus* creature for the rest of your *sun-turns*…

Peffa – (adj) Very.

Pid-pad – (v) To walk. You humans go *bud-thud*; whereas we, more delicate creatures of Winchett Dale simply *pid-pad*. Except Proftulous, who for obvious *dworped* reasons, lump-thrumps along, instead.

Piff-tosh – (n) Fire, of the kind that you have in your home, to settle in front of when the *sun-turn* has left you *peffa-juzzpapped*. Needs a gently *greeping foffle* to guard it while you're *nifferduggling*, though! From the noise made by the fire as it burns in your grate.

Russisculoffed – (n) Irritated. From the gutteral noises made by *russicers* if you go too near while they are hoarding *shlomps*. Be warned, they much prefer their *schlomps* to you!

Scrittle – (v) How *oidy* creatures and *flappers* get around on the ground. From the slight scatching noise of *vilish* feet.

Saztaculous – (adj) Something that is quite *peffa*-wonderful.

Shindinculous – (adj) Something that it so *peffa-saztaculous* that it shines out from anything that might be at all *glopped*.

Sisteraculous – (n) The absolute being of you! The complimentary part of your *softulous* that if you really listen hard to, has some truly *saztaculous* answers to questions you never thought to ask. Something so many have forgotten how to trust, but we at Winchett Dale rely on every sun-turn!

Softulous – (n) Body; be it furry, scaly or otherwise…

Sluffsday – (prop n) Monday. From the generally disappointed *sluffing* heard across Winchett Dale as we realise it's another five *sun-turns* before we can say *'Thank Oramus it's Yaayday!'*

Snutch – (n) A few.

Sploink – (n) *Ganticus* raindrop, tending to fall from a *peffa*-dark *lid* and landing with an audible *sploink*.

Splurk – (n) *(Parlawitch slang)* A fool, a *clottabus*.

Spuddle – (n) A tale, story, or legend, sometimes told by parents to their cubs, kittens and leverets. The *spuddle* of the *Berriftomus* is one, which tells of a *peffa-yechus* creature that will come to you at night while you *nifferduggle* if you've been naughty.

Sun-turn – (n) A day. The period of *time* it takes for the sun to rise and fall, before leaving just the *saztaculous twinkling-lid*. What you would call a 'day'.

Sweeniffs – (abrv) Sweet-Nifferduggles. Said to cubs, kittens and all manner of young creatures in the Dale by exhausted parents as they finally put their offspring to bed at the end of each *sun-turn*.

Trikulum – (n) Highly explosive purple powder, used to make *ganicus cracksplosions*. Must be handled with *peffa*-care at all times! Can sometimes be found in the abandoned *Trikulum* mines running under *Foffle Mountain*.

Tricky-Ricketts – (n) *Peffa*-intelligent garden weeds that only grow in completely inaccessible places. Can be heard *chickling* when you try and remove them.

Trinkulah – (n) *Crumlush* willow-harp that Matlock will sometimes play to the wind.

Twinkleabra – (n) Ornate candelabra, often lit with *saztaculous* candles in different colours, depending on what festival is currently being celebrated.

Twinkling Lid – (n phr) The *shindinculous* sky at night, alive with *saztaculous* stars.

Tweazle – (n) Rodent-like creature, a *peffa*-distant cousin of *dripples*, that won't stop *griffling* in a way that makes them sound peffa-important. Nearly always at the front at *public-grifflings* of any kind, keen to air their views, but also to be safe from any hungry *dworps* in the nearby vicinity.

Twizzly – (n) To feel scared, nervous, or an oidy bit ill – when your *softulous* and *Sisteraculous* aren't properly aligned, and you sense danger lurking somewhere close…

Tzorkly – (adj – *Parlawitch*) Literal meaning – 'to rise above', but used amongst witches to mostly mean '*Peffa-fuzzcheck* and witchy'.

Uggralybe – (n) A *Peffa*-lazy plant, that will only decide to grow if you sing softly to it at the end of each *sun-turn* – what we first called an *uggralullyby* – and the origin of your human word *lullaby*.

Vilishly – (adv) Quickly. From the noise made by a woodland creature

rushing through the undergrowth, searching for berries, or trying to escape a hungry predator.
Vroosher – (n). A wand-assisted majick spell. From the *saztaculous vrooshing* noise they make!
Whupplit – (n) an *oidy* rain-drop. From the sound it makes when falling on leaves, or even *whuppling* into the Thinking Lake.
Yamantally-spious! – (excl, slang) Used by the creatures of the dale, when something's gone *peffa-fuzzcheck*.
Yechus – (adj) Something that is truly *glopped-up* and *horrendous*.

The Dale Bugle.

➡ Where it is always peffa-good news │ Every sun-turn!

LEGENDARY!
BRAND NEW ATTRACTION OPENS TO GANTICUS ACCLAIM

Dale-creatures everywhere were peffa-excrimbly yesterday with news that *The Saztaculous Hall of All Legends* is to open its ganticus doors to showcase the remarkable skills of the many majickal-chisels that work within this most mysterious and shindinculous building.

Chief spokeschisel Barry Chipper opened the creakers in a ceremony led by Lord Garrick and a committee of arguing colley-rocks, allowing hoards of eager, drutt-paying visitors inside for the first time.

HAMMERS

'Basically,' he griffled, 'all us chisels had a bit of a griffle about it, and thought 'Why not?' Ours is a highly skilled, but largely ignored profession, and we thought it was about time folk should be able to pid-pad around and see just what we're up to. The hammers weren't so keen, but then again, they've never really moved with the times, I'm afraid.'

Mr Chipper went on to detail some of the many attractions inside. *'We've recently had a bit of a clear-out and got*

(CONT. OVERLEAF)

STILL DON'T HAVE A Dudge-Whammet? WHY NOT? THEY'RE SAZTACULOUS!!!

rid of a lot of the older legends, which frankly, were all looking a bit tired, replacing them with three new saztaculous statues that really demonstrate our skills to the peffa-highest levels. We've also got floors, ceiling, and a roof. All in all, it's the peffa-perfect sun-turn for all the family. You will print that bit, won't you? Only the hammers would love to see this all go glopped.'

Inside, visitors gathered to marvel at the ganticus statues of Ledel Gulbrandsen; former Vroffa-Tree Inn owner, Laffrohn – and some old majickal-hare called Chatsworth that no one really knew about.

GLUBBSTOOLED

Some visitors, however, were less than impressed. 'I think that overall, it's a pretty glubbstooled waste of a sun-turn,' Hibble Tuck, a slow-jarrock from Alfise Dale complained. 'I mean, you get up early, pid-pad all the way here, then hand over your drutts expecting something more than just some spuddles and statues. I think they should have been moving, or had a big fight, or something.'

Lord Garrick last night responded to criticisms. 'Folk have been griffling that the whole thing is simply a way for my brother-in-law to recoup his losses from the flooded Estuary Festival. This couldn't be further from the truth. It's my uncle.'

Just how long this latest dale-attraction can stay open is now the main griffling point – creatures remembering similar ventures which also gobflopped far too vilishly.

'I once wasted a whole sun-turn at The Officious Krate Experience,' a disheartened disidula told us. 'Turned out to be truly dreadful. The café was a disgrace, and the officious gift shop only sold old wheezes in jars.'

However, Barry Chipper was insistent the attraction will continue to expand with new exhibits being added all the time. 'We simply need a few more folk to loose their lives saving everyone and becoming legends, really. It's a supply-and-demand thing. But if you fancy seeing yourself up here one sun-turn, perhaps now's the peffa-perfect time to get out there and do something heroic.'

Last night, the hammers were unavailable for comment.

PLUFF-O-CHAIR — EXTRAPLUFFS GUARANTEED* — *SOMETIMES

FELIC TO APPEAL

The dales were rocked this morn'up with news that majickal-hare Felic from Ceedius Dale is set to appeal the Dale Vrooshfest decision that declared Ledel Gulbrandsen to be the winner and 'Briftest of all Majick-al-Hares'.

'For a start,' a russisculoffed Felic told us yesterday, in between glopped stretching exercises, 'he was a wizard – not a hare. Secondly, he's stroffed, so how is he going to be able to turn up and shake creatures' paws and open things? Thirdly – his ears were terrible. The whole thing's a complete farce, and I should be made the winner, as I think you'll find that despite the ganticus flood, my saztaculous vrooshing performance is the only thing that really sticks in creatures' minds.'

However, a resident from Ceedius Dale who wishes to remain anonymous, told us, 'I tell you where we'd all like to stick Felic – anywhere but here. If there's any dales out there that could take the clottabus out of our paws, we'd be most peffa-grateful.' A spoke-screature for the Dale Vrooshfest committee griffled. 'Like all controversial decisions, Felic's appeal will come down to much peffa-serious thought, consideration - and how many drutts he has.'

A griffle-pole for The Dale Bugle found that 97% of readers find Felic to be completely unappealing in the first place.

Classifieds

THE NUMBER ONE DIRECTORY FOR ALL THAT'S SHLONKED AND PEFFA-GOBFLOPPED IN THE DALE...

LOST

BAG OF TEDIUM-CARROTS
Somewhere in Wand Woods, I think – but to griffle you the truth, I was so peffa-bored, I can't really remember.

BLURF
Always known where it's been for years, but the moment I need to use it, can I find it?

JEERING-CHUSS
Small for his age, but really jeers splendidly. Many saztaculous years of jeering service given - especially to unexpected visitors at the creaker. Fits discreetly into a pocket or sleeve and simply jeers. A must for those glubb-stooled dinner-parties.

LAST SCRUFFSDAY
I can't for the life of me remember where I put it, or even if we had it in the first place. Any ideas?

INVISIBLE UMBRELLA
given to me by Fragus at Dale Vrooshfest. Feel quite cottabussed pid-padding around in the lid-splashy with nothing in my paw, now.

FOUND

LENGTH OF DROOL.
From Chapter 2, most probably Jericho's, who would also just like to point out that no majickal-hares or creatures of any kind were harmed in the telling of our story, we're all peffa-good friends, really - and it's just meant to be an oidy bit of fun...

AWKWARD SILENCE.
Just sort of scrittling around, looking forlorn. Says it would be more than pleased to turn up to any potentially embarrassing occasions you have planned.

HIGGOTT-CLAMP.
Together with meruttle-bars, groff-valves and matching, double-wired whammet-points. Please come and collect, as I don't have the oidiest idea what they are.

SERVICES

CRUFF-REMOVAL
- by experienced, qualified cruffer. Yes, it's 'Good-bye cruffs; hello invitations to the most saztaculous events in the dales!' once you've had those unslightly cruffs removed. Be the cruff-free envy of your cruffed-friends, with just one peffa-painful, fully-unregulated treatment. NB - may cause excessive whap-irritation, permanent scarring and burns.

PLORPING CLASSES
- Learn to plorp like the professionals. Full range of classes given - from 'Beginners - Oidy Plorping' to 'Expert - My goodness! How did you do that, without crying for a whole week?' Please bring own cushion and neffle-hammer.

QUESTION EVEN'UP!
Every Sluffsday! Winchett Dale Inn.
INCLUDES
Tweazle-raffle and *peffa-glopped* entertainment.
Witches welcome!!
(though not clever ones!)

MATLOCK THE HARE

will return when the story concludes...

Get ready to chickle, eyesplash and drudge your whammets one final time as Matlock the Hare returns for his most ganticus challenge yet.

THE TRIAL OF THE MAJICKAL-ELDERS

To discover more about Matlock the Hare and Winchett Dale, visit www.matlockthehare.com this very sun-turn…